A MARK OF IMPERFECTION

A DCI EVAN WARLOW THRILLER

RHYS DYLAN

WYRMWOOD
BOOKS

COPYRIGHT

ISBN 978-1-915185-11-2
eBook ISBN 978-1-915185-10-5

Published by Wyrmwood Books.
An imprint of Wyrmwood Media.

EXCLUSIVE OFFER

Please look out for the link near the end of the book for your chance to sign up to the no-spam guaranteed **VIP Reader's Club** and receive a **FREE DCI Warlow** novella as well as news of upcoming releases.

Or you can go direct to my website: https://rhysdylan.com and sign up now.

Remember, you can unsubscribe at any time and I promise won't send you any spam. Ever.

BOOKS by RHYS DYLAN

The Engine House

Caution Death At Work

Ice Cold Malice

Suffer The Dead

Gravely Concerned

CHAPTER ONE

THE WOODLAND SAT in a sea of open moor. A dark-green island brooding against the gunmetal sky. The coniferous trees were not native to this unforgiving landscape, planted as commercial crops in the wake of the First World War to establish a timber reserve. These days, conservationists moaned at the loss of delicate heath and bog, while waxing lyrical about how red squirrels had moved in to populate these artificial habitats.

And though sheep grazed the bare hillsides around the plantations, fences, cattle grids, and closed steel gates kept them out of the forest. These islands were places of silent solitude, rarely visited unless by contractors and the odd determined walker. Those that passed through them did so quickly, as a means to an end. Dense and dark, these clumps of forest offered little in the way of invitation or appeal.

The old roads and paths in this southern corner of Powys led only to reservoirs and holes in the ground where intrepid cavers fed their addictions. All in all, this bleak expanse of the southern Brecon Beacons National Park provided an ideal area to get lost in. Or to hide things in.

If you were so inclined.

Of course, hiding could be a good thing, because being caught out on the moors when the weather changed was never the best of ideas. And there were groups of volunteers who gave of their time to rescue those unfortunates who lost their way. An all too easy occurrence in the mist when it descended without warning. A mountain brume that brought with it an insidious threat in the way of two deadly companions: the damp and the cold. If you were not prepared, such a combination could, like an ethereal quicksand, drag you down into that slow and lingering precursor of death: exposure.

Spring came late at this elevation. And on this bitter April day, the two people sitting in a small clearing in one particular patch of forest had no thoughts of cavers or grazing sheep. They had long given up hope of rescue. Their minds – what was left of them after days of starvation and torture – were preoccupied by harrowing thoughts of what would happen next out here in the wilderness, exposed as they were to the elements: the biting wind and the driving rain. And, when the mist lifted and night fell, the cold, uncaring stars would follow.

They'd pleaded, of course they had. The man, especially. Using his illness as a lever in attempting to prise an ounce of sympathy from their captor. But his pathetic words fell on deaf ears. As did those of his wife's. Not a small woman, she'd struggled with the half-mile of dirt road their captor had made them walk up. He hadn't made them climb the locked steel gate. He'd cut through the fencing instead. Herding them like animals on a miserable, wet day until he'd found the spot. Somewhere he'd been before, judging by what had already been placed in the clearing.

And now they sat, this miserable couple, naked, bound and gagged, secured to a couple of rickety wooden chairs, watching as the man who had abducted them from their home and brought them here fulfilled the ritual he'd made them a part of.

They were not young, these victims. Unlikely candidates, one might have thought for the tableau they were now enshrined in. But neither were they hapless. Both had, in turn, displayed their own brands of cruelty. And so, they watched, shivering, desperately thirsty and hungry, aching from their wounds and bruises, pinioned by duct tape and their own weakness to chairs in a glade.

They watched and moaned as their captor dragged in the carcasses: a dead sheep, a dead crow, a maggot-riddled badger. Each placed on their own seat, facing inwards towards an upturned log at the centre. Like a family meeting for a tea-time meal.

But it was as their captor stood back to admire his handiwork, hands on hips, that a wail escaped the throat of the sick old man tied to the chair. As if he realised then and only then what was in store for them.

People said that the worst thing about exposure, at the beginning anyway, was the awareness of the cold. What soon followed, the uncontrollable shivering, losing coordination, the numbness, the slow descent into hypothermic irrationality, often ended with a preternatural calm. But that kind of information could come only from survivors.

Who truly knew what the hours of decline might be like?

A kind of hell, perhaps.

Only one thing could be certain. It promised a slow and painful death.

CHAPTER TWO

DCI Evan Warlow sat in the sunroom of his cottage with the back door open, looking out over the estuary. The sun was up, and the birds were singing on this June day in Pembrokeshire. Traffic on the A48 had been heavy over the weekend as tourists poured in with the promise of a few dry days in the forecast. Warlow's rule of thumb during these periods: Easter, spring break, Whitsun – the current culprit – and most of July and August, kept him away from anywhere within a two-mile radius of a campsite, caravan park, or beach. Still, he would not complain. Good for the area's economy. And he had the four counties of Powys, Carmarthenshire, Pembrokeshire and Ceredigion to himself for the rest of the year. Let the visitors enjoy them for a couple of months while he played Ostrich.

Cadi, Warlow's black Labrador, stood sentry on the threshold of the back door. On the lookout for stray gulls or the odd crow who might mistake Warlow's back garden as a safe haven. Prepared, with intent, to teach them otherwise. Though it wasn't yet 7.30 in the morning, he and the dog had been out for a stroll around the quiet lanes. The cottage was well off the normal tourist routes and immune from the holiday madness. Mostly.

Man and dog sat, both breakfasted and prepared for the day ahead. In Warlow's case, that meant a day at Dyfed Powys HQ in Carmarthen, ensconced in a meeting. For Cadi, it meant the start of a five-day camping holiday courtesy of one of her many fans. Warlow didn't mind. Cadi would love it and she, unlike him, had no hang-ups regarding outsiders. Besides, this holiday was taking place just a few miles west in Dale. Not too far in case something went south, such as the West Wales weather not playing ball.

The dog pricked up its ears and looked at Warlow, as if sensing his thoughts. She got up and padded over to where he sat, nudging his hand in the way she did when she wanted him to fondle her head and ears.

'You'll be fine,' Warlow said. 'And anyway, text me if you're desperate.'

The dog tilted her head, sensing something in his tone, her brown eyes never leaving his.

Warlow spoke softly. 'So, you can't talk. Big deal. We both know you can understand every word I say.'

A noise on the lane leading up to the cottage drew Cadi's attention. She turned her head, alert and poised to repel all boarders, or lick them to death in her customary greeting.

Warlow glanced at the clock. Bang on time. He got up and went to the front door to greet his visitors.

The Nissan Navara that pulled up had farm vehicle written all over it in the form of mud-spattered wheel arches and the odd scrape and dent. He'd never seen this car before, though he'd heard all about it from the daughter of the passenger who got out of the back seat. She normally drove a smart-looking Golf, but DI Jess Allanby's car was in for its MOT and a service. The bank holiday had put a spanner in the repair works and the required part would not be in until today. She therefore needed a lift to work. Warlow was happy to oblige and had suggested she cadge a ride to his place with her daughter and boyfriend when they came to pick up the dog. Jess stood in the sunshine, her dark hair gleaming, smart in a dark suit and pumps, her white blouse bright against her sun-kissed olive skin.

'Morning,' he called out.

Jess brushed a few specks of straw from her trousers and smiled back just as the front passenger door opened and a younger version of the same woman stepped out in wellies and cut-off jeans. Molly Allanby looked dressed for the part. At seventeen, she was already her mother's coltish doppelgänger.

'Where is she?' Molly asked, pretending not to see the dog.

Cadi, whose tail had already gone into overdrive as the car pulled in, now bounded forward at full speed. Molly dropped to one knee and engulfed the dog as she caromed into her.

The driver's side door swung open and out stepped a boy of Molly's age. Bryn Humphries had a shock of dark hair and a quick smile. Not a big lad, but lean and fit-looking in shorts and T-shirt, as befitted a farmer's son. But as well as helping with his dad's dairy herd, Bryn was about to take A-levels – maths and physics – at the college Molly attended and was destined for Imperial in London if they all came home to roost. Which was a given, according to Molly.

'Mr Warlow.' Bryn nodded at the DCI and knelt to make a fuss of the dog next to Molly.

'You want a cup of tea or something?' Warlow asked.

'No, we're meeting everyone at nine in the Mill House for brekkie before we go to the festival,' Molly said.

'Okay. I have Cadi's stuff all packed. Dried food, bedding, and leads, plural, in case you lose one.'

Molly frowned. 'As if.'

'I'll get her stuff,' Bryn offered.

Warlow walked back to the house and reached inside for two plastic sacks. Bryn took them and walked around to the back of the pickup. Warlow joined him and helped him lay out a mattress for Cadi. A wire guard separated the boot area from the back seat.

'I like the setup.'

'We have three sheepdogs.' Bryn grinned.

Warlow spotted the rucksacks and tents on the back seats. 'Well organised, too.'

'Looking forward to it.'

Warlow slipped the boy his card. 'Here's my number if you need it. I know you're only at the festival for a day before you head off to the beach, but since Jess doesn't have a car, I can be your point of contact.'

'Thanks, Evan.'

'Molly's not my daughter,' Warlow murmured, 'she's Jess's. But don't do anything you might regret.' He kept it light and was pleased to see Bryn take the advice in the spirit with which it was intended.

'My dad said the same thing to me an hour ago,' the boy said. 'Right after my mother and sisters did.'

'Glad we're all on the same page, then.' Warlow stood back as Molly and Cadi approached. The dog jumped in and Warlow riffled the fur on her head. 'Behave,' he said.

Cadi licked his hand.

Bryn shut the boot. Molly gave her mum a hug and hopped back into the car, grinning from ear to ear as Bryn reversed the SUV and pulled away, leaving Jess and Warlow standing there, waving back and shouting things like, 'Have fun.'

The car rounded the corner and disappeared.

'He seems so young to be driving a car that big,' Jess muttered.

'Don't worry about him. He's a farmer. He's been driving tractors since he was twelve.'

Jess turned her grey eyes to him. 'I can see what you're thinking. She's only seventeen and I'm letting her go camping with a testosterone laden eighteen-year-old and God knows who else.'

'Could you have stopped her?'

Jess nodded. 'I could have. She asked my permission. And Bryn's a nice boy. Smart, polite and he seems responsible. Besides, there's going to be a gang of them. And I'm not that much of a hypocrite. I did the same when I was her age. The boy was called Andy Pearce, and he only had a Ford Fiesta, was not smart and in no way responsible.'

'Memorable trip?'

'I remembered his name. I've forgotten some of the others.'

'That many, were there?'

Jess folded her arms and dropped her chin. 'Careful.'

Warlow snorted. 'I wanted to see if I could make you blush.'

'I'm from Manchester. Takes a lot more than that... Sir.'

Warlow grimaced. 'Ouch.'

'But thanks for giving him your card. He'll see Detective Chief Inspector every time he looks at it.'

'Any time. Right, tea?'

'I'm fine.'

'Okay, let me get my keys and we'll get this show on the road.'

'Big day,' Jess added.

'It is. So, no point putting it off any longer. Hop into the Jeep. The door's open.'

KNOWING he'd have a passenger that morning, Warlow had made an effort and tidied up the car's cockpit, removing coffee cups, balled-up receipts and dog paraphernalia from the passenger seat. Cadi's domain was the generous boot, so the back seats, barely used, remained clear. This was where he put his and Jess's briefcases.

He had a news channel on the radio but as soon as they were seated, found something else as background noise. The world's woes could bugger off for fifty minutes. Within a mile of leaving the cottage, Robert Plant and Alison Krauss were telling him that *Someone Was Watching Over* them on BBC Radio Six.

'Molly looks great,' Warlow said. 'I liked the festival uniform. Or does that qualify for fashion?'

Jess shook her head. 'Uniform is precisely the right word. She's taken a month to choose those wellies.'

'Not from Wynnstay's bargain bucket, then?'

'Uh, no.'

Warlow grinned. 'When do her exams start?'

'Two weeks. They're only ASs but she deserves a break. She's been working hard, poor kid. I hate to say it, but Bryn's a good influence.'

'He seems a likeable lad. Does he stay over?'

'Sometimes. But he's busy helping on the farm, so early nights and early starts are his reality.'

Warlow navigated the narrow lanes, heading towards the quicker A-road that would take them across country towards Carmarthen. 'Have you met his parents?'

'Only to exchange pleasantries if they've called to drop him off or pick him up. They seem normal and nice.'

Warlow nodded, aware of the little dance he and Jess were doing here. Being polite and respectful, not wanting to discuss what was ahead of them at work yet. And

Warlow sensed that Jess seemed happy to keep Molly and Bryn as the topic for now.

'Weather looks good for a change.'

'They should be fine in Dale,' Warlow agreed. 'You a camper, Jess?'

'God, no. I need a proper bed and a shower as a bare minimum. You?'

'Can't say I'm a huge fan. We did a bit when the kids were smaller. Abroad mainly, though. Somewhere that the boys could do their *Lord of the Flies* thing with thirty other juveniles, away from parents, and where the sun shone. South of France.'

Jess nodded, but her eyes were focused elsewhere. 'Holidays were always a flash point for me and Rick. He had the romantic notion that sodding off into the wilderness was a holiday. We did the Highlands once and then North Wales. Lovely places but rain magnets the both of them. Molly didn't seem to mind. Presumably because of the extra mum and dad time. I mean, we were playing cards in the tent as much as we were walking the hills.'

'Kids are resilient.'

'Unlike adults.'

Warlow shot her a glance from the corner of his eye. 'You okay, Jess?'

'I'm fine. I signed my divorce papers on Saturday. So that's another box ticked.'

'Oh.'

Jess extended her fingers and examined her nails. 'I haven't told Molly yet. Though she's been the adamant one. She says she'll never forgive him. Unfortunately, her dad thinks we should all be friends and play happy families.'

'How do you mean?'

'I suspect… I assume, that his new partner wants a bit more than a bunk-up in the car park. Knowing him, he's getting cold feet. Greener grass and all that crap.' She glanced at Warlow. 'This is from Manchester friends. He hasn't spoken to me about it. But he wasn't keen on signing the papers, I know that. And yes, before you say it, it is a bit rich.'

Jess's ex had decided to indulge in some extra-curricular activities with a female sergeant while on duty and had paid the price, both in terms of his promotion prospects and his relationship with Jess. He was still in the job, which told Warlow that the Force was more forgiving than Jess Allanby would ever be.

'Has he suggested you and he should get back together?'

'No, not in so many words. But I know the sod too well. He's pestering Molly to go away with him in the summer holidays and, get this, said I might join them somewhere for a weekend, to iron things out.' Her eyes flashed as she said this.

'Wow.'

'I could not have put it better myself.'

'If there's anything I can do…'

'You're listening to my whingeing, that's enough.' Jess sucked in air and let it out. 'Right, how about we talk about something more cheerful, like today's briefing?'

'Hobson's choice that, if ever there was one.' Warlow grunted.

'Not from where I'm standing. I'll take an enquiry into police corruption over thoughts of my ex any day, thank you very much.'

CHAPTER THREE

NOT AN INCIDENT ROOM, not this morning. They'd been allocated a meeting room, one with a big oval table so that everyone had a seat. Flip chart on one end and hot water in big vacuum flasks next to trays of plastic cups at the other. Warlow knew that the coffee sachets would be stiff and crackly with age since they only ever saw the light of day when HQ had guests. And today, a Chief Superintendent from West Mids had the dubious pleasure of doing the honours on that score.

The rest of the team were already in the room when Jess and Warlow arrived: Gil Jones and Rhys Harries scrubbed up in suits and ties; Catrin Richards in dark trousers and a light-grey shirt. She had her red hair stroked behind her ears as she sat, laptop open. Gil and Rhys, the younger DC towering over the older sergeant, had cups in their hands, bobbing like chickens over the tray of wrapped biscuits next to the hot water.

'Morning all,' Warlow said, and zeroed in on the refreshments. 'Is that water hot?'

'Don't be silly,' Gil sneered.

'Warm bordering on tepid, sir,' Rhys added. 'Probably been here an hour already.'

Jess shook her head. 'Why do they do that? Bring the hot water out an hour before the meeting starts.'

Gil, holding up a wrapped snack-pack of digestives and studying it suspiciously, said, 'I have a theory, ma'am.'

Jess waited. In Gil's case, it was generally worth it. Especially when it came to mid-morning snacks, which would be Gil's Mastermind chosen subject, if ever it came to it.

'When considering refreshments,' the DS said, 'just because they are provided does not necessarily mean that the provider wants you to enjoy them.'

Catrin didn't look up from her screen, but she raised an eyebrow and tutted. 'That's so cynical.'

Gil tore open the packet, removed a single digestive, nibbled at it, and scowled. 'If anything is cynical, it's this biscuit. No sell-by on these tiny packs. A temporal ship, IMHO, which has long since left these shores, given the lack of crispness in the crumb.'

'So what? We should get our tea now and bypass the biscuits?' Warlow asked.

'I would, sir. By the time the *crachach* arrive I suspect the tea will be warmer coming out of the drinker's bladder than it will be going into the drinker's mouth.'

Rhys choked on his brew.

Catrin, again without looking up, muttered, 'That's disgusting.'

Jess put her briefcase on the table and leaned in. '*Crachach?*' she whispered to the female DS.

Catrin was Jess's go-to source for translating Gil's random little dives into the Welsh language. Something he couldn't help sprinkling into his conversations. 'He means gentry, lords and ladies, or the senior staff, ma'am.'

Jess mouthed the word to herself, and then addressed the room. 'Everyone have a good bank holiday weekend?'

Rhys, full of it, answered first, 'Not bad, ma'am. Me and Gina went up to the zipwire in North Wales. Longest in Europe. It was amazing.'

Gil made a noise like a deflating tyre. 'Wouldn't catch me on that thing.'

'I'm sure the poor wire would be very pleased to hear that,' Catrin quipped.

Rhys chortled but choked it off after a glare from Gil. He bounced the question back to Jess to deflect attention. 'You, ma'am?'

'Nothing much other than traipsing around shops looking for festival wellies. Who knew a boot made of rubber could cost the GDP of a small country?' She added a fixed smile for good measure.

Warlow, tea in hand, pulled out a chair. 'I spent the day chopping wood, walking the dog and avoiding tourists. Job well done, too. How about you, Gil?'

'Oh, the usual,' the DS said. 'Had my nails done, my hair coiffed and put on a dress.'

'Drag night at the rugby club, was it?' Warlow asked.

'At least that would have served a purpose. Unfortunately, my manicurist is five, my hairdresser is seven and my stylist eight. Fantastic imagination but lacking in application. *Diawled bach*. The current Mrs Jones saw fit to supply the grandchildren with experimental makeup. I bought them a rugby ball. But, in the interest of inclusivity, I volunteer as their model.'

'I hope there are photographs,' Jess said.

Gil cocked an eye. 'There are, but they are subject to a non-disclosure agreement on pain of dire penalty, namely not being taken to Oakwood or Folly Farm during the summer holidays. The most severe form of punishment known to man… And girls under ten.'

'You love it, don't pretend you don't,' Warlow said.

'I think I look pretty good in blue chiffon.' Gil batted his eyelashes.

Jess turned to the one remaining officer who had volunteered no information. 'How about you, Catrin?'

'Nothing much. Craig worked on Sunday, so we couldn't go anywhere. Yesterday we mooched around, and I tried not to think too much about today.'

'You're not worried about this, are you?' Jess asked.

'I don't like being the target of an enquiry, ma'am.'

Jess shrugged. 'None of us do. But it goes with the job. Especially when we lose one of our own to the other side.'

Catrin shivered. 'I have a bad feeling about it, that's all. Craig says it has something to do with my previous incarnation as a witch.'

'He's got a point there,' Gil said, and earned a scathing look for his mutterings.

'Well, we've got two minutes before we find out if anyone's for the chop,' Warlow said. He sipped his tea and made a face. 'I'm not drinking that.' He glanced at his watch. 'I wonder if there's time for Rhys to go on a tea run?' He looked hopefully towards the DC.

Just then, the door opened, and half a dozen people traipsed in. Warlow glanced down at his paper cup and sighed.

———

'My brief, at the request of the Independent Office of Police Complaints and your own Force Watchdog, was to review the circumstances surrounding the death of Detective Sergeant Mel Lewis, with reference to his likely involvement in criminal activities. This included conspiracy to pervert the course of justice, conspiracy to murder, and misconduct in a public office.'

Chief Superintendent Marcus Davenport wore a uniform as he delivered this dire explanation. He stood at the flip-chart end of the oval table, hair cut short, broad in the chest and wearing a snazzy pair of glasses that somehow didn't gel with his jowly face. He was the only non-Dyfed Powys officer in the room. Warlow learned Davenport had requested meetings with several groups, including drugs squad officers and the Sensitive Policing Unit that dealt with witness protection. In fact, everyone that might be involved with Lewis in some shape or form. He was in for a busy day.

Apart from Warlow's team, Superintendents Buchannan and Goodey were in attendance as well as a clutch of other officers, including Detective Inspector Kelvin Caldwell. A man whom Warlow placed one notch above two-month-old roadkill in terms of his desire to be in the vicinity of.

Davenport shuffled some papers. 'I don't think I need to go over the details leading up to Sergeant Lewis's suicide. Several people in this room were witnesses. Both the coroner and the public prosecutor are satisfied with the explanation and circumstances of Lewis's death. My brief has been to investigate the events leading up to it.'

Though the Chief Super began to summarise events, Warlow hardly needed reminding of what led to the detective sergeant's death. He'd been standing next to the man on the edge of a cliff pleading with him not to jump when it happened. But Lewis had been in too deep.

'I can't go to prison, Evan. Not with the lot I'm dealing with. I'm too much of a risk.'

Lewis's words on that clifftop had been tantamount to a confession. No details, but reason enough to end it there and then. Warlow half-listened as Davenport outlined the harrowing case of two missing walkers on the coastal path whose graves had inconveniently been revealed by a landslip on the stretch between Poppet Sands and Newport in Pembrokeshire. Not missing but murdered and buried. The reason that Warlow had never found them. And part of the reason that Mel Lewis had jumped.

'The full thirty-page report will be released to the press tomorrow, but I felt I owed it to his colleagues to come and speak to you all before the media gets hold of it. Suffice to say that Lewis's involvement with organised crime remains part of an ongoing investigation. We also suspect him as directly responsible for the murder of Kieron Thomas, a known drug dealer, in Pembroke Dock. Phone records and movements link the two and put Lewis in the same location where Thomas's burnt body was found. We also have admissions from the men involved in running and hosting the marijuana farm that Lewis was their source for informing them of ongoing investigations. His role as part of the review team into the missing persons case effectively allowed him to camouflage the Engine House site and allow the drug farm to flourish.'

No one spoke. This wasn't news to anyone in that room. But hearing it delivered again from an outside source made for uneasy listening.

'I can also tell you we have considered everything carefully and find no evidence of any wrongdoing involving anyone here today. You have nothing to answer for. We found no evidence of a breach of professional behaviour and no officer here faces disciplinary action.'

Warlow felt a collective exhalation. Some people had clearly been holding their breath.

'Not that Dyfed Powys comes away squeaky clean. The possibility, indeed, the likelihood, that Lewis was not the only link to organised crime remains. In cooperation with the IOPC and the local Regulator, we are continuing with a county-lines investigation across several Force areas. Your cooperation in this would be very much appreciated.'

Davenport stopped and surveyed his audience. 'I'm happy to answer any questions you may have.'

Silence followed. The kind of silence that comes with great relief. It was broken by the least likely source, as Rhys piped up. 'You still think that organised crime has a presence here, sir?'

Out of the mouths of babes and sucklings, thought Warlow, catching Gil's minimally raised-eyebrow glance.

Davenport nodded. 'Mel Lewis was extremely stealthy in his approach. We think that the links to the Engine House drug operation came from a Midlands OCG. Hardly surprising, since your patch borders on ours. We have Covert Human Intelligence Source information that leads us to suspect that all ties did not die with Lewis.'

'Thank you, sir,' Rhys said, looking appropriately shocked.

Goodey turned to Rhys. 'The report being released to the press has been redacted since references are made to serving officers in sensitive roles. No doubt some of the cannier press will attempt to put two and two together to make mayhem. Do not be drawn into answering any questions. The press officers here can handle all enquiries.' She nodded towards a woman in a grey suit with piled-up hair who gave her a quick toothless smile in response.

'Yes, ma'am,' Rhys said.

'Okay,' Davenport drew himself up, 'I have other meetings like this to attend. Superintendent Goodey has been briefed and I'm sure can answer any of your questions. I've been impressed with the professionalism of this group. A result-orientated culture can sometimes be fraught. But from what I've seen, you have strong leadership and good cooperation. Keep up the good work.'

Davenport smiled and nodded at Buchannan who stood up. And he, with Goodey, the press officer, and four other people, including Caldwell as entourage, followed the Chief Super and left the room.

'Well,' Gil said into the loaded silence, as the team looked at one another, 'don't know about you lot, but that's the worst X Factor audition I've ever seen.'

CHAPTER FOUR

IT WAS Gideon's turn to be in charge. Given that it was a four-day, three-night expedition, and this was day three, they'd decided on half a day each as team leader. That morning, Sophie had run the show for a couple of hours. She'd developed two massive blisters after their first day in the Beacons, and, Gideon suspected, had deliberately slowed everyone down to a crawl as she dragged them through the valley towards Penwyllt, trekking up from the Sleeping Giant Bunkhouse where they'd spent the night. He'd volunteered to take over because of her 'injury'. Now they were aiming for the Roman road, Sarn Helen, which would take them to Sennybridge before nightfall. But Sophie's route had strayed way too far west, taking the easy walk along the old railway line parallel to the A4067. When Gideon took over after lunch, he'd announced that they had to cut east if they had any chance of getting to where they were needing to be.

After all, the Duke of Edinburgh Gold award was all about challenging yourself, learning new skills, time management and getting people to do the difficult things they 'rilly, rilly don't want to.'

#rillyrillydontwantto had become Sophie's new nickname.

They all had the same amount of kit to carry and, yes, blisters were a problem. Worse than that had been yesterday's rain, which seemed to blow straight into their faces for four solid hours until they reached the campsite. Gideon had never seen weather quite like it. At least, he'd never been made to walk for hours in weather quite like it. It simply didn't rain like that in Sussex. Yet he'd found being out in the elements strangely exhilarating. You had to push yourself and he'd done his best to encourage the others, though with some it had been literally an uphill battle.

But today was a better day. No rain, and only a few flitting clouds in the sky.

Gideon took the lead. He'd asked Jasper and Dan to hang back with the girls, Sophie especially, to chivvy them along. Rachel was okay but felt a degree of loyalty to Sophie. The seventh member of the team, Hetty, stuck close to the other two girls in a herd mentality. Meg, on the other hand, walked with him. She'd been the surprise of the expedition. He'd always thought her the quiet one, but she had guts and stamina. Plus, she hadn't complained. Not once.

Whereas the others, even rugby-playing Dan, had whinged at how tired they were, or wet, or hungry or pissed off. Ringing up the negatives.

But Gideon had lapped up the challenge. Everyone else, bar Meg, kept on about how they were going to sleep for a week and binge out on Netflix and chocolate once they got home. Meanwhile, he was wondering how he might swing it with the 'rents to do this all over again next year instead of swanning off to their villa in Portugal. He'd have an extra-long summer if exams went well, and he got into Durham. There'd be plenty of time.

His route took them uphill along a forest track to a padlocked gate.

'It's locked,' Dan said, as the stragglers arrived at the gate. Gideon leaned his map on the top bar.

'It is, but it's marked as a path. Once we get through to the other side, we can branch left and take the road, then it's left over one hill towards the Devil's Elbow.'

'It's so hot,' Sophie said. 'Can't we stop for drinks?'

'There'll be shade in there,' Gideon said. 'We'll stop under the trees. Be nice and cool.'

Jasper, the biggest and heaviest in the group, wiped his brow. 'Hope so.'

They climbed the gate and, forty yards further on, entered the coniferous forest. The sun was high, and the wind had dropped. Only a faint easterly breeze wafted over the group as they slowly ascended. After another hundred yards, Jasper threw off his backpack, took a step into a patch of shade and slid out his drinks' bottle.

Everyone, bar Gideon and Meg, who were a dozen yards in front, followed suit. The two leaders exchanged an exasperated, knowing look before turning back to rejoin the others, who had found various upturned logs and stumps to sit on.

'What's that smell?' Rachel wrinkled her nose and lifted her chin.

'It's a bad one, whatever it is,' Dan said.

'Are there deer up here?' Hetty asked.

'It's all fenced off,' Gideon said. 'I doubt it.'

'It's not, like, bear poo or something disgusting like that, is it?' Sophie made a face.

'No bears here,' Meg said. 'They disappeared three thousand years ago.'

'How do you know that?' Jasper asked.

Meg shrugged. 'I could repeat it in my David Attenborough voice, if you like.'

'No, you're alright,' Jasper answered, already losing interest.

Another gust brought a fresh dose of the rich aroma to the group. 'Phwah,' Dan said. 'I caught a whiff that time. I reckon something's died.'

'Ugh,' Sophie said.

Dan got to his feet, licked a finger, and held it up. 'Wind's coming from that direction.' He picked up his map and compass from his backpack and pointed. 'That way, northeast.'

'Is that the way we're going?' Rachel asked.

'We veer right.' Gideon, who hadn't bothered to take off his backpack, pointed east.

Dan kept looking at his map. 'Why don't we follow our noses? See if there is anything there?'

'I don't think there's enough time, mate,' Gideon said.

Dan frowned. 'What? It would take like ten minutes to walk across the whole of this patch of trees from north to south. Look,' he pointed to the map, 'there's a trail there.'

'Does everyone want to?' Gideon asked.

'I'm in,' Jasper said.

'I'm not,' Sophie said.

But Rachel looked excited. 'Come on, Soph. It'll be a laugh.'

'Those who don't want to explore stay here. We'll be back in fifteen.' Dan took a few steps, walking backwards up the trail, cajoling the others. 'Come on.'

In the end, only Gideon, Meg and Sophie stayed guarding the backpacks while all the others hurried off with Dan in the lead, heading left along a path towards a little hollow. Within five minutes, they were out of sight.

'Can blisters get infected?' Sophie asked.

'I suppose,' Gideon said, sliding off his backpack. Since they were now going to have to wait for the others, he decided he might as well take a break. Meg followed suit.

They drank from their bottles in silence for a while. Sophie took off her left boot and pulled down her sock to peek at the back of her heel.

'They can get pretty inflamed, but infection is rare,' Meg said.

'How come you know so much?'

'My dad walks. I mean, me and my dad and sometimes my mum. Long hikes. I've had loads of blisters. Compeed is the best.'

'I've got a plaster on mine.'

'I've got the good stuff if you like. Makes it much easier to walk. Acts like a second skin. I always carry a couple of box—'

The scream cut Meg off.

'That's Rachel,' Sophie said, her head up, searching.

A second scream followed. A different voice. This time it kept repeating three, four times in quick succession.

'What the hell?' Gideon turned and ran up to the trail. When he got there, Hetty and Rachel were running back, white-faced, terror in their eyes. They were both crying. Behind them, Dan came sprinting out, Jasper behind him, suddenly stopping to throw up.

Gideon grabbed Dan's arm. 'What's up?'

'Jesus, man, fuck… Jesus.'

'What is it?' Meg's voice emerged from behind Gideon.

'Don't go… Don't look. It's… Shit. Oh, *fuck*!' Dan shook his head, using his palm to wipe away tears.

Gideon hurried to Jasper, who'd fallen to his knees. 'Jasp? You okay?'

Another coughing heave and the noise of liquid spattering the floor came in response.

Gideon grimaced. He looked back at Meg and wanted to tell her to go back. But something inside him was glad she was there. For once, this was not a wind-up. He glanced at Meg, who nodded once.

They walked on.

The path turned left and then right through another stand of trees and opened out into a natural clearing.

But there was nothing natural about what this clearing contained. Gideon sucked in a breath and caught a full mouthful of the stench because he was looking at its source. Looking and hardly comprehending what it was he was seeing. Behind him, he felt Meg's hand on his arm and heard her shocked, rasping gasp.

Five chairs. Five dead bodies. Three animals. Two humans. The animal carcasses looked old. The human corpses not so. They'd been tied and their heads were back, their faces turned to the heavens. Turned and pinned by a wooden stake driven into the ground behind them, its spiked end protruding through the corpses' open mouths.

Gideon took a step, but Meg held him back.

'Don't,' she said.

'But—'

'You can't help them. And they wouldn't like it if you did.'

'Who?'

'The police. I know about crime scenes. And this place is a crime scene on acid.'

She pulled out her mobile. 'I'll take photos. You dial 999.'

For a moment, Gideon could only stare. But then he nodded and reached into his pocket, wondering all the while why he'd never realised how super-cool Meg Hayter actually was.

CHAPTER FIVE

'So, no one for the chop then,' Jess said, as they sipped proper tea from proper mugs, courtesy of Rhys. They could have all gone back to their desks, but they'd booked the meeting room for another twenty minutes. Rhys had volunteered to do a tea run, and Gil had fetched the HUMAN TISSUE FOR TRANSPLANT box – his biscuit tin camouflage.

Warlow wasn't much of one for debriefs, but today it would do no harm to have an open discussion about the long-awaited report. Even if he had nothing much to say about it, the others might.

'Well, personally, and speaking as someone who had the least knowledge of Mel Lewis, I'm disappointed with Chief Superintendent Davenport's lack of acronym use,' Gil said, dunking a Hobnob. 'I mean, he only used CHIS and OCG when we all know from TV programmes about this sort of thing that a sentence without at least half a dozen impenetrable initialisms doesn't cut the mustard. I mean, look at us, a crack MIT…' Gil looked at Rhys, who grinned.

'Murder Investigation Team.'

'All sitting around discussing BS after our DC has done a TR…'

Rhys frowned in concentration. 'Bullshit, Detective Constable and… Tea run?'

'Spot on that, man.'

Warlow let out a snort. 'Are we all happy?'

Nods from everyone except Catrin. 'I didn't like the bit where he said that Mel Lewis might not be the only link.'

'There's always some dirt, Catrin,' Jess said. 'Always someone bending the rules. And that can range from accessing information on the PNC for the wrong reasons to nicking stuff from crash scenes. I've seen that happen. Moments of madness.'

'I suppose.' Catrin nodded.

'But for us, it's a clean slate,' Warlow said. 'Time we all stop worrying and get on with things. Speaking of which, if anyone has leave owing, since we have a lull, now might be a good time to—'

His phone's ringtone, recently changed at the request of the team and with Rhys's help from the irritating default IOS marimba to the deep riff of Led Zeppelin's *Heartbreaker*, broke in. Warlow still wasn't quite used to hearing Jimmy Page coming from his pocket, but he had his phone on his desk and picked up almost immediately, only to see his old colleague, Owen Tamblin's name appear as his caller.

He waved the phone to show he needed to take the call and stepped out of the room. He walked along the corridor and into the stairwell before answering.

'Owen, what can I do for you?'

'You sitting down, Evan?'

'I was. Now I'm not.'

'Hold on to your hat, then. It's the Geoghans again.'

'Oh shit, have they surfaced?'

'In a manner of speaking, yes. A walker found them early this morning up in Penwyllt. Know where that is?'

'Vaguely.'

'OS maps have it officially listed as AEOB – the arse end of beyond. Not that it made any difference to the Geoghans since they'd been up there for several weeks. Dead as doorknobs.'

Warlow stopped walking and looked out at the fields visible through the window, lush and green and invisible to him as he tried to make sense of Tamblin's words. 'What?'

'Hang on, I haven't told you the worst part yet.'

'There's worse?' Warlow asked and leaned on a windowsill to steady himself.

Owen Tamblin enjoyed the tease, but eventually he relented. 'There was a note with them. And guess who it was addressed to?'

'Father Christmas?'

'Almost as jolly. But you don't have a red coat or a team of reindeer. And you'd have a hell of a job getting down any chimney.'

'You're kidding me.'

'About the chimney or the reindeer?'

'Jesus, *Live at the Apollo* must be beating down your door, Owen.'

'Wish they were. At least then I wouldn't have had to see the photos of the Geoghans. The name on that envelope was DCI Evan Warlow, in case you hadn't already guessed.'

A flummoxed Warlow could not find anything to say.

'I could meet you up there?' Tamblin offered.

'Where is there exactly?'

'A forest up past Abercrave. North of an old, abandoned railway line. Ystradgynlais would have the nearest DP station.'

Warlow massaged his neck. 'And this morning was going so well.'

Tamblin laughed out loud. 'And well done on finding that kid last month. I almost drove over the Lougher Bridge to buy you a drink myself.' The genuine delight in the South Wales Police DCI's voice came over loud and clear. Warlow and the team had cracked the case a few weeks before. One in which a rogue police officer had abducted a child in the process of getting at, and almost succeeding in, killing his estranged wife. It had been a touch-and-go case.

'We got lucky,' Warlow said.

'Count this as a heads-up, then. Unfortunately, where the bodies are located is on your patch. But since they were our mispers, I got the nod early. Their belongings were still with them, so preliminary ID came through to me. They've asked me to go up there and take a look. I'll keep you informed.'

With that, Tamblin signed off. Warlow kept his gaze on the Carmarthenshire countryside visible through a corridor window, wondering yet again at how fickle this job was. One minute you were top of the heap – or at least not for the chop – the next you were a rat in a maze again.

'Bloody Geoghans,' Warlow muttered and walked back to the meeting room. When he opened the door, he almost did a double take. The room had filled up again. Buchannan, Goodey and Caldwell had returned.

'Ah, Evan, glad you came back.' Buchannan stood up. 'Something's come up.'

Warlow nodded. 'The Geoghans. Owen Tamblin's been on the phone.'

'Ah, you already know.' Buchannan glanced at Goodey. 'It's a little delicate, so I'll let Superintendent Goodey explain to everyone else.'

Buchannan sat between Caldwell and Goodey. Her

turn to stand. She took the flip-chart end of the table; the team watching her every move with identical, quizzical frowns.

'Are we sitting comfortably?' she asked. 'Cue Twilight zone music. Two dead bodies found in a clearing, trussed up, tortured, and left to rot in a forest near *Carreg Cadno* in the southern end of the Beacons. This one is both freaky and delicate.'

'Where does the delicate come into it?' Jess asked.

Goodey turned her gaze to Warlow. 'Care to elaborate, DCI Warlow?'

Warlow didn't stand up. But everyone's face turned his way. 'This isn't Jack-a-bloody-nory,' he muttered.

'No,' Goodey agreed. 'But you are our resident expert on these two. And no time like the present, eh?'

'What's Jack-a-bloody-nory?' Rhys whispered to Catrin.

She shrugged, prompting Gil to say, 'Something from the olden days. Storytelling for kids. Very last century. Pre-Kindle and way before your time.'

Warlow sighed, not sure why he felt so reluctant to tell them. After all, they'd heard bits and pieces from him over the last few months. The Geoghans had never strayed far from his mind, largely thanks to the threatening letters he kept getting from them. But there was no escaping it now. Might as well give them the cut-down version and get them up to speed.

'Karen and Derek Geoghan,' he said. 'Both convicted criminals, aka pieces of human filth. Both imprisoned in 2008. Karen Geoghan for fraud and Derek Geoghan for manslaughter of James Kinton. Karen got four years, Derek twenty. He came out a couple of months ago on medical grounds after nearly fourteen years. Karen had once been a nurse but lost her job due to pilfering from patients' lockers. She was not charged, but never worked as a nurse again after a disciplinary hearing. Derek had been a fraudster, conning people out of money, usually elderly people. He'd pretend to read a meter or check the gas, get inside, and rob them. Then Karen met Derek. A match made in hell if ever there was one. Their specialism was following carers on their rounds, then putting themselves forward as extra help to the people in the houses once the carers left. They'd worm their way into homes and look for valuables. We suspect they got more than one elderly patient to change their wills. Never big stuff, but enough. And there'd be inexplicable withdrawals from bank accounts, usually only ever coming to light after the death of the elderly victim. All very difficult to trace. And we only scratched the surface of all that. But with James Kinton, they moved into his house. He had no relatives; was a recluse. An ideal target. They locked him in a shed, chained him up, fed him, until they forgot to and let him waste away. Kinton was the case we charged them with. Everything else emerged afterwards. The difficulty here was that they'd used false IDs, pretending to be official-dom, or from the care agencies. And their targets were never reliable witnesses. That was their MO. Pick on the weakest in the herd.'

'Charming,' Jess muttered.

'Karen never forgave me. She never forgot Christmas or my birthday. I've kept all her cards.'

'We'd better look at those,' Goodey said.

Warlow nodded. 'Owen Tamblin informed me a few weeks ago that the Geoghans had gone AWOL. Derek failed to check in with the parole officer. There was some evidence of violence in the house they lived in. It was assumed they'd argued and one of them had buggered off. From what we know now, that may not have been of their own volition.'

Goodey nodded. 'And the note left with them at the

scene was addressed to you.'

'What does it say?' Gil asked.

'We'll get intel once forensics examines and opens it.'

'I doubt it's your invitation to Hogwarts,' Gil said.

Rhys let out a wistful hiss of air and got an eyeroll from Catrin in reply. He sunk a little lower in his seat. Something he achieved with great difficulty, given his stature.

'The scene is on our patch,' Buchannan explained. 'That means we need to take ownership. The only trouble is that you're materially involved, Evan.'

'As in, put them both away?'

'No. As in receipt of threatening letters. Jess, you happy to take it on as an acting?'

Jess blinked, surprised by this new turn. She was yet to get her SIO accreditation, but Warlow was confident she was more than capable. 'Of course.'

Buchannan turned his gaze back to Warlow. 'We can't ignore the fact they'd communicated with you.'

Warlow frowned. 'What? Am I a bloody suspect now?'

'No,' Buchannan explained, but the soupçon of hesitation in the Superintendent's reply told Warlow that they had to factor in his previous involvement. 'You know the case better than anyone. And you know the area. I want you in on this, but not as SIO. The CPS won't have it.'

'Fine,' Warlow conceded, but he did so reluctantly.

'How come you know the area?' Goodey asked.

'This is the top end of the Swansea Valley,' Warlow explained. 'Where worlds collide. It's a junction of three counties. A mile south of Ystradgynlais, which is the nearest police station to where they found the bodies, you can walk a hundred yards in any direction, and you could be in any one of those three counties. I grew up around there.'

'So, we need you on the ground,' Buchannan said.

'And because it's a tricky one, I'm sending Kelvin along

as an extra pair of hands. We don't think it's wise you work alone at any stage, Evan.' Goodey nodded as if she was doing him and the team a big favour.

From the expressions on the other's faces, she might as well have anointed them in dog dirt.

'Do we really need all that manpower at this stage? I mean, this could be a picnic gone badly wrong,' Warlow objected, knowing it sounded lame. But he didn't care if KFC took offence. Nor if Two-Shoes did.

The Superintendent chuckled. 'I'll pretend I didn't hear that because normally you'd be howling for more help. Besides, from what I've been told so far, this is no picnic. Not by any stretch. Kelvin can work with DS Richards. You and DC Harries pair up. That'll leave DS Jones to run the Incident Room with DI Allanby conducting the orchestra.'

Warlow avoided Catrin's glare by keeping his eyes front. Next to him, Rhys Harries was grinning, obviously pleased at the pairing. One glance from the DCI wiped the smile from his face.

'I suggest you get over there as soon as possible,' Buchannan said. 'The crime scene techs want to move the bodies before there's any more deterioration. If you want to see the horror show, you need to go now.'

'So much for accrued leave,' Gil said.

'YOLO, Sarge,' Rhys said.

But Warlow was only half-listening. He was watching Catrin, her face stern and unhappy.

'I'll nip home and get the correspondence from the Geoghans.' Warlow turned to Catrin. 'There is something else I'd almost forgotten. Someone started a petition to get signatures to prevent Geoghan's release from jail. An unlikely lead admittedly, but it's an 'I' to dot.'

Catrin nodded. She didn't write anything down. Once told, she never forgot.

'Right, I'll meet the rest of you up there.' And with that, Warlow left them to it.

CHAPTER SIX

CARS WERE an issue when you travelled to a crime scene some distance away. For DI Jess Allanby, it was more of a problem than usual because her car was in for repairs. They agreed that Gil would take his and Catrin hers. Rhys opted to go with Catrin because Gil needed to finish a few things before setting off, and the DC was keen to get to the scene. Which meant that Jess, now Warlow'd gone off on his own little jolly back to Nevern, travelled up with her fellow Detective Inspector, Kelvin Caldwell.

Caldwell drove a red BMW with alloy wheels and leather seats. It smelled faintly of fresh laundry thanks to a scent-soaked cardboard tree hanging off the rear-view mirror. Unfortunately, the air freshener didn't mask the powerful aroma of whatever aftershave/deodorant combination Caldwell doused himself in. Jess had always been aware of the man's predilection. One only had to follow him down a corridor to know that. And better that than BO, she supposed. But it was a close call. There was nothing subtle about the aroma and there was way too much of it. She wondered if he topped himself up whenever he got the chance. Nothing wrong with a nice aftershave. In fact, there were some she wouldn't have minded wearing herself. But whatever Caldwell wore wasn't alluring. If any of the big perfume houses had come up with something called 'Desperation', this might well be it.

Though Caldwell had been an Inspector longer than Jess had, he'd come in via the direct entry route on a twenty-four-month course. She knew that there remained a degree of scepticism about this scheme in the rank-and-file, but she'd worked with a couple of great officers in Manchester who'd come in on similar schemes, and who'd brought skill sets with them that proved to be invaluable. She kept an open mind. But Caldwell's career stuttered after a couple of less than stellar outcomes in the cases he'd been involved in. He'd been re-routed as a result, towards something more office based. Her surprise at seeing him seconded to a case like this was therefore genuine.

Kelvin Caldwell's nickname was KFC, not that anyone used that to his face. There might even be an F for Freddy in Kelvin's signature, but the F in KFC, when used by his fellow officers, usually had a different connotation. Kelvin Fucking Caldwell left little to the imagination.

'Jesus,' Caldwell said, when he'd finished typing an address into his satnav. 'This place really is the back of beyond. And I'm never going to get used to these sodding names. Is-trad-ginless is the place we're setting up shop. Is that how you say it?'

'It's not how Gil pronounces it,' Jess said. 'And it's spelled with a "Y", so it's an "uh" sound, not an "eh".'

Caldwell tossed her a glance. His flat, saucer-shaped face hung under a wide forehead and a chin that curved forward. Behind his thick, short-sighted glasses, his eyes had an almost constant pop-eyed look. Jess wondered if he'd had a thyroid problem. 'What? I suppose you're up to speed with the lingo then, are you? Impressive. I've been here for years, and I can't stand the sodding thing meself.'

His voice carried a vague Brummie whine, but it was more his carping attitude that failed to endear him to his fellow officers. Well, to Warlow, certainly. And dismissing a language which had been in this land far longer than English had been spoken probably summed him up.

Jess caught herself. She needed to try. Like it or not, they were going to be colleagues on a murder investigation.

'You've been heading up the Economic Crime Team for, what, eighteen months? How's that been?'

Caldwell shrugged. 'Eighteen months, yeah. It's been great. Though we're pissing into the wind when it comes to cybercrime. Punters are Capital G gullible.'

'So, you've been there as long as I've been here, then?'

'Probably why we haven't bumped into each other much, yeah?'

They headed up the A48 to hit the M4. The satnav gave them a couple of options, but Caldwell chose the major arteries before heading north towards the hills.

'You have no problem with me being the SIO, though?' Jess believed in being direct. 'I'm due for my course in a couple of months. The Buccaneer probably thinks it's a good idea I get another case under my belt.'

'Nah, knock yourself out. I'm happy to tag along. Goodey thinks I ought to get back into major crimes, too. She's the one who recruited me for the Economic Unit. Wanted to harness my expertise there. This'll be a change from staring at a screen all day, that's for certain. And they're right about Evan, by the way. He can't be running this one. Shit sticks, as they say.'

Not in Jess's lexicon, it didn't. 'What do you mean?'

'Only that the Mel Lewis thing leaves a proper bad taste, doesn't it? They were mates back in the day, after all.'

'I was there, don't forget. I saw Mel jump.'

'But you didn't hear what was said between them. Am I right?'

'No.' That aspect of it had come up more than once in the interviews she'd had with the West Mids detectives under Davenport's remit. She hadn't heard. What she'd seen was Warlow pleading and Mel Lewis shaking his head. It tied up exactly with what Warlow had said took place. She had no reason to doubt that. 'The idea of Evan Warlow being a part of some OCG is laughable. Still, I'm aware there is no love lost between you two.'

Caldwell smiled. 'Oh, that's just banter. Me and Evan worked some big cases together before you came along.'

Jess thought about that. Banter would not apply to the way Warlow, on the rare occasions he'd even mentioned Caldwell, described working with him. The DCI had been particularly critical of how KFC missed the drug farm they'd eventually unearthed that triggered Mel Lewis's demise. Caldwell had been part of the review of the missing persons' case on the Pembrokeshire coastal path that was at the heart of the whole sordid mess. That review had left much to be desired and allowed Lewis to manipulate the investigation, therefore, allowing the OCG to operate unchecked for years. Caldwell was not solely to blame, but Warlow's approach to working with him was to make strenuous efforts to ensure they were never on the same case.

But this was different. This was big.

'What were you doing before you joined the direct entry scheme?' Jess asked.

'I worked for a company in Redditch for fifteen years. Logistics management. Good money, but I got bored.'

'Married?'

'Was. Not anymore. We parted ways a few years back. Dodged a bullet there, I can tell you. She's fifteen stone and diabetic now. How about you?'

The loaded misogyny in describing his ex rankled in

Jess's ears, but she was in no mood for a fight. Not yet. 'Separated.'

'But you have a kid, right? I think I've seen her at HQ with you?'

'Yes. Molly. She's seventeen going on twenty-eight. You?'

'No, thank God. We decided against that early on. It would have been complicated.'

'Yeah,' Jess mused. 'It can be.'

Caldwell changed tack. 'I'm looking forward to this case. Sounds an intriguing one. Tell me about the rest of the team. I've heard good and bad.'

Jess frowned. 'What do you mean?

Caldwell didn't flinch. She'd been told he was thick-skinned. Warlow had used the phrase in describing KFC, but without the skinned bit and with added adjectives.

'I'm going to be working with them. Best I find out their good and bad points. Strengths and weaknesses in HR speak. We've talked about Evan, so let's go with DS Jones.'

'Gil? He's old school. Or pretends to be to wind people up. Which he does with good humour. He's hugely valuable in terms of morale. Has a secret biscuit stash he brings out for the team. Very experienced and sharp as a tack. He worked on Operation Alice for years. A good man to have at your back.'

'He's a slob though, isn't he?'

'Not a term we've ever used to describe him. He's carrying a few extra pounds, but he was in the forces before joining us. He can handle himself.'

'He can love-handle himself certainly.' Caldwell laughed at his own joke.

Jess didn't.

'What about the DC... Umm, Roy, is it?'

'It's DC Rhys Harries. And he's brushing up nicely. I have high hopes for him.'

'I've heard he's a bit cack-handed and naïve.'

'No, he's neither. He's a big lad, that's all. A little over-enthusiastic, perhaps. But I'll take that over some of the lazy sods I've come across. He's conscientious and fantastic with people.'

Caldwell kept poking with a smile that suggested he was enjoying goading her. 'Two short planks, I'd heard. All brawn and sod all else.'

'Then you've heard wrong,' Jess replied, a little more sharply than she'd intended. Caldwell, however, seemed not to notice. His smile didn't slip. He was doing a steady eighty on the A48 by now. She could point that out, but a little part of her suspected old KFC knew what he was doing well enough.

'And then there's Catherine Richards.'

The second time he'd got their names wrong. Warlow was right. Either this was a deliberate ploy to wind her up, or he really was thick.

'Catrin is a gem. She's bright and keen and a hard worker. But you know that. You've worked with her before, haven't you?'

Caldwell said nothing, so Jess probed, 'Come on then, aren't you going to tell me what you've heard about her?'

'I have worked with her before, so I have first-hand knowledge, but the word on the street is she's changed. Become a bit of a victim, as is fashionable. Lacking in humour. Likes to play the feminist card whenever things get tough.'

'Jesus,' Jess said, turning in her seat to glare at him.

Caldwell looked surprised. 'It's not me that's saying this. You asked how she's perceived by other officers.'

'Is that right?'

'Just saying,' Caldwell muttered. 'From what I've seen

of her, she's a straight arrow. Could do with smiling a bit more, but otherwise a good, solid copper. I'm looking forward to working with her again. Looking forward to working with them all, in fact.' He turned and smiled at her. 'You included.'

Oh God, please don't let that be anything more than your clumsy way of being pleasant. Because if it's anything else, I'm going to slap you here and now.

The awkward moment lasted only a few seconds. Caldwell turned back to looking straight ahead. But his supercilious little smile persisted. It looked like his default expression. One that made you want to wipe it off with a thwack of a studded gauntlet.

'How about some music?' he asked. 'I'm into classical. You okay with that?'

Jess wasn't but swallowed and shrugged. Anything was better than his excruciating attempt at small talk.

'I'm a big André Rieu fan.' Caldwell pressed some buttons on the steering wheel and the entertainment system lit up in the centre console of the dash.

'The bloke with the curly mullet?' she asked, unable to quite mask her surprise.

'Seen him live four times. Unbelievable. Has the audience in the palm of his hands.'

Jess nodded, suppressing the urge to suggest what else he might often have in the palm of his hands. She really was spending too much time with Gil.

André Rieu.

She had an eighty-four-year-old aunt who had all the violinist's CDs. Mind you, she had a display cupboard full of Beatrix Potter figurines as well, which said a lot about her taste. The Germans had a word for what Rieu aspired to by adding glitz and pizzazz to orchestrated music. One of the few foreign words Jess had no difficulty in remembering: *Gesamtkunstwerk*.

She also knew exactly what Gil would do with the deconstruction of that term. She half-turned to look out of the window to hide her smile.

A schmalzy orchestral version of the theme from the *Titanic* filled the car. Caldwell misinterpreted Jess's expression as appreciation. 'Yeah, this is one of my top five, too.'

She sat back and closed her eyes, wondering if the combination of Caldwell's driving and aftershave was making her slightly nauseous, or the prospect of another thirty minutes in the car with him humming along, in an out-of-tune voice, to classical kitsch.

CHAPTER SEVEN

Rhys Harries stood in the HQ car park next to a 'pool' grey Ford Focus. He'd only been involved at a very junior and peripheral level with the Engine House case involving Mel Lewis. Though he'd been interviewed by West Mids too, he'd had little to contribute. He remembered the sergeant as a funny guy in the pub, but his work remained a bit of a mystery. He'd always seemed to be away on task force business. Now that his connections with OCGs had come to the surface, those absences took on a very different connotation.

Still, his job was not to reason why.

His phone buzzed. A message from his mother.

Will you be home for supper?'

Don't know yet. Will keep you informed.

You should have eaten a bigger breakfast.

He didn't reply to that one. But she was right. He should have. Perhaps he could persuade DS Richards to stop at a garage so he could stock up on snacks.

He looked up towards the door she'd be coming through. She was late. Ten minutes, she'd said. It had already been fifteen. He let his gaze drift up to the sky. A fair enough day. No rain due. Not exactly a scorcher, but it might get up to twenty degrees. A good day to be outside, though he'd packed a coat just in case. You never knew what it'd be like on the side of a mountain, which was where it looked like they were headed.

'Is it a bird or a plane?' The question from behind him took Rhys by surprise. He pivoted to see Catrin approaching.

'Hi, Sarge.'

'You drive,' she said, tossing him the keys.

He caught them on his chest, juggled for a bit, but then grabbed them safely. 'You want me to drive?'

'You *can* drive, can't you?'

'You know I can. It's just that you normally want to drive.'

'Yes, well, I have a few things to work on.'

'Okay,' Rhys said, squinting as the sun peeked out from behind a cloud. 'You okay, Sarge? You seem a bit… Edgy.'

Catrin gave him one of her steely looks. 'Two-Shoes wanted a word about Davenport. I'm always edgy after speaking with her.' She opted to use the common nick-name for Goodey. The one everyone knew her by.

'What did she want?'

Catrin's mouth flattened into a thin smile. 'Oh, the usual.'

'She never speaks to me.'

'Lucky you,' Catrin muttered. 'This Mel Lewis thing… It's a gift that keeps on giving.'

'I thought Davenport gave you, gave us, the all-clear.'

'It sounded like that, didn't it? But there are always loose threads that need tying up.'

Rhys frowned, not comprehending.

'Are you going to unlock this thing or not?' Catrin demanded.

Rhys pressed the key fob, and the car alarm blipped

twice. Both officers got in. Rhys fired up the engine and drove out.

'Motorway or cross-country?' he asked.

'You know the way?'

'Yep. I've played rugby against Abercrave. It's only a few miles from the scene. We can go up through Ammanford, Brynamman and then Cwmtwrch—'

'Right,' Catrin cut him off, irritated. 'Let's do that.' She opened her laptop on her knees.

'So, what did Two-Shoes say?'

Catrin shut her eyes, sighed, and then opened them again. 'Don't ask because I cannot tell you. In fact, forget I ever said anything about Two-Shoes, okay? It's too... Complicated.'

'Fine.' There was a pause before he asked, 'Think there'll be a post-mortem? On the bodies, I mean?'

Catrin did not glance up from her screen. 'No. They're going to slaughter a squirrel and look at the entrails. That'll tell us what killed them.'

Rhys glanced across. 'Is that a thing now?'

After a long moment, during which she may have been counting silently to ten, Catrin said, 'Of course it isn't a thing.'

'Heh.' Rhys laughed. 'You got me there, Sarge.'

'Oh, God,' moaned Catrin. She let out another sigh. 'There will be a post-mortem. And yes, I'm sure you'll be able to go.'

'Yes.' Rhys made a fist.

Catrin shook her head. He'd become the team's willing ghoul. Happy to attend post-mortems when no one else wanted to go anywhere near them.

'Any chance we can stop at a garage for snacks?'

'Yes.'

'Can we have music on?'

'No.'

Silence.

Catrin's brows furrowed as she thought. 'But that doesn't mean you can tap out the tunes you hear in your head, either.'

'I don't do that,' Rhys objected.

'Yes, you do. And your mouth moves to the words.'

'No way.' Rhys grinned. 'You made that up.'

'I wish.'

'Funny that. Gina says the same thing.'

'Gina needs a medal.'

They lapsed into silence. After two minutes, Rhys started tapping his thumb on the steering wheel.

'Okay, okay. Music,' Catrin held up a hand, 'but low volume, please.'

Rhys found a channel. Nineties hits. Will Smith's *Gettin' Jiggy Wit it.* Catrin reached for her backpack from the rear seat. She took out some earbuds and slotted one into each ear.

'Does that mean I can sing now?' Rhys asked.

Without looking up from her screen, Catrin nodded.

When Ace of Base's *All That She Wants* started up, he joined in. Except in his version, what she wanted ended up being 'another bagel' instead of the intended offspring.

Luckily, Catrin didn't hear that bit.

———

WARLOW GOT BACK to Nevern and picked up the correspondence from the Geoghans. He had them in a black box-file with a yellow poison skull and crossbones label stuck on it. A tad melodramatic, but he'd found the label on a sheet discarded near a fly-tipping site and the idea of using it tickled him. He threw a change of clothes into a bag, locked up and got back on the road for the trip up to Penwyllt.

But he didn't go straight there. Not that the stop he wanted to make first meant much of a detour. In fact, it was very much on the way. The Geoghans operated in the run-down areas of the post-industrial valleys. Areas where terraced housing ran up mountainsides and lined narrow streets. Mining communities stripped of their livelihood, chewed up by politicians and spat out to survive, fragmented and directionless. With no work for the younger generation, as one century died and another was born, the older people who'd been the community's heart were abandoned with little or no support. It became difficult to recruit doctors to these towns and villages left ugly and ravaged by years of decline. As always, the elderly and the mentally challenged suffered the most.

Karen Geoghan read the runes on this, and she and Derek saw easy pickings. Their hunting grounds were the western edge of the South Wales coalfield. Where Carmarthenshire's rolling pastures transitioned into brash and brittle mining towns on its north-eastern border. A borderland abutting the old West Glamorganshire – now renamed a utilitarian Neath Port Talbot – pushing ever up against the mountains.

Once Warlow got to the outskirts of Carmarthen, he followed Rhys's route northeast, towards Ammanford and then skirting the southern edge of the Black Mountains at the head of the Amman and Swansea valleys. Heavy industry still played its part here. The gigantic East Pit Opencast Mine remained active, gouging out coal in an ever-expanding operation to the east of the village of Cwmllynfell. Shifting the millions of cubic metres of covering soil using giant buckets and hundred-tonne dumper trucks. But Warlow held no interest in the mine. His journey took him to the next village, Cwmtwrch and east along a narrow lane towards the foothills of the Black Mountains over the River Twrch at a bridge. He didn't cross the river but kept to the bank along a dirt track, pulling in a hundred yards further on through an entry once guarded by a gate, and parked up in front of an abandoned cottage.

This was where his relationship with Karen and Derek Geoghan had begun.

Warlow got out. The day had opened out and the sun warmed his neck as he stood in front of the property once known as *Ger yr Afon*. Appropriately translated as 'near the river'. This was where he and Owen Tamblin found James Kinton.

The sun triggered another memory, anchoring it in time. They'd finally found the place in mid-July. After agreeing on meeting up here, Tamblin from Swansea, where he was based and Warlow from Carmarthen on a joint venture, they'd got there sometime before eight in the morning. The sun had been high, the air clean, the burble of the river the only sound. Back then, *Ger yr Afon* had been just about viable as a property. Flaking paint, a couple of boarded-up windows, no attempt at keeping the weeds at bay in the garden. Warlow recalled a photograph of the place from the mid-eighties when the Kintons had moved here. A very different image of a freshly whitewashed cottage with flower borders and a neat path. But when he and Tamblin turned up, the Kintons who'd bought this place were long gone.

Five years had passed since they'd died and left the property to their only son, James. He, always reclusive, withdrew almost fully from a society that saw fit to pillory him and poke fun. Partly because of his appearance, the old clothes, and his lack of personal hygiene, and partly because he frightened people. On the streets of the village, he'd have conversations with himself or the people he heard in his head, out loud.

In the main, he had groceries delivered. The mental

health team and the local GP who were meant to keep an eye on him, failed to, driven away by his poor cooperation and absences. He broke no laws. Kept himself to himself, walked the woods for hours on end, and had never been a danger to anyone. Sadly, as far as James Kinton was concerned, the authorities took no news as good news. But a neighbouring farmer also supplied him with milk and would look in now and again. Or wave at James if he'd be out and about. If anything, the farmer was relieved to see some new faces in the form of the man and woman team about the place. Both wore lanyards that made them look official. And though the farmer never exchanged a word with them, they seemed pleasant enough on the odd occasion he drove past.

It was the farmer, after not having seen James nor his helpers for nigh on two weeks, who raised the alarm. Calls were made, preliminary inquiries too. Uniforms were despatched, but they saw no sign of James or anyone else at *Ger yr Afon* during a cursory visit.

What they did find were starving chickens.

Owen Tamblin picked up the case because the village was on his patch. Warlow got the nod because he knew the area and the property sat just over the border in Carmarthenshire. What Warlow remembered most was the smell. Dead animals in the heat. A locked chicken coop with one bedraggled surviving bird pecking at the remains of the others in cannibalistic desperation.

But the smell came not only from the chicken coop. James Kinton was in the garden shed at the rear of the property. It hadn't taken rocket science to find him. Both detectives literally followed their noses. Kinton was chained up next to a bucket full of his own excrement and urine. He wore a dog collar around his neck, hands behind his back tied together with bailer twine. From the state of the bucket, it looked as if it had never been emptied. Scattered over the floor were the remains of frozen pizza boxes and cheap white bread packages. Half a mouldy loaf in one corner looked tantalisingly out of reach of the short chain that tethered Kinton to a concrete post. They found no sign of water bottles, but a dry dog bowl sat upturned in one other corner.

The post-mortem suggested that James Kinton had been dead for seven days.

The Uniforms had called to *Ger yr Afon* eight days before. At first, Warlow wondered if Kinton had been too weak to call out. But later he learned that Karen Geoghan saw the response car arrive and had gone into the shed and gagged the hapless man before hiding behind some trees.

He'd been twenty-nine years old when he died.

Warlow and Owen broke down the door of the house. They'd found the Geoghans passed out upstairs, the house full of drug paraphernalia and booze; all bought from Kinton's emptied bank account. An account set up for him by his parents so that their troubled young man would want for nothing.

Warlow thought about walking around to the rear and looking at the shed again. He didn't need to. You didn't forget cases like James Kinton. Just like he could never forget the total lack of any remorse from either of the Geoghans throughout the whole of the investigation and the layers of criminality he and Tamblin went on to discover.

Two-Shoes was right to be wary. For years he'd fantasised about what he might do to the Geoghans if ever he found himself in a position to act. But he was a copper and as yet, there was no compulsory annual psych evaluation that made you confess your inner thoughts. If there was, he'd have been out on his ear. But he and Owen had at least got the Geoghans off the street for a while. He'd had to be content with that.

But someone else obviously was not.

Ger yr Afon, its walls crumbling, stood forlorn. There might yet be some answers here, but somehow Warlow didn't think there would be. He turned away and set off to meet, for one last time, the Geoghans.

CHAPTER EIGHT

GIL SENT through some directions for Warlow. It meant him driving up the winding valley and out on the Brecon Road past Craig-y-Nos Country Park with its famous castle once owned by the late Victorian opera diva Adelina Patti. Somewhere she went to recharge her batteries away from the theatres she filled. At least that was the accepted narrative. She'd be out of the public eye up here. No bugger would hear her striving for that top 'C' for miles around. Warlow stared again at the text, squinting his eyes because he wasn't wearing his cheap reading glasses.

> Branch right at Crai reservoir and then take a sharp right again across the mountain.

Of course, there was hardly any need for directions since there were police vehicles at the turning points. Par for the course as they stopped traffic, trawling for information from regular users. Did they travel this way often? Had they seen anything odd over the last few months?

Warlow got waved through and headed up across the open moor with views of Swansea Bay way off to the south. The road curved around and down to the edge of the forest at the opposite side to where the Duke of Edinburgh crowd of kids had entered.

He parked up next to the grey Focus and flashed his warrant card to the crime scene duty officer, who ticked him off on a clipboard.

'Through the gate and along the logging road, sir. It's up and down for half a mile but then you should see some activity off to the right.'

The Uniform was right. He could see some activity. A Crime Scene van, a Mobile Ops unit and some tape on marker poles leading off through a patch of trees. Thankfully, the paths were dry; Warlow hadn't bothered to change his shoes. The way felt springy underfoot from layers of pine needles. Once he broke through the screen of low conifers into the open space, the usual crime scene melee confronted him. Probably more people than this patch of forest had seen since it had been planted. And all of them wearing white paper suits, some of them with the hoods up and masks on. Those were the techs. The others, bareheaded, he clocked as the other members of the team. The notable exception being Gil, who'd gone straight to the police station at Ystradgynlais to set up a room.

Warlow donned a paper suit and walked across to join Jess, who stood with Rhys at the edge of the horrific tableau at the centre of the space. It looked more like an art installation of some weird family party than a murder scene, what with the table and the dead animals. Across the way, KFC and Catrin were talking to a dog handler.

'Am I too late for cake?' Warlow asked, narrowing his eyes as the genuine horror of the set up sank home.

'You are. But just in time for the quiz.' Jess waved at a white-clad body who emerged from one tent. Alison Povey was the senior crime scene coordinator running the techs.

As usual, she had her hood pulled tight around her face, but she removed her mask as she walked across to them.

'Evan, nice of you to join us.' The delivery came sarcasm-free. Warlow and she were old friends.

'Wouldn't miss it for the world,' Warlow said.

Povey turned back to glance at the sight that had so shocked the youngsters who'd discovered it. 'Okay. We have two corpses, male and female, one at each end of the table. In between, we have the menagerie. Three other carcasses, all animals. Sheep, badger, and a very moth-eaten crow. All dead without injury, as far as I can see.'

'So not killed for this purpose?'

'I'm no vet, but they all seemed to have died some significant time before the principal members of the party.'

'What about them? The Geoghans?' Rhys asked, joining the senior officers to peer at the lurid scene.

That earned him a stern glance from Povey. 'It may be a reasonable assumption to name these two based on the ID we found. But confirmation will only come from dental or DNA.'

Rhys nodded.

'But to answer your question, there is significant wasting in the bodies that show a lot of excess skin. At their age, rapid weight loss does not go hand in hand with skin shrinkage.'

'The Shar Pei effect,' Jess muttered.

'Is that one of those dogs that looks like it needs iron-ing?' Rhys asked.

'That's the one,' Jess said.

'So how do you read this, Alison?' Warlow eyed the nearest corpse. From the length of hair, he judged it to be Karen Geoghan, though her sunken face and sightless eyes, which would, no doubt, have ended up as crow Hors d'Oeuvres, rendered her unrecognisable otherwise.

'Like a Stephen King novel,' she replied. Povey had a

stomach like iron and for her to be shocked, spoke volumes. 'Starved, garden ties fixing their limbs to the chairs. Eyelids removed with a sharp object so that they would not blink. So that they'd see the birds when they came down to feed. The arrangement of the pole is interesting in that the head is pulled back and resting on that sharp end of said pole which is buried in the earth. My feeling is that as they lost consciousness – and Lord knows how long that would have taken – the weight of the head would press into the point and, either wake them up, or, as has happened, eventually push right through.'

Someone swallowed loudly.

'How much does an unconscious head weigh?' Warlow asked.

'Separated from the body, about five kilos,' Povey obliged.

'So, this get-up was designed for maximum suffering?'

Povey considered the statement. 'That's the one thing we can be certain of at this stage. We'll know more once the PM has been done.'

'Dare I ask who the HOP is?' Jess asked.

'Tiernon.'

Warlow's lack of response, other than a grunted, hmm, spoke volumes.

'I like Dr Tiernon,' Rhys said. 'He's a good teacher.'

He's a Class A prat, thought Warlow, but he kept his powder dry. The Home Office pathologist was notorious for getting young officers to inspect the more gruesome and gory aspects of his work in the hope of 'generating a heave' – his words. But in Rhys, who had developed an "appetite" for want of a better word, for that most unedifying of the forensic sciences, he'd met an apt pupil who wasn't put off by anything of any colour, oozing from any orifice. Warlow looked forward to seeing the disappointment in Tiernon's face when Rhys pitched up for the PM on these two. But he felt a little for Jess. As the SIO here, she'd need to attend, too.

'Thanks, Alison,' Jess said. The CSI smiled and walked back towards her tents but stopped after five yards. 'If you want a closer look, you have fifteen minutes before we start moving them out. Tiernon wants them there this afternoon.'

Warlow stepped across and stood next to the table, far enough away so as not to contaminate anything, aware that they'd delayed everything as a concession to him. But he wanted a feel for things. Breathe in the view, see what the perpetrator had seen while he'd set all this up. Elaborate was the word that sprang to mind. Convoluted even. And it would have taken hours, if not days to get everything in place. There was a hint of real madness about the whole thing.

The Geoghans, impaled on the sharpened poles, made for grisly viewing. Warlow didn't tarry. There were better people than he who would come up with the true cause of death. Five minutes later, when he got back to Rhys and Jess, he turned to the DC. He'd been mentoring the young officer for several months. Time to see if some of the teaching had rubbed off. 'Thoughts, Rhys?'

The DC nodded. 'It's planned. So, of the five Ps for motivation, this one is either passion... Some sort of revenge or a hate crime, sir, or psychosis.'

'Agreed, though at this stage we shouldn't rule out protection – the Geoghans might have been blackmailing someone and gone a step too far. But that doesn't explain why they were left here to be found. Anything on the traffic enquiries?' Warlow turned to Jess. 'I presume a helicopter did not drop them in?'

'Not as far as we know.' She turned and strode back along the track. 'We assume whoever it was drove them in. Marched them up here, trussed them up and left them.'

'What about the note?'

'Povey promised me it'd be ready this afternoon,' Jess explained. 'Now I need to interview the kids who found them. If we divvy it up, we'll get through them quickly.'

'Be delighted,' Warlow said. 'Where are they?'

'They have a minibus waiting to take them back to their school in Sussex. They're in the caving club a couple of miles from here.'

'Problem is, the crow doesn't drive,' Rhys said. 'That means we have to go north and then come south in a loop.'

'I know it,' Warlow said. 'Next to the old quarry, right?'

That brought Jess up short. 'Of course, this is your old stomping ground, isn't it?'

'Almost. I grew up ten miles from here. But I wouldn't say I came up here often. It's like a different world.'

Back in the Jeep, Warlow backtracked, went south at the reservoir, and took the Penwyllt turn off the A4067. The winding road took him back up the mountain to a disused limestone quarry and its railway station, its tracks also long since gone. He drove on to the large parking area and waited for the others.

'Bloody hell,' Rhys said, as he exited the Focus. 'What is this place?'

'Penwyllt. Wild headland. Or the one I prefer, the edge of the wild,' Warlow replied.

'They got that right,' Jess said, zipping up her coat.

The view from where they stood was indeed wild and open. To the north and out of sight beyond rolling hills stood the forest. All around them was a vast, empty land-scape dotted with the crumbling remains of buildings and industry. A handful of houses still stood, now in the owner-ship of caving clubs and the like.

'Difficult to believe this was a thriving community once,' Warlow said.

'When? The year dot?' Rhys asked.

'Before the Second World War nearly five hundred people lived up here. Quarrying and making bricks. A hard life.'

'What did they do for entertainment?' Rhys asked.

'There was a pub.'

'There'd have to be,' Jess agreed.

She pointed towards an isolated row of terraced houses, and the vehicles parked in front. 'I take it that's where we're heading?'

Warlow nodded.

'Right, let's do this,' Jess said and started walking.

CHAPTER NINE

LUCKILY ENOUGH, there were three members of staff accompanying the kids from Erdingford College. They had their own transport by way of a Mercedes Sprinter van with the school's logo and name emblazoned on the side. Arcing over the top of said logo was the school motto. *Nulla tenaci invia est via.*

'Okay, Rhys, your first job is to find out what that means,' Warlow said.

'Easy, sir, I've got an app.' Rhys busied himself with his phone.

'Really?' Jess asked.

Rhys shrugged. A shrug full of the kind of incredulity a cave dweller with fire would give someone who hadn't quite mastered the flint and spark trick.

'The only Latin I know is *non deisistas non exieris,*' Warlow said.

'Your school?' Jess raised an eyebrow.

'Oh, yeah.' Warlow chortled. 'My school motto was "first in the queue gets most gravy". I'm not sure how that translates. You got an app for that, Rhys?'

'Probably,' the DC muttered, still glued to his phone.

'No,' Warlow explained. 'It's a quote from one of my favourite films, Galaxy Quest. "Never give up, never surrender." Ever seen it?'

Jess grinned. 'Of course, I've seen it. Alan Rickman and the flaking lizard-head makeup. I love that film.'

'Honestly? Most people I speak to never seem to have heard of it. Hidden depths, Inspector.'

'Bottomless,' Jess replied.

'Got it, sir,' Rhys said. '*Nulla tenaci invia est via* means, for the tenacious no road is impassable.'

'Hmm.' Warlow grunted. 'That's not true for a start. Otherwise, they would have walked straight through that forest without finding a bloody set from *Saw*.'

There had been offers, in some cases, threats, by parents to come and collect their kids from the mountain but the school had fended them off by promising to get them back as quickly as possible. By the end of the day even. Though it would be a good four-hour journey. By the time Jess, Warlow and Rhys arrived, both staff and students were keen to get on.

It was agreed that the staff could sit in if any of the pupils so desired. Though Jess pointed out the police did not need permission from parents or teachers to question anyone, even a child, who'd seen or been a victim of crime. And the Erdingford Sixth Formers were all over sixteen. They were voluntary interviews and they cautioned no one. They tasked Rhys with getting all photographs from mobile phones forwarded to him, and to issue warnings that these were not to be posted anywhere as they formed part of a murder investigation. Anyone who did post might end up being liable to prosecution. Jess suggested he leave the details of what they might be prosecuted with deliberately vague. The idea might be enough.

Warlow had a difficult fifteen minutes with a girl called Sophie McKee who spent most of the time describing how she was sure one corpse 'actually, like, moved' when she'd first caught sight of it. She might even have heard one of them 'actually, like, moan'. There were lots of OMGs, half a dozen 'totally, like, disgusting,' comments accompanied by dry heaves and, a cataract of tears triggering hugs from Miss Burns, the teacher who rubbed Sophie's back while staring daggers at the DCI.

He wasn't hoping for much when the next name, Meg Hayter was called out. But the girl who walked into the pokey little office and sat on a bench opposite Warlow held herself straight and looked calm and poised. Warlow shifted his weight on the wobbly chair they had given him as Miss Burns, possessed of a long face framed by greying hair which was now set into a look of milk-curdling disapproval, took her seat off to the side.

'Meg, my name's Evan. I'm one of the investigating officers. Thanks for talking to me.'

'Got to be done,' Meg said.

Warlow nodded, a little smile of appreciative surprise curling his lip. Pragmatism as opposed to hysteria. He liked Meg. 'So, in your own words, tell me what you saw.'

Meg composed herself, wiped off a smear of dried mud from her walking trousers and returned Warlow's gaze with an intelligent one of her own. 'Gideon was leading. He'd plotted a route for us to get back on track. Literally. Sophie'd been leading but she'd got blisters so Giddy took over since he was next up on the rota. He cut east through the forest. Seemed sensible.'

'And no one had ever been there before. Not uh… Giddy, was it?' Warlow pressed.

'Gideon. No, none of us had been there before. That's the whole point of D of E. Plotting the route is what it's all about. We walked into the forest but some of the others, Sophie mainly, wanted to stop in the shade. That's when we noticed the smell.'

'Smell?'

Meg nodded. 'A bad smell. Terrible. Dan wanted to find the source, so he and everyone except Sophie, me and Giddy went off to look.'

'How long were they away?'

'Only five minutes. Then there were screams and me and Giddy ran and met the others coming back. One person threw up, so you'll find some bodily fluids on the track.'

Warlow, who'd been jotting down notes, stopped and looked up. 'Bodily fluids?'

'Yes. Vomit. Jasper's.'

Warlow made a note. 'So, the two of you went on to the scene while the others ran back?'

'We did.'

'Did any of the others say they'd touched anything?'

Meg pondered and then shook her head. 'No, no one touched anything. I'm pretty sure of that. They were all too shocked.'

'But you and Gideon went to look anyway?'

'We did. Partly curiosity, I suppose, but partly as support for Giddy. I mean he was team leader, so he had to make decisions. I went because it seemed like the right thing to do.'

Warlow looked up at the girl. Rare enough to hear these sage words from a burly adult, let alone a slight seventeen-year-old. He liked Meg a bit more.

'And what did you see?'

Meg frowned. 'Do you want me to describe it? Or can I show you a photograph?'

'You took photos?'

'I did. My mum says first impressions are important at a crime scene—'

Warlow pulled her up on that. 'Your mother?'

'She works for Sussex police. She's a DI there. I got into Erdington on a full scholarship. None of the others know that.' Meg took out her phone and found her photos. 'I've already sent these to DC Harries,' she explained. 'And I didn't see anyone or anything else. I don't think anyone was watching.'

Warlow took the phone and scrolled through twenty photos in all. Different angles. Some very much like the ones he'd taken. 'These are useful. Thanks.' He glanced at his notes. 'I talked to Sophie, she said she'd seen some movement when she saw the bodies.' He stopped and waited.

Meg's jaw shifted to one side, and she blinked. 'Sophie didn't go anywhere near the bodies. She sat under the tree and became hysterical. She thought she saw all kinds of things moving in the forest. Including a wolf and a Big Foot.'

Warlow's turn to blink. The next note he made involved a lot of crossing out under Sophie's name before looking up again. 'What happened when you got to the site, Meg?'

'I stopped Gideon from walking everywhere, but of course the others might have. Though most of them bolted as soon as they saw the bodies.' Meg shrugged. 'Giddy will tell you the same thing. We got to within a dozen yards and then phoned 999. I spent the next hour trying to stop the others from going back there. What worked was telling them they might need to be questioned over the summer if they contaminated the scene. Most of them have got holidays abroad planned.'

Warlow snorted. 'Good thinking.' He threw a glance over at Miss Burns, whose eyebrows had gone up and stayed up the minute Meg had spoken. 'How about you? What are your plans for the summer?'

'The plan is to come back here. To Wales, I mean. My

brother is eleven. He likes the beach, so we'll end up on the coast somewhere.'

Warlow tidied away his notebook. 'Keep up the good work, Meg. Your mother would be proud of you. So should the school.'

'Thank you.'

Warlow glanced at Miss Burns who gave him a thin-lipped nod as an acknowledgement that the interview had ended. 'Right, Meg. I'm sure that's all DCI Warlow needs. We've given your mobile number to DC Harries. If the police need to question you again they can—'

'Do you think the sheep and the crow and the badger are significant?' Meg asked, cutting off the teacher.

Warlow had thought about that, but so far, he'd found no answer. 'Perhaps,' he said. 'Significant to whoever put them there, no doubt. Or they might have been what he'd found on the mountain.'

'They're not messages? Like some sort of hidden code?'

Another excellent question. That idea had occurred to Warlow, too. 'We'll only know that when we ask whoever it is who put them there. And we will do that when we catch them. Why, do you have any theories?'

Miss Burns looked as if she was on the point of object-ing, but Warlow stilled her by raising his hand.

Meg seemed unfazed. 'Only that the crow and the lamb is one of Aesop's fables. We've been doing some Greek classics in English as an option and—'

'Really, Meg?' Miss Burns stood up. 'This isn't some Dan Brown novel. Now, we've troubled the Chief Inspector quite enough without you theorising on dead animals and their significance.'

'It's no trouble,' Warlow said.

Miss Burns turned a tired-looking face to Warlow. He read the weariness and anxiety etched there. A weekend jaunt to the hills had turned into a nightmare for all concerned. 'We'd like to get the pupils back to Sussex PDQ. Meg is the last to be interviewed. I'd appreciate it if you'd let us get on.'

'Of course.' He turned to Meg and offered his hand. 'You've been great. Maybe we'll discuss Aesop another time.'

CHAPTER TEN

THE INCIDENT ROOM at the station in Ystradgynlais was in the newest part. The old station, little more than a bay-windowed house on Station Road, was now linked via a corridor to the more modern section. All rendered in off-white with a classic old, blue and white police lantern above the front door. Warlow had a soft spot for the lantern, and he wondered if it was the original reposi-tioned from the Station House itself. He hoped it was.

The Incident Room could have been bigger, but it had all the necessary. Desks, PCs, and a wall-mounted white-board. Not quite the Gallery and the Job Centre he preferred, but then he wasn't running this one.

Gil had already installed himself and made some intro-ductions to the local Uniforms when Jess, Warlow and Rhys arrived. After that, it was a question of finding out where to make tea. They'd be working in this room for the duration and Warlow chose a desk at random while they waited for Catrin and KFC.

'Cosy bordering on sardine tin, isn't it?' Gil said, when Rhys brought in a tray. 'I brought some mugs across in case they'd be short.' He'd already laid out a tray of biscuits. Away rations, as he called them, consisting of shortbread, Hobnobs (plain) and custard creams, with a centre pyramid of ginger nuts. In response to Rhys's raised eyebrows, Gil explained, 'All from the top twenty of the UK's choice. Shortbread remains number two, the Hobnob is in everyone's top ten, as is the custard cream. I've added the ginger nut since we'll all be travelling around a lot and they're good for settling the stomach.'

'You mean there's a science to all this flour and sugar?' Warlow asked, looking at his custard cream with sceptical interest.

'Indeed, there is, DCI Warlow. In much the same way one appreciates a good wine and the viticulture involved. Never underestimate the power of a biscuit. Even the Garibaldi, which my granddaughter recently described as a bread soldier full of squashed flies. One of the many things I've enjoyed as a father of girls over the years is when they'd get their spray tans done, the house would smell of biscuits for days.' Gil sighed before shaking his head and mentally coming back to the room. 'Now. I've seen the photos, but what did I miss on the mountain?'

'Not much, Sarge,' Rhys said, his mouth full of shortbread. 'Unless you're into weird.'

Just at that moment, as if fate had decided on an exquisite gem of stage direction, the door swung open and Catrin and DI Caldwell walked in. The DS looked like she'd been slapped with a herring. The DI wore his standard semi-smirk, an expression that made Warlow want to slap him with a herring – or something larger and spikier. Caldwell zeroed in on Gil's display immediately.

'Ah, biscuits. Don't mind if I do.'

Warlow watched as he took one of each of what was on display. When he realised that everyone was looking at him, he seemed surprised. 'Oh, is there a kitty?'

Without a moment's hesitation, Gil said, 'Yes, sir. It's a fiver each. That should see us through the week.'

'Of course.' KFC reached for his wallet.

No one said anything. Even though no other member of the team had ever contributed more than a pound a week.

'Tea?' Rhys asked.

'Please,' Catrin replied, as if he'd offered her a thousand pounds.

'Not a tea man, myself,' Caldwell said. 'But a cup of hot water would be great.'

Rhys's mouth dropped open. 'Hot water?'

'Yeah, from the kettle, as per,' Caldwell said. 'Caffeine makes me jittery.'

The room descended into small talk about the station and the mountain. Only after Rhys came back with the hot drinks did Jess stand up and address the team. 'What we ought to do now is go around the room. Pool our information and generate some actions.' She turned to Gil. 'Has Povey come back with details of the note left for DCI Warlow?'

Gil shook his head. 'Any minute, ma'am.'

'Okay, so let's press on.' She nodded at the whiteboard where some A4 sheets of paper were pinned up. 'Gil, I see you've been busy. Why don't you start.'

The DS took a sip of tea and brushed a few crumbs from a custard cream off the front of his shirt, picked a ballpoint pen up from the desk and stepped over to the board. The A4 sheets were grainy printouts from police mugshots. They showed Derek and Karen Geoghan in prison uniforms from fourteen years ago. Exactly how Warlow remembered them. Derek, a jowly man with puffy bags under his small eyes. Karen, her hair cut short, staring at the camera with a hateful defiance and her skin pockmarked from teenage acne that had left its mark.

'The Geoghans,' Gil said. 'There may be more recent photographs, but we are not in possession of any. Safe to say they did not take these on a location shoot for Hello magazine. And no, they were not wearing Addams Family masks.'

'Wouldn't have wanted to meet those two in a dark alley,' Caldwell observed.

'Trust me,' muttered Warlow. 'You would not have wanted to meet them in full sunlight, either. Not unless you had a baton in one hand and some PAVA spray in the other.'

'I've printed off copies of their records as they apply to DCI Warlow and his involvement in their arrest and subsequent incarceration. They released Derek Geoghan on compassionate grounds after being diagnosed with leukaemia. The rest you already know. There's been a warrant out for him since he broke the conditions of his licence some weeks ago. Last seen by his probation officer on April 6th.'

'And we don't know where they were in between?' Jess asked.

Warlow replied, 'I'm in contact with Owen Tamblin. I said I'd call him after this, and we'll put our heads together. He'll be ahead of us in trying to establish their movements up to the point of their disappearance since the probation officer had reported Geoghan AWOL.'

Jess nodded. 'Gil is the only one who hasn't been to the scene. But the photos will be coming through soon. I suggest you refrain from eating when they do.'

'That bad?' Gil asked.

Jess nodded. She turned to KFC. 'Kelvin, any thoughts?'

'Tortured and killed? Forget the theatrics for a moment. Could it be that someone wanted information?'

'What sort of information?' Jess asked.

KFC shrugged. 'Could be they hid some money. Could be he'd shot his mouth off in prison and someone has come after him for it.'

'What about the dead animals?' Rhys asked.

'Might be nothing but a distraction. Something to send us off down a garden path.' KFC stuffed a custard cream into his mouth and chewed.

Catrin, sitting closest to him and slightly behind, only just managed to contain the disgust obvious in her face.

'It's a fair point.' Jess sipped her tea. 'Let's find out who he was pally with in prison. Where was he again?'

'Cardiff, ma'am,' Gil answered.

'Worth a quick call, I reckon. Catrin?'

'Happy to, ma'am,' Catrin said, though she looked like she'd rather eat a bucket of frogspawn at that moment.

'We ought to chat with his probation officer, too. See if they're aware of any visitors etc,' KFC added.

Warlow listened. Hardly ground-breaking stuff. But the way KFC presented it made it sound like no one had ever thought of it before.

Gil's phone chirped. 'Hang on, looks like Povey's come through on the note. Let me have a look.' He went to a desk and swirled the mouse around. 'Tidy,' he said, and a printer in the corner of the room started chattering and chugging out some sheets of paper. Gil picked them out, glanced over them and said, 'Hmm.' Then pasted them up on the board.

Everyone sat forward to study the three sheets. 'According to Povey, the envelope was inside a clear plastic sleeve – presumably to avoid the weather – and attached to Karen Geoghan with wire that had been pushed through her flesh and cinched behind her. She doesn't know if that was done when Geoghan was alive.'

Rhys grimaced. Warlow stood for a better look. The

envelope had his name and nothing else written in felt-tipped pen.

Warlow.

He was no handwriting expert, but it looked enough like Karen Geoghan's for him to be convinced of its authenticity. He turned to the third sheet. The letter itself had no handwriting. Instead, the one word it contained was constructed out of blue stickers of the kind they used on wall calendars. The strips stuck together to form letters.

'Tâl,' Warlow read it out loud.

'What does it say?' KFC pushed his way in front of Warlow to stand a few inches from the board. 'Tall?'

'No,' Warlow said. 'It's a Welsh word. It means payment. Or compensation. Or perhaps, retribution.'

KFC turned to Warlow. 'Someone out for revenge, then?'

'Maybe,' Warlow agreed.

'Or payment as in for services rendered.' KFC went back to his seat.

'How, sir?' Rhys asked. 'I'd say this sounds more like revenge.'

'Or someone wants us to think it is. A double bluff.'

'No point second guessing at this stage. We need more information,' Jess said, seeing Warlow's lids going to half-mast. She glanced at her watch. 'Right. Gil, get this stuff onto HOLMES. I've not heard of anything like this MO out there, but we won't know unless we ask. Rhys and I are heading to Cardiff for the PM. Catrin chase up the prison and Kelvin the probation officer.'

'I'll get on to Owen Tamblin again,' Warlow said. 'He doesn't know about the note.'

'Funny he isn't mentioned, isn't it?' KFC said.

No one commented except for Warlow. He turned away and went to the desk he'd picked out. 'Yeah, hysterical. Only I don't hear anyone laughing except you, Kelvin.'

CHAPTER ELEVEN

WARLOW MADE the call to Owen Tamblin outside the Incident Room. Some fresh air wouldn't do any harm after being in the same room as KFC. Did brown-nosing bumptiousness have a smell? If it did, it probably came in a spray can with an exotic animal stamped on its side, and KFC must take a bath in it every morning. The DCI stood outside the Station watching the traffic and the odd pedestrian walking towards the shops on Commercial Street while he called.

Tamblin answered after half a dozen rings. For once, he wasn't in his car, but from the background street noises, not in an office either.

No greeting from good old Owen. He launched straight into it. 'Evan, you bugger. I expect you're not ringing me to tell me this is all a big mistake, and those kids stumbled across a film set by accident?'

Warlow snorted. 'I wish. I'm ringing you from the station in Ystradgynlais. I've been a busy boy. We've set up an IR and I've been up to the scene, had a look and managed to keep my breakfast down. Though that was a struggle.'

'As bad as they say it was, then?'

'Yep.'

'Hang on. Let me get off the Kingsway. It's like Billy bloody Smart's in town today.'

Warlow waited, wondering how many people in the room he'd just left would have any clue as to the reference Owen had just made. Billy Smart! Were circuses even a thing these days? Owen's footsteps got louder as the street noise faded.

'That's better. I'm in an alley,' Owen said in the relative quiet. But just then something, it could have been a Howler monkey or someone high on an illicit substance, whooped in the background.

'Anything special going on there today? Sounds a little lively?' Warlow asked.

'No. It's summer in Swansea, mun. They just unlock the doors to the cages and the sun brings all the sods out to feed. Either that or the buggers have a "cray cray" WhatsApp group that knows I'm in town. You know, Tamblin's on the Kingsway let fly the zombie hordes.'

Warlow chuckled softly. Owen was Swansea boy who used mun as a slang filler word for emphasis.

'Anyway.' Owen reset. 'The Geoghans.'

'Yeah. Post-mortem's this afternoon, but from the look of it, both Derek and Karen did not end up in Penwyllt at a scout jamboree. Forensics got the note open. Looks like Karen wrote my name on the envelope, but inside someone used stickers to spell out T.A.L with a little roof over the A.'

Owen waited. When Warlow didn't say anything, he volunteered some suggestions.

'T.A. L for Taliban? Talent? Talking heads? Talfryn Thomas?'

'Who the hell is Talfryn Thomas?'

'You know, Talfryn Thomas. Swansea-born, buck-toothed actor who egged the Welsh accent to the hilt. Big pal of Ken Dodd. Private Cheeseman in Dad's Army.'

'Jesus Christ,' Warlow said. 'You are talking about what, an early seventies sit-com? Are you regressing in your dotage?'

'No, I am simply trying to be helpful by making polite conversation while you drag your heels with the intel. Spit it out, man. Some of us have work to do. Or at least coffee to get from Greggs.'

'Tâl with a little roof over the a.' Warlow repeated the explanation slowly.

Tamblin hissed. 'You know me and the language. Both my kids are fluent. But all I manage are the swear words and the National Anthem, which I know better than half the sods on the team who just move their lips like goldfish.'

Warlow elaborated, 'Okay. Tâl means payment, retribution, payback maybe.'

'Oh, shit.'

'Couldn't have put it better myself.' An ambulance roared past, blue lights flashing. Warlow turned and walked around the building, away from the noise.

'Right, well, you'll be glad to know that I have not been idle down here, either.'

'First time for everything—'

'And,' Owen ignored the jibe, 'I may have come up with something. About a month ago, we got a report of suspicious activity in an empty house not a million miles away from where you are now. Owner was a widow that had to go into care. The place has been empty for a couple of years. Neighbours saw some lights late at night and called it in. I've just pulled up the report. The Uniform that went up there found the place empty but the lock on the back door was snapped.'

'And?'

'No sign of robbery, but definite occupation. Looked

like someone had squatted for a while. There was a carton of milk and some empty Asda sandwich packets in the kitchen bin. But oddly enough, the Uniform commented that there were items scattered over the table.'

'If you're going to tell me it's chicken bones or entrails—'

'Jesus, let me finish, mun. Envelopes and a Sharpie.'

Warlow's breath seized. 'What?'

'See, told you it was worth it.'

'Where is this place?'

Owen wheezed out a throaty laugh. 'This is the bit you are really going to like. It's on the edge of a little place called Ystalyfera.'

'You're kidding?'

'I am not. I can be there in half an hour. It'll take you ten minutes if you fancy it.'

Warlow said he did. He went back inside but couldn't find Jess. So, he told Gil he was off to meet Owen. Five minutes later, Warlow was heading down the road to the next village along the Swansea Valley. Into a different county. Towards a different time. The spot on the map where he was born and grew up.

———

CARDIFF PRISON IS a Category B prison and has room for five hundred inmates but holds over seven hundred. Doubling up was inevitable. Over the fourteen-odd years he'd been inside, the list of inmates Derek Geoghan had shared a cell with was not extensive. A couple of names within Dyfed Powys Force area came up and Catrin decided to start with these. Of the others, two were still serving sentences and one was living in Norfolk. It made sense to begin locally.

Jess wandered over while she pinned the information to the Job Centre.

'That was quick,' the DI commented.

'Best way, ma'am. It'll be worth asking them if Geoghan ever talked about someone while they shared the cell with him. If he was ever threatened.'

Jess nodded. 'Got to be done.'

'Or we could just go up to the roof and start pissing into the wind.' KFC walked up behind the two women. 'What were these two in for?'

Catrin explained that of the two names, one belonged to a petty thief and drug addict from Llanelli. The other to a local man serving a sentence for dangerous driving.

'Great,' KFC muttered. 'A junkie and a boy racer. They'll probably clam up as soon as they see us.'

Jess's smile didn't waver. 'Process of elimination, though, right?'

KFC held Jess's gaze, but he had the sense not to say anything. Yes, it might be fruitless, but these names were of people who probably knew and had spoken to Derek Geoghan the most over the last few years.

'Might as well do it now,' Catrin suggested. She turned to KFC. 'If you're busy, sir, I can take Rhys.'

Jess glanced at her watch. 'DC Harries and I are off to the Heath for the post-mortem in ten minutes. Kelvin will go with you, won't you, Kelvin?'

KFC shrugged. 'I think it's a waste of time, but we will go together, Sergeant. Tell you what, you drive. Give me time to read up on the vics.'

Catrin's over-bright smile didn't slip, but it stayed about as far away from her eyes as it was possible to be.

Thankfully, KFC was as good as his word and spent the journey east to Llanelli, either reading a file or scrolling through his phone, leaving Catrin to concentrate on the driving, which she was happy to do, despite the excessive watering of her eyes, courtesy of KFC's industrial strength cologne.

———

BRADLEY MASTERS' address on Ann Street, Llanelli sat almost opposite the abandoned Calvaria Baptist Church. Like the place of worship, the terraced house they pulled up in front of had seen better days. The front door opened onto three feet of pavement, which immediately abutted tarmac road. One of the windows on the first floor was boarded up and a makeshift blanket hanging from a wooden rail acted as a curtain for the first-floor bedroom facing the street.

'This it?' KFC wrinkled his nose.

'Yes, sir.'

The DI looked around, arching his back in the passenger seat, taking in the narrow streets and scruffy houses. 'We are still in Britain, are we? You didn't take the wrong turn and end up in sodding Beirut.'

'The town has seen better days, sir.'

'Boo sodding hoo.' With a sigh, KFC opened the passenger door and got out.

Three steps took them to the front door. Catrin knocked. Firm, no nonsense. A dog barked inside. KFC gave her a side-eyed look of disdain.

She knocked again.

A sluggish, nasal voice told the dog to shut up. The door didn't open. From inside, they heard. 'What do you want?'

'Bradley Masters?' Catrin asked.

'Could be.'

'It's the police, Bradley. We need a word with you about something.'

'Nah, I never did it.' Master's words slurred into one long denial.

KFC shook his head. 'We're not accusing you of anything, mate. Just open the door and talk to us.'

'Nah, I don't think so. Every time I do that I end up in the nick. Fuggit. I never did it.'

Catrin tried again, 'It's about Derek Geoghan, Bradley. Not about you.'

'Jabba the fucking gut? He's inside. I haven't seen him.'

'He's not inside, Bradley. He's outside and—'

'Someone's killed him, mate,' KFC steamrolled over Catrin's sentence. She half-turned away and squeezed her lids shut. Not the way to get a drug user's cooperation.

'What, like dead?'

'Top of the class, mate,' KFC said. 'That's what killed generally means. No flies on you are there, Bradley?'

'Na, nothing to do with me. Jabba's inside. I'm out.'

'You high, Bradley?' KFC asked.

No, he's just mentally exhausted from sitting his MENSA exam. Catrin wanted to say those words out loud very badly but managed to stop herself.

'No,' Bradley said. Then thought about it and added, 'Okay, I done some linctus, yeah? I'm knackered, that's all. You woke me up.'

'Open the door, mate!' KFC yelled, and then pared back his aggression with an insincere, 'That's a good junkie.'

'No way. I'm not being fitted up by you two.'

KFC turned to Catrin. 'I think our work here is done, Sergeant.' He dropped his voice and added, 'Get the Uniforms to pick this twat up the next time he goes outside.' Without further ado, he turned away and walked to the car. Catrin took out a card and pushed it through the letterbox. 'Bradley, when you come down, there's a number on the card for the Incident Room. We only want to know if Derek Geoghan felt threatened in any way. If he told you about anyone or anything, that might help. It's not about you, I promise.'

Bradley didn't respond. Cursing quietly, Catrin turned away and got back into the car. KFC was already scrolling through his phone. 'Right, that's one wild goose chased. Where next?' He spoke without looking up.

For a very, very short while, Catrin wondered what sort of noise her hand slapping his face might make. Then she put the car in gear and drove off.

Thirty-five minutes later, she'd reversed the journey and headed back up the Swansea Valley, following her satnav, boomeranging the route that Warlow had taken that morning, but unaware of that fact as she entered the village of Cwmtwrch.

In the passenger seat, KFC was getting very antsy. 'Another unpronounceable name. What exactly are we looking for, Sergeant?'

'A turning to the left, sir, across the river. It's signposted *Rhiwfawr*.'

'And what does that mean?'

'Big hill, sir.'

KFC sighed. 'Jesus. As if we haven't had enough of them already.'

'It's not far now, sir. Five or six minutes at the most.'

'Great. I cannot sodding wait.'

CHAPTER TWELVE

CATRIN KNEW they were in no-man's-land here when it came to area boundaries. But *Erw Foel*, though in South Wales Police's territory, was the other ex-con's last known address.

'So, what's the story here, Catrin?' KFC shifted in his seat. He put just enough emphasis on her name to imply that whatever she said, he would not be impressed. Underlining the disdain that he'd already expressed over their expedition in a thousand different little ways.

She began the climb out of the village and gave him the lowdown.

'Iwan Meredith had a string of traffic violations and dangerous driving fines leading up to the offence that got him imprisoned. He tailgated a Subaru driver and when they pulled over, Meredith drove his car straight at him. The victim broke both legs and hip. Meredith got six years. He served three years and got out eleven months ago.'

KFC shook his head. 'How old was he?'

'Twenty-five at the time of conviction. Bit of a petrolhead.'

'Boys and their toys, eh?'

Catrin cringed. From the notes she'd read, it had been touch-and-go for the victim. It could so easily have been manslaughter. 'According to the prison officer I spoke to, Meredith shared a cell with Geoghan for about four months a couple of years ago.'

'Let's hope this Meredith was a good listener then, eh?'

The road took them up over the mountainside and branched off onto an unnamed lane. Catrin overshot the turning she was looking for and had to reverse. But eventually, she turned off along another narrower track to an isolated ramshackle property on the edge of a stand of trees.

Erw Foel meant open or bare acres. Pretty appropriate for this high, flat moorland. Though the house, if it could be called such since it looked more like a mishmash of cobbled-together corrugated-tin sheds, sat in a low hollow. Its half-hidden location and a dark roof melding with the dark tress behind, explained how she'd missed the entrance when she drove past the first time.

KFC stared out of the window; his mouth open in dismay. 'Jesus. Someone lives here?'

A white Berlingo sat parked on some rough stone chippings to the left. The yard they'd pulled up in front of needed a bulldozer to clear it. The entire space, apart from a narrow path to a door, seemed packed with broken chairs, plastic bags, upturned bins, and a sofa bed on its side, its stuffing hanging out like a gutted animal. It looked more like the aftermath of a plane crash than a house. If Meredith still lived here, he'd get 'null points' for tidiness. The words 'null points' in a bad French accent, used as a habitual tick by Gil, made Catrin long for the relative comfort of the Incident Room and one of her fellow sergeant's bad jokes. She shook her head. Things must be bad for her to even allow that thought to intrude. But compared with present company, Gil was charm personified.

KFC got out of the car with uncharacteristic enthusiasm.

'I need a pee,' he said, looking around. He made for a tumbledown outhouse and disappeared behind it.

Catrin turned towards the front door guarded by an open porch whose panel windows had long since fallen out. The door itself might well have been blue at some point in its past, but now had nothing but the odd fleck of paint on its weathered surface as a reminder of what had once been.

She searched for a knocker and found, to her surprise, a modern doorbell on the frame, oddly positioned at waist level. She waited until the DI returned before pressing it.

KFC took in its low position.

'Who the hell lives here, R2 sodding D2?'

A loud chime accompanied the press of the bell. A hailing voice followed. 'Hang on, I'm coming.'

The voice sounded loud, but it took a while before the door opened. When it did, revealing a six-inch gap limited by a safety chain, the reason for both the delay and the doorbell's position became immediately clear.

'Help you?' The man asking looked up at both police officers from a wheelchair.

'Mr Meredith?' Catrin asked.

'Who wants to know?' Only half the man's face was visible through the gap.

'I'm Detective Sergeant Catrin Richards, this is Detective Inspector Kelvin Caldwell.' She held out her warrant card for him to see.

The man leaned forward to peer at the card, the chair creaking in protest. Most of the face appeared to be hair. It frizzed out, beginning at the crown, and extending down way past his shoulder, completed by an untrimmed beard.

Above that was a pair of thick glasses correcting an appalling degree of long-sightedness. But, as he leaned forward, Catrin stifled a gasp on realising that the right side of the face between his eye and his ear looked grossly distorted. As if someone had poured red candle wax over it and allowed it to set. The eye in the middle of all this damage, miraculously, looked sharp and clear. 'My name is Meredith, yes.'

'Iwan Meredith?'

The man shook his head. 'I'm Rhydian, Iwan's brother.'

'Is he in? Your brother?'

Rhydian shook his head. 'Iwan don't live here now. He's up in Scotland, working. Went nigh on seven months ago. Why? What's he done?'

'Nothing,' Catrin replied. The wind had picked up, and a curtain of rain was visibly moving up the valley. She hoped it was far enough away to avoid them. 'Can we come in for a minute, Rhydian?'

'Sure.' The safety chain rattled.

But KFC shook his head. 'Hang on. When was the last time your brother came home?'

'Not been home since he left. Still, don't blame him. No work here. Nothing for him here. Not now.'

KFC threw Catrin a glance and she read impatience in his eyes.

'And that's your vehicle outside?'

'Aye. It's been adapted for me.' Rhydian paused, and then asked, 'What's this about?'

KFC shook his head. 'That's okay, Mr Meredith. It's your brother we need to speak to. Do you have his mobile number?'

Rhydian nodded. 'On my phone. I can get it—'

'That's okay,' KFC interjected. 'Here's my card. Text me the number when you find it.'

'You're sure you don't want to come in?'

Catrin wanted to say yes, but KFC to a sideways step and shook his head slowly out of Meredith's view. She smiled down at the man behind the door. 'No need. The number will be fine. Sorry to disturb you.'

KFC walked off and Catrin followed him to the car in silence. As they drove away, she saw that the door to *Erw Foel* was fully open and Rhydian Meredith in his wheelchair filled the space. As they crossed the river bridge, KFC's phone buzzed. He read the message.

'Good as his word.' He waved the phone at Catrin.

'Why didn't you want to go in, sir?'

'We are not here to entertain the sad and the afflicted of this world, Sergeant. Besides, did you see the state of that place? There's a point at which being too friendly with punters becomes a health hazard. Didn't look like the Phantom of the Opera there was capable of much housework, did it? God knows when he last cleaned any surfaces.'

'That's a bit—'

'What? Truthful?'

'Unkind was what I was going to say, sir.'

'Bollocks. We got what we needed. And it's Kel while we're in the car, like I said. Now, I think I saw a Co-op on the way here. Fancy a sandwich? My shout. We can eat in the car and then I'll ring this number and we can all go back to the station like good little robots and tell Jess Allanby we did everything that was asked of us, okay?'

It wasn't okay. It wasn't the way Sergeant Catrin Richards did things. Not by a long chalk. But Caldwell was the senior officer here. She had no choice.

'Fine,' she said.

In the passenger seat, KFC lifted his chin.

'Fine, Kel,' Catrin said, adding his name.

KFC sat back, nodding. 'Right, what's your poison? I

could murder a prawn and mayo, but I expect we'll be lucky to get stale cheese and pickle in this backwater.'

———

WARLOW ARRIVED before Owen at the address he'd been texted. Unlike Catrin, he did not need any satnav instructions. He knew these roads from his childhood. He'd spent a good part of his formative years in the primary school, not a mile away from the hill he was now parked on. The iron and coal works that drew people in their thousands to work this valley a hundred years before meant that the slopes of the hills were as developed as the flatter valley floor. The ways were steep and winding. *Allt y Grug*, or Heather Hill, had given its name to the road that traversed it.

The rows of semi-detached council houses petered out as he'd climbed, giving way to private housing and bungalows, gradually thinning out towards the summit. Penmaen Street was nothing but a single track on a bend halfway up the hill.

Cân y Gwynt – Windsong, named when irony was still in its diapers – sat squarely in its grounds at the end of the street. A thirties-built, white-rendered property with a red-brick portico, protected from the worst of the winds by mature conifers. Warlow parked outside and sat in his car to await Owen. A few cursory glances told him that the spot was not overlooked. The nearest property stood on the other side of the road some thirty yards away. At night, the road was lit by two streetlights. Bored, Warlow got out and walked back along the short drive to the junction with the hill and noticed an unmarked dirt road twenty yards up, heading off into the trees behind the houses, just before the hill curved away to the right, He had a vague recollection that somewhere in the middle of that hill was an old cemetery.

Ten minutes later, a Black C-class Merc pulled up behind his Jeep and flashed its lights. Owen Tamblin exited. Taller than Warlow, his fellow DCI had a flat face with a nose that had never quite gone back to its proper position after too many opposition rugby players had tried to rearrange its structure. He walked with a rangy lope and his hair looked too suspiciously rich in colour to be natural.

'Evan Warlow, loitering with intent again.' Owen's voice boomed out.

Warlow waited for the man to join him before offering his hand. 'Owen. Good to see you. Though a few too many kebabs have found their way past your lips since we last met, by my reckoning,' Warlow glanced down at his friend's tight waistband.

'Cheap suit. Shrunk in the wash,' Owen quipped.

'You get what you pay for.'

'That's obvious from the car you're driving.' Owen turned towards the house. 'This must be a blast from the past for you, Evan?'

'You can say that again. I bunked off school a few times up on these mountains.'

'Don't believe it.' Owen shook his head. 'Angelic kid like you?'

'Cowboy country up here, Owen.'

'Well, I've got the key to the saloon. Neighbour left one with the Uniforms. Shall we?'

Owen lifted the latch on an iron gate. He needed some force to loosen the rust, and it gave way suddenly with a loud clang.

'What was that for?' Warlow asked. 'Scare away the ghosts?'

'Funny you should say that. The kids on the estates below all say this place is haunted.'

Warlow looked up at the dark windows. 'Did I ever tell you I was superstitious?'

'No.'

'That's because I'm not. I think the chance of seeing a ghost is about as likely as that hair on your head being a natural colour.'

Owen's hand strayed self-consciously to his fringe. 'Low blow, mun. The wife does it. Says it keeps me looking young.'

'Yeah, that's the one thing I remember about your Sandra. She's a terrible bloody liar.'

CHAPTER THIRTEEN

OWEN OPENED the front door to *Cân y Gwynt*. Leaves had blown into the open porch and the wind had sculpted a mini-Snowden in the corner. The door opened easily enough, but a pile of flyers and the odd letter whispered across the tiled floor behind the door. A musty, un-lived-in odour assailed Warlow's nostrils. Still, better that than the sickly-sweet smell of decay he'd come across so often in his career on entering buildings. As a young Uniform, he'd been to his fair share of abandoned corpses. People who'd passed away with no one to care. And as a detective, that smell had led him to bodies hidden away by perpetrators, hoping they'd never be found. But they never factored in the stench of corruption. They always forgot a cadaver dog could sniff out a body ten feet underground.

Even KFC's aftershave was preferable to encountering that smell in an empty old house.

'You okay, Evan?' Owen was already in the hallway when he stopped to ask.

'Fine,' Warlow answered. 'What's the story with the owner here?'

Owen looked around. 'Widow. Lost her husband to

pneumoconiosis in the sixties. No kids. Lived alone for fifty-something years.'

Warlow nodded. The hallway had a definite retro look. Flowered wallpaper, a dark mirrored bureau, the patterned tiles on the floor. He guessed that when it was sold, it would go as a doer upper.

'You been here before, Owen?'

'No. But the Uniforms who came for a shufti took some snaps. The kitchen is through here.'

Warlow followed along the passage with dark-brown varnished doors leading off to the parlour, the living room, a small W.C. and at the end, the kitchen. Everything was wood, except for the black range, and stained with a lighter varnish than the dark-brown furniture of the hall. Every handle on the drawers and cupboards was thin chrome, many of them now losing their sheen from use. At the centre of the room sat an oval table with six slatted, ladder-back chairs. None of them were under the table and stood at odd angles in the room.

'That's them.' Owen nodded towards the table. 'The envelopes, I mean.'

Warlow took a step closer, but then thought better of it and slipped on a pair of gloves before doing anything else.

'Good idea,' Owen said. 'I've got some overshoes in the car, too. Let me get them.'

Alone on the threshold of the kitchen, Warlow stared at the table. A torn package lay where it had been left, the cellophane ripped, with a few envelopes strewn over the table's surface. Warlow turned his attention to the chairs and the floor. Two were further away than the others. Something had dried into a dark stain under one of them. He took out his phone and started taking photographs and a video of the scene.

Owen came back with the overshoes and Warlow slipped a pair on, using his gloved hand on the doorframe for support. Suitably clad, he went directly to the chair to inspect the stain before peering at the back spindles of the chair above it.

'There's some white stuff here. Looks like adhesive from tape.'

Owen came around behind him and looked for himself.

'And I'd put money on the fact that this stuff on the floor is either blood or the concentrated contents of someone's bladder,' Warlow added.

'Jesus,' Owen said. 'Always did have a way with words, Evan.'

Warlow stood and leaned in to inspect the packaging around the envelopes. Underneath the spilled half a dozen or so was one with markings on it. 'Look at this. Black felt-tip. I can't see because it's hidden underneath the others. You got a pen?'

Owen obliged. Warlow inspected the cheap ballpoint and its chewed cap with distaste. 'I hope you didn't take this off some scrote.'

'Grandson,' Owen shrugged, grinning.

Warlow used the closed pen to gingerly push away some envelopes to reveal the bottom one. The black markings were letters, but little more than a scrawl. Nonetheless, he could make out a 'W', an 'R' and an 'L'. All that was missing was an 'A', an 'O' and another 'W'.

'Looks like whoever wrote this wasn't in much of a state if they had to practise your name,' Owen observed.

'Agreed.' Warlow stood up and looked around the room. Nothing else here suggested violence. Nothing that might alert a busy Uniform confirming a break-in anyway.

'Worth having a look around?' Owen asked.

'Yeah.'

They went together, and not because of any fear of ghosts. Both men were experienced detectives. Best they disturb things as little as possible. Every room they visited had all the hallmarks of a life that had come to an abrupt halt. The TV was old, with no hint of any link to a streaming device. The owner, Mrs Parry, had obviously not been interested in, nor capable of, modifying the technology of her old analogue set to adapt to digital broadcasting. Warlow wondered when she'd last watched TV.

Towels still hung in the bathrooms. There was no sign of vandalism in the form of emptied drawers or ransacked cupboards. The beds, apart from in the main bedroom, remained made up. Sadly, that bed still had the old bedclothes ruffled in an untidy heap. Mrs Parry, when she left, had gone quickly, it seemed. Whoever had stayed here and triggered the nosy neighbour seemed to have confined their visit to the kitchen.

Half an hour later, they were back in the passage. 'We need to get a full forensic assessment.' Warlow spoke for both of them. 'Povey's still up here. I could get her team over. So long as you have no objection.'

'Why? Because it's my turf?' Owen grinned. 'Maybe it is on paper, but it's yours as much as mine. Go ahead.'

Warlow nodded.

'What the hell was he doing with them up here?' Owen asked.

'Not playing bloody Pictionary, that's for sure.'

They moved outside, breathing in the air. Though there had been no smell of death in the house, something else had pervaded it. Something dark and noisome.

'I'd like to say it's good to be back here with you, Evan. But I'd be lying if I said I'm enjoying this.'

'You know me, laugh a minute. Fancy a cuppa? Gil Jones is running the office.'

'I wouldn't say no.'

'Right. Follow me. I know all the shortcuts.'

———

Rhys was in the driving seat as he and Jess took their leave of Cardiff. They'd had a busy afternoon. Tiernon had been his usual acerbic self, but, as before, his inability to shock or disturb Rhys had taken much of the wind out of his pompous sails. Even when he used a silver artery forceps to poke it through the wound made by the sharp-ened wooden pole at the back of Derek Geoghan's neck, pushing it, with some effort, so that it emerged through the open mouth, Rhys, goggle-eyed, had simply mouthed, 'Wow.'

Jess hadn't looked away, but she'd grown used to Tier-non's theatrics and had steeled herself. She didn't even take notes as, despite it all, Tiernon's report would be thorough. If she needed any detail recalled between leaving the University Hospital Pathology department and the report dropping into her computer mailbox, she had Rhys. He had taken notes but would also remember, in detail, every aspect of the post-mortem if asked. It was, by definition, a morbid fascination he had with all things relating to the cause of death. But better that than vomiting on his shoes. Which had happened to more than one rookie after a couple of hours in Tiernon's company.

They'd then called in to Cardiff Prison after Jess's earlier phone call to the Prison Liaison Officer managed to secure for them twenty minutes each with the two long-term prisoners who'd also shared a cell with Geoghan. Neither of them had provided any useful information regarding Derek being especially concerned about anyone outside prison seeking to do him harm. No overt threats. Not even from the relatives of those he'd done harm to himself. But both men had also volunteered the fact that Geoghan enjoyed the thought that when he did get out, he was going to 'get the bastards who put me in here.'

By that he meant, of course, Warlow and Owen.

But then there was nothing new in this information. Prisoners often harboured resentment for the officers who'd investigated and arrested them. Especially where the flames were fanned by a prisoner's family or friends during the time they were inside. Step forward, Karen Geoghan.

So, even though they'd achieved a lot in one day, it was with a vague sense of frustration that Jess stared out of the window at the capital's Wharfside apartments speeding by as Rhys took the central link road out towards the dual carriageway that would eventually take them back west.

'Had a nice time, Rhys?' Jess asked.

Rhys shifted in his seat as if deciding on just how to answer. When he did, it was with his usual endearing earnestness. A trait which rendered him wide open to teasing from Gil, Catrin and, now and again, Warlow. 'I'm not sure if "nice" is a word I'd use, ma'am. I'd say more enjoyable as a learning experience than giggles, if I'm honest.'

'You certainly don't flinch away from the pathology suite.'

'I do find it interesting, ma'am. And quite often the small details are what help. Like there was oil on the tips of the stakes. Made it easier for them to slide in.'

Jess grimaced. 'Yeah, I picked up on that, too. Seems like whoever did this thought of almost everything.'

Rhys shook his head. 'But they don't, do they? Think of everything, I mean. And it's the one or two things they forget that trip them up.'

Jess smiled. He was right. But her smile was also tinged with a smidgen of pride. Rhys Harries was shaping up to be a bloody good detective.

Rhys screwed up his face. 'The two prisoners didn't help us much, though.'

'Agreed. They told us nothing new, did they?'

'Only that Mr Warlow wasn't Geoghan's favourite person.'

'That's an understatement if ever there was one.'

They'd reached the roundabout that led to the docks, and Rhys headed down through the tunnel past Techniquest. As they came back up, Jess's phone played a tone with a typewriter's bell at the end. She glanced down and scrolled to a message app. The text from Molly covered more than one screen's length. For a few minutes, the only sound was the car's tyres drumming on the asphalt as Jess's thumbs responded. When she'd sent her reply, she sat back with a sigh. 'Sorry, Rhys. Family stuff.'

'Everything alright, ma'am?'

'No. Molly is on a camping trip and she's texting me to tell me that her father has found out and is threatening to come down from Manchester because she's far too young to be alone with older boys.'

'Is she? Alone with older boys?'

'Her boyfriend is a year older than her if that counts. But they, as a couple, are with a gang of others at a festival. That same gang is going camping for a few days. I mean, she's alone with him a lot at his house and at mine. What does that prove?'

'Right.' Rhys stayed silent for a while, and then asked, 'Did she ask—'

'She doesn't need anyone's permission. She's seventeen. Though she did ask for mine, mainly because she wanted to borrow some of my wet-weather gear. But she lives with me, not her father. He relinquished his say in decision making when he left us.' It came out much sharper than Jess had intended.

Rhys kept his eyes on the road and his mouth sensibly shut.

Jess sighed. 'Sorry, Rhys. This isn't your fault. It's the last thing you want to hear, too.'

'It's alright, ma'am. Families are complicated.'

'True that, as Molly would say. Now, I think there's an Asda around here somewhere. Why don't we pull in and you can get snacks while I try to calm my daughter down and text my ex to tell him what a complete prick he's being.'

'Yes, ma'am.'

Out of the corner of her eye, Jess saw Rhys's face brighten.

The magic word had been 'snacks'.

CHAPTER FOURTEEN

GIL HAD the teas waiting for them when Warlow and Owen got to the Incident Room at Ystradgynlais. Gil and Owen knew each other from training courses and a couple of nasty cases they'd worked on together, including an acid attack by a jealous boyfriend that had involved painstaking CCTV evidence.

Warlow filled the sergeant in on their visit to the house near Allt y Grug Road.

Gil listened and posted an addendum to the note up on the board. 'I've got some Uniforms parked outside. Povey and her team are on the way there now. She said I ought to tie you down, so you don't find any more work for her.'

'You'd think she'd be glad of an inside job after being halfway up bloody Kilimanjaro with the Geoghans.' Warlow sipped his tea and smacked his lips with pleasure.

'There is no pleasing some people.' Owen shook his head.

'And the house has been empty for a good couple of years?' Gil asked.

Owen took out his notebook and flicked through it

until he found what he was looking for. 'More than that. Mrs Parry went into care in September 2018.'

'So, it would be common knowledge that the place was unoccupied?' Gil, still standing at the board, queried Owen.

'Not exactly densely populated up there, but yes. People would know. It's a close-knit community. But there was something…' He kept reading his notes. 'Got it. Three months after she went into care, we caught someone trying to break into that property. Again, a keen neighbour saw something suspicious. A van travelling up and down the road and then parking in a lay-by half a mile off. Marius Stoica, a labourer, was caught trying to jimmy the lock on the back door. His van was full of TVs and cameras he'd nicked from burglaries up and down the valley. He got three years for that. I daresay he's out now.'

'Mrs Parry has no relatives, then?' Warlow asked.

'Not that we know of, no.' Owen bit into a ginger nut he'd already dunked and paused to savour the moment. 'Ages since I had one of these.'

'Gil looks after the biscuit side of things,' Warlow said.

'Is that in the job description?'

'It's a free service I offer.' Gil held up his hands in mock modesty.

'Think we need to investigate this Stoica, then?' Warlow asked.

'We do. I'll get back to town and get on it. Or get someone on it. He'll be on the PNC of course. And something tells me he may have ended up in Cardiff nick, too.'

Warlow put his tea down. 'That may link him to the Geoghans.'

Owen gave an eyebrow-raised nod.

'Tidy. The SIO is going to be doing cartwheels over this,' Gil said.

'Heard from her yet?' Warlow asked.

'Rhys rang in. Said he'd had a good time at the post-mortem.'

Owen almost choked on his tea.

'Don't ask,' Warlow said. 'We have a DC who looks like a lankier Thor and who everyone wants to either mother or marry. Present company excluded. He also has a rare gift in that he actually enjoys post-mortems.'

'Gift? You've had him checked out from the neck up, have you?' Owen asked.

'Don't mock it,' Gil said. 'He's first on the team sheet for any slicing and dicing.'

'You don't think he's funny about the dead bodies, though?'

'What do you mean, "funny"?' Warlow sounded genuinely puzzled.

'You know? Has a thing for the old "dead flesh".' Owen shook his head and his mouth curled down in distaste at what his mind was recalling. 'I had a case once. An electrician who had access to mortuaries. Bad case of necrophilia.'

'I've got something for that,' Gil remarked. 'The missus had a touch of whiplash once. She got a brace that worked wonders for her.'

Owen chortled. 'Wasn't funny at the time, I can tell you. I'll never forget the undertaker's face when we told him what had been going on in his Chapel of Rest.'

'Hope the bloke got a stiff sentence,' Gil said.

Both the DCI's groaned at that one.

'As for the prison visit, no joy,' Gil explained. 'Rhys said the only thing Geoghan's cellmates remembered was that he had the knives out for you two.'

'Best we wear a stab vest then.' Warlow finished off his tea. 'So, it looks like this remains a cross-boundary case.'

Owen nodded. 'Happy to help out. You know me. I'll make sure you're copied in on anything we find on Stoica.

Funnily enough, I seem to remember vaguely that he had an address in Brecon, but last I heard he'd moved in with his partner in Ammanford.'

'Christ, this case is like a game of squash. Every time you hit a ball the thing bounces back at you off the wall.' Gil packed up the biscuits.

'Squash?' Warlow spluttered. 'The only bloody squash you know anything about comes in a bottle with a picture of some fruit on the label.'

'I still play a bit of walking squash I'll have you know.'

'Is that a real thing?' Owen asked.

'Oh, yes.' Gil ladled on the seriousness. 'You use a red dot ball, and it has to bounce in the back part of the court.'

'What, and you don't run?'

'No. It's designed for people with injuries.'

'Right. So, you just stride really quickly, is that it?' Warlow asked. 'Like those buggers in the walking race at the Olympics that look like they're desperate to find a toilet?'

Gil adopted a hurt expression. 'Has anyone ever told you how unattractive a trait sarcasm is, DCI Warlow?'

Owen laughed and said his goodbyes. Warlow walked him to his car and waved him off. A grumbling in his gut told him he'd completely forgotten to eat any lunch. Okay, there'd been biscuits, but he fancied something savoury. He looked up. The centre of the village was only a stone's throw away.

'Why not?' Warlow muttered to the sky and started walking.

———

RHYS SAT in the car waiting for DI Allanby to finish her calls. He'd parked in a bay set aside for shoppers away from the pumps and gone inside while she stood on the grass verge nearest to the air and water dispenser, phone to her ear. He'd already eaten two Hot Peperamis and a Mars bar and drunk a can of energy drink. He could feel the sugar pumping through his veins. But outside, the senior officer seemed to be having a hard time, judging by the way she was using her free hand to emphasise whatever she was saying. He hoped things were okay with her daughter. He'd met Molly only a couple of times, and she seemed like a nice kid. A little scary, but still a nice kid. Good-looking, too. Like her mother.

Rhys caught himself and shook his head. What the hell was wrong with him? He knew what his mother would say. Too much sugar by far.

He fiddled with the radio and found a station he liked that played chilled-out tracks. Gina liked female singers. He liked them, too, mostly. But six tracks of angst in and he was ready to jump off the nearest bridge. He liked more upbeat stuff. Didn't mind a bit of rock now and again, either. And there were some good new bands out there. He had his phone linked up to the sound system and found some Dream State. He was banging along with his head when the passenger door opened, and Jess Allanby stepped in.

'Sorry, ma'am.' Rhys quickly turned the music down.

'Who were you listening to?'

'Welsh band, ma'am. Lots of guitars.'

'Lots of energy, too. Molly'd like these.'

'I'll text you a link.'

Jess nodded.

'Are we okay to go, ma'am?'

'I thought you wanted some snacks?' Jess asked.

'I'm all snacked up.'

'Of course, you are, silly me.'

'I got you some water, ma'am. Like you asked.' Rhys handed over a plastic bottle.

Jess let out a sigh. 'Cheers, Rhys. And yes, let's get going. We're bound to hit the commuter traffic as it is. But let's switch off the music while I catch up with Catrin.'

'Of course, ma'am. Everything alright with Molly?'

Jess unscrewed the water and took a deep draught from the bottle before replying, 'Her, yes. Her father, not so much. The sod isn't answering his mobile. Not much I can do about that. Can I hook up my phone to the car speaker?'

Rhys pressed some buttons and, a moment later, he pulled out onto the dual carriageway again as the Focus's sound system hummed with the noise of a phone ringing. Catrin answered promptly.

'Afternoon, ma'am.'

The background drone and slight delay on the speaker told Rhys that Catrin, too, was in a car.

'You driving?' Jess asked.

'On the way back to the Incident Room, ma'am.'

'Us too, but you'll get back way before us.' She exchanged a forlorn glance with Rhys as the traffic slowed to a sluggish twenty ahead of them and brake lights lit up.

'How was the post-mortem?' Catrin asked.

'Brutal. But Rhys will tell all tomorrow. We'll have the full report by then, too. But no joy from the prison visit. I don't think either of Geoghan's cellmates liked him much. What about your end?'

Kelvin Caldwell answered this time, 'As expected, Jess. *Nada*. The hophead from Llanelli didn't know what day it was, and I've been on the phone to the other guy, uh Meredith. He's up in Inverness. I confirmed that half an hour ago. He was happy to talk, but nothing useful. Says Geoghan was a resentful slob but gave no hint that anyone was waiting for him outside with a sharpened stake. Box ticked but a lot of time wasted.'

Rhys saw a mirthless smile flicker over Jess's face, but she didn't rise to the bait. 'Okay. Anyone heard from Evan?'

'Not yet, ma'am.'

Jess looked at her watch. Somehow, four pm had come and gone, and it was now nearer half past. They wouldn't get back to Ystradgynlais much before six at this rate.

'Okay, I'm calling it for today. You two get back to the station and check in with Gil and then get off home.'

'What about your lift, Jess?' KFC asked.

'I'm staying up here for the night. Gil has me booked into an Inn somewhere nearby. It made sense since I'm without a car.'

'Fair enough,' KFC said. 'For a minute there, I thought it was something I'd said.'

Rhys wasn't sure if that was a statement or a question. Either way, it hung in a vacuum, slowly twisting like a dead spaceman waiting to be collected for burial. Jess, however, was in no mood for games.

'Well, the last laugh is on me since I'll want to get going tomorrow at half eight. That means early starts for you two.'

KFC said nothing. It was left to Catrin to sign off.

'No problem, ma'am. There is one other lead we ought to follow through on. The campaign not to get Geoghan released. Run by a relative of one of their victims.'

'Ah, yes.'

In the background, Rhys thought he could hear KFC muttering, 'More wild geese. Jesus.'

Jess signed off and turned to the DC. 'Right, what was that band called again?'

'Dream Time, ma'am.'

'Get them back up. I need some distraction while I get my thoughts in order. But not too loud, okay?'

Rhys pressed some buttons, and the car filled with noise as the traffic finally began to regather some momentum.

CHAPTER FIFTEEN

It had been some time since Warlow walked this street. As a kid, this had been the next village along from his. Different county, people, schools, rugby club. The competitive, almost tribal, nature of existence when he was growing up in this valley meant that this little town had been out of bounds as a teenager. Not exactly a gang culture, but you learned pretty quickly to stick within the confines of your own square mile if you wanted to avoid trouble and a bloody nose.

Things changed. Money had been spent to bolster the communities, keep them ticking along on life support after their innards were torn out with the loss of the mining industry.

But, at least on the surface, the treatment seemed to be working here, and this town looked alive. He strolled to a crossroads to a Greggs with a queue almost out of the door, passing hair salons, estate agents, the odd gift shop and a couple of decent-looking cafes with outside seating, which lent the place a curiously European feel. He strolled up and down a few streets, then doubled back and plumped for a café called *Bara*, meaning bread, rejecting the alfresco option on the pavement for a seat inside in the corner. So that he could keep one eye on the door.

Old habits.

A neat server brought him a menu, a carafe of water and a clean glass, and he ordered some soup and a sandwich. And not your usual cream of tomato, either. This was a curried sweet potato and celeriac job. And the bread at the counter looked crusty and homemade, too.

While he waited, he pondered the afternoon's events. As so often was the case this early in an investigation, initial inquiries threw up more questions than answers, but working with Owen again felt good. Because he wasn't running this investigation, Warlow felt obliged to get stuck into the nitty-gritty, though Two-Shoes' warning of needing to use kid gloves stuck in his head as much as in his throat.

Not easy being the soldier and not the general. Not his style. So having DCI Tamblin to work with was a godsend. Owen, like Gil, was a good man to have in a tight corner.

Warlow took out his notebook and jotted a few thoughts down. When someone appeared at his table, he assumed his food had arrived and leaned back to make way before looking up. But the person who stood there wearing a striped apron with the café's logo on the front pocket was not the waitress who'd taken his order. Nor did she have any food.

Intrigued, Warlow smiled, but then frowned as something, a faint flicker of recognition, sent a search party along his synapses to plunder his memory bank… Damn, he knew this person, didn't he? Panic flared. Knowing he knew made things worse. Next came trying to place the who, the where and the why. He re-read her face, saw the amused expectation there. About his age, he reckoned, and wearing it very well. Great skin, big eyes, hair tied back in a functional ponytail, fit from the gym or walking.

And then it registered, and he blinked as recollection came flooding back with a giant dollop of embarrassment in its wake. Evan Warlow, grown man and DCI, blushed.

'Betsy? Bloody hell.'

The woman smiled and showed a row of good, even teeth. 'You remember, then?'

'Christ… of course I remember.' What he didn't add, and didn't think he needed to, was that you didn't forget the first girl you fell in love with. At fourteen. His only excuse was that he'd been thinking of other things when he'd seen her. Things to do with murder and death that no right-minded person should ever have to think about,

'I thought it was you when you walked in.' She tapped her head. 'It didn't compute for a minute, but then I remembered about those bodies up in Penwyllt and it all clicked.'

'I can't deny it.'

She nodded. 'Someone said you'd retired.'

'Someone was right. But they made me an offer… you know how it is.'

Betsy sat down opposite him, her bright eyes never leaving his face. 'You haven't changed,' she said.

'Oh, please, I'm sure I saw a Specsavers up the street. Want me to book you in?'

She laughed. 'Still Evan the joker, then.' Her gaze took him in. 'You're older. We both are. But I knew you straight away.'

'You beat me to it there. What are you doing here? Wrong town for a start.'

'I know.' She scrunched up her face. 'I went over to the dark side when I got married and moved three miles up the valley to here.'

Warlow glanced around. He'd been lucky to get in. Though late in the afternoon, every table was full. 'This is your place?'

'Yep. Five years now. Once the kids left home, I needed something to do.'

'It's great. Nice feel to it.'

On an adjacent table, a customer threw him a surreptitious glance, but his eyes slid away when Warlow returned his stare. Not with any aggression or hostility. Just a copper's wary acknowledgement. Enough to send most people running for the hills.

'It's not often we have a famous detective in here,' Betsy said in a low whisper.

'Where is he then?' Warlow made a show of looking around.

She huffed out a noise that might have been a laugh. 'Nice try. I've seen you on TV and in the papers. When you found that little boy a few months ago.'

Warlow grunted. There'd been no escaping the press in the Osian Howells case. They'd encamped in the village of Cwrt y Waun, though even calling the cluster of houses a village was a stretch. He'd had to make a statement to the hyenas. Correction – had been ordered to make a statement as the SIO.

'I did speak to the press, sure, but a lot of other people were involved in that case.'

'Still the team player, then. God, how many years is it since we spoke?'

'One or two,' he replied.

She laughed properly at that. And her laugh took him back to dark nights when they'd clung to each other for warmth under the old school changing rooms. Because there'd been nowhere else to go at age fourteen on cold Saturday nights. And the briefest echo of the excitement and thrill of their time together made him shudder. It lasted only a second, but it made his insides swoop.

They'd gone out together for almost a year and he could still remember the crushing despondency that had clouded his days when she'd broken it off. Or rather, one of her friends had on her behalf. The way he'd sucked it up and buried it because it was what you did. They'd been teenagers and older boys were a bigger draw than the quiet Warlow. But being trapped in the same school as a girl he'd carried a torch for, and seeing her every day with other boys, had not been easy. All the stupid songs about heartache and pain, with lyrics you never noticed until they spoke to you, seemed to be the only things he heard on the radio until he turned eighteen. He'd taken it hard and not found another girl during his time at school. Warlow last saw Betsy on the day they'd picked up their A-level results in the school hall. She'd been disappointed that day. He remembered that.

He'd been quietly pleased.

But she'd been eighteen, too, and a stunning beauty. He'd sometimes wondered what her life had been like. Especially in those early days after leaving school. Imagining her ending up with some wealthy bloke with a big car and no worries. Such thoughts hadn't lasted because life intervened and other girlfriends came and went until Jeez Denise and he began their tempestuous relationship, tied the knot and produced a family. In truth, thoughts of Betsy had not intruded for almost a quarter of a century.

But suddenly, here she was, and these discombobulating thoughts rushed through Warlow's brain like a sandstorm, as he searched for something to say.

He finally managed a trite gem. 'Too many to count.'

'Lots of water under several bridges,' Betsy said, sounding equally disjointed.

'So how are you? You mentioned kids?'

'Three. Two girls and a boy. All away. How about you?'

Warlow rearranged the cutlery on the table in front of him. 'Two boys. One in Australia, the other in London.'

'Your wife?'

A reasonable enough question, though Warlow had still not quite got used to his answer. Largely because of the horror, it usually evinced in the questioner.

'No. She passed away, I'm afraid.'

Betsy's eyes got larger, and her smile faded. But he'd learned to nip this in the bud before pity rushed in.

'She'd been unwell for some time, and we weren't together. Not for some years.'

Betsy blinked. 'I'm sorry. For both things.'

'How about you?'

She did a mini-eye roll. 'Married, still, to Martin Mullins.'

Warlow picked up on the little something that remained unspoken but didn't probe. Partly because it was none of his business and partly because his soup arrived with the server. Betsy stood up. So did Warlow. 'I'll leave you to it. Good to see you, Evan.'

They leaned in and hugged like old friends should. He watched her as she moved off back to the kitchen before sitting down and tucking into his soup.

He wanted it to be awful. So that he'd have no reason to come back to this café. But it wasn't awful, it was bloody delicious. He finished it in five minutes and checked his watch.

Four thirty. Very late as lunches went.

He paid, left a hefty tip, and walked back to the station to check on any intel that had come in from any source, doing his best not to give in to the strange feeling he had that he'd opened a time capsule. First, the streets around his old junior school where someone had possibly kept the Geoghans, then an old girlfriend. There'd be a third something, he felt certain. There was a Scrooge-like inevitability about another spectre from the past waiting to surprise him.

He chortled quietly at that. From what his sons were

always telling him, and Gil, come to think of it, he'd be a shoo-in for Dickens's curmudgeonly miser at the best of times.

Halfway to the station, he paused and turned back to look in the direction he'd come. Towards the café. He could have asked for Betsy's number. It might have been good to talk some more about the old times. Or about life outside his existence as a DCI. She'd said she was married, but not with any great conviction. Or had he got that tell wrong?

God, she'd been a pretty girl at fourteen.

Was still a lovely woman.

A car horn sounded a few yards away. Short and sharp. Not a warning. Someone signalling to a passing friend. Warlow turned and saw a raised hand and a smile.

The jarring noise brought him back to earth. Christ, what was he thinking? He'd go back to the café another time. Eat Betsy Mullins's great food and chat to her like an old friend.

Nothing more.

Because that was how it must be for him. There was no getting away from it. Whatever his hormones said, and that brief blast from the past had awakened a few, he'd told himself to put all such thoughts to one side. The dark little secret of his HIV reared its grinning death's head in his mind. Ever since his diagnosis, he'd been wary. Of work, of tainting anyone near him, and especially of any relationships.

He kept the HIV secret inside. Very few other people were privy to it. Not even his sons. He cringed at the realisation. Telling them remained a task he was yet to complete. How many times had he sat with Cadi in his Nevern bolt hole and stared at his phone, willing himself to tell Tom and Alun and somehow always finding a reason not to? But the disease, so far, hadn't stopped him from functioning. He was asymptomatic.

But it also meant a self-imposed moratorium on intimacy.

Not that Betsy Mullins and he would ever be intimate again.

And at fifteen, their intimacy had been constrained, though not without him trying his utmost to un-constrain it at every turn.

But any prospect of that ship relaunching with a new crew could not exist. Sighing softly, Warlow turned again, like a weary Dick Whittington this time, and headed for the station. But when he got there, he didn't turn in. Instead, he kept on walking, letting his thoughts tumble, hoping they might settle into some kind of order. But not holding his breath while they attempted to do so.

CHAPTER SIXTEEN

CATRIN PULLED into the car park near to the caving club's headquarters in Penwyllt. The Erdingford crowd and their swish minibuses had long gone. But DI Caldwell had asked that she drive back up here and so she had done. She switched off the engine, unbuckled her seatbelt and had one hand on the door handle when Caldwell spoke.

'No need for that.'

Catrin swivelled in her seat. 'For what?'

'Getting out.'

Catrin removed her hand from the door and frowned. 'Sorry? I thought you wanted a wander around?'

'I can see what I came to see from here.'

Catrin looked out of the window. They were alone. She'd parked facing the little post and rail fencing that marked the edge of the parking area. In front of her, the land fell away in what might have been the remains of a quarry, but beyond that, a disused tramway snaked up the hill towards open moorland. The converted cottages of the Club were hidden by trees off to her right. One isolated building perhaps half a mile away was the only sign of habitation. Other than sheep, she could see no living soul.

'Am I missing something, sir?'

'Kel, or Kelv, up here, Catrin.'

'What am I missing, Kel?'

'Nothing. And that's the point. Look at this place.' The DI shook his head. 'I mean, who the hell would bring bodies up here?'

Catrin shrugged. 'Someone for whom this place has a meaning, I'd say.'

KFC held up a finger and dropped his voice. 'Exactly. I mean, you and me, we'd never come near this place in a million years if it wasn't for work.'

Catrin nodded.

'But the other reason for coming up here was for us to get away.'

Catrin felt a little fluttering deep in her abdomen. Whatever this was, she didn't like it.

'No, no.' KFC waved his hand. 'Don't worry. We're both attractive adults, and I can see where your mind might be tempted to go.'

Taken completely aback by the conceit, all Catrin could do was blink and replay the words. Had he really used 'both' in that sentence?

'As I say, this is completely professional,' KFC added.

'I don't quite underst—'

'Yes, you do,' he cut across her. 'But you won't admit it to yourself. What is the common denominator here, Catrin?'

'Prison. Derek Geoghan had—'

KFC made a noise like a quiz show buzzer to indicate how wrong she was. 'Let me rephrase that. *Who* is the common denominator?'

She concentrated but ended up shaking her head.

'Who is it that knows the victims and the area?'

'I suppose Iwan Meredith—'

'Forget him. He lives in sodding Scotland,' KFC

blurted out the words and then lowered his voice again. 'Think closer to home.'

She did and still came up blank.

'Okay, let me give you a clue. Why do you think I'm here?'

'Because it's a nasty case. We need all hands on deck and…'

'And?'

For the first time since leaving Carmarthen she replayed in her head the little scene in the conference room. The fact that the higher-ups had not wanted Warlow as SIO. Something must have shown in her expression because KFC latched on to it, his own features softening into a knowing smile.

'Good girl. I knew you'd get there, eventually.'

She trod on her irritation at his patronisingly clumsy attempt at encouragement, because now she was intrigued. 'DCI Warlow?'

KFC nodded. 'This is why we needed this little chat away from nosy eavesdroppers. You're a good detective, Catrin. I like you. The Supers like you. You have potential. But I need you to understand that this case isn't like the others you've been involved in. You heard that we have evidence to suggest that Lewis wasn't working alone.'

'Surely Sergeant Lewis's death has nothing to do with the Geoghans?'

'Not directly. But corruption is an un-lanced boil. It festers. Take a step back and consider what evidence there is regarding the Geoghans. We know they had no love for Evan Warlow and Owen Tamblin. We know they sent threatening letters. If that had been anyone else, we would have interviewed the recipient of those letters to exclude them from the investigation.'

The world seemed to tilt for Catrin then. The sky lost its brightness, the angles of the mountains seemed off-kilter. She swallowed and found nothing in her mouth to lubricate the movement. 'You think we ought to question DCI Warlow?'

KFC shook his head. 'I can hear the barriers coming down. But listen to yourself. What I'm saying is that I, and Superintendent Goodey, are asking you to keep an open mind. It may come to a point where we'll need to interview Evan. Who knows? But the important thing, the only thing, is that we want you as a facilitator, not as an obstruction. Can you do that?'

Catrin took a deep breath in and let it out through puffed cheeks. 'Sir, I've—'

'Kelv.'

'Sir,' Catrin insisted. 'I've worked a lot with DCI Warlow and this doesn't… I mean, why would he do something like this?'

'Who knows? Corruption is like an octopus with lots of tentacles. Maybe he needed to send a message to others who harbour a grudge.'

'I don't see it. I can't—'

'Oh, yes you can. Because you're a smart copper, Catrin. I'm not asking you to be disloyal. I'm asking to you be honest and work with me. But this must stay under the investigation's radar.'

'What does that mean?'

'It means no one else needs to know. Not Jess, not DC Harries or Sergeant Jones. Certainly not Evan. Just you and me.'

The fluttering in Catrin's gut became a frantic bird trapped in a cage. 'I'm not sure I can do that, sir.'

'You can and you will. Remember what Davenport said? Lewis was not the only link to organised crime in this Force, and that it, the Force, remains under investigation.' KFC's eyes glittered with a kind of feral excitement. 'This, what we're talking about now, is part of that investigation.

I had hoped you'd come on board, but if you can't, then take what I've said as an order. We keep one eye on Evan Warlow the whole time. If you see or hear anything that doesn't fit the narrative of the case, I need to know.'

'Sir, DCI Warlow is—'

'Not a saint. He's just a bloke. A bloke with needs and wants and weaknesses like the rest of us. All we're asking is that you do what you are good at, Catrin. Eyes and ears open.'

Catrin turned towards the front, breathing hard. Part of her wanted to push the door open, get out and suck in a lungful of fresh air. She'd got used to KFC's smell, or at least the sensory cells in her nose had been numbed by it, but now she became acutely aware of its cloying nature again. Outside there'd be mountain breeze and miles of space. She felt the urge to run until she couldn't see KFC or the car. Until she found a place to hide in. Or a hole to fall into. Somewhere she would not have to contemplate the ideas that KFC had put into her head. That made her stomach churn. She turned back, flushed in the face. 'I'm not a spy. What if I can't?'

'Then we'd be very disappointed,' KFC said, and glanced at his watch. 'Half five. Home time by anyone's watch. Let's get back to that place I cannot pronounce, then we can both sod off home. You heard Jess. She wants us in early tomorrow.'

———

He watched the police come and go to the house on Penmaen Street. Saw it all through high-powered binoculars from his hide in the trees on the hill behind. They'd find evidence that the two pigs had been held there. But they'd find nothing to give him away. He'd made sure of that.

He'd kept the pigs alive in that house for almost a week while he

prepared the killing ground, going out before dawn, using a quiet elec-
tric fat-tyred bike to get to within half a mile of where he'd set the
table. Quick and silent, he'd met no one on the dozen trips he'd made.
And he'd bided his time for when he'd taken the pigs to slaughter.

They'd squealed at the house. Through the tape he'd wound
around their heads. Squealed until they were hoarse. But no one heard.
They'd squealed a lot more out on the moor in the forest once he'd
taken the tape off. But they were too weak to squeal loudly. Besides,
only the crows heard them. And for the crows, their croaky cries for
help were akin to a dinner bell.

It had taken the police a lot less time than he thought to find the
house. Not that it mattered. These were breadcrumbs he'd left for them
to feed on and follow. And slowly, surely, they were coming ever closer
to what waited in store. He didn't consider himself a vindictive man,
but there had to be a balance to things. He had some misgivings, of
course he did. After all, these were the same officers that had put the
Geoghans inside. But they surely could have done something, anything,
to ensure that Derek Geoghan stayed inside. They'd failed the world in
that respect.

Failed him, too.

Failed his family.

Failed everyone.

And so, they had a price to pay.

He got up from his hiding place, almost invisible in his camo
trousers and jacket. He packed away his camera and binoculars, slung
the backpack over his shoulder and went to his bike.

No one had visited the cemetery today. Few people did because of
its remoteness.

No one saw him.

No one amongst the living, at any rate.

He pumped the pedals and crossed the empty wasteland in silence,
unobserved.

Like a ghost.

———

THE ONE THING that Warlow missed on his walk was the companionship of a black ball of fun who went by the name of Cadi. Still, he met a couple of other dog walkers as he climbed out of the town and got a fix from an exuberant Golden Retriever called Horace, who was happy to get his ears fondled despite remonstrations and apologies from his owner.

'He's three but still thinks he's three months,' the woman said, as Horace rubbed his head enthusiastically into Warlow's leg.

But the repetitive physicality of walking and the distraction of being outside allowed the DCI's mind to take its own path. One that eventually led him back to the communication he'd received from the Geoghans. He'd handed over the cards and letters to the evidence officer when he'd got to the Incident Room. Having someone else examine them and be responsible for them had seemed the right thing to do. They were not the kind of thing he usually gave much thought to, other than having the foresight to hang on to them once they popped through his letterbox. His instincts had told him that might be a useful approach, though sometimes he forgot and confined them to his number one filing cabinet, the bin. But he'd kept enough. And these were not treasured keepsakes he took out periodically to study. His normal reaction, once he recognised the handwriting on the envelope, was to scan the contents once, throw anything that might rot or looked too toxic, bag everything else and file the bundle away in a box.

As a result, his memory of exactly how many there were, and their exact nature and content remained hazy. Troublingly so because something about the little collection was bothering him. Something important that registered at the time he'd received it, but that he'd forgotten once he'd filed it away.

He ought to have another gander at them all, though the prospect held little appeal.

He looked at his watch. Almost half five. That meant he'd been walking for almost an hour. He flicked on his phone's home screen.

Nope. No one had been trying to get hold of him.

Still, he'd gathered enough wool now to knit a jumper. Time to return to the fray.

CHAPTER SEVENTEEN

BACK AT THE STATION, Warlow walked into a room depressingly devoid of much activity. Gil, glasses on, poked at a keyboard as he read a report on his screen. He looked up when Warlow arrived.

'Don't tell me you and Owen went for a cheeky pint?'

'Okay, I won't. Because we didn't. I needed time to think. Where is everyone?'

Gil pushed back from the desk and arched his back. Beneath him, the swivel chair creaked ominously. 'DI Caldwell, Rhys and Catrin have all ridden off into the sunset. Rhys wants time to prepare for tomorrow's early morning briefing. Catrin seconded the task of searching for the Geoghans' social media trolls to moi. Sergeant to sergeant favour, she said, though she had a face on her like a pitbull terrier chomping a lemon when she left here. I swear that girl needs to find her happy place soon or she'll forget what a smile is.'

'Bit harsh, Sergeant Jones.' The voice from behind Warlow drew both men's attention.

Jess stood in the doorway with her eyes directed at Gil

and a very old-fashioned expression on her face. The kind a schoolmistress might give a troublesome toddler.

Gil held both hands up in surrender. 'Apologies, ma'am, but something's getting to her.'

From the small silence that followed, it seemed as if everyone present had a theory about that but was too polite to voice it.

'Hang on,' Warlow said. 'Kelvin Caldwell's gone too? Wasn't he your lift, Jess?'

'He was. But I got Gil to book me into a place just up the road. Not much sense in me traipsing all the way back to Pembrokeshire tonight. Molly's not there, so I thought I'd stay here.'

'The loneliness of the SIO,' Warlow muttered.

'Let it be known that we have more than one spare room at chez Jones. You may be in the Presidential Suite, DCI Warlow, but we have also the converted attic room for visiting dignitaries.'

Gil had already offered a bed to Warlow. An offer he'd accepted without hesitation. Gil lived in Llandeilo, a forty-minute drive away. But still an hour's less driving than to Nevern on the coast, where Warlow had his cottage. It would not be the first, nor the last time Warlow would accept Gil's hospitality.

'You could cancel the room,' Warlow suggested.

Jess smiled at the two men. 'I could, but I won't. I want to spend the evening getting my mind straight on this one.'

'Fair enough. You want to be Billy-no-mates, that's fine by us. Right, Sergeant?' Warlow threw the question at Gil, not expecting an answer. He also didn't push the point. He understood where Jess was coming from here. He'd been in this position enough times himself to know that too many distractions were not a good thing.

'So long as you wipe your feet on the way in and pretend

that anything home-baked is delicious, you are welcome anytime. Mi Casa es Chewbacca, as my granddaughter, who watches far too many cartoons, likes to say. *Diawl bach.*' He turned back to the screen and slid his glasses, which had somehow migrated to the top of his head, back down.

'What about eating?' Warlow said.

'I'll grab something at the Inn,' Jess said.

'Okay, then at least let me keep you company for that.' Warlow turned to Gil again. 'Mrs Jones isn't expecting us for dinner, is she?'

'No. She'll have plated something up for me to reheat since I have no idea what time I'll be back. But you are a free agent.'

Warlow turned back to Jess. 'Shall we?'

For the second time that day, Warlow took the Brecon Road. The Cae Inn was a lovely old, stone longhouse off the A4067 with benched tables under umbrellas in the front garden. Warlow hung about in the bar while Jess was shown to her room. Ten minutes later, they were sitting on high-backed chairs at a table in a vaulted room with exposed beams.

'Not bad for out in the sticks,' Warlow said.

'We can't be far from the scene, here, can we?' Jess looked out of the window at the hills that seemed to surround them.

'About four or five miles, I reckon.' Warlow glanced at the menu, fully aware that he'd had soup and a sandwich only a couple of hours ago.

'Halloumi burger without the bread for me.' Decision made, Jess put the menu down.

In the end, Warlow chose a Caprese salad from the specials board. The food came quickly, and they chatted about the case and about how little they yet knew.

'Did Tiernon suggest a cause?' Warlow forked some mozzarella into his mouth.

'Dehydration, exposure or blood loss were his top three.'

'A charming combination if there ever was one,' Warlow muttered darkly. 'Ah well, let's not steal Rhys's thunder on that one.'

Jess smiled, but it appeared a half-hearted affair to Warlow. That and the way she chased bits of halloumi about her plate with her fork with little or no enthusiasm prompted him to ask, 'Jess, it's none of my business and feel free to tell me to take a running jump, but are you okay?'

She paused with her face down for a long couple of seconds before looking up. 'You've been doing this for too long, Mr Warlow. Reading people is a poisoned chalice.'

'Like I say, running jump is always an option.'

'No, it's okay. It's Molly and her dad.'

Warlow listened as Jess outlined the new tensions in the fraught relationship between Molly and her father. Her stubborn rebelliousness and his overbearing guilt manifesting as protectiveness were proving to be an explosive combination. The trip to the festival and beach camping had been the final straw. 'And here I am, stuck miles away, hoping that it'll all work out.'

'Anything I can do?'

'Not unless you have a magic wand or fairy dust. No easy answers here.'

'You shouldn't keep this stuff to yourself, you know?'

Jess let out a rasping laugh. 'You're a fine one to talk when it comes to secrets.'

Warlow snorted. Jess was one of the two other people aware of his HIV status. 'I told you though, didn't I?'

'Yes, you did. But only after you'd physically assaulted me.'

He'd dragged the DI out of a building slowly filling with nitrogen gas that had all but displaced every bit of oxygen in the room she'd been locked in. They both knew he'd saved her life. Warlow opted for full-on irate. 'You weren't breathing, woman. That was mouth to mouth.'

'Like I said.' Jess's eyes danced with amusement. 'But I appreciate the offer. One you may come to regret when I finally unburden the ton and a half of crap that is my personal life on your porch.'

'Looking forward to it.'

Her face softened and once again Warlow got the distinct impression that a door had creaked open two inches. All it needed to swing it wide was for one of them to exert a little pressure. But neither of them budged.

Jess's head dropped, and she emitted a groan of frustration. 'I promised myself I wouldn't let all this interfere. I swore to myself to make the job come first. It has to because the Buccaneer has given me this one. I daren't cock it up.'

'Not always that easy though, is it?'

She massaged the skin around her eyes with the palms of both hands and took a deep breath. 'No. But I'm determined to give it a go.'

'Good. But there is one thing I can do for you.'

'Oh?' Jess tilted her head.

Warlow took out his phone and typed a message. It flew into the ether with a whoosh. Five seconds later, the phone chirped to indicate incoming intel.

Warlow read the screen and nodded. 'Right. Gil is coming to pick me up. I'll leave the keys to the Jeep with you. Just in case.'

Jess smiled. 'There's no need, Evan.'

But they both heard the relief in her tone.

'There's a bit of noise on the passenger-side front wheel-arch. I've had it checked, and it's nothing serious.'

'Are you sure?'

'I am. I've made a note of the mileage, too, so I'll know if you take her for a spin.'

Jess grinned. 'Ever the detective. I appreciate it.'

'Right, I said I'd meet Gil outside in five minutes. His text said I'd probably hear his stomach before I saw him. He's that hungry.'

Warlow got up. Jess got up too and gave him a quick hug with an added squeeze at the end for emphasis.

As he left, the one thing Warlow remembered was that she smelled a hundred times better than KFC.

––––––

GIL'S CAR, on the other hand, smelled weirdly of rotting fruit, the nidus of which was a pink-coloured, smiley-faced-emoji air freshener dangling from the rear-view mirror.

'I know,' Gil said, seeing Warlow's nose wrinkle. 'But when you're a taxi for three girls under nine, you have no choice in such things. Especially if you make the mistake of taking them with you into a garage to pay for fuel. Their eyes go everywhere. Strawberry and mango fresh, it said on the label.'

'Strawberry and mango buried under a pile of manure would have been more accurate.'

'I'll get rid of it when we get home. We have some moths in an old cupboard. This'll see them off.' Gil needed no satnav to negotiate the roads. Like Warlow, this was back-of-the hand territory for him. 'Jess okay?'

'Yes. She's on it. Having no car is a bugger, though. Especially with Molly out camping somewhere. Jess feels happier knowing she can jump up and go if she needs to.'

Gil exhaled a deep and ominous sigh. 'I have that to look forward to when the three stooges grow up.'

'Hang on, you already have daughters. You know the score.'

'I do, but it's different when you're full-on grandparent-ing. Anwen did most of the shepherding for our daughters. I turned up on weekends and played the fool. But Anwen was the guiding hand. Did a bloody good job, too. But with the little ones,' he shook his head, 'I'm going to be retired by the time they hit their teens. There'll be no escape.'

'Don't worry, you'll have lost all your marbles by then. You won't care.'

'There is that.'

Led Zeppelin's *Heartbreaker* struck out from Warlow's pocket. He read the caller ID and answered the call.

'Catrin, what can I do for you?'

'Sounds like you're in a car, sir. Driving?'

'Not this time. I have a chauffeur. I left my car with DI Allanby. Gil is kindly hosting me for the evening.'

'*Shwmae,*' Gil called out.

'Ah.' As 'ahs' went, it passed muster as disappointment and wariness rolled up into one vowel sound. A humorous response from a woman who tolerated Gil's teasing with a feigned frostiness. But this time, Warlow thought he heard something else in the tone.

'You okay?'

'Yes sir. Wondered how you got on with DCI Tamblin?'

'Great. Awaiting confirmation from Povey's team on the house we found.'

'That's good, then.'

'You?'

'Let's just say I had an interesting day, sir. Mainly ticking boxes. DI Caldwell does things a little differently.'

'In what way?'

A beat of hesitation. 'In not wanting to waste time on things he doesn't believe will bear fruit.'

'Not methodical enough for you, then,' Gil called across. Though the phone was up to Warlow's ear, his conversation was clearly audible in the car.

For once, Catrin didn't have a riposte. And that, more than anything, made Warlow wonder what this call was about. 'Sure you're alright, Catrin?'

'Yes, sir. I was curious, that's all. We're chasing up one of the Geoghans' victim's relatives who's been very active online in trying to prevent Derek Geoghan's parole.'

Gil grunted. 'I'm on it.'

'Find her?'

'Not quite.'

'Never mind. I'll work on that tonight.'

'You are allowed the night off, Catrin,' Warlow said.

'I know, sir. See you tomorrow.'

'What was that all about?' Gil voiced the thought that plagued Warlow after he'd finished the phone call.

'She misses us,' Warlow replied.

'Maybe, though I think you're being a little optimistic using the word 'us' there.'

CHAPTER EIGHTEEN

THERE WERE tired-looking faces in the Incident Room the next morning, but everyone made it on time. Armed with mugs of tea and one hot water for DI Caldwell, the assembled team waited for the morning to begin.

Jess handed Warlow his keys as he found a seat and murmured, 'Not needed, but thanks,' before heading to the front of the room and addressing the assembled officers.

'Thanks for getting in so early. There is a lot to get through, so I suggest we get started. Rhys, let's kick things off with the post-mortem.'

Rhys bounced up off the desk he was leaning on, his face freshly scrubbed and, since it was summer, no scars or bruises from any weekend rugby games.

'You don't need to look so damned enthusiastic,' Gil said.

'But it was really interesting, Sarge,' Rhys replied. 'Dr Tiernon's preliminary report is in everyone's inbox, but the main findings were as follows.' He pointed to one of the crime scene snaps of Karen Geoghan.

'We have a positive dental record match for the female. It is Karen Geoghan. Some signs of superficial knife wounds to her arms and legs, all inflicted before death.'

'So, she was tortured?' Gil asked.

'Thirty-two wounds in all,' Rhys said with a sage nod. 'There are other findings common to both bodies. Significant reduction in weight of all organs. Distended gall bladder and empty stomach and intestines. These all point to withholding of food for prolonged periods.'

'Why would he starve them?' Catrin asked.

Gil answered, 'Compliance. I've seen it in cases of child abuse. Starving kids will do anything. I suspect the same would apply to starving adults. Could be how he got them to trek up to the forest. From what I've seen of them beforehand, neither of the Geoghans were exactly mountain goat material.'

'Derek Geoghan has also been positively ID'd. He had not been stabbed, but the evidence of starvation was similar. And in both cases, there was substantial blood loss.' Rhys glanced down at his notes. 'We know that from organ pallor and wrinkling of the spleen capsule—'

Gil folded his arms. 'It's like an episode of Doggie Howitzer.'

'You mean Doogie Howser,' Catrin said.

Gil nodded. 'That's him. Precocious teenage medic twerp.'

'Hang on,' KFC interjected. 'So, did they die of starvation or blood loss? I'm confused.'

'Dr Tiernon thinks they probably lost consciousness from dehydration and starvation and were too weak to hold their necks up once the sharpened stakes started to penetrate.' Rhys reached for a chair and sat with an arched back and his neck extended, using his middle and index finger to mock up the pointed end of the stake. 'Oh, and whoever it was oiled the tip of the stake, too. Just to make it easier to penetrate skin and eventually brain—'

'For God's sake, Doggie. Some of us had a big break-fast.' Gil scrunched his face up.

'Sorry, Sarge. These are the facts.'

'It's not so much the details, it's the way you're enjoying telling us about them.'

Rhys got up and put the chair back where he'd found it and then stood with an impassive, almost smug, smile on his face.

'Thank you, Rhys,' Jess said. 'One thing is clear from the MO. Whoever did this had planned the whole thing for some time.'

'And Derek Geoghan getting out might have been the trigger,' Warlow added.

Jess turned to Catrin. 'Did you get anything useful in talking to Geoghan's cellmates?'

Catrin stood up and walked forward, her face composed into an appropriate mask of dejection. 'Nothing useful, ma'am.'

'It was nothing but a fishing expedition anyway, you have to admit.' KFC sat slouching in a chair, one arm over the back of the one next to him.

'We're still waiting to hear back from one source,' Catrin added.

'Yeah, a junkie thief who doesn't know what day it is,' KFC muttered.

Catrin ignored him. 'I contacted Iona Michaels. She's been very active online in trying to prevent Derek Geoghan from being released. She's the daughter of one of the Geoghans' victims.'

'I thought you wanted me to do that?' Gil asked, pretending to be miffed.

'I had a few spare hours last night.' Catrin shrugged.

'Is she coming in?' Jess watched Catrin pin Michaels' name up on the board under the words 'Geoghan Activist'.

'She can't, ma'am. She lives in Chepstow and has small

children.' The DS dragged up a resigned smile. 'Our best bet is a visit.'

'Okay, I'll leave that with you and Kelvin.'

'Oh, good. Another day trip looking for wild geese.' KFC arched his neck. 'Quack bloody quack.'

'Are you suggesting we ignore this lead, Kelvin?' Jess cocked an eyebrow.

'There's such a thing as Zoom.'

'There is.' Jess nodded. 'But then you might miss the little subtleties. Like the fact that she might possess a load of outdoor gear in her garage or is a potholing freak that knows the mountain around here like the back of her hand. You can't see that through a computer screen.'

'Fine.' KFC's flat delivery left no one in any doubt that he did not think this a good use of his time.

'I could go alone, ma'am,' Catrin offered.

'You could, but you won't. Four eyes are better than two here.'

Catrin nodded, the muscles on the side of her jaw clenching and unclenching as she made her way back to her desk.

'Evan?' Jess called out.

Warlow got to his feet.

'Owen Tamblin remembered a suspected burglary from some time back at an empty property on a hill on the opposite side of the valley.' He pointed to an A4 print-out of the house on Penmaen Street off Allt y Grug Road. 'Memorable because the report from the attending officer found some signs of a break-in, but not much in terms of burglary. He also mentioned envelopes scattered over the kitchen table and fresh sandwich wrappers in the kitchen bin. Owen and I visited last night, and I don't doubt this is where the Geoghans were held.'

Everyone sat up. Everyone bar KFC who seemed to be

treating all the information with a studied degree of boredom.

Warlow ignored him. 'Povey is over there now with a team. The envelopes had been recently bought; the packaging was still there. And there were some signs of an address having been... Attempted. Almost illegible, but I'd put money on it being an attempt at my name.'

KFC sat up at that. 'Bloody hell, Evan. Been a busy bee.'

'Stroke of luck and the advantage of having Owen involved. We're chasing up a B and E artist who was arrested trying to break into that same property several months before. A recidivist called Marius Stoica. We'll see what he has to say for himself. Owen's leading with this. I'm waiting on him to come back to me.'

'Sounds like a good idea.' Jess nodded. 'Rhys, I want you to go back to the Geoghans' property. See if we can find anything useful there. Oh, and chase up their phone records, please.'

'Got it, ma'am.'

'I'll come with you, Rhys,' Warlow offered.

The young DC's face lit up, but then fell again. 'Am I going to need my stab vest, sir?'

'Not if I can help it,' Warlow muttered. 'Where is it we're going again?'

Rhys slid his mouse over the pad on his desk and read the screen. 'Uh, Townhill in Swansea, sir.'

'Ah. Second thoughts, stick your stab vest in the car's boot and bring one along for me. You're driving, by the way.'

Jess turned to the board again, pleased with the way it was filling up. 'Okay, looks like we all have enough to do.'

———

Rhys drove with Warlow in the passenger seat, reading through the notes from when the Geoghans were reported missing. Or rather, when a neighbour thought it odd that Karen Geoghan had not been out in the street shouting abuse at all and sundry, which was the norm, and the postman noticed parcels were piling up outside the front door of their semi.

Rhys wisely went for Radio 6 music but kept the volume low.

'This is like old times, sir.'

Warlow didn't look up to reply, 'What, you and me in a car on the way to a job?'

'Yes, sir.'

Warlow sucked in air. 'Ooh, let me think, it must be all of four weeks since we last did this.'

'That's what I mean, sir. Our paths haven't crossed lately.'

Warlow sent him a sharp look. 'Don't tell me you'd rather be in the car with me than with DI Allanby.'

'What? No, I don't mean that.'

'Oh, so you prefer her company to mine. I see.'

'I didn't say—' Rhys clamped his mouth shut. 'You're pulling my leg again, sir.'

'I can't resist an open door, Rhys.'

They drove on in silence for a while before the DC spoke again. In fact, Warlow was amazed he'd kept quiet for the whole two minutes it took for the words to bubble. 'I think we have a good team now, sir. Two different, but fantastic, sergeants.'

'Since it's a popularity contest, which of those two do you prefer?'

Rhys smiled. 'No, I'm not going there. Catrin, uh Sergeant Richards, she's very particular, sir. I think I'm learning a lot about discipline and process from her.'

'Agreed. What about Gil?'

Rhys couldn't help the smile that curled up his lip. 'Sergeant Jones takes a different approach. I've learned a lot about biscuits since I started working with him.'

'I'd keep that off your CV if I were you,' Warlow muttered.

'No, sir. It's interesting stuff. Did you know biscuits were the first food to reach the South Pole with Amundsen in 1911?'

'I have to admit, I did not know that.'

'And a biscuit recovered from the Titanic sold for over three thousand pounds at auction.'

'Really? That one must have passed me by, too.'

'But DS Richards, she's a great teacher.'

'But loses out on the biscuit knowledge side of things, eh?'

'Everyone has their good and bad points, sir.'

'Hmph.' Warlow turned back to the report. 'It says here that there were parcels on their doorstep delivered a week before the Geoghans were reported missing. So that gives us a timeline of sorts.'

'How many weeks was it since that report and the finding on Penwyllt, sir?'

Warlow flicked through some pages. 'The last post date on the parcels was 18th April. It was an Amazon delivery. We checked, and that order was placed the day before from Karen Geoghan's Amazon account.'

'What was it?'

'Ritter Sport variety mini-box.'

'Great choice.' Rhys nodded.

Warlow's expression didn't change as he voiced his thoughts. 'It's mid-June now. Tiernon reckoned they'd been dead at least a week, yes?'

'A week, yes. Lucky that the temperatures haven't been sky high. That's what he said.'

'Right. So, we assume they'd been held for almost two months.'

'That's some crash diet, sir.'

There could be no mistaking the horror in Rhys's voice. But Warlow knew this was nothing but vicarious terror. Imagining going without food for over three hours sent the DC into a hangry tailspin.

Warlow looked up. 'Aren't we coming up to Cross Hands?'

'Half a mile, sir.'

'Right. I see the Golden Arches up ahead. Flat white and a McMuffin for me. What about you, Rhys?'

'I'd go for the cheesy bacon flatbread, sir.'

'Does that mean we have to sit in?'

As hang dog looks went, the one appearing on Rhys's face was a beauty.

Warlow sighed. 'Fifteen minutes, maximum.'

'I can usually polish a big brekkie off in eight, sir.'

'Your mother must be so proud.'

CHAPTER NINETEEN

TOWNHILL AND MAYHILL in Swansea had never appeared in any Sunday supplement list of places to move to. Rows of council houses lined the hills as Warlow and Rhys drove in, the bays and beaches of the neighbouring Gower peninsula a light year away.

The areas' claims to fame were inglorious. Townhill formed the backdrop to the late 90s film Twin Town that had the tagline, 'pretty, shitty city', as a parody of Dylan Thomas's description of Swansea as ugly and lovely. And Mayhill exploded into the national and international consciousness when the streets caught fire during a spate of anti-police riots in mid-2021.

The Geoghans were not from this area. They were incomers from East of Cambridge. But housing was cheap. And though the sense of community was strong on some of the streets, in others, people kept themselves to themselves. Which suited the Geoghans.

Once the officers pulled up in front of the property at the junction of two roads, Warlow saw immediately what the draw had been.

It was a corner spot, and, though described as semi-detached, this was a duplex, with one half of the building on one street, the other half on another. You walked up to one front door, down to the other. Both halves of the duplex were boarded up now and the Geoghans' place, accessed by the lower street, also had a narrow opening in the hedge leading to a garage with its shutters down. The opening now also had blue and white crime scene tape fluttering across it.

'Are we going in, sir?'

'No. South Wales Police have been and gone and I have their report. I wanted to see the lie of the land, that's all. Besides, look at the top window there.' He pointed to where one of the side windows had its square covering of marine ply gaping open slightly. 'I suspect anything that had been left has long disappeared. Down here they call it recycling.'

'Are we knocking on doors, then?'

Warlow looked up and down the forlorn street. Most of the houses were rendered and in dire need of a pressure wash or a new lick of paint. The idea of randomly knocking held little appeal. But his mind was on the hardstanding in front of the garage. You could back a van in there and be just a few yards from the front door. In these times of everything delivered, no one walking, or driving past would have batted an eyelid at the sight of a vehicle in here.

'No. Drive up and back,' Warlow said eventually.

Rhys complied, driving up the road and around the sharp corner before looping back on himself at the end of the next street. Warlow wanted to check access.

'So, the Geoghans had the lower half of the duplex which is screened off by conifers from the people next door down, and the houses across the road are further down the hill. Despite the density of housing, the place is surprisingly secluded. In fact, not overlooked at all.'

The street outside was on the curve of the road and, opposite, the back fences of the houses further down had dense hedges as walls.

Warlow took photographs on his phone and then instructed Rhys to find the nearest newsagent, which, like most of the rest of the world, was downhill from where they had parked.

Town Stores was a Sell Fresh Foods franchise. As well as being a newsagent as advertised, it sold everything a corner shop was supposed to sell, from snorkels to condoms. The shopkeeper obviously had a sense of humour because he'd written those very words in thick blue felt-tip pen and stuck it in his window.

Everything Inside, from snorkels to condoms.

Warlow paused for a fleeting moment to wonder at what point in anyone's life those two items might appear on the top of a shopping list. A diving trip to the Seychelles with your significant other, maybe?

Not much chance of that in Townhill.

'The mind bloody boggles,' Warlow murmured as he stepped inside to the tune of a two-tone warning note. No one could sneak in and out of Town Stores without the shopkeeper knowing. He glanced up. CCTV cameras covered every angle.

'Fancy a Twix, sir?' Rhys asked, his eyes straying to a well-stocked confectionery shelf.

'I'm fine.' Warlow headed for the counter which was rammed with the kind of things you never knew you wanted until you were about to pay for the things you actually did. Chewing gum, left-over mini-Easter eggs, scratch-cards, paracetamol. But everything looked clean and neat. Stuffed to the rafters, but an organised stuffing.

The man behind the counter wore a turban above a grey-flecked beard and moustache. He glanced up from the magazine he was reading, and with both hands on the counter, looked Warlow squarely in the eye.

'Cigarettes, is it?' There was still a trace of an accent there, but years of living in Swansea had taken the edge off it and simply added a different tone to the lilt. Some people, usually from across the Severn Bridge, ended up sounding more Indian than Welsh when they attempted the accent. Truth was, they weren't a million miles away from each other to start with.

'What?' Warlow frowned.

The shopkeeper nodded at Warlow's hands. 'You don't have a basket. Usually, that means you're after booze or fags.'

'That's very observant. But no, I'm not after buying anything.'

The shopkeeper waited while Warlow retrieved his warrant card. 'DCI Warlow, and the pick and mix artist over there is DC Rhys Harries.'

'If it's about my sons chasing that drunk out of here, I've already given a statement.'

'No, nothing to do with that, uh…' Warlow narrowed his eyes and jutted his chin forward to encourage a response.

'Gagan Singh,' the shopkeeper obliged.

'Mr Singh, we're here looking into the disappearance of Karen and Derek Geoghan. Am I right in assuming that this is the shop she bought the winning scratchcard from? I remember reading about it on the news.' Truth was, Karen had gloated about it in one of her letters. Expounding on the fact that her newfound windfall was going to be spent getting her beloved Derek out of prison, with a sizeable amount allocated to appropriately vicious retribution for Warlow daring to bring the two to justice.

Mr Singh positively lit up. 'Oh, yes. That was us. I

stayed out of the limelight. My manager Mick spoke to the press. I like to keep the low profile.'

'But you knew the Geoghans?'

'I knew her. Big Fruit & Nut fan. We have little nicknames for our regulars. She was definitely Cranky Karen. No harm meant, of course. But she was definitely cranky.'

'She bought Fruit & Nuts here?' Rhys joined Warlow at the till. A brace of Twixes and a packet of cheese and onion crisps in his big hand.

'Every week. But always encased in the dairy milk. The 90-gram bar, normal recommended retail price of one forty-nine. Mostly she waited until they were on special offer at ninety-nine pence and then bought ten. I do that when the sell-by date gets a bit close. We keep it at that to fight off the Amazon, who sells it at one pound. After she won the lottery, she splashed out on the giant box of pralines covered in sprinkled nuts. Twenty-five quid's worth. We only sell those at Christmas usually. So, the mid-year sale is always a nice surprise. Mind you, as praline-based confections go, I think it is overrated. I much prefer the seashells.'

'They are lush.' Rhys nodded.

Warlow quelled him with a look.

'Did you meet Derek Geoghan?' Warlow asked the shop owner.

'Only once. Maybe three months ago. He came in on one of those scooters.'

'A mobility scooter?'

'Yes. A purple one. We had the ramp put up outside for that. Not for him especially.' Mr Singh grinned. 'We have a lot of people on the estate use those. He bought booze mainly. But he didn't look well.'

'Did you ever chat with Karen?'

'Sometimes. She was a complainer, you know? About the cost of things. About the noise on the estate. About the weather. So, yes, a chat with Karen was me listening to her complain.'

'But she never spoke to you about anyone on the estate threatening her?'

'Good God, no way.' Mr Singh sounded suddenly more Welsh than Indian. 'And she was a big woman. I used to joke with Mick that she'd be better off walking down from Ceri Road than driving. She drove everywhere. Lots of people do now, don't they? Much better if people walked. Get a bit of exercise.'

'All uphill on the way back, though,' Rhys said.

'It is. But she would have benefitted. I mean, she isn't a small woman. She did walk it a couple of times. I could tell because of the sweat. I almost managed to offload the Nadal sweatband we have in the window. Dirt cheap display stock in case you are interested. I even asked her if she was trying to get fit.' Mr Singh paused for effect. 'She told me to eff off, only using the full four letters, not only the eff.'

'What did people think of her?' Warlow asked.

'Kids can be cruel, you know? They call her Mrs Porker. She wasn't very good with youngsters. Rude, miserable, never smiling.'

'So, no fan club then?'

Mr Singh thought and then answered, 'More a cross-the-street-if-you-see-her-coming, kind of club.'

Warlow zeroed in on that. 'But no actual threats, were there?'

'Not that I am aware of.' Singh hesitated before continuing, 'Wait a minute, she went missing. But these questions… Have you found them, the Geoghans?'

'We have?'

'Are they alright?'

'Honest answer? No, they are not.'

'Oh my God. They have an accident?'

'More an encounter, let's say.' Warlow knew that if he gave too much away here, word would spread like wildfire. He was here, asking these questions because of the shop's pivotal role in the community. Shopkeepers heard all sorts. But the opposite was true, too. Shops were a good way of disseminating information.

'So, will they be coming back? I mean, she still has a *Sunday Express* on order. Should I cancel it?' Singh asked.

'I would,' Warlow said, dropping a heavy hint.

'Okay.' Mr Singh grabbed a notebook from the shelf behind him and flattened out a page. He fished out a pen from an 'I Love Swansea' mug and ran an inky line through an entry. When neither of the officers said anything for half a minute, the shopkeeper took his cue and nodded down at Rhys's haul and then up at the young officer. 'Job done. Will that be all, Detective Constable? Or can I interest you in some special-offer Fruit & Nut for under a quid?'

Back in the car, Warlow made Rhys stand outside to eat his crisps. The man was unable to masticate soft fruit under fifty decibels, and the noise he made when eating flaked fried potato could wake the dead. Or at least irritate the hell out of Warlow. He, meanwhile, took the opportunity of a moment's solitude to dial up Owen Tamblin's number.

'Evan, help us.' Tamblin's voice boomed through the speaker system, making Rhys look around. Warlow turned down the volume.

'That joke is so old.'

'Makes me laugh.'

'Says it all. Any news?' The noise of rustling paper came through loud and clear, prompting Warlow to ask, 'Christ, you're not eating bloody fish and chips, are you?'

'I am at my desk I'll have you know. That noise is me digging for my notes on Stoica.'

'You found him?'

'Not exactly. We had a number for him. I explained why we wanted to speak to him. But he's not that keen. Says he's working and there's no way he can have time off to come and speak to us, or for us to go and speak to him.'

'Where is he?'

Tamblin rustled some more pages. 'Last known address is Ammanford. That's the good news, the bad news is that I had a word with Gil, and he sent some Uniforms up there. But my phone call spooked him. Our friend Marius is in the wind.'

'Gil will put the word out. Stoica'll surface at some point. But we've got nothing on him.'

'Not yet. But he's all we've got.'

Warlow took a beat before asking his next question. 'Was there any sign of a struggle when you visited the Geoghans' property after they were reported missing?'

'No. But there was rotting food on the table. It looked like they left in a hurry. In the middle of a meal. And given their sizes, that would have been a wrench.'

'Were they disturbed?'

'Possibly,' Tamblin agreed. 'Neighbours neither saw nor heard anything strange. But then we are talking about Townhill. Strange has a very different connotation up there.'

'I've noticed.'

'You up there?'

'We are. I wanted to see their place.'

'Then you know what I mean. But back to Stoica. His default response is to run for the hills whenever we sniff around, so that doesn't prove anything. Meanwhile, I'll keep digging. See if he rings any bells anywhere else.'

'How come you get all the glamorous jobs?' Warlow said, and ended the call before Tamblin could get past the first three oaths that came down the line.

Rhys got back in the car, still with crisp debris peppering his lips. Warlow tapped his own mouth.

'I won't tell anyone, sir,' Rhys said.

Warlow shook his head. 'I'm not asking you to keep a bloody secret, man. Wipe your mouth. You look like you've just eaten two Twixes and a packet of crisps.'

Rhys fished out a tissue and obliged. 'I kept you one finger of Twix, sir.'

'No, you're alright. Keep it for when you're hungry. Like in about ten minutes' time.'

'Shame we didn't find much out here, isn't it, sir?'

'You think we didn't?'

Rhys looked puzzled.

Warlow let him off the hook. 'We know that Karen Geoghan wasn't liked. We know their house isn't over-looked from the front or the side. Unless they went to meet their abductor, which I doubt very much given Derek Geoghan's parlous state of health, my bet is that someone forced them from that property under duress. An innocuous delivery van parked outside would not have been noticed at night.'

'Wow, that is a lot of information, sir.'

'Observation, Rhys. We also know we can get a Fruit & Nut for under a quid at Town Stores. So, not a completely wasted journey by a long way.'

Rhys put the car in gear. 'Are we heading back up to Ystradgynlais, sir?'

'We are. I want you to chase up the Geoghans' phone records and help Gil find Mr Stoica, our burglar.'

'Sure you don't want that Twix, sir?'

'I am. I don't want to spoil my appetite for when Gil gets out the biscuits.'

CHAPTER TWENTY

Iona Michaels met with Catrin and KFC in a Starbucks on the outskirts of Chepstow. She exuded maternal competence in that she'd commandeered a corner spot with a table and four chairs. In one sat a toddler busily colouring in with the slow and studied back-and-forth technique that only fully engaged three-year-olds had. Next to the toddler was a buggy containing a sleeping baby.

The police officers took the seats opposite.

'Thanks for agreeing to speak to us, Mrs Michaels,' Catrin said.

'No problem.' Iona smiled. She was a lithe thirty-something with dark hair and a no-nonsense air about her.

'We would have come to your home,' KFC said.

'No need. Jake's nursery is this side of town. He's mornings only, so this seemed the best option.'

KFC looked around. 'Bit noisy and impersonal for what we need to discuss, don't you think?'

Iona's smile didn't slip for one instant. 'I'm here, and this is the only way I can fit you in. I suggest we press on before Jake turns into the hungry monster. You don't want to be here to witness that.'

KFC sat back, not trying to hide his disapproval, disinterest dulling his expression. 'Yeah, right. Can I get you anything?'

Iona shook her head. 'I'm fine.'

The DI stood up. 'Well, I could do with a decaff. Catrin, you want?'

'Americano would be great.'

'Want one of those granola bars as a chaser?'

'No, thanks.'

He shuffled off towards the queue for the coffees.

Iona dropped her voice. 'I suppose it is a bit impersonal, but I keep everything Geoghan-related away from the house. It's a rule I have.'

'Fair enough. Looks like you have your hands full, too.'

'My choice.' Iona leaned forward to check on the sleeping baby. 'I wouldn't have it any other way.'

'What's the baby's name?'

'Ronwen. My husband isn't Welsh, so he calls her Ronnie. But it's Ronwen on the birth certificate. I made sure of that.'

'You're not from around here, I take it?'

Iona came back with a lopsided smile. 'Can't you tell? I'm a Cardi. Born and bred in Llangrannog. But Andrew works in Bristol. So, I've compromised. Still this side of the bridge. Just.'

'As I said on the phone, we're here about the Geoghans.'

'What do you want to know?'

Catrin had run through all of this with KFC on the way up in the job car. They'd agreed that Mrs Michaels had to be told, even though the press remained in the dark. Best they take the direct route. 'Karen and Derek Geoghan were found dead two days ago.'

Iona Michaels' poise slipped for only a second, but it

was enough to tell Catrin that she had no idea this was why they'd come to see her.

'Dead? Both of them?'

Catrin nodded.

'Car accident?'

'No. You need to understand that this is as yet not common knowledge and I'd appreciate it if you did not broadcast the news.'

Iona may well have heard Catrin's words, but she seemed not to listen. 'If it wasn't an accident, what was it?'

'They were murdered.'

This time, Iona reacted. She fell back in her chair, her eyes never leaving Catrin. 'Bloody hell.'

Jake stopped crayoning and looked up at his mother. She patted his arm. 'Sorry, *cariad*. It's a naughty word. Silly Mam. Why don't you make the grass green instead of yellow?'

Jake looked at his work, shrugged and went back to his colouring.

Catrin explained a little more. 'We're making enquiries and your name came up.'

Iona hissed out some air. 'Am I a suspect?'

'Been anywhere near the Black Mountains in the last two weeks?'

'I've been to Waitrose and Morrisons. That's about the only adventure I've had.'

Catrin nodded. 'We're more interested in your petition.'

Iona breathed out a sigh. 'I have done nothing wrong with that.'

'We're not saying you have. But you'll understand why we wanted to ask you some questions.'

'Okay.'

KFC came back with the drinks. The Americano for Catrin and something with a leaf drawn in the foam for himself. He unwrapped a granola bar and took a bite. 'We up to speed, then?' he asked with his mouth full.

'Yes.'

'I'm with you on this,' KFC said to Iona. 'Bit of a waste of time. Still, we are but pawns, right?' He took a slurp of his coffee.

Catrin took out a file from her messenger bag. 'You started a petition on Stopthis.com four years ago?'

Iona nodded. 'That was when it was first suggested that Derek Geoghan might be eligible for parole. I wanted people to know that this man had no place in our society.'

'Remind me what your link with him is?'

'He cheated my gran out of her life savings. He pretended to be from social services and went to her home once a week for three months. Said he was making sure that everyone's bank accounts were safe from being taken over. She was getting confused by then. She didn't even tell us he was calling because he told her that she shouldn't trust anyone who didn't have an identity card. My mum was in the process of getting power of attorney. By the time she did, Geoghan had taken £37,000 from Gran's accounts. We got none of that back. It broke her heart because it was my grandad's savings. Money he'd put away for her.'

'In your petition you called him the "night terror".'

Iona nodded. 'She said he'd come at night, sometimes while she was sleeping. He must have got a key from her somehow. Geoghan said she was a confused old... He used the "c" word in court. But I believed her. That monster was capable of anything. He'd wake her up to tell her that there'd been reports of cyber-attacks and if she didn't do anything about her money, she'd lose it all. My gran was eighty-seven. When we found all of this out, she had bruises on her arms and legs. We think Derek Geoghan did that, too. But she wouldn't talk about it. But then, we know what he did to that poor man they killed.'

'That was manslaughter.'

'It should have been murder.' Iona's lips became thin lines.

'Your petition got lots of signatures,' KFC said.

'Four hundred and fifty thousand at the last count.'

KFC swallowed a mouthful of granola and said, 'You must have been doing cartwheels when you heard he was being released on grounds of ill health.'

Iona didn't flinch. 'I wasn't happy. But then I consoled myself with knowing that his condition was terminal.'

Catrin took out a sheet printed off from the Stopthis website. 'We realise this has been running for a long time, but I see that there is room at the bottom where people can tell the organiser their reason for signing.'

'Some namby-pamby lawyer said Geoghan deserved a chance of reintegrating into society. Before he became institutionalised.' Iona squeezed her eyes shut and shivered. 'Some people wanted to vent their feelings.'

Catrin nodded. 'Anyone special?'

'You're kidding. We had a few who suggested bringing back hanging. Quite a few more who suggested other things. Very… Descriptively.'

'Any way we could access that information?'

'The petition closed when he got out.' Iona shook her head.

'But they stay on the website. The people who commented. Plus, there must be a way of tracing who contributed. You're the organiser. You can access those posts,' KFC said.

'You want me to trawl through them?'

'And pick out the crazies,' KFC said.

Iona gave him a frosty stare. 'I read all those reasons for signing, and none of them sounded crazy. People were angry. Not always with Derek Geoghan, but with what he represented. A failure in the system to look after those vulnerable people. It should never have been allowed to happen in the first place.'

KFC had stopped eating. Iona's voice had gone up a few notches and people were staring.

'Sorry,' she said. 'I'm still very angry at what happened. I'm not sorry to hear they're dead. They both deserve it. Whoever did it should get a medal.'

Catrin kept her gaze impassive.

Iona glanced at her two children. 'Are you going to write that down?' she asked the officers.

'No,' Catrin replied. 'But we'd appreciate your cooperation.'

'Okay. I'll log in.'

'Or we could log in for you,' KFC suggested.

'No. That won't be necessary. I'll let you know.'

They left Iona Michaels to it and went back to the car. KFC got in and, for once, didn't say anything for several minutes as he stared out of the window.

'You're quiet, sir,' Catrin said, as they hit the motorway.

'For once, Catrin, I'm lost for bloody words.' His Midlands accent sent the words up and down along the sentence.

'Not what you were expecting?'

'Au contraire, exactly what I was expecting. Another wild, bloody goose chase. That's us out of the fray. For what?' He read his watch. 'A good three hours by the time we get back. She was never going to cough up a list of names.'

'She did say she'd go through them, though.'

'Yeah, she did. But you've seen these sites. You don't have to give your real name in the comments. And there is no way we'll get access to anyone's bank details or address, thanks to data protection and all that guff. We'd go to court, and we'd lose.'

'So why did we come up here?'

'An "I" to dot if I remember correctly.'

Catrin frowned. The sentence rang a bell as something Warlow had said to her.

KFC waited until the penny clattered home. When it did, Catrin's frown deepened.

'Yeah, that's right. DCI Warlow has DI Allanby's ear. She threw us this bone. And we've chased after it like the good little dogs that we are.'

'We don't know that—'

'Yes, we soddin' do. And it's about time you accepted that. Very convenient that Evan and Owen Tamblin have buddied up, don't you think? They can keep sending us off up garden paths until the sodding cows come home.'

'There's no evidence that they're doing that, is there?' Catrin's voice sounded strained.

In the passenger seat, KFC turned towards the junior officer. 'That's where we have the advantage. They don't know we're investigating them. I've applied for and obtained permission to request their phone records for the last six months.'

'Their? You don't mean DI Allanby's too?'

'No, I mean Tamblin and Warlow. I want you to go through them. See if they've been communicating. Or if they've dragged someone else in to do their dirty work.'

Catrin threw him a look of horror. 'Me? Why me, sir?'

'Because you're good at your job, Catrin. We need to find out if they were in contact at or around the time of Geoghan's release and afterwards.'

Catrin looked horrified. 'They were, though. They've already said that. How does that help?'

KFC dropped his chin. 'Like I say, we don't know until we look. That's for you to find out.' He picked up on her shock. 'What if it is Warlow and Tamblin? What if they set it all up to appear as if some soddin' madman grabbed the Geoghans and locked them away in an abandoned house that, again very conveniently, is on Warlow's home ground?'

Catrin shook her head. 'It's going to be difficult to work on the records in the same room as Mr Warlow—'

KFC threw up a hand. 'Stop right there, Sergeant. I have an answer. Take a sickie. Take everything home with you and take a sickie. I'll tell Jess you've been throwing up.'

'But I haven't, sir.'

'Then it'll be our little secret, eh?'

Catrin drove on in silence. She hated secrets. She hated lying. But worse was the thought of working against Evan Warlow. The car ate up the miles while her guts did the Zumba. Twenty minutes later, she pulled up at the Magor services, opened the car door and threw up, one hand on the door handle.

KFC watched for several seconds before rummaging in the glove box and handing Catrin a tissue. She didn't argue. She felt too sick to argue.

'That was good. You'll be on a CCTV camera doing that. Good thinking.' His eyes narrowed. 'You're not carrying a bun in the oven, are you?'

'What?'

'You know what I mean.'

'I am not pregnant. But I wasn't pretending to be sick, either. The thought of investigating—'

'Orders from above, Catrin. Suck it up.'

She dabbed at some spittle left on her chin. Her breath ratcheted in her throat as she let it out. 'I think I'm going to be sick again.'

'Fair enough. Better get it all up. When you're done, I'll drive. We need to get you back because there is no denying you are not a well woman, Sergeant Richards. You need to go home and rest.' He opened the passenger door and stepped out.

Catrin looked up, swallowing back another wave of nausea. KFC was standing near the bonnet, phone in hand. He whistled as he dialled up a number. Grinned as he joked with whoever answered his call, completely preoccupied with his own agenda.

He didn't see the venomous glare of contempt she gave him just before she leaned forward and deposited the rest of her stomach contents onto the tarmac.

CHAPTER TWENTY-ONE

WARLOW AND RHYS arrived back at the station in Ystradgynlais to find a familiar face in the Incident Room.

'Ah, Evan. Great timing.' Jess looked up from where she and Gil were standing next to a woman with cropped black hair and a weather-beaten face. Alison Povey spent a lot of her working life on her hands and knees in inhospitable places that smelled of death and corruption. But on her weekends off, she and her partner and their toddler son spent almost as much time outdoors as in. Warlow had concluded that being in the open air was necessarily life-affirming for a woman whose day-in and day-out job as a forensic lead dealt with death in all its manifestations.

'Your hunch on the house in…' Jess peered at the address.

Gil put her out of her misery. 'Ystalyfera, ma'am.'

'There,' Jess pointed at the recently posted images of the empty kitchen and the table strewn with envelopes. 'Was a good one.'

'We've run some onsite DNA tests. That stuff you found under the chair was Karen Geoghan's blood,' Povey explained. 'Samples from the other chair matched Derek Geoghan. Not blood but sweat or some other body fluid.'

'Anyone else's?' Warlow asked.

'Not yet.'

'What about the envelopes?'

Povey smiled. 'They're cheap. Probably bought at a big retailer. We're on it.'

Warlow returned the smile. 'Don't doubt that for a minute.'

Gil had begun a snaking timeline across the top of the board with spaces where there were gaps. 'So far, I have the Geoghans going missing in April and turning up in Penwyllt a couple of days ago. Since the post-mortem results indicate they'd been dead for a week at least, that means they were kept somewhere from mid-April to the end of May.'

'Do we think they were at the house all that time?' Jess asked.

'We found an empty Tesco milk carton at the rear of the property dated 22nd May,' Povey said.

'What are your thoughts on that?'

The crime scene manager compressed her mouth. 'The carton was found at the corner of the property, half-concealed by some ferns. Given how careful the abductor has been to conceal their presence, either the carton has nothing to do with the case, or, it may have been displaced while being removed and, because we're in the period of maximum plant growth, the ferns might have covered it up.'

Gil nodded. 'Makes sense.' He wrote *milk carton 22/05/23* on a strip of paper and pinned it up to his time-line. One more piece of the jigsaw.

'Anything else from the site at Penwyllt?' Warlow asked.

'Nothing much. Oh, except for the fact that the oil on

the tips of the sharpened stakes was a mixture of linseed and engine oil.'

'Linseed?' Jess asked.

Povey shrugged. 'Common enough. Look in anyone's garden shed, and you might find a bottle. Engine oil you can get from most garages.'

'What about your trip to Swansea?' Gil turned to Warlow.

'The Geoghans' house lends itself to surreptitious activity. We parked on the street outside in daylight for fifteen minutes and saw three cars go past and no pedestrians. The Geoghans did not have many fans locally. Unlikely to be many callers, and Karen was not citizen of the year. But I need to get Owen to knock on some doors again. Someone might have seen something.'

'Good,' Jess said.

Warlow exchanged a few non-Geoghan-related pleasantries with Povey before Jess walked her out.

In the lull that followed, a Uniform manning the phones took a call. A moment later, she held her hand over the mouthpiece and spoke to the officers still clustered around the board.

'It's a Bradley Masters from Llanelli. Shared a cell with Derek Geoghan in Cardiff nick.'

'I'll take it.' Rhys went to his desk and picked up the handset.

Warlow tuned out the DC's one-sided conversation as Gil pointed to a photo of the empty house again. 'I sent someone to look for your B and E artist.'

'Mr Stoica. Yes, we need a chat with him. Any word on that?'

'Nothing yet. But I've got someone pulling Stoica's sheets. You don't think he has anything to do with the Geoghans though, do you?'

'Nothing would surprise me in this case.'

Jess came back into the room, looking troubled. 'I've just had a call from Kelvin Caldwell. He doesn't think that the woman who organised the petition to stop Geoghan's release has anything to contribute. And Catrin isn't feeling well. He's sending her home.'

Warlow stamped on his disappointment. Losing Catrin would be a blow. 'Nothing serious, I hope?'

'He says she's thrown up a couple of times.'

'Something's probably upset her.' Gil's exaggerated innocence almost made Warlow smile, but he managed to keep a straight face.

'Yes, maybe,' Jess said. 'Kelvin's on the way back. I've suggested vespers.'

Both Gil and Warlow nodded. The euphemistic term for a late afternoon catch-up gave everyone a chance to get some work done.

A few yards away, Rhys ended his call and looked up, his trademark blinking giving away his state of mind to the other senior officers. Gil often said if anyone needed a live-action Tigger, Rhys would be one.

'Anything?' Warlow asked.

'I don't rightly know, sir. Catrin had been to see Masters, but she got nowhere because he's a user and was high when they called.'

'Confused.com, is it?' Gil asked. 'You as well as him, by the looks of it.'

'Uh, no,' Rhys said. 'He said he had shared a cell with Geoghan. I asked him if Geoghan ever spoke about enemies. Masters said no, but he had become upset once shortly after his wife's car caught fire. He got frustrated because he couldn't do anything about it.'

'What?'

'Exactly, sir.'

Jess turned to Gil. 'Have we seen anything about Karen Geoghan being involved in a car fire?'

'No, ma'am. Not to my recollection.'

'How did Masters sound to you, Rhys?' Jess asked.

'I've heard worse. I mean, he didn't sound high.'

Gil shook his head. 'Surely an arson attack would have been flagged up?'

Warlow remained non-committal and grunted out a. 'Hmm.'

Jess sighed. 'Right then, Rhys. That's you sorted for this afternoon. Find out if your friend Masters is hallucinating or not.'

SOMETIMES, you got lucky. Or, as Warlow would often say to Rhys, 'sitting on your arse and thinking is a very underrated aspect of police work.' Nothing on the PNC linked Karen Geoghan to a car fire. But then, unless a criminal act had taken place, why should it? Instead, Rhys spent fifteen minutes on a search engine and came up with several reports, and even amateur footage of a car fire in the car park of the new-ish Aldi in Parc Tawe, a retail park on the west bank of the river towards the eastern side of the city of Swansea. The car, a 2012 Citroen C3 had, according to witnesses, spontaneously burst into flames with no one inside, in October of last year.

Two other reports mentioned that the car's owner, Mrs Karen Geoghan, was not in the vehicle when passers-by noticed the flames and called the fire brigade.

A local radio website still had a post up.

MID AND WEST WALES FIRE and Rescue Services were called to the scene at 13:47. Firefighters used three hose-reel jets to fight the fire, which was extinguished at 14:07. There were no casualties. The cause of the fire is yet to be determined.

RHYS SHOWED Gil what he'd found. As it happened, the sergeant had heard a report of another fire in Brynamman on the local radio news that morning. A quick phone call had confirmed that the Fire Investigation Officer was in attendance.

'Why don't you pop up there and have a chat,' Warlow suggested, looking up from behind his desk as the two officers chatted.

'What, me, sir?' Rhys had tried not to sound too incredulous, but his lips kept breaking into a smile despite his best efforts at trying to remain professional. 'On my own?'

Gil wagged a finger at the young officer, who was a good six-plus inches taller than the sergeant. 'Don't play with any rough boys and make sure you're back by teatime.'

Warlow suppressed a chortle. 'Do you want me to come with you?'

'No, sir.' Rhys grimaced at the vehemence of his own response. 'I mean, there's no need, sir. If you think—'

'I do think. Time to fly the nest. And this is one where you will not need your stab vest.'

'Thank you, sir.' Rhys beamed and grabbed his coat. As he left the room, he heard Gil's loud voice. 'And try not to bugger anything up.'

———

THE FIRE in an old paint store at the rear of a workshop in Brynamman had burned through the night and smoke still spiralled up from the blackened concrete and breezeblock remains. It made the place easy to find. Rhys walked across to a red Land Rover and hailed a short stocky man in a hi-vis jacket and hard hat.

'Hi. Jeff Saunders, is it?'

Saunders looked up from the computer he had balanced on the bonnet of the vehicle.

'DC Harrison?'

'Harries,' Rhys said. 'Thanks for seeing me.'

Saunders turned back to his screen and clicked to clear the page. 'What can I do for you?'

Rhys explained about the Geoghans. When he mentioned a car fire, Saunders stopped him dead with a raised hand.

'Got it.' Saunders scrolled through his phone and showed Rhys a photograph of the burning Citroën, with a backdrop of shops and other cars nearby. 'No need to say anymore. For some reason, I remembered the name as Greengage, but it must be the same one. Car caught fire in Aldi's car park. Woman was inside the store when it happened. Yes, uh, October 10th, 2021. By the time the crew got there, it was well alight.'

'Any idea why it happened?'

Saunders' lips curled into a wry smile. 'Lots of reasons why it might have happened. Electrical fault is high on the list, but in this instance the wiring looked okay, what was left of it. My best guess is that Mrs Greengage—'

'Geoghan,' Rhys interjected.

'Her, tried to top up the oil, spilled some and left an oily rag behind. Once the engine temp goes up.' He used the fingers of both hands, tips to tips, to mimic an expanding conflagration accompanied by a subdued vocalisation of a mini explosion.

'Is that common?'

'Not that common. How many cars do you see burning out?'

'I've never seen one.'

'Well, I have. But then, that's my job. Here, everything had burned away, but we found some oil residue on the axle. Lots of people deny or don't remember topping up the oil or using rags, but there it is.'

'Did she deny it?'

'In between the spitting anger and swear words, yes. She blamed us for not getting there quick enough, passers-by for throwing petrol on her car—'

'What?'

Saunders nodded slowly. 'Oh, yes, Mrs Geoghan got an F for fail from charm school. In the end I gave up ringing her. I decided it'd be less painful to walk across a hundred yards of hot coals.'

'Is that a thing?'

'Only in my head.'

Rhys wrote in his notebook. 'So, to sum up, as far as you're concerned, this was likely an electrical or oil-related fault?'

'That's usually the case.' Saunders paused, his expression suddenly wary. 'I mean, we had no reason to believe otherwise.'

'So definitely not a bomb, or some kind of incendiary device.'

This time, Saunders' brows shot up. 'Whoa. There was nothing to suggest arson here. It was a crap car, but there are better ways to get an insurance pay-out. And with oily rags, there's no telling when the things would catch fire. There's no possibility of control. She could have been halfway to Cardiff on the M4 when it happened. Probably been a worse outcome then. And the way she reacted didn't tie in with arson. At least not with her as the arsonist. She was mightily pissed off. Some of the men have kept her best quotes. "Useless fucking turd-sucking wet-wipe wankers" is a particular favourite. Someone's got it on a T-shirt.'

Rhys wrote it all down, thanked Saunders and took his leave, knowing full well that Gil would have him reading out the quote half a dozen times when he presented all this.

CHAPTER TWENTY-TWO

VESPERS TOOK place at around 5:15pm with Gil providing refreshments from the away box in the form of the usual biscuit array, but this time supplemented by some millionaire's shortbread from the local café. A donation from a woman called Betsy Mullins, who turned up with a dozen in a cardboard box as 'donation to the effort'.

'She's an old friend,' Warlow had said. That and nothing more. It earned him a couple of quizzical looks, but everyone had the sense to keep quiet.

Rhys had already eaten two when KFC breezed in. Jess immediately wanted to know details about Catrin.

He gave a vague shrug. 'One of these stomach things. Sick as a dog she was. Something she's eaten, you know.'

'But she was well enough to drive home?' Jess asked.

'Oh, yeah. She insisted on doing that. I did try to talk her out of it, but she felt too rough to hang on for the end of the day.'

'I'll give her a ring later,' Jess said, looking troubled.

'I'll have a tea, mate.' KFC nodded at Rhys. If he noticed the irked look on Gil's and Warlow's faces for neither a please, nor Rhys's name being added to the order, he ignored it.

'I thought you didn't do caffeine?' Gil asked.

KFC reached into his jacket pocket and brought out a small pouch, from which he retrieved a teabag, and dangled it from his fingers. 'Caffeine free.' He held it up, and Rhys took it from him before scooting off. He came back a minute later with a steaming mug containing a floating teabag in milky water. Written on the side of the mug were the words: *Don't be a Richard*. KFC looked at this and gave Rhys a venomous glare. 'Are you trying to be funny, DC fucking Herring?'

'Sorry, sir. It was the only one there. You can swap with mine if you w—'

'No need,' Warlow said. 'Come on, Kelvin. We've got more important things to talk about than what's written on the side of a bloody mug.'

'Honestly, that was the only one in the kitchen,' Rhys said, appealing to the others. He got a nod from Gil and a shrug from Jess. Warlow kept his mug in front of his face, desperately trying to suppress the urge to hoot with laughter.

KFC scowled and sat, fuming silently.

'Okay,' Jess began. 'I know that there are a lot of strands to this one and a lot of actions since this morning. Thanks for coming back. It's late, I get that. But keeping everyone in the loop is important. I've been on too many investigations where the right hand doesn't even know there is a left hand.' Jess nodded at Warlow. 'Present company excluded, Evan. But some cases in Manchester left me wondering if I was even in the same book, let alone page.'

Warlow took the lead and, mainly for KFC's benefit, went over the details of the house Povey's team had confirmed as a definite location for where the Geoghans were held.

'And you like this Stoica for the abduction?' KFC asked.

'Who knows? He's not keen to talk to us, that's for certain.'

'Does he have any links to the victims?' KFC chewed on a shortbread as he spoke.

Gil shook his head. 'Not that I can see. He was in Cardiff nick for a stretch when Derek Geoghan was there. But then, so were seven hundred other people. No close contact as far as we can tell. He didn't share a cell or anything.'

'But he knows the house was unoccupied. That's reason enough to question him,' Jess added.

KFC scowled, demonstrating his usual lack of conviction. 'It's all so bloody tenuous, isn't it?'

'It's tenuous until we either discount it or it becomes something more definite,' Warlow said. 'I take it your petition raiser didn't bear fruit?'

'Nah. As expected. She's a yummy mummy with two brats and is alibi'd to her curly eyelashed eyeballs. Some nutters on the petition site said how much they hated the Geoghans, but they're just blowing hot air, I reckon. I mean hating the Geoghans? That's a long bloody queue.'

'Rhys, what about the fire in Karen Geoghan's car?' Jess asked.

'What fire?' KFC asked, spraying shortbread crumbs like a scatter gun.

Warlow shook his head.

Rhys explained about the call from Masters, the junkie that KFC and Catrin had spoken to, and outlined the conversation with Saunders, the fire investigator.

'So, there was a fire, and it was Karen Geoghan's car.

But no obvious signs of arson. Most likely an oil spill on a hot engine,' Rhys concluded.

'Well done you,' KFC said. 'That all adds up to a bag full of eff all.'

Rhys reddened.

This time, even Jess seemed to lose patience. 'What do you think we should be concentrating on, Kelvin?'

'We need to go back to basics. Find out who the Geoghans were talking to before they disappeared. Maybe they'd booked a plumber or someone who got access to the house. My bet is on them letting someone in.'

Fair enough.

'Catrin was on that,' Gil said.

'But she's not here anymore,' KFC said. 'That means wonder boy here,' he nodded at Rhys, 'will need to do a shift on the old records. Under my supervision, of course.'

Jess's phone burst into life. She looked at the caller ID, frowned and excused herself.

'Not exactly fizzing along, this investigation, is it?' KFC muttered and followed it up with a slurp of tea.

There was no mistaking who the barb was meant for. 'And I suppose it would be all tied up by now if you were running it, eh, Kelvin?' Warlow knew he shouldn't, but KFC was like a nasty rash you sometimes simply had to scratch.

'We need more bodies, that's for sure.'

'But there aren't any,' Warlow said. 'We make do with what we've got. Quality not quantity.'

'We're fucked then,' KFC said.

Warlow rounded on him. 'Christ, man, grow up. If you have nothing positive to say or do, just shut up.'

Gil and Rhys watched the exchange with expressions of frozen horror. And Warlow knew this wasn't the kind of team spirit they were used to. But then no one had picked KFC to play before.

'Hey, I'm only saying.' KFC looked almost hurt.

'You're always, "only saying". How about you stop "only saying"?' The DCI stood and walked to the board. 'I agree, we need to chase up the Geoghans' phone records. But we surely do not need to reinvent the wheel on that one. Owen Tamblin will have pulled them and probably analysed them. Let's get hold of that first. Rhys, give Owen's team a ring.'

Gil started writing actions.

'Isn't this Jess's job?' KFC had folded his arms and slid down the chair with his legs out straight in front of him. It was the kind of lazy slouching attitude that made Warlow want to shake the bugger.

'Of course, it is. And I'll run it all past her when she comes back. It's what we do on this team. Everyone has a shout.'

KFC stared back impassively.

'There is one thing I've been thinking about, sir,' Rhys piped up.

'Ooh, let's hear it then, Sherlock.' KFC affected a supercilious smile.

'How and when did they get from the house to the mountain? Sergeant Jones said they'd be easy to manipulate because of hunger. But they must have been transported to near the site. Probably during darkness.'

'Don't tell me you're on the hunt for CCTV footage?' KFC said. 'It's like the dark side of the sodding moon up here. I'm surprised they have electricity.'

'Not street CCTV, sir, but some houses might have doorbell cameras. Common these days. Sometimes they pick up vehicles driving past. I'm thinking it might be worth having a look at the houses on the hill at Allt y Grug, sir. We can narrow down the time to maybe the end of May. They'd been on the mountain a week at least, so last two weeks of May would be the window for being moved up there. If there is a camera somewhere on that street, we could start with that footage.'

Warlow grinned. 'Well done, Rhys. I agree with the timeline. Throw in the end of April, too. We'll get some Uniforms knocking on doors for that.'

For once, KFC said nothing.

Jess walked back in, looking pale.

Warlow picked up on it. 'Everything okay, Jess.'

It clearly wasn't, but she shrugged off the question with a tight smile. 'What did I miss?'

Quickly, Warlow outlined Rhys's and KFC's ideas. Jess nodded her approval.

KFC looked at his watch. 'Right, I'm off.' He turned to Rhys. 'Let's get those phone records sorted by tomorrow morning.'

'I'll get on to that, sir.'

'Make sure you do. Jess, you need a lift anywhere?'

'No, I'm booked in for another night up here. Always plenty to do.'

'Okay, *team*.' KFC emphasised the last word in that sentence so that it dripped with sarcasm. 'I need the bog, and then I'll be off.'

Warlow felt nothing but admiration for the fact that no one said anything to the closing door. It took him enough of an effort. But then a tap on his arm drew his attention, and he flicked his gaze down to see Jess's hand.

'Evan, a word outside?'

Warlow followed her out and stood in a patch of late afternoon sunshine. It was pleasantly warm; the heat tempered by a stiff westerly breeze that tried its best to rearrange Jess's hair. It must have been around twenty degrees, but Jess had her arms clutched across her chest as if she was freezing. Worse, she appeared to be trembling.

'I'm guessing that phone call did not contain good news?' he asked.

'No. It didn't. Molly…' She dropped her voice and added in a whisper with her eyes going skyward. 'That bloody twat.'

Warlow waited.

'I don't mean Molly, I mean Rick, her father. She was upset on the phone. He's only travelled down to Pembrokeshire to see her without asking. He's got something very serious to discuss with her, apparently. Now he's telling her that if she doesn't make the effort, he'll be very upset.'

'Ah.' Warlow didn't add the 'F' word, but he could have. Family. Wonderful, essential, and guaranteed to upset any apple cart at exactly the right moment.

'This is about the divorce papers. That bastard is going to talk to her about me signing the divorce papers.'

'You still haven't told her?'

'I was going to wait until she'd had her little adventure at the festival and the beach.' Jess lifted her face up to the sun with her eyes shut and let out a deep sigh. 'He knows exactly what he's doing.'

'But upsetting Molly won't help anyone, will it?' Warlow asked.

She snorted. 'I wouldn't put it past him to use her as emotional leverage. He's not keen on the "D" word. And I suspect that may have a financial incentive. He's still living in our house. That will have to be split down the middle. But Molly doesn't need any of that grief.'

Jess seemed to be talking to herself as much as to Warlow.

He said, softly, 'What can I do to help?'

His words seemed to focus her. 'I hate to ask this, but can I borrow your car? I'm going to have to go down there. She shouldn't have to do this on her own. I'll speak to her. Explain.' She growled in frustration. 'Bloody men.'

Warlow held up the keys to the Jeep.

'Sorry, Evan. That should have been man. I'm not tarring you—'

'Tar away.'

Another sigh. 'Look at me. Doing every sodding thing I said I wouldn't do. Putting personal crap before the job—'

'Hang on one minute. This is your daughter we're taking about. You need to go. The Geoghans aren't going anywhere. This thing will still be here tomorrow and the day after. It's still your show.'

'Really? KFC doesn't think—'

'Yeah, you said it. He doesn't think. He is what it says on the tin. K.F.C. Forget him. We'll get this case sorted with him or without him on board. Now on you go. And say hello to your daughter and my dog for me, will you?'

For one moment, it looked as if Jess might kiss him. She'd done it before. On the cheek. Friendly. But they were outside a police station. Instead, this time, she took the keys and squeezed his arm before hurrying away to where he'd parked his Jeep Renegade.

CHAPTER TWENTY-THREE

JESS DROVE ON AUTOMATIC, mulling over Warlow's words as she hit the M4 at Llansamlet and pointed the Jeep west. Molly would say she'd lucked out by ending up working with him and, if asked, she would have to agree. Solid, dependable, able to think outside the box. All the things that KFC wasn't. All the things Rick – she tried not to call him 'Tricky Ricky', Jess's current epithet for Molly's father – was not. She sucked in a lungful of air and let it out, slowly. Evan had her back should anything untoward come up in the investigation while she was trying to sort out the mess her life had become.

Warlow was right about lots of things, though he had his quirks. Some of them admirable, others, not so. His continued psychological battle with his 'condition', as he liked to call it, was one of the least understandable and most frustrating. Becoming HIV positive after getting deliberately stuck by a junkie's contaminated needle was real bad luck. She'd chatted to a few doctors she knew. All nonchalant stuff. Vague enquiries, off the record. Needle stick injuries, even in the most careful of surgeons, were not that uncommon. But developing HIV from a contaminated hypodermic was, according to them, extremely rare.

Warlow wasn't stupid. One of his sons was an ENT surgeon. But the fact was, Warlow caught the virus. He'd been the one case in a thousand. Concern over how that might impact his colleagues in the Force was the driver for him retiring early. Not so much the stigma of other people knowing, more the anxiety of worrying over scenarios whereby he, Warlow, might be responsible for further transmission.

Police officers dealt with violent individuals. Injuries came with the territory. Warlow's contaminated blood remained a constant concern whenever he cut himself or got cut by others. But he'd got over that minor hurdle, with Jess and Superintendent Buchannan's encouragement.

There were other means of transmission, of course. Other body fluids that could be exchanged. She'd touched on that with him. Gently hinting that there was no real reason for him to play the celibate hermit. She had colleagues and friends who lived with HIV. Some of them had families. It wasn't a terminal illness anymore.

But in Warlow's case, the psychological damage seemed much greater than the physical. The man hadn't even told his sons yet. He'd need more help on that front.

Jess shook her head. She was a fine one criticising other people. Her own dirty laundry was nothing to write home about, even if it wasn't her fault.

At least she didn't think it was. She'd spent too much time mulling over the reasons her husband of twenty years had seen fit to indulge in some rumpy-pumpy in a Manchester Police station with a buxom sergeant. Friends had consoled her by saying that men were all animals at the base level. Driven by lust, the physiological need to procreate. If that was meant in any way to excuse his behaviour, it fell on deaf ears on the female side of the Allanby family.

The evening before he'd dipped his wick on the night shift, they'd been planning a family holiday to Greece. That might have been the most difficult thing for her to understand. Easy to blame the third party, but everyone had to bring a bloody bottle, right?

Worst of all, the whole mess had made her contemplate giving up the police force. A job she still loved. And yes, she was the old cliché. Someone from a not-well-off background in a not-well-off area. Gorton remained one of Manchester's forgotten suburbs – she'd grown up in a terraced house with her brother and sister, and a mother whose life ambition was to ensure her kids ended up somewhere else. And Jess, the middle child, saw all the crap going on around her and decided she wanted to do something about that crap. Make a difference, be smarter than the thieves and the muggers, use the skills she'd learned on the streets in dealing with volatility.

Greater Manchester Police made her feel at home. But the snide grins and innuendo in the fallout of Tricky Ricky's indiscretion had almost, almost been the tipping point. When it got too much to bear, she'd talked it through with Molly and applied her skills somewhere else.

She'd done that. And done it well. Yet here was bloody Rick, still interfering with the way she did her job.

'Bastard,' she muttered as she pulled out onto the fast lane. What she should do is ring the sod. Ask him what the hell he was doing. But she couldn't trust herself not to scream obscenities and that wasn't what Molly needed now.

To distract herself Jess checked her phone. Molly hadn't rung back yet. Good. Knowing she shouldn't be doing it while driving, Jess found Catrin's number in her contacts list. She put the phone on speaker and did the one eye on the traffic dial.

'Hello, ma'am.' Catrin sounded subdued.

'How are you?' Jess asked.

'Fine ma'am. I threw up, that's all.'

'Dicky tummy, so Kelvin told us.'

'Yes. Definitely.'

'Something you ate?'

'Probably.' Catrin sounded unconvinced, but Jess put her reticence down to not wanting to talk about food.

'You alright to talk?'

'Go ahead, ma'am.'

Jess filled Catrin in on what she'd missed. Warlow's visit to the Geoghans' holding house, Stoica the burglar, Rhys's finding of the burnt-out car. She ended up asking her about the petition woman, adding that KFC had seemed dubious. 'Kelvin says that she's unlikely to produce anything useful.'

'Too early to say, ma'am. She's going to get back to me with a list of unpleasantries.'

'We can divert all this to Rhys or Gil—'

'No, it's okay. I should be fine in a day or two.'

'You still feeling sick?'

After a count of three, Jess said, 'Catrin?'

'Yes, sorry, ma'am. I… Truth is, I do feel sick, it's just…'

This wasn't the pragmatic Catrin she knew. Still, being ill wasn't fun. 'Well, you have my number.'

'I do ma'am. Thanks for phoning.'

Catrin broke off the call, leaving Jess with an ill-defined sense of things left unsaid. Catrin was usually enthusiastic and precise. But then she usually wasn't throwing up. Jess's phone rang again to end further conjecture. This time, it was Molly.

'Mum?'

'Hi, Moll. Where are you?'

'We're on the way to a pub called The Unicorn.'

'Molly, you're underage.'

'It's where Dad says he'll meet us.'

'Your dad is actually in Dale?'

'He said he is. He said if I didn't go, he'd come looking for me because he's come all this way to talk to me.'

'Okay. Fine. Yes, he's disrupted your fun, but talk to him for twenty minutes and tick the box.'

'He's stalking me, Mum.'

'No, he isn't. He's your dad.'

'But what's so freaking important that it can't wait for a few days?'

Here was Jess's chance. 'It might have to do with divorce papers.'

Silence. Jess counted twelve empty seconds in her head, grimacing as she waited for Molly's response. 'You've signed, right? About time, if you ask me. But don't solicitors and stuff deal with all that?'

Jess breathed out. 'They do. So, I'm not sure what he wants to talk to you about.'

'I expect he wants to ask my opinion. Ever since this happened, he's been wanting to know how I felt. Funny, he never wanted to know before. If he'd asked before he screwed Sergeant Big Tits, I could have told him then.'

'Is Bryn in the car with you?'

'Of course, he is. He's driving, Mum.'

'So, perhaps you could tone it down a little?'

'Bryn knows all about our family secrets, Mum. Knows all about Tricky Ricky.'

'I bet he does.'

Another beat. 'I can hear an engine. Are you driving, too?' Molly asked.

'I am. Listen, see your dad. Go and get it over with and you can get back to your break.'

'It's so unfair, though. Him turning up out of the blue like this.'

'Yeah, well, ever the spontaneous one your dad.'

'Interfering git, more like.'

'Let me know how it goes, okay?'

'Will do.'

'Is Cadi with you?'

'She is. She's on an adventure, eh, Cads?'

Jess ended the call. She considered pulling into a lay-by there and then to sit and wait to hear how the father and daughter meeting went. If it all ended up being Rick assuaging his guilt with a free pub meal, all well and good. She could turn around and be back in Ystradgynlais in twenty minutes. But she didn't pull in. She kept driving. Some instinct, or irritation, pushing her on. Google maps said it would take an hour fifty. She decided to drive half-way, then stop and ring Molly, see how it was going and either keep heading west or backtrack to the team.

That seemed like a plan. She found something on the radio to listen to and kept her eyes on the road.

———

KFC SAUNTERED BACK into the Incident Room, beaming with satisfaction. 'I'd give that at least twenty minutes or take a canary in with you.'

One of the Uniformed officers operating the phone lines looked up, her face crumpled in disgust. KFC took no notice. 'Where's Jess?'

'Something's came up with Molly,' Warlow replied. 'She's had to nip home.'

KFC had been picking up his briefcase, but on hearing this news, he stopped.

'How long for?'

'As long as it takes.'

KFC put his briefcase down and rubbed his hands together. 'Righty-ho. We don't have an SIO. That means I better take over until she gets back.'

'Nice idea, Kelvin. But I'm taking over until she returns.'

KFC tutted. 'Now, now, Evan. You heard what the big nobs said. Not a good idea to have you too involved. For the sake of transparency.'

'Yes. Well, sod that. I outrank you, Kelvin. I'm running things until Jess gets back. Decision made.'

'Should we not run it past the chiefs first?'

'No, we should not.'

A little knowing smile had appeared on KFC's lips. 'I think you're making a mistake there, Evan.'

'Won't be my first, or my last.'

'Alright. Have it your way. Guess I'll pop into HQ on the way home. Fill them in on how events are transpiring.'

Warlow's smile expanded to reveal two pointy canines. 'You do that, Kelvin. Have a safe journey now.'

The DI did not bother looking around as he left.

'Fancy a celebratory cup of tea and a biscuit, anyone?' Gil asked, twenty seconds later.

Rhys pushed back from his desk; owl-eyed from looking at the screen. 'What we celebrating, Sarge?'

Gil grinned. 'The fact of your endearing innocence, Rhys. Long may it prosper.'

CHAPTER TWENTY-FOUR

It was Gil's suggestion that they call in to Stoica's place on the way across to Llandeilo. The address, in Ammanford, was a small, terraced property on New Road. No front garden. Just a door off the pavement, straight into a sitting room, kitchen behind with a small garden and a ramshackle shed of some kind.

A red and yellow Romanian International football team shirt hung in a top window.

Gil got out and knocked on the door. The woman who opened it stared at Gil's warrant card and then identified herself as Teri Colson. She had an English accent and unwashed hair pulled back from her face to reveal all the dark roots, two inches of timeline measuring how long it had been since the dye job. She wore a tracksuit with socks over the leggings and fluffy slippers. In her arms was a baby that Warlow estimated, by the amount of hair on its head, to be around nine months old.

Gil asked for Stoica.

Colson shook her head. 'He still ain't here. How many times do I have to tell you?'

The DS went into disarming smile mode. 'That's okay. What's the baby's name?'

Not a tough question, but Teri Colson struggled with it for a moment, as if giving up the name was revealing a secret she'd prefer to keep. Grudgingly, she said, 'Gemma.'

'Is Gemma Mr Stoica's baby?' Gil asked.

'He's the dad, yeah.'

'Okay. Then tell him we want to talk to him about something we know he did already. Something he's done time for, so he can't do that time again. It's a house on Penmaen Street in Ystalyfera. All we want to do is chat with him.'

'So, he's not under arrest?'

'No. Just a chat. We could get a warrant for him, but we don't want that.' Gil nodded at Gemma, who remained impassive. 'And it must be a pain you being here all on your own with just you and the baby.'

Teri made a noise like air escaping from a lilo. 'It's not only Gemma. There's Nicu, too.'

'There we are then. Sooner this is sorted out, the better.'

'Do you work, Teri?' Warlow asked.

'I do nails. But it's hard with the kids here. Marius takes them out to the park when I've got customers. It's a real nuisance not having him 'ere.'

Gil nodded. 'Tidy. Then tell Marius to give us a ring. We need to chat. That's all.'

'He don't trust you lot, though.'

'Tell him we'll meet him anywhere,' Warlow said.

Teri looked at the DCI. 'Who are you then?'

'This is Detective Chief Inspector Warlow, Teri,' Gil said. 'He's the boss.'

Teri's lip quivered suddenly. 'Marius promised me he won't go back inside. He says he's not thievin' anymore.

He's got a job at the car wash while he does his HGV. It's not brilliant money, but it's somethin'.'

'Doing this, talking to us, that'll be a good thing to do. Tell him.' Gil had one eye on the bedrooms above, but no curtain twitched.

'I'll try, but he has these weird ideas about the police. Where he's from, the police have their own way of doin' things and not gently.'

'Persuade him.' Gil smiled at her. 'Otherwise, we may have to arrest him and you don't need that, do you?'

They left her in the doorway holding the baby.

Gil headed west again, with Warlow watching the industrialised town turn into rolling agricultural hinterland outside the window.

'Doesn't look like Stoica's our man for this,' Warlow said.

'Not unless he's lost it. Nice-looking kid.'

'Sounds like he's trying to turn things around.'

'A child is as good an incentive as there is. Two, even better. And he's one that's stayed even after Brexit. Way things are going, jobs aren't going to be that difficult to get.'

'Not if he can drive one of those big bloody lorries,' Warlow added. 'Okay. Let's hope the Gil Jones' charm works, then.'

'Oh, it will. Never fails.'

Warlow watched a hay lorry thunder past, shedding bits of straw that fluttered like injured birds in its wake. 'It isn't working with Kelvin Caldwell,' he muttered.

'No, well. You know what they say about turds and polishing?'

There really wasn't anything Warlow wanted to add to that.

———

Dale was an open heathland area bearing a western and eastern border with the sea, set sandwiched between the Marloes Peninsula above and St Anne's Head below. At the southern tip, the St Anne's Lighthouse marked the entrance to the busy Milford Haven waterway. Dale had a village, unimaginatively called Dale, one road in and one road out. There were other roads, but they petered out into rutted farm tracks. Jess stuck to the route the voice on the app told her to take. She considered herself a good driver with an unblemished accident record and had even done some advanced driver courses up in Manchester. But she felt she was pushing her luck at her current speeds. These lanes were narrow, the hedge growth verdant. All it took was one boy racer coming the other way with less experience than she had, and they'd both be crow-fodder in minutes.

She took her foot off the accelerator as she approached another bend. Crow-fodder brought to mind the Geoghans' sightless eyes, and she cringed inwardly. Not because of any squeamishness, but because thoughts of the case she was deemed to be supervising had been so far from her mind for the last God knows how many miles. Blown away by the almost hysterical call from Molly, who'd yelled and pleaded down the phone to her almost an hour ago.

Not in anger, not entirely. More in panic and fear.

The app had said one hour thirteen to Dale from the Starbucks at Cross Hands on the A48, where she'd parked up with a latte as part of her half-way plan. It had taken her fifty-three minutes. She had the map open on her phone now, propped up in front of the gearstick, resting against a little space for coins. Not that she needed instructions anymore because the green and white sign announcing her arrival in Dale loomed, and the little 'Please Drive Carefully' request, in Welsh as well as

English, sounded like a good idea. She dropped down to thirty and followed the road in to park in a pay and display.

Molly and Bryn were waiting for her, along with half a dozen youngsters of about the same age. Molly ran over as soon as Jess parked. She still had the car door open when her daughter fell against her and sobbed onto her shoulder.

'Mum, oh Mum.'

Jess hugged her while the group of friends walked over, all of them subdued, the girls in cut-offs and sweatshirts with sleeves dangling over their hands, the boys in shorts and T-shirts. She knew almost all of them. They were a merry bunch. Up for a laugh. But this evening, not one of them was smiling.

Fifty yards across the car park, the door of a black Peugeot SUV opened and a tall figure in too-tight blue jeans and a white T-shirt got out. *Trying too hard to look young*, she thought. *Pressure from the new partner no doubt*. Jess looked over at him and pushed Molly away.

'Stay here. I won't be a minute.'

A tear-streaked Molly sucked in some ragged breaths and nodded.

Jess crossed the car park and stood contemplating Rick Allanby, her soon-to-be ex-husband. He still had a full head of hair, greying a bit at the temples, a full mouth, and a complexion red from the outdoors and a little too much booze. He held both hands up, palms forward, and spoke before she could say a word.

'I didn't mean for this to happen.'

Jess gave up a sour smile. She'd heard it all before. 'No. But it has happened, hasn't it?'

'I needed to see her.' The accent she was familiar with. Straight out of Bolton. Rick's voice rubbed along like a tin sheet on a gravel road. He'd tried and failed to give up smoking a dozen times. She glanced down past his hip and felt no satisfaction at seeing the pack of twenty on the seat. 'I needed to see her and hear it from her,' he added.

'Hear what from her?'

'That she was okay about the divorce.'

'Of course she's not okay with the bloody divorce. It's the last thing a kid needs, isn't it? She hates the bloody thought of it. But I don't need her permission and neither do you.'

'I know.' He squeezed his eyes shut. 'But I wanted to ask her myself. I should have asked her outright, but I was skirting around it. We were talking about her camping, and I wanted to know what the arrangements were, that's all.'

Jess felt her lips tightening. 'Rick, we talked about this. I told you.'

Rick put his hands up either side of his head. 'You did. But since I was here, I asked if she'd show me the camp-site. For my peace of mind.'

Jess dropped her gaze and shivered. 'Jesus, Rick. That's a red rag to a sodding bull.'

'She's still my little girl, Jess.' Anger made his words gruff.

'No, she isn't. Not your little girl and not my little girl. Not anymore. She's seventeen. Old enough to vote.'

'Trouble is, she has your soddin' temper. I only asked to see the campground, and she lost it. Started shouting. Accusing me of spying on her.'

'Don't, Rick. Don't say anything else. Don't blame anyone else. Get back in your car and go home.'

His face fell. 'Perhaps I can help—'

'You can, by going home. Molly won't talk to you now. Go back to Manchester.'

His eyes drifted up and over to where Molly leaned against the Jeep.

Jess sighed. 'She'll come around. But until we—'

'I'm sorry about the dog. But we need to talk. There's something you need to know.'

'Just bloody go, will you?' Jess swivelled away and as she left, he called to her.

'I'm sorry, okay? I am sorry.'

But it was too little too late. Jess kept on walking.

Molly wasn't sobbing anymore, but she could barely talk when Jess put a hand on her daughter's arm.

'Oh, Mum,' she wailed.

'No,' Jess said. 'Stop crying. It isn't helping anyone.'

'What about Evan? What am I going to say to Evan…?'

Jess squeezed Molly's upper arm. 'Listen to me. I need you to tell me exactly what happened.'

But it was too much for Molly. Her face crumpled, and she turned away. Jess looked for and found Bryn close by and caught his eye. To his credit, he walked across undaunted.

'Talk to me,' Jess ordered.

'It's all a bit of a blur, to be honest. We went to The Unicorn.' He indicated over Jess's shoulder to a white-washed pub with black signage. 'We went in and sat down. Cadi scooted under the seat. As good as gold she was. We'd been on the beach for ages today and she was tired. Molly and her dad, they started off okay, but then he went on about the campsite and said to Molly to think about how old she was and how much trouble she could get into. He said he wanted to see the setup. I explained it was four tents, two for the boys, two for the girls. That's the truth, Mrs Allanby.'

'I believe you, Bryn. Though I suspect none of you are going to get much sleep.'

'Molly lost her rag. They were shouting and her dad stood up. He's big and the table, it shifted. So did some chairs. One fell over and must have hit Cadi on a paw or something because she squealed. I think she was as frightened of the shouting as the chair hitting her. Either way, the door of the pub was open, and she ran for it. It all happened so quickly. I barely noticed because of everything else. I ran after her and Molly came too, but by then she'd gone.'

'Which way?'

Bryn pointed back towards the pub and the road running past it, which quickly disappeared up a hill and around a tree-covered bend. 'I followed, but I couldn't find her.'

'How long ago?'

'Nearly an hour and a half.'

'Where does the road go?'

'There's a field studies centre down there. At the fort. And then the coastal path.'

He didn't mention the high cliffs. He didn't need to. Jess glanced at her watch. Almost a quarter after seven. Still lots of light left in the day.

Molly stood with her back to the Jeep, arms folded. 'Do you think someone's taken her, Mum? She's such a lovely dog. If someone found her, they might…'

'That's theft, Molly. Dog people aren't like that.' She looked around and did a head count. 'Nine of us. Let's split up. How far is it to this fort?'

'Two and a bit miles, at a guess.' Bryn looked at his companions and someone nodded.

'Right, we'll walk it. Take side roads if we have to.'

'But what if we don't find her?' Molly asked.

Jess swung her head back and forth. 'We do not worry about that until we have no choice. Everyone okay? Has everyone eaten?'

Some dubious looks and shakes of the head. Jess walked out to the road. Someone walked past with a slice of pizza. 'Where did you get that?'

The man turned and pointed to a covered space outside the pub with wooden seating. Jess turned and called to the others. 'Fuel up. My shout. Let's get to it.'

Molly didn't move. 'But what if we can't—'

'We won't find her if we don't try,' Jess said before turning again to Bryn and giving him some cash. 'Run over and order three cheese pizzas. No topping. These are emergency rations.'

Bryn set off, the others following him at a slower pace. Eventually, Molly pushed herself off the Jeep and joined Jess. 'She squealed with fright, Mum. I was supposed to look after her.'

'Okay. Let's try to make it up to her. Come on. Get to it.'

CHAPTER TWENTY-FIVE

His mother had a saying about patience. She had it framed on the parlour wall when they were growing up. When she died, they left it hanging as a reminder. It was still there, black calligraphy stitches embroidered on white canvas.

To bear with patience wrongs done to oneself is a mark of perfection, but to bear with patience wrongs done to someone else is a mark of imperfection and even of actual sin.

That was the thing about his mother; she'd been a bright woman. These days she might well have gone to university instead of staying at home and working in a shirt factory. And though they'd read the saying a thousand times, he hadn't understood it well until now. His mother hadn't known who said those words she'd sewn, but she liked them. Taught her children their meaning.

When the idea first came to him, he'd looked up the quote and had seen the words attributed to Thomas Aquinas. A reference to retribution. He cared nothing for religion but liked the thought that a philosopher and a thinker considered such things sinful to let wrongs go unpunished.

Especially wrongs done to others.

He had been patient when it came to what had been done to him. But his patience had run out when he thought about the wrongs done to others.

Monsters should not get away with what they did simply because they were monsters.

Where did you draw the line?

He'd draw theirs in blood.

And so, he did. Deal with the monsters. But now the people who let the monsters out of their cage needed to pay, too. The police needed to learn a lesson. Even they had to suffer the consequences.

He'd followed the car from the police station in Swansea for an hour. Fearing at first that the driver was going home. Doing what he needed to do with the car parked outside the driver's home was not smart. But this time, the car went to another place, picked up some small children and took them to a park where there were swings and slides.

He'd waited until no one was around before acting. It took only a few moments. If anyone saw, they chose not to intervene.

There had to be consequences for standing by while the monsters were let loose.

When what he'd come to do was finished, he got back into his car and drove away, turning his thoughts towards the other police officer.

His patience was running thin. The other one had to pay as well.

———

WARLOW GOT the text from Jess Allanby at Gil's house in Llandeilo as he sat finishing breakfast a little after seven fifteen the following morning. Gil was on his second round of toast. Mrs Jones had taken one grandchild to her pre-school breakfast club, and the house was quiet.

'Jess wants to meet me at her hotel before we chat.' Warlow studied the text for any clues.

'What's the big secret?' Gil stopped munching to ask the question. He was on a different planet etiquette-wise to KFC when it came to being able to speak and eat at the same time.

'She wouldn't say.'

'I can drop you off and go straight into the station,' Gil said. 'Must be SIO stuff. FYEO and all that.'

'Heard from Catrin this morning?'

'No.'

'Hmm.' Warlow grunted. 'Going to be a long day without her.'

Gil dropped him off at the Cae Inn at around 8:20am. Jess stood in the little reception area, chatting to a young woman. She looked up as he walked through the door. But Warlow sensed something was amiss immediately. Jess had a glorious smile. This one looked like it was being squeezed out from between two rocks.

'We can use the lounge bar. It's empty this time of day.' Jess led the way into the big room. She didn't sit.

'What's all this about, Jess?' On closer inspection, she looked almost as pale as she had the night before. 'Is Molly okay?'

'Molly's fine. It's not Molly.'

Warlow's brow creased. 'Rick?'

'I wish it sodding was.' Jess's mouth looked screwed down tight as she looked directly into Warlow's face. 'Rick met Molly in a pub in Dale. There were verbals. Somehow, in the midst of it all, Cadi took fright and ran off.'

Warlow laughed. A soft noise. He could just imagine the scene. But Jess's face didn't relax. There was no punch-line to this joke.

'I spent most of yesterday evening, until it got dark anyway, leading a search party trying to find her. I got back here at around 2am.' Jess shook her head. 'Evan, Cadi's still missing.'

Warlow's pulse thudded in his neck, all the moisture evaporating from his mouth. 'She's missing?'

Jess nodded.

He thought furiously. 'Okay. I know Dale. Not much traffic down there. A few campsites.'

'We visited them all. But there's lots of woodland and a few buildings she might have sheltered in.'

Warlow didn't speak. He didn't have any air in his body.

'I wanted to tell you face to face,' Jess said.

'Where's Molly?'

'Upstairs. I brought her back with me. She's in a state.'

Warlow had his back to the door. Not his usual position when he entered any room. He saw Jess's eyes flick up over his shoulder. Flick up and narrow. He swung round. Molly stood in the doorway, no makeup, her hair tied back, a couple of dark smudges under her puffy eyes. She seemed hunched over, looking more like a twelve-year-old than the feisty seventeen that she was, with her arms folded across her sunken-in chest, her mouth ugly with despair.

'I'm sorry, Evan. I am so sorry. I was meant to look after her. This is all my fault.'

'She's a dog, Molly. A dog with a mind of her own.'

'I know but…' A great sob ruptured her words.

'Hey, before I trained her not to worry about shotguns, she ran off as a pup. But we found her.'

'Really?' Molly's eyes widened in hope.

'The truth,' Warlow said. He hadn't meant it as a signal, but Molly took it as one. She strode across and grabbed him in a hug. He didn't speak. She didn't need words at that moment. All she needed was his forgiveness.

'Someone's bringing my car back from the garage this

morning. We'll go back late this afternoon. We have people out looking, Evan. I can assure you of that.'

'She'll turn up,' he said, his words belying the crippling anxiety he felt inside. She was only a dog. But she was his dog.

'Can't we go back down now, Mum?'

'No, Mol. I'm working. And you need to get some sleep. You look bloody awful.'

'Your mother's right,' Warlow said. 'We need her here. I'm needed here. You trust your friends?'

Molly nodded.

'Then let them search for Cadi. She'll be hungry. She won't stay hidden for long.' He might not believe the words he was speaking, but he said them for Molly's sake.

'Okay.' Jess sighed, relief bringing a little colour to her face. 'We've been dreading this.'

'She's a dog,' Warlow repeated, finding words from somewhere and voicing them even if he didn't quite believe them himself. 'A bright dog. She doesn't want to be lost. She'll work something out.'

He said little more as they drove in to Ystradgynlais Station. He was too busy desperately trying to run with his own rhetoric. But his thoughts were all over the place.

'If you want to go down to Dale, I'd understand,' Jess said, reading him like she always could.

Warlow shook his head. 'I'll be fine. Is Catrin in today?'

Jess compressed her lips. 'She texted me. Still not right, I'm afraid.'

Warlow nodded. 'Cadi'll have to wait then.'

Led Zeppelin's *Heartbreaker* crescendo'd out of Warlow's phone. He accepted the call on the car's Bluetooth speaker.

'Owen, I hope your morning's going better than mine.'

'No, it's gone totally to shit.'

'I won't argue with that,' Warlow said and caught Jess's grim smile.

'Me first. Last night I took the grandchildren to Singleton Park. Would you believe it, some bastard spray-painted my car.'

'What?'

'I know. Graffiti'd the crap out of it.'

'What's all that about?'

'Yeah, well, that's why I'm ringing. I couldn't make much out last night. I was so pissed off, but this morning, one of the Uniforms took a look. Claims he could make out letters. Scrawled all over the doors on the passenger's side they are.'

'What does it say?'

'I hope you're sitting down.'

'I'm in the car with Jess.'

'Hi, Jess. Anyway, the letters were a "T", an "A" and an "L".'

'Shit,' Warlow said in a low hiss.

'Shit the bloody bed is more like it. But the real question is…?' Owen let it hang.

Warlow muttered out the words, 'Could it be him?'

'Exactly. Is there a bloody lunatic targeting me?'

'And no one saw anything? No stray Insta or Facebook video?'

'It's a park for kids. You don't video there.'

Of course, you didn't. Not unless you wanted a lot of grief. The locals' neighbourhood watch would hang, draw and quarter you for a start and ask questions later. 'You have photos?' Warlow asked.

'I'm sending them over. I'll have to book the car in for a sodding respray. Worse than that, my car's now a bastard crime scene.'

'I've got news for you, Owen. Always has been.'

'No one's laughing, Evan. What happened on your end to make this the mother of all mornings?'

'Personal niggles, you know the kind of thing.'

'Well, you can stuff all that. "TAL" sprayed all over my car trumps any baggage. Keep me in the loop. And watch out for bloody Banksy.'

Warlow ended the call and sat in silence.

Banksy. He should have laughed at that, but someone had drained his laughter account. His head was full of churning anxiety for Cadi, but the other half latched on to this news from Owen and tried to make sense of it.

Banksy.

Owen was a funny man. But sometimes buried in his humour, there were throwaways that glittered. Gems that needed to be plucked out and polished to reveal their true value. Warlow wondered if he'd just found one.

'You've got that look in your eye,' Jess said, glancing over.

'Hmm, maybe. Let's wait until we get to the station, and I'll let you know if it's an itch worth scratching.'

CHAPTER TWENTY-SIX

In the Incident Room, Warlow went directly to his desk and jiggled the mouse to bring the computer he'd been using back from the dead. Once it lit up, he logged on and called up the itemised list of Geoghan greeting cards he'd brought in, all photographed and added to the case file. He scrolled through until he found what he'd been looking for.

When it appeared on the screen in front of him, Warlow caught his breath. This was it. This was what he'd been trying to remember. Hardly a Banksy unless the publicity-shy artist had started taking crystal meth with a magic mushroom chaser after a night of watching Halloween movies back-to-back. He remembered receiving it at around the same time he'd had a card from Karen Geoghan. In his head, he'd somehow buried the memory. Looking at it again, he wasn't surprised. But this card was not like any he'd received from the Geoghans.

Four mannequins – two adults, two children – sitting around a table. Each mannequin had its eyes removed and replaced with red lightbulbs. Each one, too, had one arm removed and red paint splashed on the torso near the armhole. Said arms were on a platter at the centre of the table, around which the mannequins all sat. He flicked on through the series of images that followed, inside and outside of the card, his scalp contracting.

The message inside, printed in felt-tip pen, read, *I WILL FIND YOU*. The card had a homemade quality about it. He called Jess and Gil over.

'This is what our chat with Owen this morning brought to mind.'

'*Arglwydd Mawr*,' Gil said. 'Your holiday snaps need work.'

'I got these months ago. I don't think I held onto the envelope, so it's going to be difficult to date. But look at the poses.'

'Unhappy families,' Jess said.

'And you're sure it wasn't from the Geoghans?'

Warlow sniffed. 'Karen didn't believe in symbolism. She was much more in your face.'

'What made you remember this now?' Gil asked.

Warlow explained about Owen Tamblin's car. Gil listened, staring at the image, his expression becoming ever more horrified. 'You think this could be him?'

'Who knows? There are links, clearly. The table and chairs, the posed family members. At the very least, we get forensics to take a closer look at this card. I'll speak to Alison Povey.'

'Agreed,' Jess said.

Warlow sat back. 'Okay. That's one thing done. Catrin isn't coming in today, so what was it she was working on again?'

'It's okay, sir,' Rhys piped up. 'You don't need to worry about that. We've got the Geoghans' phone records going back six months. I'm working through them with Sergeant Jones.'

Gil nodded. 'Fascinating stuff. I've brought in one of the grandchildren's watercolour paint sets so Rhys and I can take turns to daub a bit on some paper and watch it dry. Just to break the monotony.'

Warlow wanted to smile at that, but all he managed was the faintest compressing of his lips. 'I want to get back out to the house on Penmaen Street. Rhys, didn't you say you wanted to check out the houses there for CCTV?'

'I did, sir.' Rhys brightened visibly. 'I've got one promising possibility after talking to the Uniforms.'

'Then let's go. I need to stay busy today.'

'Oh, and why is that sir?' Rhys asked. A reflex response that triggered another flush of embarrassment as he tried to cover his tracks. 'Not that you're not always busy, sir. I mean, I didn't—'

'I've lost a good friend,' Warlow said, stemming the apologetic tide, but choosing not to elaborate.

If he registered the pained look on Jess's face, he decided not to show it.

———

TERI COLSON WATCHED her son Nicu on the slide in the municipal park in Ammanford. He'd been up and down it a dozen times already and showed no sign of slowing down. The council had been to repair the potholed play area in the last couple of months and there'd been a resurgence of interest now that it was no longer a death trap or a broken limb trap at least.

Nicu squealed with delight as another slide user almost reached him before he got up. It had become a competition between him and a little girl as they followed each other up the steps and then down the slide, giggling. Gemma was asleep in the stroller and there was another half dozen toddlers and mothers in the park. But Teri sat apart, pretending to be on the phone so that she wasn't disturbed.

A man walked in from across the way, entering through a gate from the street and heading in her direction on a path. Despite the warmth of the evening, the man wore a baseball cap and dark glasses and a zipped-up hoodie with the hood down. He'd have looked even more suspicious with it up as he stepped off the path and strode purposefully across the last thirty yards of grassy area and sat on the bench next to Teri.

'What did the police want?' he asked.

Teri glanced around. No one was taking any notice. 'They were nice. A Sergeant and a Chief Inspector. They said they wanted to talk about something from the past.'

'What like?'

Teri shrugged. 'I don't know, do I?' She dropped her voice. 'You haven't done anythin' stupid, have you?'

Marius Stoica wagged his head. Exaggerated movements of vehement denial. 'Teri, I swear. I am at the car wash all day. I stay with Costin until—'

'Until when, Marius?' Teri interjected.

'Until I know the police are not trying to…' He shrugged.

'Oh my God, they're not fittin' you up. It's not like that. I mean, a Chief Inspector ain't gonna come after you for breakin' and enterin', is he?'

'At home, they will get you in jail and make the case. My cousin Boian, he is in jail for stealing a car. He wasn't even in the city the day car was stolen. That is fact.'

'So, what? You gonna hide at Costin's forever?'

'No. I—'

Nicu came off the slide and recognised his father. 'Daddy.' He ran over. Marius picked him up. 'Pui Nicu.'

'They miss you,' Teri said.

'I miss them, too.'

'So why don't you speak to them? The police. Just ring 'em. Find out why they want to speak to you, at least.'

Nicu took Marius's baseball cap off and slid it onto his head where it promptly fell over his eyes. 'I do not want to go back to prison, Teri.'

Teri laughed out loud. 'You might as well be in fuckin' prison, cos me and the kids can't see you.'

Marius nodded. 'I will make it better. I promise.'

'Daddy, watch me on the slide.' Nicu slid off his father's knee and ran across to the steps.

'I watch,' Marius said. 'Five minutes. I am on break from car wash. Go. Let me see you fly.'

———

CATRIN SAT at her usual desk at HQ in Carmarthen. No one had bothered her. She looked busy, exuding an air of not wanting to be disturbed. Something she did well. Craig, her traffic officer partner, said that she could be a bit 'offish' when she was in the zone.

He'd added, 'And when I say "offish", I don't mean a place where Sean Connery did his accounts.'

She'd laughed at that the first time she heard it. But thinking of it again now did not raise even the slightest of smiles. All the mirth had leeched away from her since that discussion with Caldwell. The upshot of it all was a screen full of numbers and dates.

Pretty meaningless to the casual observer.

Dynamite if someone found out what she was actually doing.

She looked at the columns under the heading 'Subscriber Activity'.

Date, time, call date, call time, type (incoming or outgoing), duration.

This was DCI Tamblin's mobile phone record, and she'd been looking through it for almost an hour. It was tedious work, made worse by the constant fluttering of anxiety that worried away at her insides. She cross-checked common numbers and known numbers, looking for patterns and then assessing the significance of those patterns.

So far, she'd found that, apart from work-related numbers, an Indian restaurant in St Helen's Road was the most often dialled.

'Found anything interesting, then?'

The voice from behind her made her jerk, spilling her notepad onto the floor where it fanned out like a dead gull.

She looked up from reaching for it straight into KFC's leering features.

'Uh, no, not really. Nothing pertinent.'

'How much have you looked through?'

'Two months' worth so far.'

'We said six to be safe, didn't we?'

'You did, sir.'

KFC peered at the screen over Catrin's shoulder. His head was closer than she wanted it to be. His aftershave beat at her in patchouli waves, and she turned her head away.

'So, early days then.' He stood back, oblivious.

'What am I supposed to say if DI Allanby contacts me, sir?'

'Say you're still ill.'

'But I'm not. I'm here.'

'Okay.' He shrugged. 'Say you're working on something for me.'

'She'll want to know what, sir.'

'Phone records. Say it's a lead we're pursuing. All true.'

Catrin shook her head. 'DI Allanby isn't one for vagueness.'

KFC looked irritated. 'Has she contacted you?'

'No, not yet. But she's bound to ring and ask how I am.'

'Tell her you're feeling better, but not quite up to par.'

Catrin stared at him.

'Are you up to par?'

'I'm not happy about what I'm doing but—'

'There you are then.' KFC gave her his trademark empty smile.

'I'm not comfortable with this cloak and dagger stuff, sir.'

KFC's expression didn't change, but his lids dropped to half-mast. A little tic that Catrin knew meant he wasn't smiling inside. 'I'll go and tell the anti-corruption unit and Superintendent Goodey that we'll discontinue this line of enquiry because it's making one of our sergeants uncomfortable, then, shall I?'

Catrin shifted in her seat. 'Wouldn't it be better if someone outside the unit did this?'

KFC shook his head slowly. 'The reason I want you is you're thorough, so I've been told. I thought you were beyond letting misguided loyalties get in the way of good policing.' He dropped his voice. 'Do I need to remind you that two people are dead. There are probably dozens of punters in this world who are rejoicing at the fact the Geoghans are bird food, but they are still dead. Still murdered.'

Reluctantly, Catrin nodded.

KFC stood up straight but kept his voice low. 'Get on with it, Sergeant. Not every task in this job is a cake walk.'

CHAPTER TWENTY-SEVEN

NUMBER 27 ALLT y Grug Road, also well-named as *Golwg y Mynydd,* since it had a great view of the Darren Mountain across the valley, was a hillside property. The rising angle of the mountain meant that houses were higher on one side of the street, with their sloping front gardens providing an unfettered view of the road in front. From where they were standing, Warlow and Rhys looked across and down slightly towards the Penmaen Street turning. A camera might catch most of the comings and goings if the lens was wide enough.

Warlow stood back to let Rhys do the introductions. This was his project. The pebbledash rendering on the walls of the house looked to be in good nick, the UPVC windows were clean and the front door had a larger than average bell circled in blue with what looked like a small camera lens in a blacked-out area at the top.

Rhys pointed to it and grinned at Warlow, who acknowledged the DC's enthusiasm with a shake of his head.

The man who opened the door leaned on a knobbly stick and wheezed from the effort of arriving from wherever he'd come from. Not tall, barrel-chested, with a belly that ran straight down from the neck. His trousers had no chance of covering the lot and had to be constrained by a belt that looped alarmingly low beneath where a belt would normally be. He was unshaven with a grey stubble that some older men, with staggering miscalculation, thought acceptable as a last, desperate statement of masculinity. Most of the time, all it did was make them appear like lazy, scruffy old men. At least it did in Warlow's opinion. He had a wet shave even on his days off. If he didn't, he was convinced his Lab, Cadi, kept giving him funny looks.

'Help you?' the man asked.

Rhys had his warrant card out and explained who he was.

'Oh, yes,' the man sang. 'They said you might be around. One of you blokes in a wossname, came.'

'Pardon?'

'You know, one of them Panda cars.'

Rhys turned to look at Warlow, who said, 'Response vehicle,' by way of explanation. The DCI judged the man in the doorway to be mid-seventies, overweight, and challenged in the lexicon stakes. It might be fun to let the young constable struggle, but Warlow wanted to get this over with and go back up to the house where the Geoghans had been kept prisoner a hundred yards away. He stepped forward, all smiles. The man watched his approach and took a slight backwards shuffle.

'Mr Roberts, I'm Detective Chief Inspector Warlow and this is Detective Constable Rhys Harries. The officer in the Panda car explained what we might be calling for, did he?'

'Aye. Gary my name is. Something about the camera, innit?'

'That's it,' Rhys said. 'You have a doorbell security camera installed.'

'Aye. Bloody great little thing. Rings when someone comes to the door. You can even speak to the buggers from inside. Christ, when we first had it, I scared seven different colours of crap out of our posty, Nigel. He was pushing something through the door, and I said, "If you're pushing your cock through my letterbox again, I'll have you arrested." Honest to God, I thought he was going to have a stroke. As it was, he fell off the step, flat on his arse. Laugh? I had to have four puffs of my inhaler.'

Rhys wore a fixed grin as he listened. Warlow had the feeling that good old Gary had an anecdote for every occasion. The trick was not letting him get into his stride.

'Did the other officers explain that we're after any historical footage you have? Any idea how far back this thing records?'

'Might be three days, might be three months. In other words, no bloody clue. This stuff, the wossname…'

'Security camera?' Rhys asked.

'Aye. That's my son's doings. I'm not up with all this technology. I'm waiting for a hip op, me. Constant pain, I'm in. So, Ian does all this stuff.' He waved the non-stick-holding hand vaguely at the door. 'My left hip it is. Old injury from work, you know. Smashed it into a dozen pieces I did under a bloody dram in a small mine on the Darren. I've been waiting since Moses got on the Ark, mind.'

Warlow side-eyed Rhys and saw his lids drop as he tried to compute the metaphorical complexities of Moses on the Ark and failed.

'So not your area of expertise then, Gary, the bell?' Warlow asked.

'No idea. I've got my pigeons out the back. I'm good for sod all else for now. And after lockdown, there'll be men on Jutiper before I get into the orthopaedophile ward. It sounds like.'

'Jutiper?' Rhys said.

'Yeah, up there. That one with the rings.' Gary waved his hand again and began an elaborate few moments of fruity coughing that he stifled with a well-used handkerchief.

Warlow shut his eyes for a count of two before opening them again.

Behind Gary, the house looked neat and well-kept. Someone else's doing, Warlow suspected. Rhys was on the point of correcting Gary on the difference between Jutiper and Jupiter and Jupiter and Saturn, but the DCI nipped it in the bud with a question.

'Is Ian in, by any chance, Gary?'

'No. DVLA, that's where he is. One of the buggers who won't even open your application for a new licence for six weeks. Sods,' Gary grinned, 'he tells me they get memos telling them to do that sort of thing. Hard to believe, isn't it?'

'And no one else in, is there?'

Gary shook his head, making the few wisps of hair still clinging to his scalp wave in the breeze. 'My daughter calls twice a day. Lives up the Gurnos, she does. Real devil she is. Always cleaning and bringing food.'

'Lucky you,' Warlow said.

'Aye, could be worse.'

'Do you have a number for Ian? If you do, then Rhys here could give him a ring.'

'Aye. Try at lunchtime. He should be free. I've got his number on the fridge. You can come in for a brew if you like. Milk's on the turn, but it's not too bad.'

'No, thank you, Gary.' Warlow had to put a hand out to stop Rhys from crossing the threshold. 'If you could get us Ian's number, we'll be on our way.'

'You're over in Penmaen Street, are you?' Gary thrust his head forward and looked across to the narrow lane.

'We are.'

'Who'd have thought it? Devil worshippers in Ystalyfera.'

'Is that what they're saying?' Rhys asked.

'Oh, yeah. But then look at me telling you.' He leaned a little further forward and uttered a conspiratorial whisper, 'Find any goat skulls, did you? There're always bloody goat skulls, isn't it?'

'No goat skulls, I'm afraid,' Warlow answered. 'Only a dead mouse in the downstairs toilet. Ian's number, when you're ready.'

Gary hobbled off, and the officers waited. It took him five minutes to return. As well as Ian's number on a piece of paper in the stick-holding hand, he cradled a small dog that looked like it needed a haircut in the other.

'Jenny, this is. My daughter, Lisa's, dog. She wanted to say hello.'

'Hello Jenny,' Rhys said and reached out a hand. The dog growled at him.

Seeing Jenny, a bow-wearing Yorkie, brought a fresh surge of anxiety swooping through Warlow over Cadi's situation. He ground his teeth together and forced out a question. 'Get much traffic up here, Gary?'

Gary cocked an eyebrow and nodded up the hill. 'There's nothing up there past *Bryn yr Allt*. Dead end except for the Patches. It's not the M4. But Ian likes to keep an eye on things. You know, neighbourhood watch and wossname.' He handed over the slip of paper.

Rhys thanked him, and they took their leave. As they walked back to the car, he asked, 'Patches, sir?'

'Yes, I thought you'd ask me that. Let's walk up to the cemetery and take a look, shall we?'

———

Gil, alone in the Incident Room, muttered at his monitor screen. He much preferred looking over phone records when they'd been printed off. But these days, it was all about saving trees. The screen made his eyes ache and left them scratchy. His optometrist had told him to get drops for what she'd called 'evaporational dryness'. And he had, only they were in the fridge at home. Instead, he waded through Karen Geoghan's call history, highlighting likely numbers and copying and pasting them into a different file.

He had a late morning mug of tea on his desk and had put one on DI Allanby's, ready for when she returned from whoever she was talking to on her mobile, which he could see she was still doing outside in the car park. Her expression had started off anxious and had not changed.

The Incident Room door swung open, and KFC stalked in, stopped, looked around and said, 'Christ. It's like episode three of the Walking Dead. Where is everyone?'

Gil sat back and arched his back. 'Catrin is still off. DCI Warlow and Rhys are following up on some potential CCTV leads and I am finding out that Karen Geoghan preferred to do most of her shopping by telephone order. Not big on the old online platform, it seems.'

KFC frowned. 'You shouldn't be doing that. I told Wonderboy to do that.'

'Mr Warlow whisked Rhys off to the great outdoors.'

'But it's menial. Jesus, isn't there something better you could be doing?'

Gil put on his slightly hurt look. 'I thought you said this might be important.'

'I did. And it is. I mean it's got to be done, hasn't it? That's why we have plods like Wonderboy. This stuff keeps him out of mischief.'

'Mr Warlow thinks he'll get more from the job by being out and about.'

'Yeah, well, Mr Warlow isn't running this show, is he?'

Gil paused, wondering about the wisdom of continuing to engage, and deciding in a heartbeat it was. 'Very experienced officer, Mr Warlow.'

KFC's shoulders sagged with disappointment. 'Oh, don't tell me you're in his sodding fan club too?'

'I've worked with worse senior officers,' Gil said, keeping his gaze firmly on KFC's face.

'Yeah, I'm sure you have. But then I would expect you two to be all pally. You're cut from the same cloth. You have the same sell-by dates.'

Gil's eyebrows went up half an inch, but his genial grin remained. 'Like my wife says, nothing wrong with new wine, but you can't beat the old vintages.'

'Well, I'm not one of those people.'

'Really. I'm shocked.'

For once, KFC took notice of the slight. 'Always the funny man, eh, Sergeant? But you know what, I don't find you funny. I find you sodding irritating.'

'That's a relief then. Because I thought it was just me being irritated by you.'

KFC walked over and stood next to Gil's desk, looking down at the older man. 'Be very careful, Sergeant. Remember what they say about sinking ships.'

'We going on a boat ride... Sir?' Gil added the label very slowly.

'Yeah, we are. And there's a great big iceberg ahead of us.'

'Oh, right. I'd better man the lifeboat, then.'

KFC grinned. 'Don't bother. There'll only be room for the fit and the strong. We'll be letting the old and the weak drown.'

'Lovely,' Gil said. Though his genial smile hadn't

slipped, something sparked behind his eyes. 'Been a follower of Mother Teresa long, have you?'

KFC leaned in. 'There he is. Another pathetic stab at a cheap laugh. That the way you got out of fights at school, was it?'

Gil, still grinning, slid up out of his chair. He did it quickly and smoothly for a big man. Within one second, he was standing in KFC's space. Close enough to make the more senior officer rear back to avoid a collision. Although the room was empty, Gil kept his voice low. Only one person in the world needed to hear what he was about to say. 'And there's me thinking you were here to be a part of the team. Okay, now we understand one another. Fight it is. I'll let you take the first swing, as the senior officer and all that. I hope it'll be a good one. Because it will be the only one you'll get a chance to use. Against me, or anyone else on this team. I've been in lots of altercations with better men than you, Kelvin Fucking Caldwell. Though, come to think of it, not many worse than you. Take a good look. I'm still standing.'

The door opened and Jess walked in, saw the two men in deep conversation, and dragged up a smile. 'My, that looks like an interesting discussion. What have I missed?'

KFC turned and walked towards her, pale of face. He opened the Incident Room door and said, 'I think you and I need a quiet word, Jess. Outside. In private.'

CHAPTER TWENTY-EIGHT

WARLOW AND RHYS walked up the hilly road, leaving Penmaen Street behind. The road bent to the right. Just before the bend an access lane, guarded by a steel barrier swing gate more typically seen in forestry areas, snaked away through the trees. A padlock barred entry to the swing gate, but a kissing gate to the left allowed pedestrian access.

On both sides of a stoned lane, the trees were barely holding on to life and slick, dark, muddy puddles persisted at their roots. The land climbed to their left and an Enduro bike park with muddied tracks leading off into the hilly landscape took up the space on the right. Warning signs on a mesh fence kept walkers out. But ahead, the lane climbed steadily to the higher ground.

At the top of the rise, the half-circle metal kissing gate guarding the entrance to Allt y Grug Cemetery had seen better days. But as they stepped through, Rhys let out a 'Whoa.'

On either side of a broad, central grassy path, ranks of gravestones sat arranged in rows, surrounded by tall fir trees screening them from the blighted land at either side.

Both officers walked up to the highest point and looked around. To the north and east, a desolate landscape of sick trees dotting hills and hollows spread out before them.

'Has there been a fire here, sir?'

'No,' Warlow explained. 'The Patches refers to the way they used to dig iron ore out of the ground here. In patches, as it says on the tin. They discarded the spill as they went. Like some gigantic mole gone haywire. These days they'd never get away with it.'

'Looks like something out of *Lord of the Rings*.'

'You don't mean the Shire, I presume?'

'I was thinking more like Fangorn Forest after the Orcs.'

Warlow smiled at the younger officer. 'You know your Tolkien, Rhys.'

'I know some, sir.'

'You ought to chat with Molly Allanby. She's a fan.'

'I follow her on Insta. She's a big fan.'

Warlow stood in silence for a while, contemplating the despoiled land that rose and fell unevenly.

'Does the graveyard have any significance, sir?' Rhys asked.

'To the case? Who knows? But there is a road that runs through the Patches. We ought to drive it. See if it's still open.'

They got back to the car and Warlow told Rhys to get a map up on his phone. 'I'm trying to visualise this. The hill is like one side of a triangle, Penmaen Street is the base.'

Rhys made the map larger with a tweak of his fingers, and Warlow pointed out where they'd been and the land around the cemetery. A road cut across it but seemed to peter out. 'Doesn't look as if anything joins up, sir,' Rhys observed.

'Hmm. Not how I remember it. Let's go with instinct.' He put the car in gear and retraced the road to the A4067.

Just before they crossed the river, which formed the county boundary, Warlow pointed to a sign that read: *Aggregate Industries*. 'Up there,' he said.

'There's a no entry sign, sir.'

'I know.' By then they'd driven past. He headed to a roundabout and came back, took a right through the no entry sign and soon they were travelling a single lane, poorly maintained track through the Patches. What trees grew on the slopes and banks looked stunted and diseased. A mile in, some forestry workers were harvesting and looked up at the unusual sight of a car on this road. After another half mile, the lane wound down to re-emerge on a maintained road and Warlow headed down to the valley to cut across the river once more. Another right took them to the roundabout again.

'It's a shortcut, sir.' Rhys nodded.

'Yes, it is. And not widely used by the look of it.'

'Is it important?'

'I lived here over thirty years ago. Things change. But the last time I was back here, the Geoghans were the reason I came. We've been west of the River Twrch all this time. On the other side, it's a stone's throw to the Black Mountains again. Some nice spots. Quiet spots. That's where James Kinton lived.'

'Kinton?' Rhys frowned. 'I've seen that name in the files. Isn't that what Derek Geoghan went down for?'

Warlow nodded slowly, his mind going back to that trip out to the Kinton's place that he and Owen Tamblin had made all those years ago. From where he was sitting now, it was only two or three miles. Close enough to be significant. Walkable even, if you knew the shortcuts.

'It is,' Warlow eventually answered Rhys's question.

'Do you think that has any bearing on what's happened to the Geoghans, sir?'

'That, Detective Constable Harries, is a bloody good

question.' Warlow glanced at his watch. 'Let's get back to the station. By then, it'll be time for you to give Ian Roberts a ring.'

———

JESS AND KFC stood outside the station in Ystradgynlais. 'What's on your mind, Kelvin?'

'Are you having a laugh, Jess?'

'I don't follow?'

'This.' KFC waved his arm vaguely over his head. 'The whole thing. It's a joke.'

'We've only been here a couple of days. Admittedly, having Catrin off isn't helping.'

'It's not Catrin. Not only Catrin, I mean. She is your best asset. From what I've seen, she may even be your only asset.'

Jess frowned.

KFC glared. 'I'm talking about the dregs you've been left with.'

Jess looked away momentarily, trying to quell her irritation. But this was her case, and she ought to listen to everyone's viewpoint. 'Care to elaborate, Kelvin.'

'The fact that you're asking me that is the most worrying thing. Come on, Jess. You've got one officer on this squad off sick, one who shouldn't be here at all because he's had his finger in the pie, a finger that still smells strongly of fish.'

'Are you talking about Evan?'

'Evan and Owen Tamblin both.'

'I've already discussed this with Buchannan and Goodey—'

'Great. But that doesn't make it any better. We're relying on those two to provide evidence and motive, but have you thought about how selective they might want to be?'

'Selective?'

'To cover their own backs.'

Jess laughed. 'Are you seriously suggesting that Owen and Evan are implicated in this?'

KFC breathed out. It made a sound like a small horse. 'They are in this up to their necks. The Geoghans were communicating with them, for Christ's sake. What if there was more? What if there was the threat of blackmail?'

Jess stepped back to stare at KFC. 'Where the hell is all this coming from?'

'It's coming from a detached viewpoint. From someone outside the bloody gang who is looking in and seeing what no one else can see.'

Jess folded her arms. 'If you have any evidence to support this, show it to me.'

KFC exhaled through his nose. 'I'm gathering evidence.'

'We all are, Kelvin.'

'Really? And who have you got doing that, eh? Warlow, who has his own agenda. Wonderboy—'

'His name is Rhys,' Jess said, with slow and dangerous emphasis.

'—who is being led around the houses by Warlow, and Sergeant soddin' Snail in there.'

'Gil has more experience than the both of us put together. I admit that things are moving slowly, but it's the same at the start of any investigation.' For a moment, she considered telling him about Molly and Cadi, and that she could well do without his continued posturing, but she didn't. It would only give him more fuel.

'We need to move more quickly here.'

'And how would you do that, Kelvin?'

'Broaden the scope. Get some more people in. Look more closely at Warlow and Tamblin—'

Jess threw her hand up. 'Stop. Just… Stop. Listen to what you're saying. You're accusing two senior officers without a shred of evidence.'

KFC clenched his jaw. 'That might change. Sooner than you think.'

Jess's expression of horror must have made KFC take a mental step back. His next words were in a much more conciliatory tone.

'All I'm saying is that I think you are being too loyal, Jess. And I wouldn't want to see you cock this up. I know how important it is to you.'

'If you do, then you'll get on board and pitch in like the rest of us.'

KFC eased out a hollow laugh. 'Don't be like that. I'm on your side, Jess.'

'Then you know we have a vast mountain of evidence to sift through and leads to eliminate before we consider any of the more… Unlikely scenarios. What about the prison angle? Has anything at all come of that?'

Caught out, KFC looked momentarily contrite. 'Not yet. I'm chasing a few things up. In fact, I'm just about to go and see someone now.'

A face appeared at the door. A Uniform involved in indexing the case onto HOLMES.

'DI Caldwell, a call for you, sir.'

'Who is it?' KFC called back.

'A Mrs Michaels. Says she has a list for you?'

KFC's face fell, and he shook his head and muttered to Jess, 'The Geoghan hater with the online petition. More bullshit.' He turned to the Uniform. 'Okay, ask her to email it to you and get it onto the database. I'll look at it later, okay? Better still, leave uh, Harrison a note.'

The Uniform nodded.

'See,' KFC said to Jess, 'I am involved in the nitty-gritty. Just ticked another box there. I'll get Wonderboy to go through all of that crap later. Job done. Now I'm going to tick another box. Another negative that'll bring us all back around to your friend, Warlow.'

Jess shook her head. 'Don't keep saying that, Kelvin. Not without good cause.'

'Oh, I'll find good cause, don't you worry.' He gave her a death's head grin as he started to stalk off and, turning away with his back to her, waved a hand.

Back in the Incident Room. Gil held out a fresh mug of tea to Jess. 'The other one went cold, ma'am.'

Jess took it. 'Thank you.'

'DI Caldwell gone off somewhere, ma'am?'

'He has. Chasing up a lead, he says.'

'Nice to see someone so keen. Always reminds me of that song, does DI Caldwell. You know the one.' Gil started to hum the tune to *You're Beautiful.*

Jess paused with the mug an inch from her lips. 'That's a love song by, what's his name, James Blunt.'

'Yes, that's the one, ma'am.'

Gil continued humming softly, and both officers went back to their screens. Ten seconds later Jess looked across at Gil. 'There is another reason the singer of that song resonates. Not anything to do with cockney rhyming slang, is it?'

Gil, his expression the picture of innocence, glanced over. 'Oh, that I wouldn't know ma'am.'

'You are a wicked man, Detective Sergeant.' Jess, laughing softly to herself, shook her head and turned back to her work.

CHAPTER TWENTY-NINE

'ANY NEWS?'

Those were the first words that came out of Warlow's mouth when he arrived back at the station at lunchtime. He hadn't meant to blurt them out but blurt they did. Jess looked across, her anxious expression telling Warlow all he needed to know. They hadn't found his dog. But Gil, still in blissful ignorance, interpreted the question as pertaining to the case at hand and duly obliged with a reply.

'Nothing much. DI Caldwell graced us with his presence, but then shot off to chase up a lead. But he's left you some work, Rhys. I saw one of the Uniforms leave a note on your desk.'

Rhys nodded.

'What about you two?' Gil asked.

Rhys glanced at his watch. 'I'm about to ring someone about possible CCTV evidence. It looks promising.' He mimicked a drinking movement with his hand and nodded at Warlow, who replied with a thumbs up.

'Anything new from the abduction site?' Gil asked.

Warlow bit back the disappointment that threatened to

engulf him over no news of Cadi. 'We didn't go there in the end. We walked up beyond the house towards a grave-yard. The area between it and the house is a wasteland.'

'Tidy. Nice walk?'

'Not pretty. But it's an ideal spot for someone to come and go to the house unobserved on foot.'

Warlow walked to the board and picked up a high-lighter from Gil's desk. Jess got up to join him. He circled an area on the enlarged map. 'The Patches, so called because of the way they dug up iron ore in the bad old days. This valley had one of the biggest iron and tinplate works in the world in the mid-nineteenth century. Unfortu-nately, the way they extracted the ore made a bloody mess of the landscape. What we have now is a few square miles of scrub and woodland. Unoccupied, hardly travelled.'

'And you think the abductor might have used this?' Jess asked.

'Possibly. There is only one road leading up to the house at the end of a street with few other properties. It's a dead end beyond. A vehicle would have been noticed.'

'But the Geoghans must have been brought to the house somehow,' Jess said. 'You don't think they trekked across these… Patches, do you?'

Warlow shook his head. 'No. They would have been brought up by vehicle and taken away by vehicle. But there is no way to hide a vehicle on that street. My guess is he drove in, got them into the house and then drove away and left the vehicle somewhere else before coming back to the house on foot.'

'Across the Patches?'

'Possibly. It's one theory, anyway.'

Jess nodded. 'Which means our perpetrator might be local.'

'Or have local knowledge at least,' Warlow agreed. He

paused before going on. 'There is one other thing.' He leaned in and used his finger to follow a river on the map, found a road going east, peering closely until he got to the point he wanted and drew another, much smaller circle. Large enough to only surround a single property.

'What's that?' Gil asked.

Warlow sighed. 'Somewhere I wish I'd never had to visit. This is called *Ger yr Afon*. Next to, or near, the river would be the best translation. It's where the family Kinton lived. Where Owen and I found James Kinton chained up in an outhouse, dead from dehydration and starvation with his lips stapled together so he couldn't make a noise while the Geoghans played parasite and ate his food and spent his money twenty yards away from his prison.'

'But that's only, what, a couple of miles away as the crow flies?' Jess said.

'Don't say it,' Warlow warned. 'You know how much I hate the "C" word.'

Jess and Gil exchanged a knowing look.

Warlow picked up on it. 'What?'

'We've had our own "C" word episode this afternoon. Only our "C" word wasn't coincidence.'

'Let me guess, Caldwell?' Warlow asked.

'You do not want to know.' Jess clamped her jaw shut.

Rhys arrived back with the tea and handed a mug to Warlow.

'I'm going to make that call, sir.' Rhys excused himself and Gil moved back to his desk, leaving Warlow and Jess to wander over to hers. Warlow turned his back to the other before resuming the conversation.

'How's Molly?'

Jess pulled out a chair and sat. 'I don't think she's slept much.'

'Understandable. She's upset.'

'That'll be the two of us, then.' Jess sighed. 'But she has

all her friends out looking plus a gaggle of roped-in volunteers. There's a notice up on a local Facebook group. Molly wants to go back, obviously. She's desperate. I might have to drive down there after work.'

'I can do that,' Warlow said.

'No. My car's coming back at two. The garage cocked up the repairs so they're sending a driver and a support car to get him back. I can't see much happening here tonight, so I'll take her back down.'

'Cadi has my number on her collar. She's been chipped, too. If someone finds her, we'll know soon enough.'

'What if she's too scared to let anyone near her?'

Warlow laughed. 'Are we talking about the same dog? She's human-centric.'

Jess looked pained. 'I am so sorry, Evan.'

'No more apologies, Jess. Let's get on with what we can here.'

'If Catrin wasn't off and if I could depend on Kelvin to do the spade work, I'd let you go.' Jess kept her voice low.

Rhys looked up, face beaming. 'Ian Roberts says he has two months' worth of recordings on the cloud. He can get me access as soon as he gets home from work.'

Warlow swivelled around. 'Good. It's likely the Geoghans would have been transported at night. We're looking for a vehicle that travelled up and down that road in the dark. Twice.' He pointed to Gil's snaking, stuck-up notes.

'When he brought them in and took them away.'

'Spot on, Rhys.'

'So, three or possibly four weeks apart?'

'I'd say three to five to be safe,' Warlow said. 'Right, time for some paperwork. Oh, anyone heard from Catrin? How is she?'

'Nothing yet,' Jess replied.

'Okay, then maybe no news is… Wossname,' Warlow said. He got a couple of funny looks for that and a guffaw from Rhys.

———

GIL RETURNED to the phone records but couldn't concentrate. He picked up his mobile and phoned Catrin's number. It rang eight times before an apologetic voice told him that the person he was calling wasn't available. He tried texting. The message joined the half dozen others that had been received but remained unanswered. This wasn't like her. Even if she was sick.

With daughters of his own of about the same age, Gil used that fatherly knowledge to his advantage when it came to winding his fellow sergeant up. And Catrin's bluff dismissal of his attempts at irreverent humour often belied the little smile he saw playing on her lips when one of his quips hit home. All part of the suffer-no-fools armour she wore. When they'd worked together outside of the office, they played the game. But underneath the jousting, certainly for his part, there remained a professional relationship that made them both meshing cogs in a well-oiled machine.

She was sharp and analytical, where he was more methodical and cynical. His approach was to believe nothing anyone said, certainly anyone with a record, until he'd had the pudding and eaten it. And the thing about Catrin that he admired the most was her loyalty. To the team, and even to him. When she let her hair down, there was another – rarer – Catrin under the armour. He'd seen it in the off-duty situations they'd shared. Seen the ambitious young woman with the scathing glares, quick wit and quicker laughter who felt she was making a difference. In the job for the right, old-fashioned reasons.

Gil liked that. He liked Catrin. What he hadn't liked was the fact that she'd been thrown into a pit with a rattlesnake in the form of KFC.

No one in this squad liked the "C" word. In Gil's case, not in any of its many connotations.

Catrin plus Caldwell plus coincidence plus *You're Beautiful.*

He got up from his desk, mobile in hand. Everyone else seemed to be using the car park for personal calls. Why not?

The sun had made an appearance, and, in between the scudding clouds, it burned down onto the tarmac of the car park giving up a bitumen smell so reminiscent of hot summer days. Gil found some shade; his eyes weren't good enough to read the phone's screen in the glaring sunlight. He skipped through his contacts and found the one he needed.

This time, the phone was answered after four rings.

'Hello.' A bright male voice. The greeting carrying the right modicum of surprise mingled with wary pleasure.

'Craig. How are you?'

'I'm good, Gil.'

'Working?'

'Yes. On the way to a breakdown in St Clears.'

Craig Peters was a Dyfed Powys traffic officer and Catrin's partner.

'You alone in the car?' Gil asked.

'I am. Why, you're not going to tell me my girlfriend has been kidnapped again, are you?' The little laugh that accompanied this question carried a hint of concern on its tailwind. Gil had been with Warlow when they'd contacted Craig the day that Catrin and Rhys had gone 'missing' while visiting a suspect in an isolated address in the Brechfa Forest. The young traffic officer had not forgotten that.

'No. Not this time. But it is Catrin I wanted to talk about.'

'Oh, dear. Let me pull into the next lay-by. I'm one of two vehicles responding. Phil is already there, so I can take a minute.'

Gil waited. Thirty seconds later, he heard the noise of an engine winding down and then Craig's voice once more. 'Go ahead, Gil.'

'She's not answering her texts. All okay? Nothing serious is it.'

The long seconds of silence that followed told Gil more than any number of words. 'I don't think I should be getting involved in all this.'

'In all what?' Gil asked. 'She went off sick yesterday, according to DI Caldwell. And we're all concerned that she's okay. That's all this is.'

Craig's breathing came over the phone, loud and deep. The kind of excess exchange of air that came with reluctant weighing up of situations. 'She's fine.'

'Good, glad to hear it. Physically then, yes?'

'Yes.'

'What about in her head?'

'Are you a mind reader, Gil?'

'No, but I've sat in enough interviews to be able to tell when someone's being miserly with the truth.'

'Shit,' Craig said. 'She's going to kill me.'

'Shall I send over armed response?'

'Don't joke. It might come to that.'

'What's up, Craig?'

'Do I have to answer that?'

'Technically speaking, I am the more senior officer but, I can tell you're uncomfortable, so no. But if it'll help, say I ordered you to answer.'

'Think that'll work?'

'Not a snowball's.'

Craig's laugh was a thin warble. 'She wasn't looking too good last night. Said she'd thrown up. Didn't eat much of her supper. This morning she went to work, but later than usual. Said she was going in to Llangunnor to do some work for Caldwell.'

'She's in HQ?'

'She is. When I asked her what it was about, she flew off the handle. Said it's better I didn't know. I've never seen her so pissed off. She even asked if there were any jobs going in traffic.'

'Are there?'

'No. She was only kidding. But she's usually up about work. You know Catrin. No stone unturned. But this morning... She wasn't like that.'

'Okay. Thanks, Craig. That's helpful.'

'Is it? What should I do, Gil? Leave it there or buy her flowers or something. Do you know what's going on?'

Gil sensed the desperation in Craig's plea and answered truthfully, 'I don't know, That's the honest answer. But it has nothing to do with you, so get that out of your head. This is work.'

The traffic officer exhaled loudly. 'Okay, thanks for that.'

'Best we forget this conversation. This'll be between you and me, okay?' Gil said.

'Good plan.'

'Make yourself popular again and go shut down the A48.'

'Thanks, Gil.' Another sigh.

'And don't worry about Catrin. We'll soon have her whistling *What a Wonderful World* again.'

'Hah. That'll be the day.'

'Oh, a Buddy Holly fan, is she?'

'Who?'

Tumbleweeds rolled across Gil's mind. 'You have no idea who Buddy Holly is, do you?'

'Uh…' Craig muttered.

'*Mawredd.* Just Google it.'

CHAPTER THIRTY

AT A LITTLE AFTER THREE PM, Owen Tamblin stood looking at his car for what must have been the twentieth time that day. He'd had his keys back, but in a way wished he hadn't. The misshapen 'T', 'A' and 'L' were baking onto the paintwork in the sun. He hadn't given the insurance company a ring yet. He ought to do that. Though quite how they were going to classify this, he wasn't sure.

Hardly an accident. More a deliberate act of vandalism. Which meant him shelling out for the repairs most likely. 'Bastards,' he muttered. Though whether this applied to the perpetrators of the act, or to the slippery eels at the insurance company was anyone's guess.

His phone rang to break the spell, and he fished it out of his pocket.

'Tamblin.'

'Is that Detective Chief Inspector Tamblin?'

Not a local accent. Normally, Tamblin was pretty good at voices, but looking at the car had frazzled his circuits. 'It is. Who is this?'

'I am Marius Stoica. We have spoken already on the phone.'

Within two seconds, all thoughts of car graffiti disappeared from the DCI's head.

'Mr Stoica. Good of you to call.'

'I have been thinking about everything. I am not thief anymore. I have partner and baby now.'

'Marius, we know this. We're not trying to catch you out, mate. I promise you. We need to have a word, that's all.'

'Why can't you do it on the phone?'

'It's too sensitive, pal. I can't explain it over the phone. It's part of another investigation and who knows who could be listening.' It was a truth of sorts. Tamblin did not want to talk about this over the phone. Far safer to have a one on one.

'I am busy in car wash for another half an hour, then I go to friends to pick up clothes.'

'Where does your friend live?'

'Cross Hands.'

'Do you have a car?'

'No. Partner has car for baby.'

'Right. Text me your friend's address and I'll come and pick you up from there. I promise we'll run you home, too, once we have a chat.'

'Okay, I text you address.'

Tamblin ended the call. Thirty seconds later, his message app pinged. He looked at it, performed a fist pump, and then looked up into the sky and mouthed, 'You can be a fickle sod.'

———

WARLOW SAT at his desk in the station at Ystradgynlais, trying and failing to piece together the separate bits of information they had. Failing in part because they didn't fit together, no matter which way he rearranged them. And failing, too, because with each passing hour, the dreaded feeling of hollow despair over Cadi grew ever larger. And yes, she was only a dog. But a dog that had been his only real companion over the last few years of his life. She'd been with him through a cold winter while he renovated the cottage. There, as he tried to come to terms with his diagnosis of HIV. A constant presence when he'd told his sons that their mother had passed. He'd shed no tears over Jeez Denise's demise because he had none left after their tempestuous last years together. But Cadi had sensed his sadness for the boys. And no matter what anyone said, dogs had emotional intelligence. Often a great deal more than some humans he knew.

People, non-dog people, responded in bewilderment when experts explained this bond on talk shows or on the radio. But he'd never needed convincing how much a privilege it was to own a dog and have them let you be their reason for being. What would he do if she didn't turn up, he wondered? He had no idea. He'd seen relatives left behind in misper cases. Parents, partners, sons and daughters. The absence of closure was a cancer that ate at you. With care and patience, you might be able to keep it from overwhelming you. But it never went away.

When Gil tapped him gently on the shoulder, it jolted him out of his maudlin wool-gathering.

'You okay, Evan?'

Though Warlow was the younger man and rank demanded a certain formality when they were in company, they'd long ago used first names in close conversations.

'No,' Warlow answered. 'This case is eating at me.'

Gil nodded but read the lie for what it was. 'DI Allanby told me about Cadi, Evan. She'll turn up. She's not a stupid dog. Christ, she's a Lab. She'll be looking for food.'

Gil was probably right. But Cadi had a lead and collar on. What if the lead had got caught on something and she was trapped? What if some trigger-happy farmer had seen her near his sheep?

'She'll turn up,' Gil affirmed.

Warlow swallowed back a threatening lump and tried to banish the dark thoughts swirling through his head.

'Talking of the lost. I've just come off the phone with Craig.'

Warlow frowned. 'Catrin's Craig?'

'None other.' Gil pulled up a chair to make it look like they were studying the screen together. He used what he liked to call his *Last Christmas* voice. A convoluted and euphemistic reference to the erstwhile George Michael and his song *Careless Whisper*. Something Gil liked to use to warn his junior officers when they were being a little too loud and risked being overheard on sensitive matters. He'd hum the tune to *Last Christmas*, instead of the tune to *Careless Whisper* as if doing so would confuse the enemy. Usually, it succeeded only in confusing his friends. 'It's not like her to ignore texts and calls. So, I gave Craig a ring, and it's even worse than we thought.'

'She's not in hospital, is she?' Warlow asked.

'No. She's at her desk at HQ under instruction from DI laughing-boy not to communicate with us.'

'What?' Warlow's voice went up an octave. He paired it back to *Last Christmas* again. 'Does Jess know this?'

Gil shook his head. 'Worse is the fact that Craig told me she'd even mentioned putting in for a transfer this morning.'

'As a joke?'

Gil lifted one eyebrow. 'This is Catrin we're talking about.'

'Jesus. What the hell has that idiot been doing?'

'I take it you're not referring to Catrin?'

'What do you think?' Warlow sat back, pondering. It took him five seconds to decide. He got up and slid on his jacket. 'Right, this calls for drastic action. Tell Jess I'm going to see Tamblin.'

'Are you?'

'Only if he's in Llangunnor.'

An hour later, he walked through the door of Dyfed Powys Police HQ and went directly to the room he expected to find Catrin working in. He wasn't disappointed. She had her back to him as he approached and when he spoke, she didn't flinch. Instead, she simply froze.

'Glad to see you're feeling better, Sergeant.'

He gave her some space. Didn't crowd her. Waited for her to stand, turn around and face him. She did that, positioning herself so her torso blocked out the screen. Catrin was always pale. Her Celtic colouring was such that she had to be careful in the sun. Even so, there were many more freckles than usual because it was June. She had her chestnut hair tied back in a single tail, the parting unusually uneven on her brow. The smile that broke over her even teeth quivered with nerves as she regarded Warlow.

'Sir, I… Why aren't you in Ystradgynlais?' She blinked, realising the question sounded suspicious, trying to rescue it by widening her eyes to make it seem less accusatory.

'I could ask you the same thing.'

'I came down with something yesterday. I wasn't brilliant this morning. DI Caldwell suggested I stay here.'

Warlow nodded slowly. 'So, you're feeling better?'

'I am, thank you.'

'Well enough to answer your phone?'

She wrinkled her nose. 'I think there's something wrong with it, sir. It wouldn't charge this morning.'

Warlow held his hand out, phone in hand. 'Want to borrow mine? Might be worth you giving Jess a ring. She's been mithering all morning.' He deliberately used one of Jess's words.

Catrin stared at the phone in his hand as if it was a

writhing rattlesnake. 'No, it's okay, sir. I could use the land-line and phone the station.'

Warlow retracted his hand. 'You could.' He shifted his head to peer over her shoulder at the screen. 'What are you working on?'

'Nothing much. Analysing some phone records.'

'For DI Caldwell?'

She nodded, the smile quivering even more.

'Pertinent to our case?'

'DI Caldwell seems to think so.'

'And you?'

Catrin shuddered. 'I suppose I won't know until I've been through them, sir.'

'Let's have a look.' Warlow stepped forward.

Catrin didn't move.

'Step aside, Sergeant.'

Catrin folded her arms across her chest, dropped them to her side, then folded them again, as if she couldn't remember what they were for. Finally, she took a stride to the left. Warlow stepped forward and read the screen. He said nothing for three minutes as he scrolled through. He paused only once to lean forward, tut and say, 'I can't believe I spent £3.47 talking to a man about replacement tyres.' When he eventually straightened, his face seemed expressionless. 'Why don't we go outside for a chat?'

'Sir, I—'

'After you.'

She led the way – her back a ramrod, her stride a march – through the swing doors and down the stairs.

'My car's had aircon on all the way here. It'll be cool in there.' Warlow nodded towards his Jeep across the car park.

She didn't argue, and a minute later detective sergeant and DCI sat in the front seats of Warlow's Renegade with the engine running and cool air permeating the cabin.

'I'm going to be applying for a transfer, sir,' Catrin said.

'I see. Can I ask why?'

Catrin's expression moulded into something halfway between confusion and hysteria as she let out a little chortle. 'Isn't it obvious? I've spent the last eight hours going through the telephone records of one of my senior officers. I'd understand why you would not want to work with me after that, sir.'

'Why?' Warlow said. 'Find anything incriminating?'

'No, sir. Not in yours and not in DCI Tamblin's. If it's any consolation, I didn't want to do this. I suggested someone from outside the unit, but DI Caldwell... He ordered me to do it. That's pathetic, but saying it somehow helps.'

Warlow said nothing for a couple of beats and then spoke very softly. 'Let me tell you what I would like to see happen.'

Catrin squeezed her eyes shut in the same way that anyone in front of a firing squad might.

Warlow continued, 'I'd like you to apply for a transfer. And then I'd like you to watch as I rip the bloody thing up.'

The DS's eyes sprang open. 'But sir—'

'How many times did Owen and I talk in the last six months?'

'Five times.'

Warlow gave her a distorted smile. 'That's five times too many. But three were about the Geoghans. About Derek getting out. About Karen Geoghan's love letters. We keep in touch over threats. There, now you can tell DI Caldwell you even corroborated the intel.'

Catrin shook her head glumly.

Warlow held up a finger. 'Have you seen enough of our records to write a prelim report?'

'Yes, sir.'

'Then do it. How long will it take?'

'There's nothing much to report.'

'Good. Then I'll wait here for you. We need you on the case, Catrin.'

'But—'

'That's an order, Sergeant. And the last time I looked I still had more clout than KFC.'

She nodded, but still hesitated. 'Things aren't the same though, are they? In the team, I mean. Not with—'

'You don't have to say it. We both know what's causing the dysfunction. What isn't clear yet is why he's being so divisive. It might be because he doesn't like me. But this isn't my case. It's Jess's.'

'I think he really is convinced that you and Mr Tamblin are responsible, sir.'

'Yes. He'd want you to believe that. Now, are you up for this?'

Catrin looked away, through the windscreen of the Jeep and the rolling countryside and seemed to make up her mind as she snapped her head around. 'I am, sir. And thank you for coming to get me.'

Warlow was delighted to note the little fiery glint in her eye. 'Don't thank me. Thank Gil. He's been anxious about you.'

Catrin blinked. 'Gil?'

'Yes, Mr Softie. Gil's old school, Catrin. I realise that sometimes he gets to you. But he's a firm believer in the Three Musketeers principle.'

Catrin frowned.

Warlow shook his head. 'One for all and all for one. Something DI Caldwell has never appreciated.' He glanced at his watch. 'Go on. The clock is ticking.'

Catrin, looking a great deal better than when she'd got into the car, nodded and got out. The smile she gave Warlow this time was a genuine one.

She hadn't reached the main entrance doors before Warlow's phone rang.

'Owen Tamblin. Speak of the devil.'

'Evan, I hope you're sitting down.'

'Story time, is it?'

'It is, and this one's got a great happy ending.'

'Disgusting. It's too early for porn, Owen.'

'Shut up and listen. I am on the way to pick up our friend Stoica.'

Warlow grinned. 'He's seen the light then.'

'He's seen his missus, and she has been telling him a few home truths. Said I'd pick him up from Cross Hands.'

'Cross Hands? I could have picked him up on the way back. I'm in Carmarthen.'

'No worries, I'm five minutes away. I'll take him straight up to Ystradgynlais if that's the best option?'

'Good idea. I'll let Jess know. We'll see you up there unless we overtake you.'

A derisory grunt followed. 'In that bloody thing you drive? No chance.'

CHAPTER THIRTY-ONE

In the Jeep, Warlow filled Catrin in as best he could, without mentioning the personal baggage weighing him down. Catrin had enough to worry about.

'The house that the Geoghans were kept in has significance in other cases?' Catrin asked.

'Perhaps. Geographically maybe. I haven't put it all together yet. My hope is that Stoica might be able to help.'

'But he isn't the perpetrator?'

'We have no reason to think that. The way the Geoghans were killed,' Warlow shook his head, 'that has to mean something to whoever did it. A significance we can only guess at.'

'And Stoica hasn't exactly been on the run, I suppose.'

Warlow considered this before answering. 'No. He's been coy, but he hasn't run. So, either he doesn't give a monkey's, or he has nothing to do with it directly, other than being connected to the house. Personally, having seen his domestic arrangements, I'm veering towards the latter.'

Catrin turned to stare out of the window at the passing view. A view her eyes didn't register. When she spoke, the words emerged in a low monotone, as if voicing her thoughts. 'Whoever did this doesn't care about getting caught, does he?'

A good point. 'If you do not want to get caught, you hide the bodies. You don't put them on display. Victims are a cornucopia of clues. By definition, and however fleeting in some cases, they're the one thing that has been in contact with the perpetrator.'

She turned to Warlow. 'So, what does it mean? That he wants to be caught?'

'Perhaps. Or his compulsion has taken over all sense of normality. I suspect he realises that the net is closing in. The question is, will he be content with just the Geoghans?'

They lapsed into silence, each of them trying to disentangle the knot of thoughts the conversation had knitted in their heads. Eventually, Catrin broke the silence.

'What am I going to say to DI Allanby, sir?'

'Tell her what you told me.'

'But I feel terrible about that. I'm going to get into trouble either way. If not with DI Allanby, then with DI Caldwell. I feel so disloyal.'

Warlow threw her a challenging glare. 'You were partnered with Kelvin Caldwell for this case. He is the senior officer. Now, he may have good reason to believe what he believes about me and Owen Tamblin. Or he may be a card carrying...' Wisely, he didn't finish the sentence, recalculated, and started again. 'He may have reasons of his own to want to implicate me. But that's his agenda, not yours.'

'And all this because he doesn't like you?' Catrin sounded incredulous.

'Pride and arrogance are a dangerous mix. And I don't pretend to like DI Caldwell either. But not being on my Christmas card list is not grounds for dismissal.'

'Not liking you is one thing, but this is a vendetta.'

Warlow turned down the corners of his mouth. Good word, vendetta. 'What do we really know about anyone or anything, Catrin? We look in the mirror and think we know ourselves, but all we can know is the version we want to see. Nine times out of ten, we're wrong on one level or another. Because I can guarantee it isn't how others see us.'

Catrin sat, pensive. 'How did Gil find out I was at HQ?'

'He's a detective. Ask him.'

She mulled that over, brows lowering. 'He rang Craig, didn't he?'

Warlow nodded. 'He rang Craig. So that's two people who care enough about you to risk incurring your wrath.'

She compressed her lips together. 'I don't do wrath, do I, sir?'

Warlow said nothing. His silence triggered a slight smile from his sergeant. 'I have no right to be angry, do I?'

'Remember that when you see them next.' Warlow's foot tapped the brakes. 'Hang on, we're running into some traffic.'

They'd passed junction 47 on the M4 but traffic had slowed both ways approaching a vehicle on the hard shoulder with smoke billowing up from its bonnet.

'Oh, dear. Someone's overheated.' Warlow looked to pull out and overtake the rubberneckers, but there was too much traffic. Their speed dropped from seventy to a pedestrian twenty.

'Look at this lot just gawking,' Catrin said.

But Warlow could only stare at the stopped vehicle, his brows bunched. The car, a Merc, looked to be in a bad way. Not simply overheating, because the smoke pluming out from under the bonnet and billowing from both open front doors wasn't steam, this was black and oily. As they passed, orange flame began flickering underneath the front wheel-arch.

'Sir, there are people in that vehicle.' Catrin said as they drove past.

But Warlow hardly heard her. His brain was too busy making sense of what his eyes had seen on the vehicle's paintwork. A streak of yellow that looked suspiciously like the letter T.

'Shit! Shit! That's Owen's car.'

He slammed on the brakes and veered into the hard shoulder thirty yards from the smoking car. 'Call it in,' he yelled to Catrin.

He was out of the car in an instant. Running back and seeing a figure on the driver's side leaning in, engulfed in the dense black smoke. Warlow yelled. The figure didn't respond. Couldn't because it was taking all their effort in trying to pull something from the car.

Warlow was feet away when, with a groaning effort that sounded almost feral, the figure pulled back and another shape came with him. This a flaccid torso that hung unmoving. One more yank and the rest of the body followed in a crumpled mess, with the legs still inside the vehicle.

Owen Tamblin's legs.

The man that had pulled him out fell back, coughing and spluttering, hands over his eyes, tears streaming down his blackened face. Grunting, he got on his haunches and began pulling Tamblin back, struggling from the smoke and his constant coughing.

Warlow sprinted forward, grabbed Owen's jacket, and yanked him backwards, away from the car. The other man tried to help but another bout of coughing and retching drove him to his knees. The smoke was thick, stinking of oil and plastic. It caught in Warlow's throat, burned his eyes. How the hell this other man had been able to put his head inside the car to reach Tamblin, he'd never know. But they were too close to the conflagration.

Warlow's efforts had only managed to get the unresponsive Tamblin as far as the back tyre. Now flames were jetting out from underneath the engine and all over the bonnet.

Warlow grunted and heaved once more. Tamblin was a dead weight, unable to help. The other man looked spent, shielding his eyes as a fresh gout of flame gushed upwards.

'Come on.' Warlow growled to himself as he braced for another yank at Tamblin. He managed three feet and then had to reset, his feet slipping on the gravelly hard shoulder. The Merc had become a fireball. How could it have caught so quickly? Warlow didn't want to be this close to something that had a tank full of God knew how much fuel.

He bent his knees, shut his eyes against the heat, grabbed Tamblin's jacket and pulled. Somehow, he seemed lighter. Warlow half-stumbled. He looked down. Other hands. Another four. Other people had seen and stopped and helped. Two young men. Strapping lads.

'Lift,' Warlow yelled.

This time, they half-carried Tamblin and got him back a good fifteen yards. Warlow went back to help the second man. Led him away to the crash barrier behind where Tamblin lay. And all the while, faces in the passing cars looked on in horror.

That only lasted a few more seconds. Until a crack of exploding glass made Warlow flinch, and a fresh eruption of orange flame and smoke drew everyone's attention away from the men.

The car had become an inferno.

Tamblin convulsed, his breathing ragged and stertorous. But at least he was breathing. His right hand looked blistered; his eyes were open but unseeing. He didn't speak when Warlow spoke to him. Shock had robbed him of that ability. Warlow talked to him, kept him awake for a long three minutes until the ambulance arrived and the paramedics took over.

The DCI moved back to sit on the barrier as the emergency services did their jobs. The fire crew arrived four minutes after the ambulance. By that time, the black Mercedes was a vague dark shape inside a dancing orange ball of flame. Traffic officers shut off one lane. Three minutes later, the fire was out under a blanket of foam. Tamblin's Merc had become a dripping black carcass. Warlow wondered what might have happened if they'd arrived a minute later than they had.

Warlow thanked the two boys who had stopped to help and made sure the Uniforms took their names. They'd been on the way home from the gym. Samaritans who had an urge to help and not simply ogle.

Warlow hoped that he might have done the same even if he hadn't recognised the car. He waited while the paramedics checked Tamblin's passenger over. The man refused to go to hospital. He wanted to go home. And apart from some superficial burns on his arm, he seemed fine.

A stoic.

Well-named then.

Twenty minutes after he'd driven past the burning car and screeched to a halt, with the scene awash with blue and whites and fire engines, Tamblin was already arriving at Morriston Hospital's A&E department. But the passenger, Tamblin's saviour, walked with Warlow to his Jeep and got into the back seat.

Catrin, who'd sat in the car coordinating the services on the phone, looked from the DCI to the man.

Warlow made the introductions.

'Sergeant Richards, meet Marius Stoica. After he's answered a few of our questions, which he's happy to do, I am going to buy him a bloody big drink.'

CHAPTER THIRTY-TWO

BACK IN THE station at Ystradgynlais, they treated Stoica more like a member of the team than a suspect. Not that he was a suspect. But Gil and Rhys had tea at the ready and Gil had opened the emergency rations box with the addition of a further contribution from the café. This time chocolate brownies.

'Looks like the owner has a soft spot for you,' Gil said, when Warlow expressed delight on hearing she'd called round again.

'We're old friends.'

That earned him a raised eyebrow from Catrin, but nothing more.

Warlow sat out the interview. Though physically fine, the DCI remained shaken from the burning car episode. He and Jess watched on a monitor as Gil and Catrin spoke to Stoica.

The monitor sat in a tiny space next to the interview room. If they'd turned the volume down on the speaker, they would have easily heard the conversation anyway. Jess was already seated when Warlow joined her. So, it was only he who saw Catrin turn to Gil just before they entered the interview room. She said something in a low voice to which Gil rumbled a reply. Then she pulled him into a hug. Warlow counted nine seconds before Catrin let go, turned away, smoothed down her blouse and opened the door, while Gil simply stood there shaking his head with a whispered, 'girls.'

On camera, in the interview room, Catrin wasted no time. 'First, thanks for talking to us, Mr Stoica.'

'Marius,' Stoica said. He'd washed up, but there were dark stains on his arms that would require a scrubbing brush and white spirit to get off. He coughed once or twice and kept dabbing at his right eye, but otherwise seemed incredibly unscathed by events.

'We'll try not to keep you long, Marius,' Gil said. 'Tea okay?'

'Is good.'

Catrin quickly outlined why they wanted to speak to him, going over the crime he'd committed in breaking and entering Mrs Parry's empty house on Penmaen Street, which subsequently led to his arrest and conviction.

'It's a while ago now, but how did you know the house was empty?'

Stoica let his head drop. 'I am not proud of what I did then. She was old lady. I had labouring job in house nearby. I see ambulance take her. People on street talk. I wait a week and go back.' He held both hands up. 'I got caught.'

'Can we talk about your time in prison?'

'In Cardiff Prison?' He frowned. 'Why?'

'While you were there, did you ever come across a man called Derek Geoghan?'

The frown deepened. 'No. That is not Welsh name. Not Romanian name either. I would remember.'

'You've never heard the name Geoghan before?' Gil prompted.

'No.' Stoica coughed. This bout lasted a little longer than the others and he had to turn away and let it run its course.

'Was there anyone else involved with you in the breaking and entering?'

'No, I work alone. But when I was in court, they read out the address. Many people know where it happened.'

It was a good point.

Gil continued with this line of questioning, 'And when you were working on Allt y Grug Road and saw the ambulance, did anyone else comment? Your fellow workers?'

'No. They all up on roof. I don't talk about it. I keep it to myself. Back then... My head was not in good place.' The coughing returned with a vengeance. Stoica took a gulp of tea and it seemed to help.

'Can you tell us what happened in the car?' Catrin asked.

Stoica nodded. 'We were driving. Detective Tamblin has very nice car. Mercedes. Leather seats. Comfortable, you know? We are driving and suddenly we smell burning. Quickly, like in seconds, we see smoke coming from bonnet and coming in through vents. We are in fast lane. We cannot stop right away. By the time we can move, smoke is already thick. I get out. I wait for Detective Tamblin to get out, too. But he doesn't. I am coughing. He is coughing. Smoke is thick in seconds. Black smoke that smells bad.'

Stoica took another gulp of tea. This time, his hand shook as he held the mug and he used the other to steady it. 'It happens so fast. I call to Detective Tamblin, but he doesn't come out. So, I go to help him. I pull him out. He is breathing not good. Like you say, wheezy. And then Detective Warlow comes, like miracle.' He put the mug down and it clattered on the desk. It signalled another bout of coughing.

Catrin looked up towards the camera mounted in the

corner of the room and shook her head. Five seconds later, Warlow pushed open the interview room door and walked in.

'Marius, you sound a little rough. Are you sure you don't want us to run you down to the hospital?'

'No. My throat is dry is all. Scratchy. Now I feel tired.'

Warlow nodded to the other two. 'Best we finish this another time, don't you think?'

Gil and Catrin stood up while Warlow addressed Stoica again. 'I'll be back in ten minutes to run you home, okay?'

Stoica coughed softly. 'Thank you.'

Jess was waiting for them in the Incident Room.

'I've just come off the phone with the hospital. Owen is in the burns unit. He has some smoke damage to his lungs and a nasty burn to his arm. He's on oxygen, but conscious and responsive. They wouldn't say anything else.'

No one commented. Warlow was no expert in inhalation injuries, but he knew enough. Tissues swelled; tubes narrowed. Sometimes, they induced unconsciousness to allow the patient to recover with minimal distress.

'What about Stoica?' Rhys asked.

'Bloke deserves a bloody medal,' Gil said.

'I believe him when he says he's never heard of the Geoghans, sir. It is an odd name. He would have remembered,' Catrin said.

Warlow reluctantly agreed. 'It's not a technique I'd recommend but interviewing someone after a close encounter with a car fire is as good a way as any to peel away their defences. We will not get anything useful out of him like this. He's too traumatised.'

'What about the "C" word, sir?'

They all turned towards Rhys, still sitting at his desk.

'Explain,' Warlow ordered.

'The Mercedes, sir. Karen Geoghan's car caught fire in

a car park. But the Fire Officer told me it could have caught fire anywhere along the journey it had taken.'

A long and thoughtful silence fell on the room.

'Bloody hell, Rhys. Out of the mouths of babes,' Gil muttered. 'Coincidence be damned.'

Jess turned to the board. 'What haven't we done here?' she said. 'What are we not seeing?'

'Or what haven't we done properly?' Warlow grunted.

Jess pivoted and pierced him with a look, her eyes narrowing. 'Where is DI Caldwell? Anyone?'

Some shrugs, a few shakes of the head.

Jess looked at her watch. Almost five. 'It's late, but I would like to go over everything again while DCI Warlow takes Marius Stoica home.' She sent him a glance. 'By the time you're back we'll have something. I can feel it.'

———

AFTER WARLOW LEFT, Jess excused herself, explaining that she needed to phone Molly and tell her there'd be no early finish this evening. No chance of getting back down to Dale to search for Cadi.

Rhys watched her leave and pulled Gil to one side. 'Has something happened to Mr Warlow's dog, Sarge?'

Gil saw no point in trying to hide it. 'She went missing during a camping trip. Molly was in charge. It's complicated.'

'I had no idea. He must be worried.' Catrin walked up to the board and scanned all the additions there'd been since yesterday but had picked up on Rhys's attempt at an inside voice.

'He's bearing up,' Gil said.

Catrin shook her head. 'Feels like I've got a lot of catching up to do. What's all this about car fires for a start.'

Rhys filled her in, citing the Fire Investigation Officer's

suggestion that Karen Geoghan's car might have caught fire because of an oily rag.

She returned a scathing look. 'But we are not seriously thinking that could happen twice?'

'No,' Gil said. 'Like I said, don't mention the "C" word. But it could mean that we have a method for arson here. I mean, had you any idea you could set a car on fire by leaving an oily rag on the engine block?'

Rhys shook his head. 'But then how do you get access to the engine without lifting the bonnet?'

Gil had the sense to realise, from Rhys's smirk, that this was rhetorical.

'Bonnet releases sometimes break or get stuck,' Rhys replied to himself in an almost gloat. 'I googled it. Mechanics and such have ways of opening them.'

'The quickest way to get the car to catch fire is to use rags soaked not in engine oil but in linseed oil,' Catrin explained. 'Craig showed me a report once of—'

'Linseed oil.' Rhys cut her off. He ran to his computer and played an arpeggio on the keyboard, blinking repeatedly as he waited for the information to load. 'Yes, it's there. On the forensic report. The sharpened stakes used to impale the Geoghans. There were traces of linseed oil.'

Another momentary silence descended as they thought all of this through. Catrin embellished her explanation with a video of linseed oil-soaked rags spontaneously combusting on a warm afternoon. 'Imagine what they'd do in a hot engine.'

'He's targeted DCI Tamblin,' Gil muttered, voicing everyone's thoughts.

'But why?' Rhys asked.

'Tâl,' Gil explained. 'He even marked the bloody car. This is payment, retribution, take your pick.'

'But for what?' Jess's voice came at them from the doorway.

Gil shrugged and offered a vague reply, 'For something to do with the Geoghans. That's the only thing we can be sure of for now.'

'Okay. Let's do as DCI Warlow suggested. Let's go back through everything we do know. Perhaps we've overlooked something. Catrin, go over what the indexers have added to the case file. It'll be a good way to catch up. Rhys, the CCTV. Gil, have a look over what DI Caldwell was supposed to have been dealing with.'

'Where is DI Cald—' Rhys's question turned to stone from the looks he got from his fellow officers. The youngest member of the team was learning when to keep his mouth shut.

The room went quiet. The team eased back into the bread and butter of the investigation. The hard yards. Yes, it was turning into a long day. But they were all convinced that this was where they were going to find the answers, too.

CHAPTER THIRTY-THREE

He approached the cemetery from the east, climbing through the wasteland, crossing the muddy bike track, black from the coal waste and ore spoil dumped there years before. Only a brown and white dog saw his approach. Something large with a bushy tail. He'd seen the dog before. It was harmless, friendly even. A mutt given free rein to wander by its owners up near the top of the hill.

The dog he didn't mind.

The heat of the late afternoon hung heavy in the air. The sun had gone, and thick clouds were accumulating in the west. The forecast promised thunder before nightfall. But not yet. Now was only stillness and the promise of a storm to come.

He'd seen the car fire on the motorway, astonished at the speed at which it caught. He'd followed Tamblin from Swansea, surprised that the officer travelled west, out of his patch. Even more surprised to see who he'd picked up at the address in Cross Hands.

Marius Stoica of all people.

Stoica wasn't a target, and he'd felt a moment's regret at what might happen if all went to plan. He had no argument with Stoica. If it hadn't been for him, he wouldn't have found the house. The convenient hiding place for the pigs.

When he saw the car veer towards the side of the road and the billowing black smoke, he knew he'd succeeded. He'd pulled onto the hard shoulder fifty yards back to watch through binoculars. But then Warlow appeared out of nowhere and ran to the car and pulled Tamblin away. Warlow's feats triggered others. And so, he had to assume that Tamblin might not be dead. Nor Stoica.

He was pissed off about the one; pleased for the other.

But there would be other chances. Other days when he would make Tamblin pay.

He crested the little rise at the rear of the cemetery. Through the trees to the right, up on the hill, houses looked down. But the foliage on the bushes and trees that surrounded the cemetery was summer-thick. No one would see him.

He crouched low, patted the dog. He could look down the length of the cut grass that made a central avenue through the gravestones. He sat and waited. No sound. No movement.

He was alone.

Staying close to the outer border, he hurried to the right, to his first stop. Two graves, side by side. His parents, separated by thirty years. His mother's death dated recently, only a couple of years ago. His father's twenty-eight years before hers.

He'd been six months old when his father's acute shortness of breath turned out to be a massive pulmonary embolus. Of course, he could not remember that. He'd been a baby. His mother told him this. Taught him it along with her wisdom. Read to him. All the old stuff. The fables and stories that she loved as a child growing up in the sixties. Did it all while her own health started to fail.

He came to her grave for atonement. To apologise for the mess he'd made of everything.

For how he'd been a terrible son.

To explain how he was making amends.

He hadn't been able to tell her this while she was alive. He hadn't been there for her in those final months. Something he regretted more than anything.

When he'd finished, he crossed the central path to a different part of the cemetery where three identical gravestones were laid, two at the back and one in front.

He stood at the base of the newest grave, its stone still untarnished by the elements, though it had been here far longer than his mother's had. But as with his own parents, he made sure these three stayed clean.

The family Kinton.

He'd barely known the elderly parents. He hadn't spent any time at the riverside cottage. That wasn't where he and James would play. He always thought of James as an older boy, though in truth he'd been in his early twenties when his own parents died. He'd looked like a boy, though. Slight, wiry, and with the mind of a boy inside that older head. Someone who didn't mind endlessly kicking a ball on the rugby pitch. Someone with a bike willing to explore the nooks and crannies of the rivers and old factories.

He knew that people thought it strange. He heard the rumours that it was a dangerous kind of friendship. But James Kinton had no motive, other than a desire to remain a child, the way his mind wanted him to stay. There'd been no suggestion of a sexual element to their relationship. Much later, when he understood these things, he would understand that James Kinton was a misfit: poorly understood, mercilessly bullied and teased during his miserable school years for what should have been classified as some kind of syndrome.

Autistic spectrum disorder were the words the coroner used at the inquest.

Peter poxy Pan was how James referred to himself, referencing something a teacher once said to him when he was expelled from a classroom for the hundredth time. But what he, the fourteen-year-old loner and James, the twenty-year-old child, shared was something he had never been able to share with his own family.

They'd been two outliers who'd found a mutual love of playing games. Not inside on a computer. His mother could never afford such things, anyway. But outside. In fields, on railway tracks, on the edges of rivers.

The Geoghans took all that away. And the police would have let them do it all again.

They had to learn.

'I'm on it, James,' he whispered. 'I'm on it.'

CHAPTER THIRTY-FOUR

Rhys took his car. He'd brought his own since his lift, namely Catrin, had not been available to share one this morning. This time, there was no discussion as to who drove as Catrin climbed into the passenger seat.

'You okay then, are you?' Rhys asked as they headed to Allt y Grug Road again.

'Fine,' Catrin said.

'Good, because they were all worried about you. As you weren't answering your phone and stuff. Imagining A&E or ITU or something.'

Catrin sat primly, facing forwards. 'No need to worry. As you can see, I've made a remarkable recovery.'

'You can though, can't you? Make a quick recovery. I went to visit my grandmother in hospitable once. Next day they shut the ward because of norovirus. Too late for me, mind. I got it. I mean, I've been sick before and I've had the squits, but this was like mega. Both ends at the same time. Double jeopardy. Bucket for the front, bowl at the back. I must have thrown up twenty times and gone through a roll and half of toilet paper. Like turning on a tap at the back end. Pouring out. I'll never forget it. Must be terrible to get that if you're already ill with something in hospital. It left me weak; I can tell you. Lucky my Mamgu didn't get it. You ever felt like that?'

Catrin, open-mouthed in horror, had turned to stare at Rhys during his extended description of diarrhoea and vomiting. 'I do now.'

Rhys ploughed on. 'What I'm saying is that by the following morning, I was A1 again. I scoffed a three-egg omelette, two sausages and a black pudding for breakfast. Plenty of room for all of that, obviously.' He grinned at the recollection. Food, either eating, talking or thinking about it, tended to make him happy. 'So, you know, you can feel better really quick.'

Catrin sighed. 'I don't feel better because I wasn't ill to start with.'

Rhys frowned. 'Hang on, I thought…'

'Best not to. Think, that is.'

'But—'

Catrin turned back to face front. 'KFC wanted me to do something for him at HQ.'

Rhys threw her a questioning look. 'What sort of thing?'

'Do not ask me that.'

'Something bad?'

'Bad enough.'

Rhys nodded. 'Sergeant Jones and DI Caldwell had a row. A bad one.'

'About what?'

'About the way he calls us all names. You know, KFC's always trying to be funny.'

'Very trying,' Catrin said. Under normal circum-stances, she might have added something along the lines of Gil being a fine one to talk. His attempts at being funny seemed to appeal to almost everyone besides her. But after today, she was beginning to wonder if the trouble was her, not him. A sobering assessment on the verge of being an existential crisis.

'Anyway, Sarge didn't back down. DI Caldwell doesn't like him very much.'

'Think that worries Gil?'

'No.' Rhys grinned. 'Funnily enough, he looked happy afterwards. Kept whistling that soppy tune, um: *You're Beautiful.*'

Catrin shrugged. 'It takes all sorts.'

———

ALONE IN THE INCIDENT ROOM, Gil pondered Warlow's words again. *Or what haven't we done properly?*

The business with KFC and Catrin irked the sergeant. Not his job to deal with DI Caldwell. That pleasure lay with the higher-ups. And though he'd considered going for an Inspector's job over the years, something always got in the way. Like kids, or looking after his dying father, or Operation Alice, or life. When he saw prats like KFC and what they seemed to get away with, justification for not scrambling for a foothold on the ladder always blossomed in his head. Not that he didn't take pride in the job. And part of that pride included mopping up the mess when someone hadn't been too careful.

HE STOOD up and walked to the board and checked on the actions laid out for KFC and Catrin. Normally, things left for the latter were a no-brainer. But she'd been distracted. Deliberately so, it seemed. Still, the prison angle remained an unticked box. Something Jess asked him about as well, and he hadn't yet done anything about it.

He remembered that one of Geoghan's cell mates had rung in with information about Karen Geoghan's car fire.

Information which Rhys took and ran with to good effect. After what had happened to Owen Tamblin and his car, Gil felt a strong urge to chase that one up again.

He found the number, went back to his desk, and dialled it.

'Yello?'

'Mr Masters, this is DS Jones, Dyfed Powys Police.'

'Right.'

'I'm following up the call you made regarding information on Derek Geoghan.'

'Jabba the gut. Yeah. What's he done now?'

'Thanks for the heads-up regarding Karen Geoghan's car. Turned out to be very useful.'

'Pissed off by that, was old Jabba. We used to call him that on account of him being big, like.'

Gil filed away this example of biting prison wit and pressed on. 'You were his cellmate when it happened?'

'I was. Went apeshit he did. Mind you, that was a fuckin' improvement on when he wasn't apeshit. Bit of a creep, like.'

Gil stayed silent, hoping Masters would expand on that. He did.

'I mean, you got to play the game in the nick. Try to get on, like. People said he was a creep, and he was, but he was alright with me. Worst thing about him, he liked to talk about the stuff he done. Braggin' about how he did the robbin'. Takin' the piss about people in wheelchairs and shit. I switched off, like.'

'You didn't mind that?'

'I did mind, but what can you do? Sometimes I'd just zone out and let him drone on. He used to say they was easy pickings, and people were thick. It got on some people's tits, mind. That's why no one lasted long in with him. I can't say I enjoyed it, but I played the game. I knew I'd be out of there in fourteen months, like. And 'cos I stayed with the old bastard, the screws were good to me. Perk of doublin' up with a dirtbag. And some people couldn't stand bein' in with him. Some asked to leave. Others, it got to them, like. I can understand it, too. Once or twice, I felt like throttling the bastard.'

Gil filed that way, but he was more interested in the fire. 'Did Derek Geoghan give any clue who he thought might have been responsible for setting Karen's car on fire?'

'Nah. Oh, hang on. He did go on about some woman who had a petition going to stop him ever gettin' out. He thought maybe she got someone to do it. But I don't remember any names, like.'

'Well, if you do, you have our number.'

'Yeah, sweet.'

Gil ended the conversation with that. Nothing new there, except a confirmation of what a miserable excuse for a human being Geoghan had been. But it led on to the petition woman again. Gil went back to the board and found her name before turning back to the case files once more.

———

HAVING SURVIVED three minutes of more 'wossname' from Gary Roberts and having made a fuss of Jenny the dog, Rhys and Catrin found themselves upstairs with his son Ian in what they could only describe as a games room. Had Gil been there, he might have told them that in days gone by, such a term applied to a room containing a billiards table, a bagatelle, a jukebox or a foosball table. But since it was now 2023, the better term was Gaming Room.

Ambient lighting from a vertical lightsabre lamp illuminated a curving desk. Rhys recognised the wheeled Secretlab high-back chair as a Gamers' must-have. Three screens made up the visual side of the home cinema get-up. Joysticks and control units had been stored away on an under-table shelf, leaving only a keyboard on show. Over-all, the impression was of a gamer who looked after his equipment.

'Wow.' Rhys's admiration shone through.

'A man cave,' Catrin said. 'Craig would love this.'

Ian shrugged. Unlike his father, he was a mid-thirties geek with all his hair and thick-rimmed glasses. 'Dad lives downstairs now. Because of his hip. I'm self-contained up here.'

'This is a nice setup,' Rhys said, nodding.

'Cheers,' Ian said. He moved a mouse and the screens lit up with a page from OCULONE filling the screen. 'Everything from the CCTV is on the cloud, but I've signed in, and the rest is up to you. It's organised by date so… Cup of tea?'

They gave their order, and Ian trotted off downstairs.

Catrin glanced around and spied a soft downtime chair in the corner.

'You can drive,' she said to Rhys and pulled the chair across.

Grinning, Rhys sat in the chair and started scrolling through the files. They had a date for when the Geoghans had last been seen in and around their home in Townhill. They had the date of the Amazon order, too. To be safe, Rhys worked forwards from there.

'We assume that he would have come up after dark?'

'Yes,' Catrin agreed. 'Let's go from 18th April.'

'What time was it dark on 18th April?'

Catrin tapped buttons on her phone. '8:28pm. That's sunset anyway.'

'Okay.'

Not often in investigations did they strike gold at the first attempt. Rhys had the replay on fast-forward, and every time he saw a car go up or down the road, he froze the frame and called out what he thought it was. But the majority did not turn off into Penmaen Street. Most drove straight uphill. The camera angle was such that they saw each vehicle side-on and only in black and white as they turned and before they swung out of view. No chance of a licence plate. After twenty minutes, they had thirty vehicles that had travelled up the hill between the hours of 9:30pm and sunrise at 6am. But only two had turned into Penmaen Street and only one had come back within an hour. A light-coloured van.

And that hour had been between 2:30am and 3:30am.

'The witching hour, as my dad calls it,' Catrin observed.

Ian came back with teas. Rhys asked him if he knew anyone who owned a light-coloured van living on Penmaen Street.

'There're only five houses up there. I don't know anyone with a van.'

Rhys and Catrin exchanged glances.

'Okay, so we do the same for the next week,' Catrin said. 'Then we fast-forward four weeks, see if we can find that van again.'

CHAPTER THIRTY-FIVE

Marius Stoica spent most of the journey from Ystradgynlais to Ammanford sipping from a bottle of water and coughing intermittently. Warlow steered the subject away from Tamblin and the fire and asked him about his HGV licence.

'Yes, I drive at home in Romania, but here, I need medical and CPC tests. I pass those and theory. Now I need to take the fresh course.'

'Refresher course?'

'Yes. The driving. I need practise. Is expensive but quickest way. I work at car wash to get money. But with family is not easy.' He stopped and coughed gently into his fist.

'How expensive?'

'Nearly two and a half thousand pounds. I am thinking of loan.' The words came out slowly and painfully. 'Many cars need washing to save enough, you know?'

Warlow nodded. He suspected that Heavy Goods Vehicle training schools would be cashing in on the demand for drivers. Wasn't it always the way?

Heartbreak's chords drifted up into the car.

Warlow took the call through the speaker.

'Evan, it's Molly.'

The skin on the back of Warlow's neck contracted. 'Molly, any news?'

'No. None.' Her voice sounded small. 'Mum said I should ring and tell you that. Sorry.'

'Can't be helped, Molly.'

Anger sparked in Molly's voice. 'Yes, it can. I could be helping find your dog. All my friends are out looking, and I'm stuck in the middle of nowhere because Mum has to work. She said she'd be taking me back down to Pembrokeshire this afternoon. Now she says it might be tomorrow.'

'Your mother is running a murder enquiry, Molly.'

'Yeah, but why does she have to? Why can't she be a stupid teacher or work in a factory or something? Then at least she'd have normal hours.'

'Hang on, am I still talking to the Molly who is considering a criminology degree at Uni?'

That stopped her for all of ten pensive seconds before the need to vent took over 'How can you be so calm? Why aren't you shouting at me for being so stupid and a feckless teenager?'

'Feckless teenager?'

'Yes.' She was spoiling for a fight. He could hear it in her voice, though he suspected the simmering anger was all self-directed.

'I'm a detective, Molly. So is your mother. That puts a whole different spin on feckless teenagers. The kind we meet have robbed their grandmothers to feed their habits. You are about as feckless as penicillin.'

That made her think. 'How can penicillin be feckless?'

'It can't. In fact, it's the exact opposite. It's saved millions of lives. The embodiment of effectiveness.'

'So now I'm penicillin?'

'Yes,' Warlow said, searching for the best way to extend his creaky metaphor. 'A bit furry round the edges, but all in all, good to have around.'

He could almost hear her smile. 'That is the worst example of trying to cheer me up I have ever heard.'

'Hey, I'm running pretty low on cheer-up juice myself.'

Next to him in the car, Stoica coughed and soothed it with another swallow of water.

'Is that Rhys with you?'

'No. Someone else.'

'Okay, then I'll leave you alone. If I hear anything, I will let you know. I promise. And I am still sorry.'

'I know you are. She'll turn up.'

Molly rang off without adding anything else.

Stoica lifted his face from a handkerchief. 'You lose dog?'

'Yes. She's been missing for a day now.'

'Is hard.'

'It is. I can't deny that.'

————

GIL AND JESS were busy at their desks when the door to the Incident Room opened, and Kelvin Caldwell walked in.

He paused, looked around, and cupped a hand to his ear. 'What's this, a Yoga class?'

'Hi, Kelvin. Good of you to call in,' Jess replied.

'I got lost. All these mountains look the same.'

'Re-training as a Sherpa not on your bucket list, then?' Gil said.

'Is that meant to be funny? Because if it is, it's stony ground.'

Gil shrugged. Jess cocked her head, bemused by the vitriol in KFC's reply. But she was saved any of his further rancour by the door opening again, this time more forcefully. Rhys strode in, all arms and legs, Catrin following behind.

'Result,' Rhys said, grinning.

'We think,' Catrin qualified the DC's enthusiasm with a more circumspect response.

'Christ, if it isn't Wonderboy and...' KFC paused, searching for an insult, finally settling on the ineffectual, '...Catwoman.' His retort brought the two younger officers up short. Catrin looked the more taken aback, shocked more by his presence than his biting wit. Rhys merely looked bemused.

'Afternoon, sir,' Catrin said.

'Oh, so you can tell the time, then,' KFC replied, glaring at her. 'Funny, I thought you had an appointment elsewhere.'

'Unfortunately, I was ordered back to the Incident Room by someone of higher rank, sir.'

'Who?'

'DCI Warlow.'

KFC wheezed out a laugh. 'I might have soddin' guessed. Did you stop to ask yourself why, Sergeant? Did you?' His belligerence brought Jess to her feet.

'Rhys, we'll have vespers in ten minutes. Can you get the kettle on? Kelvin. A word, please.'

'I'm listening.' KFC made no effort to move from where he was still staring down Catrin.

'Outside,' Jess ordered.

For one moment, it looked as if KFC might refuse. But then he muttered something too quiet for the others to hear, pushed open the door and walked out, not bothering to hold it open for Jess.

'Charming,' Gil said.

Jess paused in the doorway and turned to him. 'We'll definitely be needing emergency rations after this.'

KFC loitered in the corridor. Jess walked past him and

through the exit to the car park. A space that was turning out to be way busier than their interview room.

'So, what?' KFC asked. 'Couldn't you find the naughty step?'

'We're out here to save your blushes, Kelvin. Owen Tamblin's car caught fire as he was driving along the M4 with a potential witness. He's in the Burns Unit at Morriston.'

'No shit,' KFC said, but with a lack of any genuine feeling suggesting that, despite it being a sad day for Owen, this had bugger-all to do with him. And something in his eyes flared and flickered like the guttering flame of disappointment.

'We're treating it as a potential arson,' Jess explained.

'Really?'

'Yes, really, especially since Karen Geoghan's car caught fire in an Aldi car park. Something one of the prison witnesses told you, but which you declined to follow up.'

'Oh, come on.' KFC dripped with derision. 'How the hell was I supposed to know that would be significant?'

'You couldn't. No one except Rhys did. He talked to the Fire Officer. And whereas I agree that spontaneous combustion can occur, the chances of it occurring twice in the same case are nigh on infinitesimal, wouldn't you agree?'

'But arson?'

'Yes, arson.' Jess half-turned away and looked up, her exasperation showing in the way she ran a hand through the hair on top of her head. 'Which part of steady police work don't you follow, Kelvin? Rhys followed up a lead. He follows up on lots of leads. He does that in the expectation that most of them will get him nowhere. But he also knows that occasionally it will ring a big and a very loud bell.'

'Who is the arsonist?'

'We don't know, Kelvin. If we did, we probably wouldn't be having this conversation. Or are you going to suggest to me that Owen Tamblin, as a suspect in your mind, set fire to his own car and almost died in the process?'

KFC's mouth pouted. 'Could be he underestimated. Got it wrong somehow.'

'For God's sake, listen to yourself, man. This ends here. Whatever vendetta you have against Warlow and Owen went up in flames with Tamblin's Merc.'

The wind, still warm, gusted and blew a waft of Caldwell's cologne, sickly sweet, over Jess. It reminded her strangely of incense covering up the decrepitude and decay inherent in a Chapel of Rest.

'People don't change, Jess.'

'You sound like one of those idiots standing in front of a live feed from the International Space Station telling us they still believe the earth is flat. Get a grip, Kelvin. And those two members of my team that you insist on childishly insulting may have the only real lead we've had in this case. So, you have a choice now. Either go away and don't come back. Or come back in and do your job.'

Jess turned and left KFC with what she suspected was a smirk on his face. But what he really had was a lot of incense smelling egg.

Inside, Jess took hold of the tea Rhys had made for her and glanced at her watch. 'Okay, it's getting late, but I would really like to go over what progress we've made here.' She took a gulp of tea. 'Nice brew, Rhys.'

'Thank you, ma'am.'

Gil had laid out a display on his table. Jess took a custard cream, split it in half, dunked each in turn, and ate each half in two bites. She stood for a moment, with her eyes shut in near ecstasy. 'That is so good,' she said. 'Okay. Gil, you start us off—'

The door opened and KFC walked in. He avoided eye contact with everyone and walked to a desk where he sat attentively.

'Gil?' Jess prompted.

'Right. I've been going through the information Iona Michaels sent us. For those of you who have forgotten, she is the lady who set up an online petition to stop Geoghan's parole. Catrin asked her to collate a list of comments that might be construed as negative.'

'Or inflammatory,' Catrin said.

Gil sent her his classic one eyebrow-raised look. 'You've just hit the nail on the head, there. There are three entries from perhaps six months ago from someone who signed himself in as Charles Bronson, but who left three messages.'

Jabba the gut or his missus don't deserve to be let out. I would not piss on them if they were on fire.

I would piss on them first and then set fire to them.

I would like to see the f*****s burn.

'Who is Charles Bronson?' Rhys asked.

'An actor famous for one of the first citizen vigilante films: *Death Wish.*'

Catrin nodded. 'Oh, yeah. That's the one where his wife is killed, and his daughter attacked after a home invasion.'

'Exactly. Brutal in its day,' Gil added.

'How does that help?' KFC asked. 'It's an alias.'

Gil shook his head. 'It is. But there'll be a trail here. An electronic imprint.'

'I agree. We need to get the nerds onto this.' Jess nodded. 'Good work, Gil.' She turned to Rhys. 'You look like you're about to burst, so tell us what you found.'

Rhys stayed seated at his desk. 'We'll get the actual footage, but I used my phone to take a video of what the CCTV showed. It's in my emails now.'

He quickly outlined the scenario and dates while he clicked onto the email. Catrin stood at his elbow as they blew up the image to fill the screen.

'This vehicle drives into Penmaen Street on April 17th at 2:37am, stays one hour and then drives out. The same vehicle does exactly the same thing on May 23rd. At the same time, just after 2.30am, stays fifty-four minutes and then leaves.'

'No licence plates?'

'No ma'am. But as it swings round, I think I can see something in the windscreen. Some sort of permit. I think we might blow that up if we get a good enough still.'

'What sort of van is that?' Gil asked.

'Not sure. Might be worth a quick whizz around Google,' Catrin replied.

'Tidy,' Gil said, beaming at the two younger officers.

'Any joy with the Geoghans' phone records?'

Gil shook his head. 'Nothing stands out.'

Jess turned to Caldwell. 'While these three chase up their leads, why don't you put some fresh eyes on the phone records?'

'Good old scut work, eh? Why not?' KFC turned to his PC and jiggled his mouse with as much enthusiasm as a street cleaner after a rugby international in Cardiff.

CHAPTER THIRTY-SIX

WARLOW PULLED the car into the kerb at Stoica's partner's house in Ammanford.

'We'll probably need a statement about the fire,' Warlow said. 'But we can do all that here. No need for you to come back to Ystradgynlais. I'll send someone out.'

'Thank you.' Stoica undid his seat belt.

'If anything else strikes you, if you can think of anything to do with the Geoghans, give us a ring. Your partner has my number.'

Stoica nodded and stifled another cough. 'I am sorry I cannot help. I did not like prison. I do not want to go back there.'

Both men flicked their eyes across to the front door, which opened to reveal Teri Colson standing there, waiting.

'Sounds like it's worked as the deterrent it's meant as, then.'

'Not good to be foreigner in prison, you know? The funny accent. They call me Igor. Lucky for me I know someone in there at same time. Local boy. We do not share cell, but I spend time with him outside of cell during meals and in recreation room. He is young. Likes cars. Fast cars.'

'What was his name?'

'Iwan. Iwan Meredith.'

Nicu Stoica broke free from his mother's arms in the house doorway and ran towards the car. Stoica got out and, coughing still, swept the boy up in his arms.

'We'll be in touch,' Warlow said through the wound-down window and waited until Stoica disappeared inside the house before pulling away from the kerb and wondering why Stoica's last words bothered him so very much.

Molly's apology had brought Cadi back to his mind, but he needed to forget her now. Easier said than done, but something buried in his subconscious kept flickering like a failing torch. Flickering maddeningly but never quite lasting long enough so that he could see the detail of its light. There were many distractions in this case. Far too many. Some simply bizarre, like the elaborate way the bodies were treated, and the horror of the Geoghans' captivity and ultimate death. Some personal, like losing Cadi and dealing with Molly Allanby in a way that wouldn't jeopardise his relationship with her or Jess. And some unnecessarily foisted upon them, which was as good a way as any to label KFC – Kelvin Foisted Caldwell – for once. Warlow had to get his eye back on the ball if he wanted to help sort this case out. And yes, it was Jess's case on paper, but with what had happened to Owen, he knew with a gut-twisting certainty that both the injured DCI's and his own figurative DNA was plastered all over this one.

On the way back up to Ystradgynlais, Warlow took a left in Brynamman and headed up the mountain road to a spot where he could park the car and look out onto nothing. Look out and let whatever deductive juices he still had marinate in his brain.

It sometimes worked. Then again, it sometimes simply ended up in a nap. Both had their own significant merits.

———

'Sarge?' Rhys called out without letting his eyes leave the screen. 'What's this on the windscreen?'

Gil got up from his desk and walked across to where Rhys was sitting. The DS leaned forward and adjusted his glasses. A very grainy, pale rectangle occupied about half of the screen. An even more smudgy blue blob sat in the lower left-hand corner of the whitish rectangle.

'It's blue,' Gil said.

'I'm thinking football clubs,' Rhys said. 'Uh, Man City?'

'Nah, they're light blue. This is royal blue.'

'Oh,' Rhys sat up, eyes wide, 'Chelsea?'

'Yeah,' Gil conceded. 'Possibly. But the Bluebirds are closer to home. Cardiff City. Though we are in the Swansea Valley, so keep your voice down.'

From across the room, Catrin called out, 'Leicester City, Portsmouth, Millwall, Everton, Rangers.'

Gil turned his head. 'When did Gary Lineker walk into the room?'

Catrin replied without taking her eyes off the computer or her fingers off the keyboard, 'Or someone capable of posting a search term in Google for blue soccer teams, UK.'

She turned to grin at her two fellow officers and got up to join them at Rhys's screen. 'Pretty dense block colouring, though. Chelsea's lion is surrounded by white. Everton has a shield shape. But there is a half-circle of sorts here…' She peered closer and then stood back, a smile pushing the frown of concentration out of the way. 'That's not a football team. That's a Blue Badge.'

'Thanks for that clarification for the colour-blind,' Gil said.

'No,' Catrin said, extending the negative with a dollop of exaggerated patience. 'I mean *the* Blue Badge. As in the scheme that allows you to park in spaces for Blue Badge holders, access city centres, that sort of thing.'

'Oh,' Rhys said, peering hard again, his face six inches from the screen. 'Spot on, Sarge.'

'Tidy,' Gil said, before asking, 'How does that help?'

'Did the Geoghans have a Blue Badge? He might have nicked it from them,' Catrin posed the question, not really expecting an answer.

'Or,' KFC's voice came from behind a screen. 'It might be someone with a Blue Badge who has sod all to do with the case. I mean, is it likely that a Blue Badge holder over-powered the Geoghans?' They didn't need to read his expression. The sneer in his voice was enough.

'Kelvin, thanks for your erudite contribution.' Jess walked over to join everyone except KFC at Rhys's desk.

'One does what one can,' KFC said without the faintest hint of sensitivity towards the sarcasm in Jess's voice.

'Could be the car was stolen,' she suggested. 'Or that the driver knew someone Blue Badge eligible. That's how it works, I think. You can use your Blue Badges in taxis if you need to. By that I mean you can transport it to whichever vehicle you are using.'

'What about the van itself?' Gil asked.

'We've got side-on views only and a bit of the front as the vehicle turns,' Rhys said. 'No chance of a plate, ma'am. But this one has a high, square back end.'

Once again, Catrin, who'd returned to her desk, called out, 'I've got a few alternatives. There's the Fiat Doblo, Ford Tourneo, VW Caddy and one or two others. If we can get a better side-on view, you can start differentiating by the window design.'

KFC stuck his head up over his screen. 'So, are we now searching for a disabled arsonist with a thing for the Geoghans?'

'Pretty much,' Gil said. 'Unless you can come up with a better idea… Sir.' The gap Gil left between the sentence and the pre-nominal honorific – as he'd termed it in a discussion with Rhys about the military origins of such things – brought a sudden rush of colour to the DI's face.

Jess's phone ringing prevented the interchange from escalating.

'Ah, Evan. Let me put you on speaker.' Jess pressed some buttons and put the phone down on a desk at full volume. 'We've had a vespers, of sorts. Rhys and Catrin have come up with some CCTV footage of a likely vehicle that may have been involved in transporting the Geoghans. Any joy with Stoica?'

'No. Bugger-all. He's a bit shaken up. Any news on Owen Tamblin?'

'Nothing more. You?'

'His missus texted me to say he's stable. But that's all.'

The beat of silence that followed was full of collective relief. Though Warlow knew stable was a catch-all term for awaiting events, good or bad.

'I told Stoica we'd need a statement from him re the fire and that we'd get someone out there for that once he's feeling better.'

'You don't think he's involved with the Geoghans?' Gil asked.

'No chance. Wants to move on. Good luck to him. He had a hard time in the nick. Says he met up with a local boy. Does the name Iwan Meredith mean anything to anyone?'

Catrin's head shot up. 'Meredith? Yes, sir, it does.'

'How?' Warlow asked.

'As an inmate who shared a cell with Geoghan.'

This time, in the silence that rushed in, someone listening might have heard the sound of the oily meshing of gears.

'That must have been after Stoica was released,' Warlow said.

'I've got the dates, sir.' Catrin looked through her notebook. 'We went out to his last known address and spoke to his brother, who told us he was working away. DI Caldwell checked that one.'

KFC came round from his desk to stand, with folded arms, in front of Jess's phone.

'Yeah, I spoke to him. The guy's been in Scotland.'

'Berlingo,' Rhys said, causing everyone in the room to look at him.

'Are you playing online?' Gil asked, hitting the DC with a daggered look.

'Not bingo, Sarge. Berlingo. It's another option. It's a van with a squared-off back that could be easily converted for someone who was a Blue Badge holder.'

'Oh. My. God,' Catrin's voice was almost too soft.

'What?' Jess demanded.

'Meredith's brother, ma'am. Rhydian Meredith. He was in a wheelchair when we called, and the car in the driveway, if you could call it that, was a Berlingo.'

For several seconds, the only noise that came out of the phone's speaker was static.

'Tell me you checked on that call, Kelvin?' Warlow's voice crackled almost as much as the line. Full of suppressed anger.

'I spoke to the guy. He was in Scotland.'

'And you know that how, exactly?'

'He said he was.' KFC looked suddenly troubled.

'So, you then checked with his employer, right?'

Warlow's question was a rhetorical one. The absence of a reply from KFC answered it, anyway.

'Christ's sake, man,' Warlow bellowed. 'Basic bloody corroboration. Where does Meredith live?'

Catrin answered, 'It's in an out of the way spot, sir. West over the river in Cwmtwrch. Up the hill and then there's this bad road over—'

'The Patches?'

'I think that's what it's called. How do you—'

Warlow didn't let her finish. 'I just do. Right, I'm on the way there now. This might all be BS, but someone needs to check it out. I'm already more than halfway there. In the meantime, get Meredith's details up and check out his employer's address.'

The line died, leaving the whole room speechless.

'Should someone go with him?' Gil asked.

'Me,' KFC said. 'Evan wants everyone to believe this is my cock up. I want to be there when he sees he's wrong. Again.'

'Do you want some company?' Rhys asked.

KFC didn't turn around or reply. Jess looked at Rhys and shook her head as the DI disappeared through the Incident Room door. 'Let him go.'

'With a bit of luck, he'll get lost again,' Gil muttered.

'What was that Sergeant Jones?' Jess asked.

'Bit of throat clearing, ma'am. Nothing more.' He turned to Rhys. 'Right. You heard the man. Iwan Meredith. Let's see what we can find through the round window.'

Catrin and Rhys waited for an explanation. All they got from Gil was a shake of the head and a one-sentence wistful reply that left them none the wiser. 'Playschool?'

In response, both younger officers looked completely blank.

'*Arglwydd mawr*, might as well reference a cave painting.'

CHAPTER THIRTY-SEVEN

WARLOW TOOK the road across the River Twrch. *Afon Twrch*, to give it its Welsh name. A waterway, like so many in this area, birthed from the bowels of the high Fans of the Black Mountains. Its name, some said, was indicative of the twisting nature of its path, like the burrowing snout of a '*twrch*' or boar. Others, of a more poetic bent, associated the river's name with ancient ideas and beliefs, inextricably tied into the legend of *Twrch Trwyth*, the monstrous and venomous boar of *Trwyth*, the hunt for which, according to legend, drew King Arthur and his men into the tale of *Culhwch and Olwen*. Their quest, first to Ireland, and back across the Irish Sea into Wales cut a swathe through the Preseli Hills and along the edge of the Black Mountains, from Nevern, where ironically Warlow now lived, to the very borders of the country at the River Severn and on to Cornwall.

Warlow was no student of the *Mabinogion*, or the dark ages of this ancient land. But he was aware that men fought against other men here, perhaps even against creatures that were not men. And the river, in its geography, had always formed a boundary. In ancient times and in men's minds, a barrier from one world into another. These days, more prosaically, at its origin a border between the counties of Powys and Carmarthenshire, and here, at the lower end of the valley, between Powys and the county borough of Neath Port Talbot.

For those living in this area, these differences were meaningless: slightly different signage on the streets, refuse collections on different days. And yet, as Warlow climbed up on the mountain road, past the turning he and Rhys had emerged from after their dismal journey across the Patches, and on towards *Erw Foel*, he couldn't help but wonder what visitors of a thousand years ago might have made of this inhospitable place. There would have been acres of woodland, no doubt. Vast forests not yet culled for armadas or houses. Ideal territory to hide a poisonous boar.

Now the trees were gone, and the moorland stretched in all directions. Though it was only a little after seven in the evening, the promised change in the weather was approaching fast from the west in the shape of heavy clouds the colour of a ripe bruise. Catrin had texted him the map she'd used to find the place, along with a warning about missing the turning. As a result, Warlow found it on the first attempt.

Invisible from the road, the property emerged in the hollow as he descended along the lane. He stopped halfway along to survey the property. Beyond the house, a stand of trees suggested that the building had somehow walked out of that place of shelter and might creep back in there at night like some kind of animal.

'No doubt on chicken's legs,' Warlow muttered to himself.

The Berlingo, more pale-grey than white, sat parked to one side, in amongst the flotsam that rendered the place as uninviting a property as Warlow had ever visited. And he had visited many a sleazy dump in his time. Rat-infested squats where the junkies who lived there had about as much idea of cleanliness as a dung beetle. Strange remote farmhouses where the owners saw nothing wrong with sharing their living room with a dozen hens and did little or nothing to tidy up after hens did what hens were supposed to do: crap everywhere.

And yet here, at *Erw Foel*, something else assailed his senses, something he couldn't quite put a finger on. There was poverty here, real poverty, as well as a sense of neglect and dereliction. The occupier had either abandoned all hope of making the place acceptable or had made a huge effort to make it appear so. He put himself in KFC's place for a moment. Easy to see how a slacker like him might want to spend as little time here as possible. Catrin, on the other hand, would have wanted to scratch the surface. Like Warlow did. Especially now that they had a connection between one of the Merediths and Stoica.

Warlow took his foot off the brake and eased the car along the final fifty yards towards the property. He pulled up behind the Berlingo, got out, and walked around to the front of the van. A Blue Badge was stuck to the lower right inside of the windscreen. He turned and picked his way through the debris to the front door and rang the bell. He was on the point of ringing it again when the door opened on a safety chain and a man's voice asked, 'Help you?'

'Mr Meredith? I'm Detective Chief Inspector Warlow. Would you mind answering a few questions about your brother?' Warlow held up his warrant card.

'Iwan? I've spoken to you lot once.'

'I know. But with this sort of investigation, we often need to double-check information.'

'Okay, hang on, I'll let you in.' The safety chain rattled, and Rhydian Meredith swung the door open to reveal himself. An Iron Maiden T-shirt covered his top half, jeans-clad legs bent in the wheelchair. All topped off by an impressive beard. Warlow did his utmost not to stare at the man's damaged face. Meredith reversed his wheelchair along a narrow passage. He did so with practised ease, reversing into an open doorway.

'Come into our parlour,' Meredith said.

Warlow followed, shutting the front door behind him. It was stifling inside the house. A glance down the corridor showed a dark kitchen, and with the door closed, no natural light reached into the passageway. From somewhere, the slightly threatening repetitive chords of a heavy metal band filled the space. The volume dropped only slightly when Warlow entered the room where Rhydian Meredith waited for him.

'Thanks for speaking to me,' Warlow said.

'It's fine. I'm not exactly busy.' Meredith kept his face down, his long hair falling like a curtain to cover some of the scars.

'You lived here long?'

'I grew up here. Me and my brother.'

There must have been something in Warlow's expression that demanded more of an explanation because Meredith obliged. 'We could have done it up, but my mother, she was into local history and that. This place has been here a long time. Out back there are more rooms lower down. Used to be a slaughterhouse at one time. People brought their pigs here to bleed them. Anyway, my mother wanted it kept like it had been. Bloody mad if you ask me.'

Warlow had to agree with that. 'Your brother, still away, is he?'

'Yeah. Up north.'

'Does he drive your car at all?'

Meredith made a sound in his throat. The descriptive term that sprung into Warlow's head was a guffaw. 'He's banned from driving. Five years on release. So, no is the answer to that.'

'When was the last time you saw him?'

Meredith shrugged. 'Couple of months.'

'Do you have details about his workplace?'

'Good question. I've probably got them somewhere.'

'Do you mind if I see them?'

'Yeah. Give me five minutes and I'll dig them out. Cup of tea?'

For one moment, Warlow considered offering to make it, but then caught himself. This man lived alone in this house and had come to terms with whatever challenges he faced. He didn't need to be patronised. 'Milk and one.'

Meredith left the room, leaving Warlow alone in the dim, musty parlour that had a peculiarly damp vegetative aroma. A heavier than usual net curtain obscured the view, and though the curtains proper were not drawn, the light that came through cast deep shadows around the heavy furniture. Pieces that looked as if they had been here since at least the sixties or seventies. An ancient box TV occupied one corner and the stuffy corduroy settee looked in need of a good hoovering. An open fireplace had unburned logs in the grate. On the walls, the flock wallpaper in a blue flowered pattern lent the room a gothic air. No photographs or paintings adorned the walls. Instead, half a dozen framed, and embroidered hangings took pride of place. Warlow could vaguely see some sewn words. Proverbs or bible quotes, he guessed. Though the light was so poor, he struggled to make anything out. He tried the light switch. Nothing happened.

He fished out his phone and fired up the light and held it up to a wall hanging.

.   .   .

To bear with patience wrongs done to oneself is a mark of perfection, but to bear with patience wrongs done to someone else is a mark of imperfection and even of actual sin.

THE SOUND of a car pulling up drew his attention back to the window. He crossed to it and pulled back the heavy net. Layers of grime on the glass of the panes meant his efforts reaped little in the way of reward. Outside, a red BMW parked next to his and KFC climbed out. Warlow sighed and considered waving, but instead of walking towards the door, KFC walked across to Warlow's Jeep and peered in through the passenger-side window. From inside the parlour, Warlow ducked away and let the curtain fall back so that only the tiniest crack allowed him a view. KFC looked up and around, like someone trying to make sure he wasn't being overlooked. Quickly, he put his hand on the Jeep's passenger-side door and opened it. Warlow had not locked the vehicle, and the door opened quietly.

'What the hell are you doing, Kelvin?' Warlow muttered before stepping out into the corridor and calling out, 'One of my colleagues has arrived. Okay if I open the door?'

The music did not diminish in volume and Warlow doubted he'd been heard. He shrugged, stepped towards the front door, and pulled it open just as KFC arrived on the doorstep. The DI blinked in surprise. 'What are you, clairvoyant?'

'No. But I've got a pair of eyes. What were you doing in my car?'

'Being careful. You left it unlocked.'

'Yes, I left it unlocked. Why is that any of your business?'

'Hey, I was only checking. For all I knew, you could be

asleep in the back seat. I've been known to grab a few zeds while waiting for backup.'

Warlow peered at KFC, aware that here was a man of devious intent. 'Except I didn't know you were coming.'

'Oh, Catwoman not tell you?'

'Catwoman?'

'Catrin, your lapdog sergeant.'

'No, she did not. And we're not all slackers catching zeds in our cars, Kelvin.'

KFC shrugged. 'So, where's R2D2?'

'Christ, man. Have a bit of respect.'

'Okay, okay, Jesus. Talk about not being able to take a joke.'

'Jokes are meant to be funny. That's where you fall down.'

'Touchy. Still not found your dog?'

Warlow turned away. If he thought the bastard had said that with a smile, he'd probably hit him. Best he remained in ignorance. 'We're in the parlour. He's gone to make us some tea.'

'Great. I hope to God he's bleached the cups.'

CHAPTER THIRTY-EIGHT

Now that they had a point of focus in the Incident Room, gradually, the pieces of the puzzle started to come together, helped in no small part by a fresh round of tea and the away box being rifled once more. While they sipped and dunked, the team worked steadily through their to-do lists.

Gil got on the phone with the liaison officer from Cardiff Prison. Catrin pulled up Kinton's file and Rhys went through the information Michaels had given them about people who'd commented on the petition in detail. Jess paced back and forth in front of the board, looking at the images and scraps of information, the timeline, the addresses.

Gil was the first to come up with something useful. He put the phone down, sat back and turned, with a slightly bewildered look, at Jess.

'Iwan Meredith ended up doubling up with Derek Geoghan. In fact, he volunteered. But he was removed for attacking Geoghan in his cell after only four hours. Lost it big time. If someone hadn't stopped him, it could have been very bad.'

Jess frowned. 'We know from your other prison source, uh, Masters, that Geoghan was an unpleasant cellmate. '

'He liked to talk about what he'd done,' Gil said. 'That could have been too much for Meredith.'

'What was Meredith in for again?'

Gil turned back to the computer. 'Road rage. Exacerbated by a history of other driving offences. Oh, hang on. The month after he passed his test, he was involved in an accident in which his brother was severely injured.' Gil read from the screen. 'Says here that the brother, uh, Rhydian Meredith, had underlying problems. A spinal deformity. Scoliosis – which Wikipedia says is a curved spine.'

'He was in a wheelchair when we called round to see him,' Catrin confirmed.

'The RTA caused burns, bilateral hip fractures, ankle, and shoulder dislocation. A spinal fracture, too,' Gil read out. 'If he wasn't in a wheelchair before the accident, he probably was after it.'

Rhys swung around in his swivel chair. 'I'm not sure if this is significant, but the "I'd set them on fire and wouldn't bother to piss on them" post on the petition site appeared the day after Meredith was released from prison.'

Jess nodded. 'He wouldn't have been able to post in jail. No access there. It's hardly proof positive, but it fits. Good work, Rhys.'

'Kinton,' Catrin announced with an urgency that drew everyone's attention.

'Who?' Gil asked.

'James Kinton. His case is what links Owen Tamblin and DCI Warlow to the Geoghans. His death is what finally sent Derek Geoghan to jail. Kinton was found starved to death and chained up like an animal on a property not far from where DCI Warlow is now.'

'Right,' Jess said. 'But how does that fit with Meredith?'

'I've been going through the Kinton file. Buried in there are interviews with people who last saw Kinton alive. One of those is from a fourteen-year-old who was often seen in Kinton's company. That's an interesting one. Apparently, Kinton had issues. He was a bit challenged, according to the files. Liked to spend time with younger kids.'

'Any suggestion of—'

'No. Nothing like that. He'd been assessed by school psychologists as having developmental delay at the social and emotional level. Autistic spectrum disorder are the big words. He was a grown man but had the mental age of a younger teenager. The point is, the fourteen-year-old who was interviewed and gave a statement was Iwan Meredith.'

'Shit,' Gil said. 'Why didn't DCI Warlow remember that?'

Jess answered, 'Evan talked to me about how the Kinton case was complicated. Ended up being run by South Wales Police in the end. Evan was involved, but the donkey work was done by Owen Tamblin and the Swansea team. They would have run the interviews. Sounds like Meredith's statement would not have been vital to the case. Just a ticked box. It's always complicated when a case spans two Force areas. My old boss used to say that border deaths were nobody's deaths.' She stopped, and so did everyone else. No point getting overexcited about this yet, but her instincts were telling her otherwise. And judging by the expectant hum that seemed to permeate the room, it was a shared sensation. She let the tiniest of thrills dance over the skin of her scalp and pointed at Rhys. 'We have Iwan Meredith's number, don't we?'

Catrin nodded. 'We do. DI Caldwell contacted him.'

'He did. And Meredith told him he was in Scotland. We know the date that call was made, right, Catrin?'

'We do ma'am. The same day we visited Rhydian Meredith.'

'Rhys, get on to the mobile provider and ask them to find out where he took that call.'

Rhys nodded. He'd asked for cell site analysis before and had a number he could dial for technical help.

Jess drew in a lungful of air and let it out slowly. This was good. She felt as if they were getting somewhere at last. She toyed with ringing Warlow with the intel, but it shouldn't take Rhys long to track down the information on where Meredith had been when he'd taken Caldwell's call. Once she had that, she'd let him know.

Sod it. she'd text him now to tell him that Meredith was looking more and more like a possible.

———

'Jesus, hard to believe people can live like this, isn't it?' KFC poked at the corduroy sofa with a gloved finger and an expression of profound distaste. Warlow noticed he'd put gloves on before he'd even entered the property.

'Some people have no choice,' Warlow replied.

'Really? Some new disease, like an allergy to the Hoover?'

'The man's in a wheelchair, Kelvin. Or is this you being disability blind for the sake of wokeness?'

'Careful. You should make sure that disability is still on the okay list. They could have you up in front of an Inclusivity Committee for that.'

'You're a fine one to talk. R2D2 my arse.'

KFC grinned and walked over to the TV. 'I believe in saying it as I see it. Otherwise, what's the soddin' point?'

'The point is in not being offensive.'

KFC pressed the on button on the TV. Nothing happened.

'Why are you even here?' Warlow asked.

'I'm familiar with the witness, remember? And I don't like the fact that you're checking up on me. Casting aspersions about how I do my job. I thought I'd come along and enjoy the moment when you realise that this is the dead end at the top of the garden path where all the wild geese live.'

Coming from anyone else, this childish suggestion of schadenfreude as a motive might have been laughable enough for Warlow to dismiss it and demand the real reason. But this was KFC. And his prat credentials and pettiness made it all too believable.

A buzz from his phone prevented any further discourse for the moment. He read the message twice before looking up at a frowning KFC.

'What?' The DI asked.

'Iwan Meredith attacked Geoghan in his cell in prison. He also gave a witness statement in the Kinton case that Owen and I were involved in. The case that put the Geoghans away.'

Disbelief crawled over KFC's features. He managed only to utter a feeble, 'What?'

'Exactly,' Warlow said. 'What? As in, what the ghanta, as my ex-partner from the Met, Ajay used to say, have you been doing all this time, Kelvin?'

'Now hang on—'

But Warlow stopped him with a raised hand and a cocked head. The music had changed, dipping slightly in volume, as if a door had been closed between where they were and its source.

'This tea is taking an awful long time to make,' Warlow muttered.

KFC hit the wall switch.

'Not working,' Warlow said and walked out of the room.

KFC followed. 'Where are you going?'

Warlow paused in the dark passage and turned back. 'There's a wrongness about this place. I felt it as soon as I walked in. And now it's gone into overdrive. I'm going to find Rhydian Meredith.'

'I thought he was makin' tea?'

'So did I. Now I'm not so sure.'

Warlow headed down the dimly lit passage that got darker the further into the house they ventured. So dark he used his phone as a torch to light the way. Not one of the light switches worked, yet the music still played.

'Someone's been selective with the fuse-box, I'd say,' Warlow grunted. As much for himself as KFC.

They entered the kitchen. A small room with the windows boarded up and as dilapidated as the rest of the house. Mismatched cupboards with clear plastic handles and a Formica-topped table pushed up against one wall. Two chairs with tubular steel frames and canvas seats stained by God alone knew what sat next to the table.

The officers scanned the room, each one taking a side to pick over.

'Aye, aye,' KFC said. 'Look what we have here.'

Warlow turned to see KFC holding out a small phone. Nothing fancy. No touchscreen. Just a bog-standard Nokia. Warlow took it and pressed the power button. The phone lit up. But the requested password stopped any further assessment.

'A burner?'

'Looks like it,' KFC said. 'I take it back, Evan. Maybe there is something fishy going on here.' He held out a gloved hand. 'Better bag it up before you cock up the evidence trail.'

Cursing silently, Warlow handed it back, took out some gloves from his pocket and slid them on, before looking around for anything else that might be useful.

A small ramp ran over the threshold of the doorway they'd walked through, and the same arrangement was repeated at the exit. A doorway that should, by rights, have opened out into a garden, or at least the outside, but instead merely showed another dark space beyond.

'Where the hell does that go?' KFC asked.

'No idea. But I suspect you and I are going to find out. Put your phone on silent and follow me.'

CHAPTER THIRTY-NINE

WARLOW LED. Outside the kitchen door, a ramp led down onto a long flagstone-floored corridor. Above, a dark, corrugated-tin ceiling, decorated with flaking paint and thick cobwebs, made up the roof. Either side the walls were of stone, or where the stone had fallen away, patched and repaired with rough breezeblock and filled in with render. A cool waft of air promised something bigger at the end. Ten yards further on, they found it. A long, low shed partitioned off, windowless, smelling of damp, perhaps twenty-five yards long, with deep shadows at the end. More rusting corrugated iron partitions separated off stalls on one side, open to the middle. And above the music, another noise, a moaning wind that rose and fell, funnelled by some quirk of topography to rise and fall like some unnameable beast calling to its lost children.

'What the bloody hell is this?'

'A place where animals were kept.'

'Animals?'

'For slaughter.'

Warlow walked on through the oppressive darkness, his phone's light strong enough only to cast a circle of light a few feet ahead. But the music drew him on. Much louder now in this enclosed space. He counted fifteen stalls before they came to a junction. More darkness to right and to left. He envisioned another shed at right angles to the one they'd walked along, but the music came from the left.

They entered a more open space. A central area with a drain at the centre of the flagstone floor. To the left, a modern sound system blared out the music. Warlow stepped over to it and shut it off, the tail end of a harsh chord ringing in his ears for seconds after the noise ceased.

'There must be power somewhere.' He searched the walls and followed the cable from the sound system. Next to a galvanised-steel plug, a pull switch. Warlow yanked, and the room filled with light from strips tied to the roof. What it showed sent a bucket of ice cascading into his gut.

At the edge of the room, next to a grimy wall, a table had been set.

Four mannequins – two adults, two children – sitting around a table. Each mannequin had its eyes removed and replaced with red light bulbs. Each one, too, had one arm removed and red paint splashed on the torso near the armhole. Said arms were on a platter in the middle of the table, around which the mannequins all sat.

He'd seen this image before, sent to him as a greeting card. Or as a warning. He realised he'd stopped breathing and heard his lungs heave as he finally gave in to a lack of oxygen.

'Jesus. Pass the Chianti and fava beans.' KFC stood staring.

Warlow took no notice. Something different about the setting bothered him. And then he saw it. Two more chairs had been set. He remembered four. Here there were six. Two empty spots waiting to be filled.

'What the fuck is this, Evan?' KFC asked.

'I have no idea, other than the fact that it looks like we've found our killer.'

'Yeah, where is Meredith?'

'I don't know. I—' It struck him then, like a blow from some unseen creature. He flinched at the recall.

'What?'

'In the parlour. There are writings on the wall. I thought they were biblical, but they aren't. They're sayings or proverbs.'

'What are you talking about?'

'I'm talking about not listening to answers when they're handed to you on a plate. We're meant to be here. At least, I am. He's been waiting for me, and for Owen Tamblin I guess.'

'You are making no sense at all,' KFC complained. 'Who has?'

'Meredith.' He used his phone and typed in the remembered words of the embroidery on the wall. *To bear with patience wrongs done to oneself is a mark of perfection…*

He got the rest of it in four seconds and read it out.

To bear with patience wrongs done to oneself is a mark of perfection, but to bear with patience wrongs done to someone else is a mark of imperfection and even of actual sin.

Not Aesop, but Thomas Aquinas, according to his search engine.

That didn't matter. There were more quotes on the parlour wall. Some of them might well have been gems from Aesop. No doubt what they were witnessing here was some kind of twisted interpretation. A meaning that perhaps only an insane mind might understand. Because Warlow was convinced now that they were dealing with an unhinged Meredith here.

'We need help.' Warlow turned and began walking out of the space.

'That's the most sensible thing you've said all day,' KFC agreed and hurried after the senior officer.

———

'Bingo,' Rhys said, loud enough to grab everyone's attention. He'd been on the line to Vodafone and his exclamation coincided with the handset being put back into its cradle.

'I don't suppose it's politically correct to say two fat ladies these days, is it?' Gil said.

'Never was,' Catrin added.

'There are some good ones, mind. Like "Keep 'em keen". That's nineteen, by the way.'

'Up north, we are more direct. "24" is "Did you score",' Jess explained.

'I wasn't actually playing Bingo,' Rhys interjected, looking crestfallen. 'It was more an expression of success. Like, yay or eureka.'

'We know, Rhys.' Catrin put on an indulgent smile. 'It's just that you are such an easy tease.'

'What have you got for us?' Jess asked.

'It's the mobile provider, ma'am. The call to Iwan Meredith's phone that DI Caldwell made was picked up by Meredith at 1:45pm. But the cell site analysis from Meredith's phone puts it in the SA postcode.'

'That's around here?'

'Yes ma'am.' Rhys walked to the board and drew a circle on the map from an image on his phone. 'Within this area.'

Jess followed him. 'What's that in the middle?'

Rhys stared at where her finger was pointing. 'That's Allt y Grug Cemetery, ma'am.'

'*Arglwydd*,' Gil said, pushing back from his desk.

'That isn't the worst of it,' Catrin said, tilting her

screen so that everyone could read it. It was a page from the Western Mail. From the height of the pandemic, when so much else was going on. And though horrific in content, it had only made page four.

BODY OF WOMAN FOUND MUMMIFIED AT ISOLATED HOUSE

THE SEMI-PUTREFIED corpse of a woman has been found eight months after she was last seen alive. Non Meredith was discovered by a postman at her home in the Swansea Valley. A long-term sufferer of chronic pulmonary disease, she had self-isolated for months. A spokesman for South Wales Police said that foul play was not suspected. A friend of Mrs Meredith's who had lost contact after moving to a care home, told the Western Mail that Mrs Meredith had been a wonderful mother to her two children. But her failing health over the last few years had been a constant worry.

THE SCREEN CHANGED as Catrin clicked her mouse. 'This is the coroner's report. Nothing to suggest anything criminal. Looks like she got the virus and became too unwell to get help.'

'Bloody hell,' Rhys said. He spoke for them all.

Gil seemed to be struggling with understanding what he'd read. 'Hang on, what about Rhydian Meredith? Where was he when all this was happening?'

Catrin answered, 'He met us at the door of the property in a wheelchair.'

'Did he?' Gil asked, suspicion adding weight to his words.

The whole team exchanged looks as they tried to tie it

all together. Catrin scrambled for her mouse, clicked and clicked again.

'Oh shit,' she half whispered as her eyes scanned the screen.

'What?' Jess demanded.

'The social worker's report on Iwan Meredith for the courts, ma'am. Home circumstances. I should have seen this. I should have—'

'Just tell us, Catrin,' Gil said, injecting some urgency.

'Iwan Meredith lived alone with his mother. She wasn't young having children. Forties, it looks like. Late marriage. His brother, because of the injuries sustained in the crash, was in a long-term rehabilitation centre for spinal injuries in Oswestry. Somewhere called Gladstone Ward.'

Gil made the call. It took three minutes for him to confirm that Rhydian Meredith was still an inpatient there.

'So, someone is pretending to be Rhydian Meredith?' Rhys asked.

'Correction. Iwan Meredith is pretending to be his disabled brother,' Gil said.

'But why?' Rhys looked at the big sergeant in bewilderment.

'Because he's been banned from driving,' Jess said, finally seeing it. 'But if the DVLA weren't informed otherwise, Rhydian Meredith's licence would still be valid. He'd still be able to use the Berlingo.' Jess pivoted away, her eyes raking the board again.

Gil reacted first, with Rhys a close second. Both officers stood up and reached for their jackets. 'We need to get over there,' Gil said.

Jess nodded. 'I'll get hold of Evan.'

Catrin got up from her seat. 'Ma'am, I might be more use—'

'Go. The more of you, the better.'

———

This time, KFC led the way back. 'So, the animals were kept here, waiting for their turn to be slaughtered?'

'Looks like it.'

'Christ, what a horror show.'

'I doubt there was much animal welfare in those days.'

KFC talked as he walked. 'But what's the deal with the bloody mannequins?'

'I'm no forensic psychologist,' Warlow said, 'but my guess is he's somehow recreating his family. Or a family, at least. Some kind of idealised facsimile. Who knows?'

A sudden drumbeat of noise stopped both men in their tracks.

'What the hell is that?' KFC looked around as if the source of the noise might emerge at any moment out of the rough ceiling and walls.

Warlow had the answer. He pointed upwards. 'Rain. On a corrugated roof. And it sounds heavy. The storm has arrived.'

'Jesus. I nearly crapped myself then. This place gives me the creeps. It's not helped by us having no idea what this bloke is capable of.'

Warlow agreed but saw no reason to embellish the DI's thought processes.

'I mean,' KFC continued, 'he might be stalking us right now.' He stopped moving. They'd gone about halfway along the stall area; the waiting room of death.

Warlow sighed. 'Are you talking out loud for the sake of it, or does this train of thought have an actual destination?'

KFC half-turned and dropped his voice. 'All I'm saying is that we need to be careful. One of us could get badly hurt here.'

Warlow's irritation flared. 'You're making no sense, man?'

KFC turned quickly, the light from his torch momentarily blinding the DCI. Warlow brought his hand up to protect his eye. 'You're right, Evan. Now isn't the time for this kind of talk. We need more action, not conversation.'

'Isn't that from a so—'

KFC stretched out the hand not holding the phone, and something hit Warlow on the right side of his chest. A slight tap. But, like the sting of a wasp, it was only after that initial awareness that the real pain came. An electroshock of fifty thousand volts seizing up his muscles. He jerked to the side and fell face first into a stall. The pain was worse than anything he had ever experienced as his muscles spasmed.

His thoughts were only of the crackling intensity of the pain. He tried to scream, but his jaw muscles cramped as he hit the ground and all he could do was lie there like a tense strand of wire.

A strand of wire that had just been tasered.

It ended as quickly as it had started. Warlow's body relaxed as he sucked in air.

'Golden opportunity mate.' KFC's voice was behind him. Warlow turned his head. He felt weak, drained, but knew he had to move.

'Uh, uh.'

Another crackle, another spasm, the pain even more intense than before. This time Warlow did scream. He had no control over it. When it stopped, he lay still, hearing his pulse jackhammer in his ears. His muscles quivered. His whole body shook.

'Thanks for putting your prints all over that burner. I'll stick that in your car so they'll find it. Picked a knife up on the way through the kitchen, too. You didn't see that. Just like you didn't see me coming.'

Warlow's breathing was a ragged gasp. He could not have said anything even if he'd had the strength. KFC walked closer. Warlow knew what was coming, but even so, when the taser fired again, he could do nothing but give in to the horrifying convulsion. This time, he tasted coppery blood and knew he'd bitten his tongue.

When it stopped, KFC laughed softly. 'Fucking killer, isn't it? Just so's you know, I planted the seed of your involvement with organised crime in Catwoman's head. Now they'll find the burner and the knife I picked up from the kitchen as the murder weapon – the weapon that kills you – which will have Meredith's DNA all over it. And none of mine 'cos I wore gloves. Schoolboy error that one, Evan. Shall we do it once more, just for kicks?'

The taser discharged. This time Warlow half expected it and gritted his teeth. Even so, it was no better than the times before. When it ended, he was not capable of moving. He felt like he'd been in the gym for a week. His muscles leaden from an outpouring of lactic acid.

'I'm going to stab you in the back now. Then I'm going to run off and call for help. Explain how I barely managed to get away. Maybe they'll find Meredith, maybe not. Who cares if he denies it? He's obviously a head-case. Davenport will have you as his OG source, he'll wet himself with joy and they'll be off my back for a good long while.'

Warlow twitched and tried to push up.

'Nah, don't move, Evan. You know what'll happen.' KFC chuckled. 'Your mate Lewis got cocky. Spent too much money too quickly. I mean, what copper, bent or otherwise, buys a yacht for fuck's sake? But it doesn't matter now. I have you to sacrifice. All good. Ready? Here comes number five.'

But it didn't come. Instead, both men heard something else. The click of a switch as the light from the mannequin room flicked off, followed by a mechanical squeak, slow and repetitive. Warlow tilted his head once more, aware that at any second KFC might fire the taser. With the probes still attached to his chest as they were, Warlow felt helpless. But KFC's torch illuminated the dark passage and lit up the source of the noise; an empty wheelchair rolling towards them. Warlow strained to peer back over his own shoulder. KFC loomed over him, but his attention was on the wheelchair.

KFC couldn't see what Warlow could see in the thin grey light behind the DI. The shape of a man with a deformed head. The silhouette of a monstrous pig. But Warlow noted that for only a few seconds. Because the shape had something in its hands. Something long and heavy.

The wheelchair stopped. As did the squeaking.

In its place came the noise of heavy breathing and at last KFC became aware of something behind him.

He pivoted, his phone clattering to the floor. But too late to shield himself from the blow that had already begun, and the axe that came down and struck him on the shoulder, severing muscle and bone, causing Kelvin Caldwell to scream like a slaughtered pig.

CHAPTER FORTY

WARLOW LAY WHERE HE WAS, hidden in the stall, unable to move any of his beleaguered limbs. He knew what tasers did. Knew that with each additional burst, the risk of his heart stopping increased. But all of that drowned beneath the sickening sound of a metal blade hitting wet flesh. Mercifully, KFC stopped screaming after the third blow.

In the darkness, Warlow waited for the axe that would split his skull. His ragged breathing rasped in his own ears, but the rain drowned most of everything else out. Until it diminished enough for the noise of something heavy being dragged to drift through to his brain. Someone was pulling Caldwell's body away towards the mannequin room. He'd seen the ferocity of those first two blows in the phone's dim light, the rage behind them. KFC would not have survived such an attack.

Warlow had no idea if the pig man knew he was in the stall. But there'd be the wires from the taser, and a simple inspection would show where they led. The need to move galvanised him. But all he managed to do was roll over onto his back. It took a lot of effort. Moving all four limbs took even more. He felt heavy and sluggish as he rolled back onto his front and tried to push up. His arms started to quiver, and he fell back, hitting his head on the floor, air huffing out of his lungs. Then he tried again and got onto his knees. The pitch blackness of the stall threatened to disorientate him, but he didn't try to turn around. Instead, still on all fours, he yanked off the taser clips and backed out.

He'd been tasered once before. All part of the training to see its effects at first-hand. But being shocked four times was not to be recommended. Everything took four times more effort than it had before, and someone had tied lead weights around his arms and his thighs.

He gritted his teeth and crawled forward until all that was left inside the partition was his head. It was then that the music started up again. He froze. Not being able to see was now a huge disadvantage. Slowly, Warlow moved into the stall again and this time turned around. Now he moved forward on all fours, his head exiting the stall first this time. He peered down the passage. A red light oozed out from where the music blared.

Not good. He had to get away from this spot. He pushed up into another crouch, his back muscles screaming in protest as he bit back a groan. He put one hand on the rough wall as support, managed to get up into a half-crouch and began to move. He almost lost his balance as his foot lost purchase. He looked down and noticed he was standing in a black pool.

KFC's slick blood

Warlow shook his head. Not only from the horror of it but from something else, less definable.

His breath heaved in and out as if he'd run a marathon. He'd gone half a dozen yards when a sixth sense made him glance back and instantly wish he hadn't.

There, silhouetted against the sickly red light on the

threshold of the mannequin room stood a man with a misshapen head and an axe in his hands.

Shuddering, Warlow turned and set off on a stumbling jog.

The music followed him. A driving, discordant accompaniment to his panic. Not Metallica now. Nothing remotely as melodious as them. This was feral music, the vocals an incomprehensible cacophony of grunts and screams. More of a death chant than a song.

He stumbled into the kitchen, yanked the chairs back and upended them in the doorway, pausing only to catch his breath, of which there seemed never enough. He turned to the door into the hall just as the boar-headed Meredith arrived. Warlow reared back and heard the axe scythe through the air, inches from his face. But Meredith's momentum was his undoing. He careened into the chairs and went sprawling. Warlow didn't wait. He scrambled through the passage towards the front door.

He was going to make it. Adrenaline surged. His breath sounded like ruptured bellows.

And then he saw the chain and the padlock.

Meredith had locked them in. Had enticed them into his lair, doubled back and locked the door.

A grunting curse drew Warlow's eyes as Meredith got to his feet but stumbled again.

Only one place left to go. Warlow ducked back into the parlour, slammed the door shut behind him and scrabbled with his fingers at the thumb lock. An ancient, flimsy brass thing. But something, at least.

He dragged the corduroy sofa over to the door. It felt like it weighed three tons. Then, somehow, he wrestled the box TV on top of it to make a barrier.

The door shuddered as Meredith smashed into it. Shuddered, but held.

'Meredith,' Warlow croaked. 'Stop this. Think, man.'

His response was another shuddering series of charges on the door. Miraculously, both it and the bolt held.

'What next, eh? Thought about that? Is this what your family would have wanted?'

The shuddering charges ceased.

'James. Was. My. Friend.' The words, muffled through whatever headgear Meredith wore, emerged disjointed and delivered through teeth clamped together.

Two seconds of silence followed, ending in a splintering crack as the axe blade smashed through the wood of the door.

Oddly, the time between withdrawing the axe and swinging it again gave Warlow a moment to think. His eyes raked the room for something, anything, to fight back with. But there was nothing besides the ancient furnishings. He could hardly fight an axe with an antimacassar. And then his eyes fell on the framed embroidery. He staggered to the curtains and pulled them open. Thin grey light leeched into the room, and he stepped towards the nearest wall hanging.

The wild boar and the fox. A dozen lines. Warlow let his eyes fall to the takeaway at the bottom.

Preparedness for an enemy as yet unseen is the best guarantee of peace.

Signed underneath. 'N. M.'

'N. M,' Warlow shouted. 'Is that your mother? Looks like she was a wise woman.'

The monotonous axe blows stopped suddenly. Warlow again took advantage of the silence.

James could only be Kinton. And this man was out to avenge his death.

'I'm sorry about James. Truly sorry. I—'

Meredith's muffled voice broke in. 'You let Geoghan out. You and the other copper. Let him out so that he could do it again.'

The next blow from the axe smashed through the door panel. Warlow had no intention of allowing Meredith a wild-eyed, Jack Nicholson, face-through-the-door moment. He moved over to the window, knowing now that there would be no reasoning with the killer. They were way beyond that. Exhaustion threatened to engulf him. His heart thumped in his chest, speeding up and slowing down to its own strange rhythm.

Years of overpainting had sealed the windows shut. His hands fluttered over the panes. Even if he could, he was now too weak to break one.

Behind him, a panel on the upper half of the door disintegrated under another blow.

All Warlow could think about was Cadi and his boys, his regret at not having had a chance to say goodbye to her, or them. He hoped the dog was okay. Hoped some kind soul had taken her in. There were things he wanted to say to Jess, too. And how he would have liked to ease Molly's pain…

Meredith's hand reached through to pull at the splintered wood.

Warlow scanned the room. His thoughts were like scraps of paper in a high wind, his eyes unfocussed, hopelessness threatening as he stared at and vaguely registered the dark fireplace with its unburned logs in the grate.

And the wrought iron fireplace set on a stand next to it.

A fireplace set with a brush, tongs… And a poker.

Warlow fell to his knees and crawled over. Three yards that felt like thirty. He fumbled for the stand and found the poker; a good one with a curved spike for rolling the logs. He turned and crawled back, hands reaching for the sofa, grabbing at the material, pulling his weight up. Dragging himself up the slope of the seat like a desperate climber on the north face of Everest.

Meredith's hand came through the door, breaking off more panel wood, searching again for the thumb lock.

Warlow raised the poker and brought it down.

The spike hit Meredith in the soft tissue between thumb and forefinger. Warlow raked it back.

Meredith screamed.

Warlow rolled away. He only had the one blow in him, and the effort sucked out what little energy he had and drained it away in heaving breaths. He had nothing left as he rolled across the floor. He hit the wall and reached up. A sudden urge to see daylight for the last time driving him.

When he got to the sill and peered out, he almost fell away in shock.

There, six inches behind the glass, was a face. A young face. Determined-looking and brandishing a crowbar.

'Hello, sir,' Rhys yelled through the glass. 'Stand back. I'm going to smash in the window.'

Warlow turned away in time to hear the crash of steel against glass. The ripping sounds of old wood breaking. The last thing he remembered was Rhys's long legs stepping through the space where the sash window had been and Gil's voice through the rain.

'Hold on, Evan. Hold on.'

After that, there was only noise and shouting and never enough air before he fell away into darkness.

CHAPTER FORTY-ONE

THE ENSUING couple of hours sped by as a jerky montage of images and sensations.

Blue lights.

Pain.

Like the taser, but short-lived. Pinpricks in his arms, sirens, and finally more darkness as a blissful release washed over him.

The darkness stayed. Thick and impenetrable, but gradually, the murky depths of his consciousness cleared enough for him to open one eye and take in his surroundings. He didn't move anything except his head, mindful of how not enjoyable moving had been the last time he'd tried it.

But once he turned and clocked the fact that he was in a room on a bed, separated from other beds by curtains, except for the bed opposite where a man watched him in silence, even Warlow's foggy mind understood that he was in a hospital.

The patient across looked up, earphones in, nodded and said, 'Alright, pal?'

Warlow pushed himself up into a reclining position,

delighted to feel the strength in his arms back to normal. Though he still wasn't quite sure why he thought it had never been anything but. He searched for the thread that dangled, but a cotton wool fug where his thoughts should have been made everything woolly.

As he manoeuvred, he noted the spaghetti arrangement of wires going from his chest to monitors on a cabinet near to him, the blood pressure cuff velcro'd to one arm and a drip feeding into a vein on his other hand. Whatever had happened, it looked bloody serious.

'Aye, Aye, Lynne, number two is awake,' the man opposite sang out.

Warlow peered across, wondering if he was addressing him. He wasn't. Instead, a woman in navy-blue scrubs came around the partition and stood looking at him.

Warlow had been a hospital visitor enough times to know that this sort of colour uniform conferred seniority. A ward sister most likely, though these days he suspected that term might have been neutralised into ward manager. Lynne gave the man in the bed opposite a thin smile. 'Thanks, Jerry,' she said, before immediately pulling the curtains around Warlow's bed.

The DCI lifted his hand up to scratch at an irritation on his forehead only to find this head swathed in a Rambo-style bandage. He explored, gradually following the wrapped material around the circumference of his head, probing with his fingers until he found a spot where pressing caused wincing discomfort.

'Eleven stitches,' Lynne said. 'You fell and cracked your head on a coal scuttle.'

'Did I? Good. For a moment there, I thought I'd had a lob… Lobot… A brain thingy. You know, a *One Flew Over the Cuckoo's Nest* job.'

Lynne, not a small lady, smiled indulgently and crossed both her chubby arms.

'No lobotomy. That's tomorrow.'

Warlow returned the smile and decided that he already liked Lynne.

'What do you remember?'

'Great question. What do I remember?'

'You're a policeman. DCI Evan Warlow. Let's start with that.'

And then, like someone threw a switch, it came back to him. Separate images to start with, unrelated snatches that gradually coalesced into a horrifying whole. The house of horrors, Caldwell, the boar-headed Meredith…

Lynne watched his face, saw him struggling. 'You were tasered. More than once, I expect.'

Warlow nodded.

'That set off a dysrhythmia. It sent your heart off-kilter. Triggered a ventricular tachycardia. Our cardiologist said you could have slipped into VF and then asystole—'

'Asystole?'

'Cardiac arrest in old money. Either way, not enough blood gets to your brain. That made you fall over and hit your head. We don't think it's concussion, though. You've been out of it for eight hours. But your heart seems fine now. Lucky for you, your team was there and one of them knew about defibrillators.'

'Defibrillators?' Warlow shook his head. Defibrillators were in the drawer marked 'not a clue' in the memory cupboard. He glanced at his watch. Not there. 'What time is it?'

'10:25am. Cup of tea?'

Warlow nodded, suddenly aware of how dry his throat was.

'You have a visitor,' Lynne said as she turned away. 'She's been here all night. The others were too until midnight, and someone sent them home.' She gave

Warlow one more dazzling smile. 'I'll be back with the tea in a jiffy.'

Warlow watched her leave, replaying the events that were jostling for space inside his head, tumbling over and over and not settling. A minute later, the surrounding curtains twitched, and Jess Allanby appeared, wearing an anxious expression that quickly morphed into relief at seeing him sitting up.

'Evan. I don't know whether to thump you or hug you.'

'Do I get a say?'

'You scared the crap out of me. Out of all of us.'

'You know me. Always craving attention.' He lifted his arm and the drip line tugged and snagged at his hand. The sudden pain triggered another memory. Painful too, but in a different way. 'Kelvin Caldwell?'

Jess shook her head. Warlow squeezed his eyes shut. The sound of metal cleaving flesh remembered with sudden sickening clarity. 'I watched him die, Jess. I was helpless. I couldn't do anything.'

'Are you up to telling me what happened?'

'Not exactly private.'

Jess stepped back and glance around. 'Bloke next door is asleep. Chap opposite has headphones on. We're good.'

Warlow nodded. He didn't know if he could, but found it got easier in the act of telling. He insisted she have her phone on record. But when he got to the part about the burner that KFC had put into his hand, she pressed pause.

'A burner phone?' she asked, puzzled.

'Stuffed with numbers pertaining to county lines, I expect. He was going to put it in my car. It has my prints all over it. That might be difficult to explain away.' The thought of Caldwell getting his way brought colour to Warlow's cheeks.

The edges of Jess's mouth curved down. 'It won't be.' She un-paused the phone. 'Professional standards were already looking at Kelvin over the way he treated Catrin. I informed them as soon as she told me what had happened. I took a call from them at nine this morning. Kelvin had three bank accounts under various names. If he was alive, he'd be facing jail.'

Warlow huffed out a puff of air. 'Even so, no one deserves to die like that. Did you get him? Meredith, I mean?'

'Rhys and Gil found him in the kitchen, bleeding heavily from a hand-wound.'

'He's in a secure unit, I take it?' Warlow grunted.

Jess nodded. 'We found rags soaked in linseed oil in an airtight box in one of the outhouses. We think he sabotaged Karen Geoghan's car and then Owen's.'

Warlow let that information sink in while Jess put her phone away.

'Your son is on his way,' she said.

'Why?'

Jess met his challenging gaze without apology. 'Because you almost died, Evan. I had to tell him you were in ICU.'

Warlow thought about protesting, but then saw his knee-jerk reaction as nothing but crankiness. He would've done exactly the same thing. He looked around.

'Is this Glangwili?'

'No. This is Morriston Hospital. It's the nearest one to where it happened.'

Lynne came back through the curtains with two cups of tea. 'Thanks,' Jess said with feeling.

'You looked like you could do with one.'

'Can I get up? To go to the loo, I mean?' Warlow asked.

Lynne shook her head. 'Bedpan only, sorry.'

'Bedpan?' Warlow growled.

Lynne grinned and clamped her lips together to minimise her smile. 'Gets them every time. Yes, you can get up once I've taken everything off your chest and the drip out.' She glanced at a watch hanging from the top pocket of her scrubs. 'You've been stable for over eight hours. Twelve is the yardstick. We do the same for cardioversion patients. The drip's got nothing but saline in it, anyway. And now you're drinking, it's all good.'

She disconnected Warlow efficiently and quickly, using a sticking plaster over the cannula entry point on the back of his hand so that he didn't bleed too badly. 'Oh, and heads-up, you are wearing a gown. So, you might want to tie it at the back if you get up. No need for any unnecessary titillation, is there?' She left them to it with arms full of the detritus from Warlow's monitoring equipment.

'She's a gem,' Jess said.

'There are some good people in this world. Trouble is, you and I don't meet enough of the buggers. Comes to something when it takes a near-death experience to remind us of the fact.'

Jess remained thoughtful as she took a sip of tea. But then her face clouded. Warlow picked up on it. 'What?'

'You hit your head, and you were bleeding. I had Gil on speakerphone reporting on what was happening. While Catrin fetched the defibrillator from the community hall on the river three miles away, Gil was helping you. There was a lot of blood, Evan. I had no option.'

The mug of tea, halfway to his lips, stayed hovering in the air as Warlow absorbed this information. *Shit.*

Shit the bed, shit on toast, just… Shit.

He knew it was going to happen at some point. It had only been a matter of time before some injury of his exposed his colleagues to the curse he held within him. Jess had been right to warn them. And now everybody knew that he was HIV positive.

'I told them that you didn't want it broadcast. I think you can trust them.' Jess watched his reaction over the rim of her mug. 'I'm truly sorry. I know you didn't want them to know and—'

'Doesn't matter.' He laughed dryly. 'Bound to happen. The worst-case scenario writ large. It's chaos theory. Like that bloke said in that film with the dinosaurs. No matter how much you plan, the fan and the crap are always creeping ever closer, laughing their socks off.'

'*Jurassic Park*?'

'That's the one. Except there was no mention of socks, come to think of it. Nor a fan or crap. All in all, their scriptwriters might have said it a bit more elegantly.'

They drank their tea in silence for a couple of minutes. But Warlow kept shifting in the bed, restlessly.

'Do you want to use the loo?' Jess asked.

'I'm not a bloody four-year-old.' Warlow glowered. But then, after another five seconds of wriggling, added, 'That obvious, is it?'

Jess raised an eyebrow.

'Know where it is?'

She snorted. 'I might do since I've been there half a dozen times through the night. That's what weak hospital tea does for you. Need me to adjust your gown?'

'No, I think I'll manage.'

Jess shrugged with a lopsided smile and pushed through the curtains.

Warlow slid out of bed, feeling remarkably well, considering. Though the bandage over his head felt awkward and lumpy. When he finally stood up, he was glad to see that he had underpants on. He managed to find two ties at the back of the gown and fiddled with them, fashioning a blind knot in several throws until they, and the gown, felt reasonably secure. He took a step forward. Nothing happened. The world didn't tilt; he didn't fall over. He opened the curtains to find Jess standing in the centre of the bay, waiting. Jerry, still with his earphones on, gave him a nod and a little wave.

'There is just one thing you need to see before you hit the loo.' She pointed towards a window at the end of the bay. Warlow walked towards it, Jess at his side. The window looked out onto one of Morriston's many and labyrinthine car parks.

Immediately Warlow appeared at the window, four people standing in front of a line of cars raised their hands to wave like demented festivalgoers welcoming a headliner. Gil, Rhys, Catrin, and one more. The fourth member was younger than the others. Molly Allanby stood holding a lead attached to an alert, sleek, black Labrador.

'Cadi!?' Warlow's tight voice almost seized in his throat. Christ, he'd forgotten all about his own bloody dog. He turned to Jess. 'How?'

Grinning, Jess joined him and waved, too. 'Molly will explain in great detail, no doubt. Facebook groups, social media, we may hate the sodding things, but they have their uses. Cadi was taken in by a family in a camper van. The young boy in the family conveniently lost her collar and lead, but his older sister found them in a hedge. I'm thinking of giving her a job. She went online and…'

He'd felt surprisingly okay after his ordeal. But now, on seeing this shower, and especially seeing Cadi, tears suddenly sprang to his eyes. He turned away, blinking furiously, and spoke to an empty bed in the corner of the room. 'You know I'm not staying here, don't you?'

Jess protested. 'The doctors said—'

'What do they know?'

'They know you almost died for a start.'

He turned back, harnessing pedantic mode to distract himself from his emotions. 'The clue there is in the almost. I never quite understood that one. I mean, death is pretty binary. Personally, I'm quite happy with dead or not dead.

And, as far as I can see, I am not dead. Besides, I have a dog that needs walking.'

'Evan, this isn't a joke.'

He used the tip of his index finger to wipe away the rest of his tears. 'Who's laughing? Obviously not me.'

Jess handed him a tissue with a disapproving frown. He blew his nose and dabbed his eyes before cocking one eyebrow. 'Morriston, you say? Does that mean that Owen Tamblin is here?'

Jess nodded. 'Burns unit. But he's about to be sent back to a ward.'

'Right, let me empty my bladder and we'll get Nurse Lynne to find me some scrubs to wear. Let's find Owen. Seeing me dressed up will be better than any bloody medicine for that sick bugger. And let me borrow your phone. I need to speak to my son. See if I can stop him dashing down the motorway from London.'

Jess gave him a sceptical look.

'I know there needs to be a difficult conversation, but I'd like to speak to them both together and God knows what time it is in Australia at the moment.'

Jess handed over her phone and there, half-naked in a hospital ward, Warlow phoned his youngest son, Tomos.

CHAPTER FORTY-TWO

THE MEDICAL TEAM CONCLUDED, after checking Warlow's cardiac enzymes and the record of continuous ECG monitoring, that he'd suffered no permanent damage. His hours of unconsciousness stemmed, not from the concussion, but from the sheer physical trauma of having been tasered four times in short succession.

'Equivalent to running a marathon,' Lynne said.

After convincing her, with a theatrical wink, that what he needed to do next was part of an investigation, she found him some scrubs, and he and Jess went in search of Owen Tamblin.

'Let me get this right,' Warlow asked as they negotiated the corridors of what had once, famously, been an emergency hospital built during the war, 'Owen is going to fully recover with no permanent damage?'

Jess nodded. 'They told me sterile bandages and pain control only. They didn't think he would need a graft.'

Warlow grinned. 'Good, that's all we need to know.'

Just before they arrived at the burns unit, Warlow caught Jess fighting a smile. 'What now?'

'It's the scrubs. They suit you, that's all. I can see you in *Casualty*.'

'On TV? As what? Corpse number three after a building collapse?'

'No, the grouchy and overworked, but underneath it all, charming and caring, trauma surgeon. Not quite George Clooney…'

'More Mickey Rooney?'

'Who?'

'Never mind. I didn't get the 'A' levels for med school. The brains went to the boys. They got them from their mother.'

'What did they get from you?'

'A sunny disposition and a love of dogs.'

'Lots of cloudy days in Wales, I've noticed.'

'Fickle bugger, the weather.'

Warlow found a mask and an elasticated bouffant-style cap in boxes conveniently situated outside the ward where Owen Tamblin was a patient. He put both on and walked into the four-bedder. Three beds occupied, one empty. Owen lay in his bed, one arm completely bandaged to the shoulder, the other bandaged from the elbow down, encompassing his hands, bar two fingers.

Warlow, masked, kept his head down and added some gruffness. 'Mr Tamblin? I've been sent to take you for your coffee enema.'

Tamblin, who'd been listening on some earphones, sent Warlow a horrified glare. 'What the hell?'

'Matron's orders.' Warlow turned his back and began fussing with the curtains.

'Christ,' Tamblin grumbled, 'I know the coffee here is a bit shit, but—'

Warlow swivelled, pulled down his mask and grinned.

'You evil bastard,' Tamblin said.

'Complete the well-known phrase or saying. Who needs enemas…'

'With friends like you.' Tamblin shook his head. 'Christ, Evan, good to see you. Narrow bloody escape. For the both of us.'

Warlow nodded. 'Meredith is in the funhouse. Will be for the duration, I reckon.'

'Do we have any kind of explanation for what he did?'

'Not yet. They'll give him a label or two, I expect. If you want my two penneth, I think he was traumatised by Kinton's death at first, and then more traumatised and guilt-ridden for what happened to his brother in the car crash. Final straw was his mother dying alone while he did penance. He wanted someone to blame.'

'Us and the Geoghans.' Tamblin lowered his chin.

Warlow let his eyes drift up over the bandages. 'How's the arm?'

'Painful. But the meds are good. They say it'll heal. I'm never going to be a hand model for Tiffany and Co but could be worse.'

Warlow eyed him. 'I was hoping you'd be bandaged up, head and all. Like the Invisible Man.'

Tamblin sucked in air through his teeth. 'I always wondered about him. Because the only way he could be completely invisible was if he was starkers. But we both know that running around with your accoutrements unconstrained by a jock strap is both uncomfortable and possibly noisy, in the flesh-on-flesh stakes.'

Behind Warlow, Jess grimaced.

'Had some practise, have you?' Warlow asked.

'No, but you get my drift. I reckon the old Invisible Man was a bit of a perv.'

'What about the old bellows?' Warlow pointed vaguely towards Tamblin's chest.

'Yep, no permanent damage. Before I gave them up,

I'd tempered the old lungs with years of fags. A bit of smoke did no harm.'

'I'm sure the respiratory physicians bought into that explanation.' Warlow grinned.

Tamblin's expression became suddenly serious, and a shadow seemed to pass over his eyes. 'Lucky Stoica was in the car with me. Otherwise…'

'He's a good bloke,' Warlow said. 'In fact, I thought maybe you and I could start a whip round. Help him with some of his HGV lessons.'

Jess, hovering a few feet away, chipped in with a tut. 'Whip round? This is 2023. You can run a GoFundMe account. People do it all the time and it sounds like he'd be a good cause. A heroic cause. I'll get my daughter on it. It'll take Mol ten minutes to set up.'

'Right, put me down for £250,' Warlow said.

'Put me down for double that,' Tamblin added.

'Once it's set up, you can put yourselves down online in a couple of clicks,' Jess said.

Warlow set his bandaged friend a look of utter disdain. 'Five hundred? Always got to go one better, haven't you? Look at the state of you. Lucky it's your left hand. At least you can use those two fingers on your right for essentials.'

'I've got news for you,' Tamblin said. 'They only freed up those two fingers a couple of hours ago. Before that, I was completely helpless.'

'You mean someone else had to—'

'Hold and wipe, yeah.' Tamblin's smile was a ghost of his usual full-on grin.

'Christ, I hope they were paying that poor bugger danger money,' Warlow said. 'He or she?'

Tamblin reddened visibly.

Warlow shook his head, ladling on the pain. 'That poor girl will be scarred for life.'

'Hang on,' Tamblin said, his eyes full of fire. 'I've been

told by the physio that I need to use my right hand as much as possible.' Slowly, with excruciating effort, gritting his teeth with the pain, Tamblin turned his arm over and slowly picked his hand up off the bed. And even more slowly made a V sign with his index and middle finger aimed squarely at Warlow.

A nurse in light blue appeared at the doorway, looked in, frowned, and said, 'What's going on here?'

Warlow opted for damage limitation. 'Two Curly Wurlys from the shop it is then, Detective Chief Inspector Tamblin.' He turned, nodded at the nurse, and left, pushing a giggling Jess Allanby in front of him.

––––––

THE NEXT COUPLE of days involved mopping up the mess. Catrin liaised with the DVLA and confirmed that there had been no formal confirmation of Rhydian Meredith's licence being revoked. Someone there tried to explain that they required paperwork, including his returned licence. With it being still active, it would've been easy for Iwan Meredith to carry on driving. Visitors to *Erw Foel*, of which there were very few, would not know any different.

Of those who knew the family, they'd been told that Iwan Meredith was away and that the house was empty. Strangers were met with Meredith in a wheelchair. The burned and coagulated skin that Catrin noticed on his face and that she'd described as appearing like molten wax was indeed exactly that. They'd found boxes of red candles at the house. As for Meredith, he wasn't talking. He was allowing the small army of analysts and specialists and forensic psychiatrists to do their thing on his behalf.

Warlow chipped in. He had his own theories as to what might have twisted Iwan Meredith's mind. A claustro-phobic upbringing in a single-parent household with an invalid brother could not have helped. Nor would the loss of a true, if unlikely, friend in the form of James Kinton. And added to all that were the lovingly sewn morals on the walls of the house. Everywhere he looked. They'd found more; tens, if not hundreds of embroideries, stored away in a bedroom.

All Warlow had to do was cast his mind back to the interview with young Meg Hayter in the caver's club at Penwyllt. She'd seen the truth there and then. The crow and the lamb and the badger had not been random carcasses. As well as dripping with maggots, they'd been dripping with meaning.

They'd found a book at the house. A battered, moth-eaten thing with illustrations. *The Fables of Aesop for children* with a publication date of 1913. Warlow had looked them up, these actors in moral tales. The crow and the lamb appeared in a story exemplifying abuse; Meredith's relationship to the Geoghans and the police in a nutshell.

Many are those who exploit the weak yet cringe before others who are their match.

And the badger was surely an emblem of Meredith's decision to act. That fish out of water moral came from a story of a badger raised by beavers, who experiences an existential crisis when told he's been living a lie.

Make peace with your own image, for to live as another leads to nought but sorrow.

There'd been little peace in Meredith's life. His decision to act, to finally be himself, may well have been a form of vengeful redemption in his tortured mind.

As for the boar's head mask they'd removed from the bleeding killer's head, it would be up to the psychiatrists to unpick that little knot. One theory suggested a link in his mind to where he lived and the fabled boar *Twrch Trwyth*. A throwback to pagan times. But Warlow preferred the simpler explanation in the samplers hanging on the wall.

Another of Aesop's tall tales where a boar explains to a wily fox why he is always sharpening his tusk for the conflict yet to come.

Preparedness for an enemy as yet unseen is the best guarantee of peace.

Meredith set up the old slaughterhouse in anticipation of one day confronting his enemies. There seemed little doubt that when Warlow and KFC turned up, he had his weapons ready.

The link with Penwyllt could be traced back to Meredith's grandfather who'd worked at the railway station until it closed in the 1960s. The line remained open for a few years after that and he'd take his little girl with him sometimes on the train to check the line until it, too, closed in the 1970s. She'd developed a liking for the place. Passed that on to her able-bodied son. Non Meredith, the NM on the samplers, wanted to instil wisdom into her children. But that wisdom had been corrupted by fate and the evil that men and women do into something vengeful and terrible.

CHAPTER FORTY-THREE

SEVERAL DAYS LATER, Warlow was back in Carmarthen and meeting with Sion Buchannan and Two-Shoes in Buchannan's office. A not entirely comfortable Superintendent Goodey was at least a little less acerbic than usual and no surprise, thought Warlow, having had her protégé, KFC, turn out to be a bloody great fly in the ointment.

'At least Caldwell wasn't married,' Warlow said after Buchannan had confirmed that £275,000 had been paid into his three accounts in varying random amounts over the last three years.

'There is that,' Buchannan agreed.

Warlow thought he saw a small muscle jerk underneath Goodey's left eye. He'd had his suspicions that KFC and she had been more than colleagues. And if there had been something, she was putting up a very brave front.

'But we've all got a lot of egg on our faces,' Buchannan said. 'You remember that Kelvin Caldwell had run the review into the Pickerings' missing person's case. He had Mel Lewis as his man on the ground. He'd arranged for Lewis to be responsible for checking over the Engine House where a marijuana farm was running. Between them, they'd pulled the wool firmly down over everyone's eyes.'

'Does Davenport know all this?' Warlow grumbled.

Buchannan nodded. 'I'm going to speak to Davenport again shortly. None of this will fall on you, Evan.'

Warlow gave a little nod.

Goodey butted in, 'Let me do it. After all—'

'No. I'm doing this.' Buchannan sounded adamant. 'You and Caldwell were close colleagues. It looks better coming from a neutral.'

Goodey looked like she wanted to say something else. Wisely, she zipped her lip.

Buchannan sat back and looked at Warlow. 'How's the head?'

'Just a little cut. That's all.'

'Right. By the way, I had an email from DS Richards. It's a few days old but it's about a possible transfer.'

Warlow shook his head. 'That's a mistake, sir. Sent in error.'

'Are you sure?'

'Ask her. She wrote that under duress. You can delete it.'

———

THE FOLLOWING DAY, Warlow fed Cadi early and sat in his chair, overlooking the estuary. The dog, favourite toy in her jaws, sat at his side. Post-fed Cadi was a grateful animal. Keen for contact, keen to show her gratitude by resting her head on Warlow's knee or sitting grinning with her paw in his hand.

Warlow enjoyed these quiet moments with the dog. An affirmation of the bond they shared. Suddenly even more special, because somehow Warlow felt they both knew they'd almost lost one another.

'Never mind, eh *cariad? Ni yma o hyd.*'

We're still here.

A knock on the door broke the spell. Cadi, ears up, dropped her toy and headed towards the source of the knock. She was happy enough to see any visitor, but these were special visitors. And Warlow had no doubt that she'd already picked up the scent.

He opened the door to find Molly Allanby and her boyfriend, Bryn, standing there. 'Hi, Evan,' Molly said, with an anxious smile. The kind that wavered between anxiety and concern.

'Molly,' Warlow said with mock earnestness, and looked past her to the boy behind.

'How are you feeling?' Molly asked.

'Fine. All good. Like you're meant to feel after ECT, I suspect.'

Molly's expression stayed blank.

'Electro-convulsive therapy. Shock treatment, you know?'

'Like in the films?'

'That's it.' Warlow saw no point in explaining that ECT wasn't a made-up thing.

Cadi was already wriggling between the boy and the girl, trying to grab their attention for a rub of some kind.

Molly looked up. 'Is it okay to take her?'

'Who? This dog? The one you lost?'

Molly's face fell, and her eyes widened in horror. 'I—'

'I'm kidding. Cadi told me you're forgiven. Let's not hear another word about it. Stuff happens.'

Molly, suddenly teary, engulfed Warlow in a hug. 'I'm so glad you're okay,' she whispered.

'It'll take more than a bolt of bloody taser-lightning to kill me.'

Over Molly's shoulder, Bryn laughed.

Warlow disengaged. 'Right, off you go. I've got stuff to do.'

'Oh, yeah, Mum said you had a Zoom call.'

'Something like that.'

Girl, boy, and dog bundled into the car and left. Warlow watched them go and let his eyes drift up to the sky. It was going to be a lovely day. Warm. Just a hint of a cooling breeze coming in off the Irish Sea. He glanced at his watch.

8:55am.

He'd scheduled the call for nine. That would make it 5:00pm in Perth. After work for Alun. The beginning of the day for Warlow in Wales and Tomos in London.

Inside, the cottage, *Ffau'r Blaidd*, Wolf's Lair, felt much like a den to Warlow. One he shared only with a fellow canine. He liked the place. Enjoyed the fact that his own sweat had raised it, phoenix-like, if not quite from ashes, then certainly from the ruin that it had been. Like him to an extent. He felt at home here. Much more so than the house he'd shared with his ex – now deceased – wife, Denise, in the most unhappy of years after the boys had flown the nest.

Warlow embraced all these musings as he made himself a fresh coffee from the machine that did bean to cup.

Bean to bloody cup. He let out a single snort of laughter.

Talk about bloody bourgeois. His father would have – what? – turned in his grave. No. His father would probably have laughed himself silly. Or ROFLOL, in today's acronym riddled parlance. Warlow's dad had worked in the coal industry and suffered as a consequence. At a time when pneumoconiosis was an inevitability, not bad luck. But he'd retained a wicked sense of humour that he'd shared with his grandsons until he'd been too ill to share anything. Warlow had found himself thinking about his parents a lot over the last few days. A pot of mixed emotions stirred by his visit to the Swansea Valley. To a different place and a different time. No mobile phones when he'd grown up there in a house with a coal shed and an outside loo. He could even remember the arrival of central heating. A lightyear away from this new old-building he'd made for himself: triple-glazed, watertight, insulated, comfortable.

And yet he still wondered if he deserved it. Or juxta-posing that idea with guilty ease, whether the place deserved better. A young couple maybe. Someone with a family. Not a grumpy, middle-aged widower too scared to talk to his own kids.

Warlow made his coffee, went into the living room for his Zoom meeting and sat down, but promptly got back up again and walked back out to look over the estuary from his sunroom.

Sunroom. Another middle-class term that rankled. He tutted. 'How the hell can you be annoyed at something you made with your own bare hands?'

He looked around for any sign of approval from Cadi, but then remembered she'd gone.

'Christ, I'm even talking to myself now.' He let out a deep sigh, recognising his procrastination for what it was and turned back to the living room.

He'd finally splashed out on a portal device linked up to the TV, which meant there was no more faffing about with a phone for a video call. He switched the camera above the TV on, sat on the sofa and pointed the control unit at the camera. One click and it would WhatsApp a video call to the boys. But somehow, his finger wouldn't move. A cold sweat prickled his forehead. He got up again, walked around the room, inhaling and exhaling deeply, as if he was about to take a run at a long jump, then slapped himself in the chest and sat down once more.

This time, when he pointed the controller, his quivering finger pressed the button.

They came online within seconds.

'You two are keen,' Warlow said.

'You said it was important, Dad,' Alun replied, serious, neat, and tanned in a tieless shirt.

'I presume this has got something to do with the hospital?' Tom, his youngest had a coffee on the go on the table next to him.

Warlow nodded and looked at his sons. They were his greatest achievement. Two healthy young men. Personable, successful, good people. When others asked him if he wished he was rich, he always answered that he already was.

'Where's Cadi?'

'Out with a friend. Didn't want her to be a nuisance for this.'

'Well, we're here, Dad.' Alun, impatient as always.

Warlow took a deep breath. 'Something happened to me a couple of years ago at work and I'm afraid it left its mark. I wanted to tell you both ever since it happened, but... I suppose I've been a bit of a coward. Too scared to tell you in case...' He let the sentence hang.

'Dad, come on, whatever it is, you can tell us,' Alun said.

'That's good to hear. Okay. First and foremost, I'm not ill. I'm actually pretty good. But two years ago, I had the bad luck to run into a junkie who hated the police so much that she'd hidden contaminated needles in her hair and clothes. And I snagged one. I'm a very unusual case. Someone who got HIV from a needle stick injury.'

'HIV?' Tom said, the incredulity evident in his voice. 'You're on meds though, right?'

'I am. The works.'

'But you said you were okay?' Alun sounded perplexed.

'I am. I'm okay. I'm absolutely fine and asymptomatic, but I've still got HIV.'

'So this is what the call's about?' Alun asked.

'Don't sound so disappointed,' Warlow attempted a half-grin but only managed a grimace. 'I'm sorry I didn't tell you at the time.'

The boys said nothing, silently processing the information, identical frowns on their faces.

'Okay,' Alun said. Quite often he was the one that stepped in as the oldest of the two. 'I suppose we'd better thank you for telling us now.'

'People at work know. After the injury to my head that bled… They had to know. I didn't think it fair for them to know and you not.'

Tom was staring at him from the phone. 'It must have been hard for you keeping all this to yourself.'

'I didn't know how you'd react.'

'How did you think we'd react?' Alun laughed.

'I don't know. It's been a dilemma.'

'I'm just relieved that you're okay,' Tom said. 'I mean, HIV is manageable these days and you don't look too worried.'

No, thought Warlow, because he wasn't. Not about himself.

'Dad, I know people. Anytime you want to see someone else,' Tom offered, ever the doctor.

'My consultant is brilliant,' Warlow said. 'There's no need for me to see anyone else. The meds keep everything under control. As I said, I'm not unwell.'

All three men took a breath, searching for what to say next.

Alun broke the impasse. 'Right, that's done then. Now, why don't we talk about something really important? When are you two coming out to Australia?'

A wave of relief washed through Warlow. The virus

had somehow made him feel terribly ashamed of himself. An outcast. An untouchable. He'd worried about this for a long time. Putting off confronting it with the boys. But now that it was done and they'd reacted the way he dared to hope they would, he felt elated and very stupid at the same time. He didn't answer Alun's question. He let Tom step into the breach and start a discussion about how much leave Alun thought he might need when he visited.

'At least three weeks. A month would be better. There is so much to see and do…'

Warlow looked on, only half-listening, but happy to do just that. Not pilloried, not abandoned. Accepted. Emotionally schooled by his own sons, yet again.

'What about you, Dad? You think you can swing a month off work when the time comes?' Alun's question brought Warlow back to the here and now.

'Why not,' he said. 'I expect there'll be a crime spree in my absence, but now and again, the sheriff just has to get out of Dodge.'

Warlow saw his sons exchange glances.

'Did you just say get out of Dodge?' Tom asked.

'I did.'

Alun shook his head. 'Sounds like you really do need a holiday.'

ACKNOWLEDGMENTS

As with all writing endeavours, the existence of this novel depends upon me, the author, and a small army of 'others' who turn an idea into a reality. My wife, Eleri, who gives me the space to indulge my imagination and picks out my stupid mistakes. Sian Phillips, Tim Barber and of course, proofers and ARC readers. Thank you all for your help. Special mention goes to Ela the dog who drags me away from the writing cave and the computer for walks, rain or shine. Actually, she's a bit of a princess so the rain is a no-no. Good dog!

But my biggest thanks goes to you, lovely reader, for being there and actually reading this. It's great to have you along and I do appreciate you spending your time in joining me on this roller-caster ride with Evan and the rest of the team.

CAN YOU HELP?

With that in mind, and if you enjoyed it, I do have a favour to ask. Could you spare a moment to **leave a review or a rating**? A few words will do, but it's really the only way to help others like you discover the books. Probably the best way to help authors you like. Just visit my page on Amazon and leave a few words.

FREE BOOK FOR YOU

Visit my website and join up to the Rhys Dylan VIP Reader's Club and get a FREE novella, *The Wolf Hunts Alone*, by visiting:

www.rhysdylan.com

You will also be the first to hear about new releases via the few but fun emails I'll send you. This includes a no spam promise from me and you can unsubscribe at any time.

AUTHOR'S NOTE

A Mark Of Imperfection takes Warlow back to his roots. To the borders of three old Welsh counties, to the edge of coalfields which fed the industrial revolution, to the moors and hills.

These areas, so often stripped of their resources, and left only with scars for nature to heal, can harbour resentments that run deep. And resentments can fester until they become impossible to contain. Even in the quiet places, the tranquil spots. But thankfully this time, Evan survives to take Cadi for a walk once more. Blimey, who'd have thought that such a wonderful place as West Wales could harbour such horror. Of course, most of the time, the worst you're going to come across is a stray sheep on the road, or a bull in a field (my advice, go around).

Those of you who've read *The Wolf Hunts Alone* will know exactly what I mean. And who knows what and who Warlow is going to come up against next! So once again, thank you for sparing your precious time on this new endeavour. I hope I'll get the chance to show you more of this part of the world and that it'll give you the urge to visit.

Not everyone here is a murderer. Not everyone… Cue tense music!

All the best, and see you all soon, Rhys.

READY FOR MORE?

DCI Evan Warlow and the team are back in…

BURNT ECHO

Shiny new things…

When reports of a putrid smell oozing out of an old mine shaft in the Cambrian hills' 'green desert' of Wales turns out to be a corpse, DCI Evan Warlow and his team quickly slip into gear.

But this is no pot-holing adventure gone wrong. Soon, Evan and the team are hunting for another missing person and discovering ghosts from the past that no one wants to confront. With the team stretched and suffering the consequences of a misspent youth and the dangers of root vegetables (yes—root vegetables), Evan has his work cut out in unravelling a web of manipulation and lies.

But there is more than one victim here. And unless he can find a way to the truth and quickly, someone else is going to fall foul.

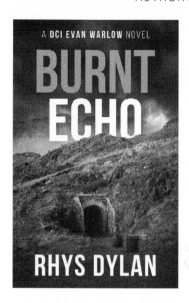

Made in the USA
Middletown, DE
18 May 2023

30846600R00203